THE *Southern* THIRST TRAP

ADRIAN R. HALE

Content Warning

This story contains explicit sexual content, profanity, may contain mild violence, and topics that may be sensitive to some readers. This story is best suited for readers 18+.

Playlist

Fallin' (Adrenaline) – Why Don't We
Heaven – Julia Michael
I Forgot That You Existed" – Taylor Swift
You Problem – Cloudy June, Emlyn
Fortnight (Feat. Post Malone) – Taylor Swift
Good In Goodbye – Madison Bear
In The Kitchen – Renee Rapp
Rumors (feat. Zayne) – Sabrina Claudio
Thot Shit – Megan Thee Stallion
Selfish – Madison Bear
Are You Gone Already – Nicki Minaj
Daddy Issues – The Neighbourhood
Lights On – H.E.R.
Bad Girls Do It Well – Ex Habit
Bathroom – Montell Fish
Play With Fire (feat. Yacht Money) – Sam Tinnesz
I'm Yours – Isabel LaRosa
The Alchemy – Taylor Swift
Streets – Silhouette Remix – Doja Cat
Only Love Can Hurt Like This – Paloma Faith
Skyscraper – Demi Lovato

God Is A Woman – Ariana Grande

I Want To – Rosenfeld

Show Me – Black Atlas

Needy – Ariana Grande

Hits Different – Taylor Swift

Dangerous Woman – Ariana Grande

Do It For Me – Rosenfeld

The Feels – Labrinth

imgonnagetyouback – Taylor Swift

Powerful (feat. Ellie Goulding & Tarrus Riley) – Major Lazer

Lights Out – Nbdy

Love Me – Ex Habit

Church – Chase Atlantic

Hey Daddy (Daddy's Home) – Usher

Check out the full playlist on Spotify

Listen to the full playlist on Spotify!

Dedication

For the moms who are doing their best, showing up every day, and battling their own inner critic while balancing the world on their shoulders – you are incredible. If no one has told you today, you're doing a great job and your best is enough.

One

Zander

"We're approaching fourteen thousand feet. Time to fly, Javi," I yell over the roar of the wind through the open door. I glance once more out at the impossible nothingness of sky stretching as far as I can see, and finally the pale glimpse of land far below.

"Are you sure this is how you want to start, and possibly end, your day?" he yells, as he attempts to loosen his death grip on the door handle.

"Ten grand says I'll have the softer landing," I toss back at his tightly set face before spreading my arms wide to fall backward into the open expanse that becomes rushing wind as gravity grabs a hold of me. I see Javi's mouth move in what has to be a curse at my expense and jerkily follow me out of the airplane before I'm too far away.

I barrel roll onto my stomach, the wind buffeting against my body, arms and legs spread wide. There is nothing like these few moments of unobstructed falling through the sky to wake you up and remind you that you're mortal. Not even a beautiful woman gets me this high or has the blood pounding through my veins in a shockingly intense rhythm.

Well, there was one woman who had an even greater effect, but I push that intrusive thought back into the vault where it belongs. I don't think about her, especially not when I'm already free-falling out of the sky. She's just as likely to get me killed as she is to save me if I start thinking about her now.

I tuck my arms and legs close against my body and rocket downward, a quick set of somersaults sufficiently setting my head spinning and thoroughly removing all thoughts of women, even that one specific woman, from my mind.

My face cracks into a grin against the blast of wind in my face, arms and legs spreading back out as I check the altimeter on my wrist. A quick tug to the cord at my side to open my chute as the ground rushes up towards me is all that is needed to stop the perilous plunge. My body jerks upwards momentarily, the canopy ballooning above me, and the sudden quiet is a shocking difference from the howling wind that had blocked out all sound. All thoughts are pushed from my mind other than surviving... and maybe an errant thought of she-who-must-not-be-named.

My head has been caught up in too much lately. I needed to abandon all thoughts of work and focus on what really matters for a moment. Falling out of the sky is a great way to put everything into perspective. Nothing but my gauges and the canopy above me working as it should have my focus now.

I keep my eyes trained below, pulling on my hand controls to angle me toward the verdant field still thousands of feet below. A glance over my shoulder shows me a bright red canopy that tells me Javi isn't far behind. I refocus on my landing, angling the steering lines and situating myself for a quick drop and running finish. I yank hard and collapse the chute as my feet connect with gravity and the earth once again, running forward toward the waiting group of SUVs and our crew a safe distance off the landing field. Piece of cake. Adrenaline rush achieved, all before the work week even begins.

A whoosh, the sound of feet smacking the ground, and a shrill scream have me turning to see what kind of spectacle Javi has made of himself.

"How? How do you manage to thump down like a rhino executing a leap when you have all the modern technology that has made skydiving smooth and beautiful right there in your hands?" I jeer at him as he untangles himself from the chute that is billowing around him while he lies on the ground.

"You're the psycho who likes jumping out of perfectly good planes. I just go along to make sure there's a witness if you kill yourself. Of course, you're better at the landing than I am." His chest is heaving, and his usually olive skin is unnaturally ashen. He's still terrified despite having done this dozens of times before, right along with me.

"I thought you'd grown to love it, Javi," I joke. "Now, get it together so we can make it back to Atlanta before the day gets away from us."

I pull off my rig and safety gear before stripping out of the jumpsuit and handing them to the waiting staff, who jogged over at our landing. My long stride eats up the distance to Javi's Land Rover Defender that will take us back to the office. Once I reach it, I change out of the casual jump clothes and into the pressed suit I have hanging in a garment bag right there in the field at the side of the vehicle, not worried about who sees me. This isn't a locker room, but no one's sensibilities will be offended by my brazen actions. Javi changes on his side of the SUV, and I can't help but smile at the freedom singing through my blood from the rush of the jump.

There's nothing like starting a Monday morning from fourteen thousand feet to put me in a good mood, even when we're dealing with shit at work. That's why I scheduled the jump. It's bad enough with the normal stress of the holidays, but work has been creeping in enough to send me running for an adrenaline fix. My brothers deal with it in their own ways.

Payton escapes to his lake house or the coast and gets up to whatever secretive things he does to blow off steam. But normally, he's at work dealing with PR nightmares or ensuring the tech side of the business is rock solid.

Hayes has been up his own ass about his upcoming anniversary with his newly pregnant wife. I can't believe it's been a whole year that Paige has been in our lives and has turned my asshole brother into a doting husband and slightly less of a workaholic, giving us all less of a headache. She's worth her weight in gold for that reprieve alone, and I should really find her a nice Christmas present this year, since I can't exactly give her another director seat on a board like we did last year.

And fuck, what a year it's been. We spent it navigating what to do with the information that Octavius Rex handed us on New Year's Eve. Turns out running roughshod over any company we wanted to acquire and dismantling family legacies and companies on a whim for years could really make people hate us. That kind of hate fuels more than just personal grudges, and a corporate cabal of angry assholes tried to take down Olympus International for good.

Had Rex not come through when he did...well, I don't even want to think about what that would have cost us. It's been a long year of picking up the pieces, revamping our image and the public's perception of our company, and leaning into new areas of expansion.

Javi's voice brings me out of my thoughts that are quickly displacing the feel-good endorphins I'd hoped would last a little longer.

"Maybe if your hobbies were soaking up the sun on a rooftop pool deck with a cold *cerveza* in hand, you'd see me actually enjoy something you drag me to. No. Instead, you jump out of airplanes and off cliffs or dive into the ocean without an air tank. You're supposed to need some downtime and peace every once in a while, man. When do I get a vacation from your intensity?" he grumbles at me across the SUV, hurrying to finish changing so we can start our trek back into Atlanta.

The last time I took a real vacation was five years ago, and even then, it had included freediving in the Maldives, but with a beautiful woman instead of Javi. Jesus, was she good in bed. My internal warning system snaps me to attention, keeping me from reminiscing too far into the memory of the long-legged Sports Illustrated swimsuit model who had accompanied me. I let that one go on far too long for comfort, spending two weeks wrapped around her sun-kissed skin and fearless enthusiasm to chase the adrenaline rush with me. I clench my teeth and focus on the present rather than she-who-must-not-be-named.

No repeats. And no attachments. Ever again.

It doesn't matter that I can still vividly recall every highlight of that trip and each curve of her body. I blocked her number and removed her from my mind as soon as I resurfaced in Atlanta.

"You can take a break when I do. Until then, be ready for any adventure. That's your job." Technically, his job is to be my Senior Vice President, but he tasked himself with ensuring I don't do anything too risky that may affect the business, so now, he's my adventure buddy, too. A good sport and a good employee. What more could I ask for?

"It's also my job to remind you that we have a meeting to close the Rosenthall deal this week. Hayes wanted you to be the lead on that, rather than a team. He said we couldn't afford to send in anyone but you." Javi jumps directly back into work mode as soon as the adrenaline works out of our systems.

I dust imaginary lint from the shoulder of my crisp white shirt as I smile to myself. "I'm the best at what I do. No mistaking that. We'll have the new enterprise in our hands before the week is over, piece of cake."

Javi jumps in the driver's seat of the Defender while I climb into the passenger side and pull my phone out of the glove box. It's nice having everything arranged so perfectly so I can get my fix of free-falling before wheeling and dealing. Just another perk of being king. My messages are currently free of any pressing matters, thanks to an impressive staff, who filter out all but the most urgent on my behalf. Not bad for a Monday.

I absently open a browser tab and see the Atlanta Haute List site that must have been there since the last story that was sent to me to read, likely by Payton, who keeps us updated with all the rumors. This gossip blog seems to be obsessed with my family, publishing even the most trivial of stories related to us. Last week, it was a story about my brother Hayes and his wife Paige's foundation or something. A quick scan of the photo below the story has me scrolling back up to the headline in a flash, and then I'm quickly reading through the story itself.

The Atlanta Haute List
Model-Turned-Chef Closing In On Atlanta Condors
Tight End

Atlanta foodie favorite, Harlowe Sorenson, knows a good ass. Whether it's her own from her scantily clad swimsuit modeling days, or her newest connection to Atlanta's newest offensive football sensation, Knox Contraire, she knows all the best angles to hit.

Sorenson and Contraire were first linked last summer at a children's benefit gala (see our story where we gushed about how cute a couple they would make), but that wasn't the last of it. Sorenson showed up to Condors home games during the season just often enough to start the whispers that she was there to see a certain player on the offense. It wasn't until recently that they've been spotted together at trendy hot spots all over the city.

It was just the two of them photographed together until this weekend when Sorenson's rarely seen four-year-old son, Hendricks, joined the pair for a trip to the zoo. Contraire made a great impression on the young boy, throwing Hendricks over his shoulder and giving him lots of tickles, much to the delight of Sorenson. Harlowe captured the antics with her own photos that she's unlikely to share on social media, given her stance on not putting her kid in the public eye, but you can see our photos of the outing below, provided by Hauties in the know.

Harlowe has come out of supermodel retirement and has been making a name for herself on her Foulmouthed Foodie YouTube cooking channel and social media accounts, sharing spicy photos and recipes alike that set the internet on fire on the regular. It's no surprise Knox has scooped her up and is making a move to potentially get serious, if this outing with Hendricks is anything to go by. With her cookbook, *At Home With Harlowe: A Foulmouthed Foodie's Guide To Eating Well* releasing today, we're sure we'll be getting a better look at Harlowe's life, and might even be seeing more of her relationship with Knox as she promotes this new venture. We at the Atlanta Haute List will be hunting down the stories and sharing everything we find with our Hauties! Hit Like and Subscribe for all the Haute gossip!

Think of the devil...

I didn't know she'd returned to Atlanta from LA, or that she's moved from modeling into cooking, but I hadn't kept up with her life after our trip. Fuck. Five years have done little to change the knock-out gorgeous good looks of Harlowe Sorenson. Even through the grainy cell phone shots taken from a distance, I can see her beauty, but she has a new softness, both to her body and her face, that keeps me staring long and hard at the photos. Still a leggy brunette with high cheekbones and a luscious pout, it appears motherhood, and maybe this new fucking football player, have her smiling more easily than I remember. I chastise myself for hovering over her photos. I don't want women I've had before.

So what if she seems happy? I should be completely unmoved by a candid photo of her and some dude, as jacked as he is. What is he, six-six? Who needs to be that big, anyway?

Should be, sure, but the weird tugging in my gut has me wondering why I would care so long after I had her for myself. I fuck beautiful women by the handful; what's one in a hundred from five years ago? Is it just because she was an incredible lay? No. Good sex isn't hard to find. Her ability to go with the flow and follow my lead, yet challenge the fuck out of me at every turn? No, that may have been unique to her, but not enough to have me wanting her now. Then what the hell is it that has me feeling anything at all about this woman now? Maybe it's because I felt a little too much for her, and in the end, had to hack out my heart to make the parting easier. *Fuck*.

"...charisma and charm," Javi says, breaking into my thoughts.

"What?" I ask, pulling the phone away from my face and finally giving him my attention.

"That Forbes piece you did a few months back finally came out today, and they said you had charisma and charm, so you must have been on your best behavior for the interview. Was it a female reporter? Were you trying to get her to go out with you after the piece? If you did, that would have been a good way to tank what she wrote later, knowing how quickly you move through women."

I run a hand through my hair, thick and wild from the dive. "I know better than to sleep with a journalist," I say, gazing out the side window. Especially one with an interest in getting a scoop on Olympus or my family.

That piece was done on my recent acquisition of a transcontinental airline catering to executives and private transportation needs. It's a pet project, really, one I didn't want to fall under the Olympus International umbrella. The journalist wanted a fresh take on sustainable travel in the modern age, something private jets generally aren't known for but meshes well with another project of mine for a cleaner burning engine that requires less fuel that does fall under the Olympus umbrella called Pegasus. I didn't come up with that technology myself, but I do own the company that did, therefore, my interview. The project is hush-hush, but we spoke at length about the need for sustainable travel and how this engine will revolutionize the industry. I'm quite proud of where it's going and know it will shake up everything once it's released.

"Remind me to send flowers to Forbes when we get back to the office." I pull a pair of sunglasses out of the center console and slide them onto my face.

"Weiss already has. She follows up with all of your interviews," Javi replies, signaling onto the interstate, thick with Atlanta morning traffic that crawls through the arteries of the city like the grease that's ubiquitous to Southern cooking.

"We pay her well, right?" I ask, half serious. Katherine Weiss is my middle-aged executive assistant and she's an invaluable asset to my team. She knows my schedule, and my brothers' schedules, better than we do. She can book absolutely anything, with anyone, is ruthless about protecting our interests and time, and she's incredibly thorough. I'd wanted to hire one of the cute twenty-somethings who applied, but Hayes put his foot down. He reasoned that our closest support staff needed to be discreet, dependable, have incredible work ethics, and not want to get into bed with any of us. Weiss checked all the boxes, and she's been with me since I took on the CEO mantle when my brothers and I created Olympus International in our twenties, from the bones of our father's mining operations.

"That you do. She seems quite content to boss you around daily at her six-figure salary."

I nod, satisfied. I turn my phone over in my hand and know I shouldn't, but I can't keep myself from opening The Atlanta Haute List story again. *Who is this fucking meathead Harlowe has been seeing?* Before I can open a new tab and Google him myself, a more pressing thought enters my brain.

Who knocked her up? I scan the story again and confirm that the boy is four years old. The unrelenting flip my stomach is doing clues me into what my subconscious is already working over. I do some quick math, adding in a nine-month pregnancy. I'll have to check my schedule from that time five years ago to be sure, but I have a sinking feeling that it could line up.

Do I have a son?

My thoughts are interrupted by blaring horns and Javi swerving toward the shoulder to try to avoid the suddenly dead-stopped line of traffic ahead of us.

Two

Harlowe

"Great. Just great," I mutter under my breath when I see the red taillights lined up for miles on the highway.

"You should *not* have taken I-85. I told you it would be a nightmare during rush hour," Paloma says from the backseat. I glare daggers at her through the rearview mirror. She meets my glance with stoic hazel eyes that scream *I told you so, bitch.* She's my best friend and personal stylist, but she likes to be in charge, and backseat driving is one of her favorite ways to rule the friendship. I ignore her.

"Alicia, I'll never make it home in time to get Hendricks to school with this traffic. I knew I should have arranged with one of the other moms in the class to pick him up," I complain, casting a glance at my manager in the seat beside me.

She's busy tapping away on her phone with a bemused twist to her lips that tells me she's responding to another press request for me. Alicia doesn't care about anyone's schedule but mine, even when it's my son who's missing out. I knew it was a possibility, but I told my babysitter that I would be back in time, and now it's too late to change the plans with school having started while I was still on set and unable to send her a message to take him in after all.

"Honey, it's fine. He's four," Alicia says, laying a manicured hand against my arm and looking up at me from heavily lashed brown eyes. "What are they going to do, give him detention for being late?"

"Well, I would've been back in time if the news segment hadn't dragged on and the producers let me shorten my cooking demonstration to just one of the recipes rather than all three," I retort.

I felt the minutes ticking by when I should have been out the door. Even TV magic with prepped bowls of ingredients, shoving the uncooked pans into the fake oven, and pulling out the pre-finished food to show how marvelous it could all look couldn't get me out of that studio on time.

"The extra air time was so worth it!" she enthuses, brandishing her phone with a page of analytics pulled up. I glance at it for a second before returning my eyes to traffic. "Your social engagement went up sixty-three percent while it aired, and you have new channel subscribers and followers," she sing-songs. Of course, she's thrilled. It's her job to see that my new cookbook, *At Home With Harlowe: A Foulmouthed Foodie's Guide To Eating Well*, gets the best press and she wants me to ride the release week momentum as much as I can.

I shouldn't have been such a pushover for the press my publisher and Alicia set up, knowing it was going to cause a scheduling conflict. I know it's really good coverage that will likely drive up sales, but it's still interfering with my son's life, and that's one promise I made to myself that I'm at risk of breaking.

"Breathe, Lolo. No use fretting over it now when you can't do anything. Just call the school and excuse his absence, or whatever. That's what I do for my boys," Callie adds to the mix from her seat in the back under a stack of cookbooks. She's never worried a day in her life, not for money, jobs, or the prospect of having her kid kicked out of school. She lives in a daydream bubble and somehow things just turn up roses for her, thanks to a mega-rich older husband who holds ownership in the Atlanta Condors football team.

I snake my phone out of my purse from the center console and fumble to pull up the school's number. It's just preschool, but they are incredibly strict with their schedule and I don't want to be on the administration's bad side. It costs an arm and a leg to keep Hendricks in this program, and there is a waiting list for years they could easily replace him with.

I never knew how savage preschool was until I looked into enrolling my kid in the best school I could find for his super smart little brain and learned firsthand that I should've signed him up when I found out I was pregnant. Lucky for me, I know the right people, mainly Callie's husband's acquaintance who's on the board, and I carry just enough of a sparkle of former celebrity status that a spot was made available when Hendricks was ready.

The phone connects through my car speakers and the call is answered while the girls grow quiet.

"Hi, this is Harlowe Sorenson, Hendricks's mom. I'm so sorry, I'm running late and won't be able to drop him off until," I pause and my eyes dart to the clock, then back to the gridlocked traffic, "probably ten."

"Ms. Sorenson, that's an hour and a half into the school day. Our policy allows late drop-offs up to fifteen minutes, but after that, the classes move quickly into their programming. Unfortunately, it's too disruptive to the students' academic and imaginative pursuits to have a peer join them later," the receptionist informs me, her voice taking on a patronizing tone.

"That's bull—" I stop myself before I curse out this woman who is probably paid minimum wage and has school policies she has to follow.

Giggles erupt, and Callie quickly covers her mouth with her hand.

"I'm sorry, but this is preschool. It's not like it's medical school. They fingerpaint and chase each other around before listening to stories and having a nap. Not exactly a rigorous curriculum of strictly academic excellence. I doubt any of these four-year-olds would be *disrupted* by Hendricks arriving late." I roll my eyes as I say it because it's my fault my kid attends a pretentious preschool. I wanted him to have the best opportunities I could afford, and this place is ranked first in the Atlanta metro. I hear a supportive hum of approval from the peanut gallery in my car.

"Despite what you may think, our classes are designed to prepare young minds for their future, shaping their development and directing milestones to best cultivate their cognitive functioning. You will just have to keep Hendricks home today and drop him off tomorrow during the specified window. I've noted the absence in his file. I hope you're aware that you only get three unplanned absences per term before you will be asked to re-evaluate your commitment to your son's future."

Alicia scoffs and stops her phone scrolling. Paloma clicks her tongue softly. I catch Callie's worried expression in my quick glance in the rearview mirror.

Damn. The preschool staff lay it on thick. Hendricks has only been at the school for a few months, and he seems to love it. Guilt gnaws at me, knowing my career has gotten in the way of his happiness and education. Every day he comes home with a new story or fact that I end up having to look up myself just to see if he's making it up. He's an absolute sponge and is doing so well. I was a good enough student, with a demanding Asian mother who pushed for academic excellence, but I didn't go to college. I just went straight into modeling after high school. Hendricks definitely got his incredible brain and aptitude for learning from his businessman father.

"Fine. He'll be in class tomorrow."

I hit the hang-up button on the dash screen and look up in time to see the line of cars stopped in front of me. Gasps sound around me as I slam on the brake pedal. Adrenaline whisks through my veins, the tingly rush of fear an instantaneous cold draft. I manage to stop with mere feet between me and the next car, but quickly I'm rocked by the slamming of a car into my rear bumper. My head snaps back painfully from the momentum and I already know it wasn't just a light scratch I can ignore. By some miracle, I was far enough back not to hit the car in front of me.

"Oh no, a motherfucker didn't," I swear, thinking of how much more this will set me behind. I don't have time to deal with a fender-bender today and all the complications that are going to add to my already haphazard schedule. I have more press interviews, and a signing at a bookstore tonight. "Are y'all alright?"

"*Ay, Dios.* I knew I-85 would be a horrible choice. It's cursed," Paloma mutters, clutching her seatbelt when I turn quickly to see if the girls are hurt.

Callie rights herself in her seat, her stack of books now on the floor and a stunned expression on her face. "Did someone just, like, hit us? How rude," she says, without any irony at all. *Bless her heart.*

"Atlanta drivers are worse than LA drivers, I swear." Alicia rolls her neck and resumes her phone tapping, hardly fazed.

"No, no, no." I signal to get over to the shoulder. "This cannot be happening."

"If we get this wrapped up quickly, we can still make the virtual interview," Alicia says, her fingers flying over her phone, likely managing some PR magic I want no part of. She's pragmatic to a fault, but damn good at her job, and I leave her to it.

I put my car in park and turn off the ignition with trembling fingers. The adrenaline is still running high and I'm not taking it well. Or maybe it's combining with all the caffeine I've had to get me through the four a.m. wake up and early morning on set, jacking me up with anxiety and making me shake like a cracked-out chihuahua.

"Look alive, ladies. A man approaches," Paloma says in her richly melodic voice.

"We are alive, Paloma," Callie assures her, placing a slim hand on Paloma's wrist with her big blue eyes opened wide.

Despite the warning, a gentle tap on my window startles me, and I look up to see the driver who hit me. He's on the tall side and of average build, with dark hair, olive tanned skin, well-dressed, and good-looking enough for me to note about someone who just rear-ended me in traffic. He motions for me to get out of the car, and I do. I hear three doors open in quick succession after mine. *Great. Now I'll have a mob to witness the exchange of insurance.*

"Ma'am, I'm so sorry. Traffic stopped suddenly and I tried to get onto the shoulder, but I still hit the edge of your bumper. I'll take care of everything, but you'll need to take photos and call your insurance."

"He called you ma'am," Paloma snorts, coming up on my left and digging her elbow into my side.

We have been friends for a decade, practically growing up together in the fashion industry. She styled many of the shoots I modeled on and became my best friend. She was supportive enough to follow me back here when I retired from the business, though it feels like ages since either of us saw that life. But I'm only twenty-nine years old. That doesn't really qualify as ma'am territory. Although, this is the South, and he's probably a good ol' boy relying on his manners. I shake it off and nod.

"It's been that kind of morning, that's for sure," I say, feeling the weight of responsibility and my schedule sitting heavily on my shoulders. I rub my neck and look at the traffic slowly creeping past us. There's a weariness I hadn't anticipated clinging to me, and that is almost more distressing than the accident, though a sore neck certainly won't help.

I've been doing non-stop press for a week leading up to the release of the cookbook, and there are still a few more weeks of events to keep the momentum up now that it's released. Alicia says we may be entertaining a cooking show option with a major channel because the pre-sales have been so high, but they want to see more engagement with my Foulmouthed Foodie YouTube and social channels.

I'm known for dropping F-bombs and maybe an ingredient or two on my tits on occasion. I make people laugh and salivate with both my food and my body. It's a narrow line to walk of funny and sexy, but it's won me a loyal following of men and women who enjoy my content. It's taken me years to embrace who I am at my core—a woman who now loves her body despite years of hating it, who wants others to embrace themselves also, and who makes damn good food that everyone can enjoy while saying the shit everyone is thinking, anyway.

It's that channel that got me the book deal in the first place, as I have grown my audience to several million subscribers who interact regularly with my videos and social media. It's been a full-time job just managing that alone, and now I have to wrestle with all of this.

"Come around back so we can get you out of here as quickly as possible," the man says, taking control of the situation as kindly as possible. Definitely a high-level businessman of some sort, if that's how he can manage even an accident.

I follow him around the back of my black Audi SUV, the girls on my stilettoed heel, and I keep my eyes trained on the bumper, looking for damage.

"Oh, fuck," I whisper, seeing the smashed-up right side of the bumper. It's completely crushed, the paint around the back hatch also scraped.

"Holy shit!" Callie shrieks.

"That's it?" Alicia drolls at the same time. I look between them and shake my head. Two sides of the same coin, these two.

"I think it's still drivable, but that'll definitely need to be fixed. I'm Javier Montero, by the way."

I nod absently. My thoughts focused on how long the car will be in the shop, if I can get a loaner vehicle on short notice to get downtown tonight, and how much it'll all cost. I do well on affiliate money and sponsorship deals with my channel and social media, and with my book advance, but there's always the worry of what could happen in the future. This is a significant expense.

"She's obviously not pleased to meet you, given the circumstances," Paloma says for me, and I give her a look to keep out of it.

"Harlowe?"

I glance up when I hear my name spoken by a familiar resonating baritone that has haunted me for five years. My heart leaps into my throat when I catch sight of the passenger getting out of the Land Rover pulled up behind us.

"Zander," I whisper, my already shaking hand coming up and covering my mouth.

I step back against Paloma, her fingers gripping my arms in support. Callie straightens in reflex next to me, her impeccably inflated chest turning to the man looking toward us. I'm not surprised by her reaction. Everything sits up and takes notice when Zander Olsen arrives. Even my nipples are straining through the lace of my bra and poking at my tight, dove gray top. His eyes clock the traitors and a ghost of a smile crosses his lips. My lips flatten in response, even if my nipples refuse to.

"Y'all know each other?" Javier asks, looking between me and the bad boy billionaire casually exiting the SUV's passenger side like it's a fancy exotic car and not a utilitarian vehicle.

Zander strides toward us with the confidence of an action movie hero walking away from an explosion scene. Too bad the explosion is the obliteration of my thong, because even my pussy is a traitor, and as much as I loathe seeing him, he still makes me impossibly wet with one fucking look, and I absolutely hate him for it.

Behind me, Paloma snorts derisively, Callie stands glaze-eyed and silent, and Alicia stays glued to her phone, uninterested.

"Barely," I answer, lowering my hand and tearing my eyes from Zander's perfectly chiseled face that has starred in far too many of my anxiety dreams over the last few years. How can he look exactly as I remember? Devastatingly handsome—the kind of beautiful that is life-altering—with eyes that take me in, yet hold no warmth for me now when they were once endless wildfires that consumed me.

Self-consciousness rises, and I'm acutely aware of the weight I've put on since he saw me last, the softness of my thighs that were once toned, the way my ass has grown and jiggles, the remaining hint of a momma belly that won't quite leave despite all of my workouts. I can't imagine how he would ever pick me now, because I'm so different from the naïve twenty-four-year-old swimsuit and fashion model he knew then. I chastise my own cancerous thoughts and repeat the mantra that has sustained me as my figure and life transformed. *I am enough.*

Fuck, I have to be enough.

I pull my eyes away from Zander and turn to answer Javier's question. "I'm shocked he remembers my name."

The coldness I'm able to infuse into my tone surprises me, given how rattled I feel, and Javier gets a look of understanding on his face. That's right, I'm just one of Zander's *many* conquests. Have a laugh at my expense later.

"How could I forget it?" Zander asks, striding closer, drawing my attention again. "You were *the* Sports Illustrated Swimsuit model of the year and on dozens of mainstream ad campaigns. Your face and name were everywhere when I met you."

His voice is unreasonably cool and collected, a hint of humor barely keeping his recitation of facts from sounding banal. I clench my teeth but manage to plaster on a perfectly calm face. We had so much more than my professional accomplishments, but why would he care to recite those facts? He doesn't *do* attachments.

"That's not all you should remember, asshole," Paloma says under her breath, defensively stepping up to shield me.

I lay a hand on her arm and shake my head. The less we engage Zander, the better. *Not now.* Maybe not ever.

She is the only one who knows to what degree Zander Olsen changed my life. She watched me struggle with the consequences of time spent in his captivating presence and saw what the sting of being completely shut out of it when he was done with me did to my confidence. Of course, Paloma would want to rip his eyes out now, even if I just want to disappear from his radar once again.

Javier's eyes widen. "I thought you looked familiar! You're *Harlowe Sorenson*! You were a Guess model, right? You did that iconic commercial in the field of yellow flowers with just cut-off jeans shorts on, the flowers covering your..." he trails off, running a hand through his hair and looking anywhere but at my face. Or my tits, which the yellow flowers barely covered in that particular ad campaign.

I cringe inwardly, thinking of my late teens and early twenties and all the brand campaigns, photoshoots with big names, swimsuit fashion shows, and cosmetic lines I desperately tried to land. It's still the scantily clad ones that stick with people. Even now, after major self-reflection and work in therapy, all the stinging rejections for being too ethnic, not ethnic enough, too big, too small, too brown, too Asian, too indeterminate, too mixed, not American enough, too loud, not having a recognizable name, and a million other reasons for rejection that were given to me while I was a working model still bubble to mind with the mention of one of the few campaigns I actually landed.

"Harlowe has had a million photoshoots. She was the face of Givenchy perfume, which is truly iconic." Callie pops a hand on her hip as if to chastise the man for not knowing.

Callie wasn't a model, but her work on a reality show allowed her to create a clothing line that is still going strong, so she's just as familiar with the industry as I am. We became friends in LA through Alicia, who manages us both. It was a stroke of luck when she met Myles Klein and he moved her to Atlanta after he put a huge diamond on her finger and bankrolled her fashion line. He is absolutely besotted with his wife, and Callie isn't complaining. And I like having my friends all in the same city.

"I think I'll just take some photos and get out of here. I have things to do and spending time on the shoulder of a major highway during rush hour isn't high on my priority list." I cast a look back at the traffic crawling by us and pull my phone out of my back pocket to start snapping pictures of the damage. "Ladies, you can get back in the car now."

I can feel the disappointment from Callie as she turns and struts back to the car. Paloma hesitates, eyeing me but saying nothing, for once. Alicia started for the car before I finished my sentence.

"Oh, yeah, sorry. I'll grab my insurance card." Javier turns back to the Land Rover, leaving me to face Zander alone.

I feel him staring at me and try hard to ignore him. This morning is feeling more and more like an episode of Black Mirror than my actual life.

"You look good, Lowe," he says, voice quiet and familiar. Too familiar for not having seen each other in five years.

I don't even spare him a look. "You look the same."

"You're a mom now."

My spine stiffens as I fight the urge to freeze, but slowly rise back up from the crouch I had taken to get a close-up photo of the bumper damage. I turn towards him in what feels like slow motion, my face set in steel, not giving away that my heart is hammering away in my chest, full of fear. Thoughts race through my mind at what he could possibly know and why he is bringing this up now.

"I am. It's nothing for you to worry about."

Zander's expression flickers, a bit of the casual openness shutters, replaced by a mask of indifference that slips forward in the blink of an eye. An eye that matches those of my beautiful son.

"Is he..." He blinks, pausing for a moment before a brief shake of his head and continuing with a wry smile. "You're with a football player, I saw. Is he good to you?"

"You seem a little too knowledgeable of my personal life for someone who doesn't do attachments." My voice is calm, but tinged with vicious malice. I don't confirm anything other than his awareness of me so long after I was told he would never care about me long-term.

"The Atlanta Haute List seems to like reporting on your life right now almost as much as they scrutinize mine. I can't help but read the stories when I'm ensuring they aren't spreading too many rumors about me."

Ah. It always comes back to how things affect him. "Feel free to skip those stories. It's of no consequence to you what I happen to be doing or who I'm with. I know you don't care about the people you've bulldozed in your quest for world dominance. No attachments and all that."

I'm glib, but the words still taste of poisonous hurts and insecurities. He can't possibly begin to understand the pain he caused me, even though I knew his "rules". *No attachments. No repeats. Short-term fun only.* I'd agreed to them, even. How was I supposed to know we would find something special in the middle of the ocean and it would change me forever? I thought it had changed him, too, but I was wrong.

I can't have been the only foolish girl to think maybe I was different. That maybe the extra time he spent with me meant something. Maybe I meant something. I quickly learned just how wrong I was to assume he would ever care about anything other than his work and his own pleasure.

Zander's face gives nothing away, and I'm surprised to feel disappointment when he nods. "Take care of yourself, Lowe. Javi will get this straightened out. You won't have to worry about a thing."

Words freeze in my throat when he turns, dismissing me, and returning to the Land Rover as Javier hurries forward, wringing his hands.

"I reported this to my insurance, and they'll cover everything. But," he says, looking away from me in hesitation, "I don't have my card on me. I can text you a photo when I get back to the office. I'm so sorry to take up so much of your morning and for causing this inconvenience."

"That's too fucking convenient," I say, hand moving to my hip. "How do I know you won't just disappear and leave me with a crazy insurance claim to take care of? Do you work with him?" I ask, nodding at Zander.

"Yes, so you know where to find me. If there is anything insurance doesn't cover, I will personally. I don't want you coming out of pocket for anything. This was my fault. Let's exchange numbers in case there is anything that comes up?" His voice belies an almost endearing nervousness.

I sigh as I enter his number in my phone, and quickly text him my contact information, just so I can check he gave me a real number. His phone vibrates, and he shows me, an apologetic half-smile softening the rugged planes of his face. "If I have to drag you out of that tower downtown to get your damn insurance card, I'm going to be pissed," I mutter.

"I promise you won't have to. I'm so sorry about this. I'll take care of everything. You won't have to pay for a thing," Javier repeats as we finish up.

I can feel Zander's eyes on me throughout the exchange, and it makes me nervous. More so because he knows about Hendricks. I wanted to stay off his radar for my son's sake, but fate has other plans, it seems.

When I finally flop back into my seat, I have three sets of eyes glued to me. "What do you nosy bitches want?" I ask, signaling to get back onto the highway in the still gridlocked morning traffic.

"Why didn't I know you dated Zander Olsen?" Alicia asks immediately.

"He's so hot. You two are like gorgeousness personified standing next to each other," Callie gushes. "I think I was just inspired for my spring/summer line from that one interaction alone! I can see it now, menswear-inspired pieces with florals and chiffon," she muses, clapping her hands and speaking her thoughts out loud.

"Oh, please. Don't wax *hoetic* about that jackass," Paloma says to Callie, before leaning forward and focusing on me. "Are you okay, Lolo?" she asks, placing a cool hand on my shoulder. I cover hers with my own for a moment and check the lanes next to me as traffic finally eases up, and the flow opens enough for me to merge

back onto the highway.

I feel more disrupted and unsure of my life than ever. I started the morning on a high feeling like I had my shit together, promoting my new cookbook on a local news channel. I began feeling like a failure for running late, ruining my son's day, and possibly jeopardizing his spot at school. It really went downhill with the weird flex of fate of being hit in traffic, both slowing down my already beleaguered schedule, then, the ultimate fuck your self-confidence, chucking Zander into the already chaotic mix.

If he only knew that I see his face every day when I look at my son, that I think of our short time together and my failure to create the sort of security for my son that a father would have provided, he may have been less casual, less unaffected. But that's not how Zander rolls, and I knew it when I agreed to a spontaneous trip with him. Stupid, naïve girl. There is so much I would change, so much I wish I had known then.

Even so, the best thing to ever happen to me came from it.

"I'm okay. For now," I answer.

Three

Harlowe

Five Years Ago

"What do I pack for two weeks in the Maldives with a man I barely know but want to climb like a tree and live in his branches like a granola hippie activist?" I ask Paloma as I throw open my closet and haul out my suitcase. It's seen the world with me as I live the crazy nomadic life of an international supermodel that I've been swept up into the last six years since being discovered by a talent scout in Atlanta while out shopping with my mom.

Yeah, that's a weird little *only-in-the-movies moment* I never thought would be my real life, but here I am, on more magazine covers than I can keep track of, letting my manager book my next deals for brands that wouldn't have given me a second look just a few years ago, and being invited by a billionaire to accompany him on a two-week trip to the Maldives.

"Lots and lots of bikinis. I don't think you need to bring anything else. You already know he is going to rail the ever-living hell out of you, so lingerie is a waste of space unless you think he'll get bored and you'll need to spice it up. Two weeks is a long time for a renowned fuckboy like him," she muses, pulling open a dresser drawer and grabbing a handful of silk and lace pretty things thoughtfully.

Those pieces probably came home with me from the countless photoshoots, fashion shows, and campaigns I've shot for various lingerie brands. I was blessed with a body made for the likes of Agent Provocateur and La Perla, brands I've become well acquainted with at this point, and a face that cosmetics companies can't wait to book. I'm lucky, so damn lucky, but sometimes I feel like the only thing I'm good for is being pretty, or having a body that turns people on. Zander Olsen is just the latest to be fascinated by my bangable body and pretty face.

"You mean if *I* get bored. He'll have his hands full with me, fuckboy or not," I joke.

I can be whatever flavor of plaything Zander Olsen wants for this trip. I know what this is. He's a bored billionaire who's interested in fucking me, and I'm just as interested in fucking him. It's mutually beneficial and I'm perfectly content to take a few weeks off to see if he can back up the reputation he's built for himself among the modeling community for being a spectacular lay and a pretty interesting guy in the small amount of time he's given women before and after taking them to bed.

I've met him a few times at industry events. He's hot, he's made me laugh, and I finally agreed to go to dinner with him after making him work for it. I wasn't going to be the typical model who went willingly to his bed, or even into his DMs. I would make him come to me. And he did, like a very good boy.

At dinner last night he offered to take me on this trip and ensured I knew there would be no strings, no attachments, just the two weeks. I know that's already way more than anyone else has been given. So I accepted. And here I am, hastily packing my suitcase and ready to see what Zander Olsen is really *packing*.

"Some of these pieces are so pretty," I say, picking up a strappy purple number I remember being a bit hard to get into, but was a total knockout. I purse my lips and toss it back in the drawer, knowing I want easy pieces to get into and out of. Easy access, and all that.

Paloma holds up an armful of bikinis in every color and dumps them on my bed. "Lolo, no one could get bored with you. Just look at you." She waves her arm up and down my body for emphasis. "I'm sure you two will be having too much fun and sex to care about much else." She sighs before she turns and scowls at me. "I'm not jealous at all. Nope. I don't need a rich as sin, hot as hell, tall drink of water to offer to take *me* away on a tropical vacation for two freaking weeks. I won't be having vivid fantasies imagining just this very thing the whole time you're gone. Not jealous one bit," she says, her voice growing more strained as she speaks.

I laugh as I throw in a wardrobe of designer dresses, shorts, skirts, and tops. "I'll be sure to bring home a beautiful souvenir for you."

"Business casual, even for vacation? You're taking this seriously, I see," I say with a smile, taking in Zander's charcoal slacks and crisp white shirt as he extends his hand and helps me out of the car he sent to collect me, pulling me onto the tarmac of the private section of the airport. He flew to LA from his home in Atlanta and we'll head to the Maldives from here.

He looks incredible, as usual, but he could be headed to a business deal in that outfit. At least he lost the tie and jacket. I'm wearing a bright yellow halter dress from the Chloé resort collection I shot last spring, and the suitcase that is being unloaded by the driver is full of fashionable clothing all suited for the tropical vacation we are headed on. I'm nothing if not the consummate model, always prepared for the job at hand, and this particular job is to be the beautiful, willing companion to this sexy as hell man who is whisking me off across the world. I know my role. I'm ready for it, not a hair out of place, and a wide smile already on my face just for him.

"Only the best for you," he says with a grin.

He wraps an arm around my waist, drawing me against his firm body. Even in my tall espadrilles, he's still a few inches taller than me, but I can look him in the eyes, and those gray depths are sparkling with sexy challenge.

"Are you ready for two weeks of escaping from reality?"

"Are you ready to spend two weeks keeping up with me?" I toss back, sliding my hand up his neck until I can cup his jaw and run my thumb over his full bottom lip. I may know my role, but I can still keep him on his toes.

"Full of surprises, aren't you," he growls, his lip brushing my thumb with the movement before he sucks it into his mouth, and I smile at the sensation.

He catches my wrist in the iron grip of his own hand so I don't pull away until he's finished swirling his tongue around and nipping at the pad. He uses his grip on my wrist to pull my thumb out of his mouth with a pop, brings my hand down behind my back, and keeps it there where he laces our fingers.

"I like a challenge, Harlowe. Keep it up. We'll have fun either way, but this way, it'll be even better."

His words are a hot promise spoken directly against my mouth, and I smile coyly at his words. I let my eyes close and run my nose along his cheek in a soft caress. "Promise?" I whisper into his ear before I bite the lobe gently and pull.

"Fuck," he swears roughly, giving into the temptation and turning his face to catch my lips with his.

Suddenly, it's like my new reason for living is to have his lips on mine, because holy shit can this man kiss. One of his arms is still around my waist, our fingers entwined together at my lower back, keeping our bodies pressed tightly together. His other hand has found its way to my throat, thumb and forefinger directing my jaw *just so* as he claims my mouth. I swallow against the tight hold he has on me and shiver, fully aware of how in control of this kiss he is while I'm plundered for his pleasure. He gives as much as he takes, and when he pulls back, I feel hazy, lust-filled, completely out of sorts and off my own game.

"You're going to be trouble," I say, hating the slight shake in my voice that gives away how affected I am by that kiss and the interaction so far.

"I was just going to say the same fucking thing about you," he says, giving me a look I'd call calculating, but it's quickly replaced by one that looks a whole lot like *fuck it*.

That second look is the one that gives me the confidence to lace my fingers in his again and pull him toward the waiting plane. "Think they will serve us champagne as soon as we hit cruising altitude?" I ask.

"Of course," he answers, sounding a bit curious.

"Good. Champagne always makes me want to suck a fat cock, and from what you had pressed against me just now, I'm pretty sure you're going to make my champagne dreams come true, and I want your eyes rolling back in your head before we're above open ocean."

The groan of longing that meets my ears has my smile curving up just as I'm about to hit the stairs to the jet. He pulls on my hand and stops me from climbing the stairs before he pulls me back against him, where I can once again feel the very large evidence I based my assumptions on.

"You are most certainly going to be trouble," he says in my ear. "Now, be a good girl and let the flight crew get everything situated before you start shocking them. Save it all for me and the private room where I'm very intrigued by this champagne claim of yours. I don't want to share any part of you with anyone else."

"Yes, sir," I say, winking and starting again for the stairs. This game thrills me, and I don't even know all the rules. We seem to be making them up as we go.

I swear I hear him murmur, "Fucking perfect," before he follows.

Zander

"Well, that's going to tank my insurance premium," Javi mutters, climbing back into the Land Rover and slinging his phone into the center console. "I can't believe I don't have my insurance card in here."

"The SUV didn't take too much damage. You'll just need to replace a headlight and maybe the bumper. It could have been worse," I offer. "Besides, you had a bunch of beautiful women with all their attention on you. How often does that happen?"

He shakes his head and ignores my jab. "Are you going to tell me about that thing with you and Harlowe? When did you date her?" He uses *date* liberally, and he knows it, but he's not crass enough to call it what it usually is and ask when I fucked her.

"I met her at a few parties and industry events about five years ago, when she was on the cover of every magazine, like I said."

I don't tell him how her presence nearly took my breath away the first time I saw her in person, or how I pursued her wildly, knowing I wanted to be near her, in her orbit, and maybe shine as brightly as she did. I even found business reasons to be in LA or New York when I knew she was working there, so I might have the chance to run into her again. I don't tell him how she is the only woman I actually went after, rather than letting her come to me. How crazy I was about her.

"Cagey bastard," Javi says, signaling and pulling into traffic after Harlowe's black Audi vanishes in the sluggish flow of Atlanta traffic, and the pang of losing sight of her makes me want to rub at my chest.

Instead of giving in to that desire, I smile as if I'm entirely unaffected and lean back in my seat. I don't kiss and tell, no matter how much Javi wants to know.

Seeing Harlowe in person rattled something loose in me. Memories broke away from the vault I had them stored in, flooding back to me even more than when I saw her photos on the Atlanta Haute List.

The rock salt rasp of her voice after diving for abalone and lobster.

The throaty laugh of hers that feels like it was connected straight to my cock.

Her slender fingers and the deft work they made of my swim trunks.

The way she would hold her breath just before she came.

Her devastated face when I told her there was no future for us, no matter what she felt.

I breathe in deeply and actively work to stop the avalanche of memories and slam the vault closed again. There's a reason it was locked up in the first place.

"Let me know where she takes her car in for service and I'll take care of her rental. She needs something safe. She has a kid to think of," I say quietly, without looking at Javi as we finally exit the congested highway. I feel him glance over at me quickly, but I don't meet his stare. A muscle tics in my jaw under his appraisal.

"Yeah man, if that's what you want, I will," he replies, a little confused.

"I'll pay for the whole repair for you both. Just arrange it with Weiss. And don't tell Harlowe I'm involved."

I'm grateful when Javi doesn't reply to that and lets me brood in peace the rest of the drive in. I'm able to work myself out of the weird headspace Harlowe threw me into before we finally pull up to the Olympus International Tower in downtown Atlanta, park, and ride the elevator to the top floors. It's a little later than I had anticipated, but I'm the CEO. I get to walk into work whenever I want. Payton and Hayes are waiting for us in the boardroom, going over figures for the deal I'm set to lead this week.

"Hey there, adrenaline junkies. How was the freefall?" Payton asks, leaning back in his seat while Hayes keeps his eyes on the paper in front of him. He's a workaholic even more so than I can claim to be, though his hot young wife has taken some of the edge off. Mostly. He's been a bit better now that Paige is pregnant. He actually leaves the office at a normal time these days.

"Awful," Javi answers for us. "This *cabrón* has a death wish." He pours a cup of coffee from the sideboard and stirs in a generous amount of sugar with his milk. His Cuban roots are showing more than usual this morning.

"I don't have a death wish. I just prefer to start the week in a way that'll get my blood flowing. I think better that way."

Weiss hands me a cappuccino and a folder, annotated and ready for my attention before swiftly disappearing to work her admin magic elsewhere. I offer my thanks to her retreating back, but she doesn't even say hello, and it almost makes me laugh. She really is the only woman on Earth I can't charm.

Javi brings his sweet coffee to the table and settles in, his attention fixed on Payton.

"To top it off, I rear-ended a car full of hot chicks in traffic on I-85," Javi continues, as if I hadn't interjected. "And it turns out this fucker slept with the driver and is being cagey as hell about the details. Did y'all know he bagged the hottest Sports Illustrated model ever, Harlowe Sorenson? She was my favorite spank bank material for two years straight. I was bummed when she mysteriously disappeared from the public eye right as she was exploding in popularity."

I barely maintain my calm and collected exterior at his words that normally wouldn't have garnered a reaction from me. Instead, unwanted feelings of possession spike through my veins and make me want to do unspeakably violent things to him for even imagining my Harlowe naked, let alone whatever depraved acts got him off.

I suppress the murderous thoughts and yank my own leash to get my thoughts away from she-who-must-not-be-named. She's not even mine to be possessive of, despite the roaring in my pulse that seems to shout it. *Mine! Mine! Mine!*

"You'll have to be more specific when it comes to hot models Zander's slept with," Hayes says, still focused on his stack of paperwork, but finally contributing to the conversation. "They're a dime a dozen and I've served probably twenty of them NDAs or escorted them out of his penthouse at one point or another when they didn't understand that Zander was done with them."

"You don't remember her, Hayes?" Payton asks, throwing a ball of paper at his head. Hayes swats it away and looks up with a scowl.

"Trying to remember all of Zander's conquests is a full-time job, and if you haven't noticed, we're plenty busy here as it is."

"Oh, come on, I can't be the only one who remembers everything! It's no fun." Payton huffs and leans back in his chair as he taps on a tablet. "You have to remember when Zander took two weeks off and went MIA in the Maldives with a model. Like, five years back. It was the last time he took that much time off, and probably the only time he's spent more than two nights with a woman."

He puts a photo of Harlowe from Sports Illustrated on the boardroom screen and Hayes looks up, his eyes widening in surprise. It's the photo that originally caught my interest. Harlowe stretched out on her back in shallow water on the beach, one arm thrown up over her head, the other covering her bare tits, her hips turned invitingly toward the camera. Her dark eyes are half-lidded, a look so feline you feel like prey just waiting to be caught, her full lips parted and almost smiling, knowing the effect she has on you. Her appeal jumps out of the still image and grabs you by the balls. There's no way to see that photo and not want what she's offering.

"Oh. Her." His ominous tone and lack of additional commentary have me instantly on alert.

"What does that mean, you inscrutable fuck?" I ask, unable to hold back my curiosity, and honestly, my intrigue with Harlowe. There's a pang of longing so strong I have to physically stop it with a hand to my thigh, gripping the muscle hard enough to bruise to distract myself and keep my cock from rising to attention any further.

"It's nothing," Hayes says evasively. "I just remember her now."

"And?" I ask, ready to chase this rabbit to its untimely end now that my brothers have been extra shitty about it.

Hayes takes a deep breath and exhales in a way that speaks volumes. *You're wasting my time and this is bullshit,* he seems to say just with that sigh and the scowl he throws my way.

"She called the office, a lot, and even went as far as trying to get into the tower after you ended things. I had to explain that you were done with her and didn't want to hear from her ever again and escorted her out. I don't think she was very happy that you cut off communication after your romantic time in the Maldives. I couldn't get her to sign the NDA." His last words are spoken ominously, like he's been holding onto that and expecting trouble ever since.

She came here? To Olympus International Tower? Why would she have done that? She knew the score before we ever left the US. We would go back to our own lives when we returned. There wouldn't be any connection or repeats. She agreed.

I didn't know any of this. I hadn't wanted to. The staff and my brothers know I don't want contact with women here at work. I guess they've been handling more than I ever knew if Hayes had to escort Harlowe out of the building himself.

"What did she want?" I ask, my voice sounding slightly eager, despite the coldness I infuse into it.

Hayes rubs a hand across his face. "She just wanted to talk to you, and only you. She didn't want to leave a message or tell me why she was so insistent on speaking with you, so I have nothing more to tell you than that. She was pretty worked up and left angry as hell. She threw a fit and scattered paper all over the conference room. She even threatened me to my face. I was impressed by her."

I look at Hayes and finally understand why he was being inscrutable before. He isn't impressed by many people, so to have a woman I fucked manage that while he was trying to clean up the situation I created says a lot. He's an intimidating fucker—a big, ruthless man with cold green eyes and a scary-ass aura, who is often tasked with the most unpleasant parts of our business, and seems to enjoy them a little too much. But Harlowe is the fiercest woman I've ever met. If anyone could go toe-to-toe with Hayes and walk out the victor with his respect, it would be her.

"You're awfully interested now, Zand. Does it have to do with seeing her again today, or is there more you're not telling us?" Payton asks, drawing my attention away from Hayes, who refuses to say any more about Harlowe.

"It's nothing. Just curious now that fate threw her back in my path. I don't do repeats." If I just keep telling myself that, it'll become true.

"Oh, we know," Hayes drawls, sounding bored and already back to flipping through his profit-and-loss sheets. Numbers and money are his drug of choice, whereas I prefer something that spikes my adrenaline a little more.

Like seeing Harlowe did this morning. It was even better than the freefall out of the airplane that had preceded it. I'd forgotten how she warms my blood and sets my pulse racing with a look. But her anger and coldness were a wall around her, and I'm the reason it had been erected in the first place.

"I think the brother protests too much," Payton says, his smile looking particularly evil as he targets me with his typical brand of middle brother meddling and my own personal hell. "You wanted her enough at one time to break your own golden rule of one night and spent two whole weeks with just her. You cut off communication as soon as you got home, which is normal, but now that she's back on your radar you can't help asking questions and seem far too invested in the answers. Could it be that you're willing to break another rule and do repeats? I think you want her. Bad." He crosses his arms over his chest and levels me with a satisfied smirk. The bastard is too spot on and he knows it. I hate my brothers.

"I think we have a shit ton of work to do and talking about a woman I fucked a long time ago and have *no interest* in now isn't going to help us accomplish anything." I grab a stack of papers out of Hayes's hands, and he makes a move to take them back, but I'm faster, and fan them out in front of me to bring home my point.

Five

Zander

"Please tell me about Harlowe, I'm begging you," Javi pleads.

I give him a measured look across the booth we are ensconced in with Luca and Diego at Dionysus, where we gathered after work for drinks. It's an upscale place with an impressive liquor list and discreet employees, close enough to walk from Olympus Tower that it's a frequent haunt for us. I sip my Underworld Spirits bourbon on the rocks before lowering my glass as my mood cools.

"There's nothing to tell." I don't want to share any of her with anyone. Every part of her that was mine stays that way. And it's safely locked in the vault.

"Why are you so interested, Javi? Other than your absolutely childish crush on her," Luca says, tracing a bead of condensation from his own glass and eyeing Javi with glacial indifference. Luca's icy persona thaws a bit when Payton's warm, golden retriever personality is around to temper him. Neither of my brothers joined us tonight, so we get the frosty version that matches his cool-blond hair and arctic blue eyes.

Hayes, of course, wanted to go home to Paige, who owns the distillery that makes this incredible bourbon. Payton said he had more work to do. He's been putting in extra hours the last year as we recover from the industrial mining accident that was part of a corporate sabotage plan intended to take our company down a year ago. We managed to bring the responsible parties to justice, but not before our company image had taken a beating, which has lasted, and we lost a newly acquired property, along with the lives of twenty-four of the mine employees.

While we were able to turn over information on the group who orchestrated the fiasco and get the main people arrested, Payton has been expecting more subterfuge. The shadowy network of disgruntled former business owners set on seeing the demise of Olympus International is large. Partly due to our penchant for hostile takeovers and ruthless business acquisitions, and partly because we have what others want—power. There's always the possibility of another fucker out for revenge looking to take us down.

"He probably wants to relive a special time in his life," Diego quips, smirking over the rim of his drink at Javi. "Lord knows he hasn't had many dates in the last five years to distract him from his Sports Illustrated subscription."

"Y'all are no fun. Haven't you ever had a list?" Javi asks, gesturing at us with his tumbler.

"A list?" Luca asks, disdain dripping from his clipped words. He cocks his head to the side as he narrows those unnervingly light eyes at Javi. He looks like a fucking

Husky. Shrewd and wolf-like. Ready to howl or hunt. A little psycho. Don't leave him alone or your furniture will end up shredded.

"Yeah, a list of celebrities you would do anything to get with if the opportunity presented itself. Models, actresses, singers, that kind of thing." He looks around at all of our faces, my own kept carefully neutral. "Oh, come on, you have to know what I'm talking about!" he says to our silence. Javi would definitely be a chocolate Lab. Something loveable and loyal. Maybe a little dumb, but intelligent when it counts.

I bark out a laugh, freeing him from his embarrassment. "Of course we know what you're talking about. We just usually clear the list and are left with conquests instead."

Luca and Diego nod in agreement, to Javi's obvious shock.

"You *clear the list*? How?!" Javi asks, perplexed. He looks to Luca and Diego next. "I know Zander clears it just by fucking everything that bats an eyelash at him, but what about you two? You're not fuckboy billionaires."

"But we're hot as shit millionaires. And it's all about who you know," Luca answers, sitting back with a satisfied grin. "I'm in PR. I have the contact details for pretty much anyone who is connected in some way to a woman I may want to cross off the list. How do you think I met Keira Jansen?" His mention of the model half-sister of the Kartwright sisters, a notoriously media-friendly family with a reality show, is a good start to the conversation.

"Or you go to galas and fundraisers and get introduced by mutual acquaintances, which is how I found myself in the bed of none other than Samantha Jeffries," Diego adds, mentioning one of the hottest up-and-coming young politicians Georgia has seen in years.

"You're telling me I could have been clearing the list rather than fantasizing about them this whole time? Fuck!" Javi says, dropping his head in defeat.

I chuckle at his abject despondency for all the pussy he has missed out on when it could have been handed to him on a silver platter due to his employment at Olympus. Money and power can indeed get you a whole lot in this world if you want it.

"Cheer up, man. At least now you've met Harlowe and can cross her off your list and start working on the others." I don't want him fantasizing about how he could get with Harlowe now. She's off-limits to everyone.

Except for that huge Condors tight end, an insidious voice reminds me. The smile slides off my face with that truth. Harlowe is dating fucking Knox Contraire, and that means he's had his hands all over her. My stomach sours and I set my bourbon down. The Atlanta Haute List says they have been linked for the last few months, which means he's already surpassed my ability to stick around, making him a much better choice for her, realistically. But a feral part of me doesn't subscribe to reality and wants to make a call to an associate, one who doesn't mind cracking kneecaps, and have him take care of Knox, so he's no longer a rival.

What the fuck am I even thinking? I'm not looking to get back with Harlowe, so I don't have any rivals that I should be considering taking out, hypothetically or not.

My phone vibrates in my pocket and saves me from the back-and-forth struggle in my brain where Harlowe is concerned. "Wishing you joined us, after all?" I say when I see Payton's name on the screen.

"I could use you guys back at Olympus," he says, a note of urgency lacing his tone.

A wave of dread passes through me and I press the phone tighter to my ear to block out some of the bar noise. "What happened?"

"Olympus is under a cyber attack. We've had over fifty attempts to breach our servers in the last half hour, and our team is scrambling to keep our firewalls and protections in place. I already called Hayes. He's on his way back to the office now. We need a plan for if they succeed. The team here has started moving assets around so they're not in danger if the hackers get in, but it's tight."

"We're leaving now. Give us five and we'll be there." I hang up and turn to the guys. "Sorry to disappoint, but we have to go back to work."

I throw some bills down on the table and stand as they gather their jackets without argument. We're all attuned to the needs of the business. If even one of them had made a disparaging remark about the time of night or the shittiness of being called back in, they wouldn't be senior vice presidents.

"Payton says our servers are under attack," Luca says, reading a text on his phone and filling in Javi and Diego as to why we're on our way out of the bar and back to work at eight in the evening.

"Do you think it's the same group that targeted Olympus last year with the South Africa mines?" Diego asks.

"Didn't they all go to jail? Who would be left to fuck with us now?" Javi answers.

"You think three people organized and executed that level of destruction?" I pose to the three of them.

We shoulder through the doors and out onto the sidewalk. My long stride takes me away from the bar as I look up at the glass and steel skyscraper that houses Olympus International a few blocks over. A feeling of foreboding looms larger than the building itself.

"Gage Geological alone had over a thousand employees unceremoniously let go. Kilowen Industries was torn apart and filtered into our own conglomerate without sparing a single thought for the generations that had created and nurtured it. Don't even get me started on Donner Investments. We took their portfolio, but dismantled the whole organization within months of acquisition."

"I hear what you're saying. We have plenty of enemies from those three acquisitions that could be continuing the work of those who headed it up." Javi's voice carries a note of anger, and I look over at him. "It's just business. They didn't have to take it so personally."

Luca laughs, the sound ringing coldly around us as we enter the tower lobby. "I think they showed us just how personally they took it last year when they collapsed a mine and killed twenty-four workers. They don't fucking care who suffers in their attempt to take down Olympus."

When we enter the boardroom, we find Payton waiting with a group of whoever was left at work when the attack started, and more are filtering in behind us. My brother is intently watching a screen of code flow by which means nothing to me, but Luca stiffens. He abruptly turns and rushes out of the room only to return a moment later with his laptop. Luca sits at the table and begins typing furiously, along with the others from our tech department.

Luca and Payton met at MIT and share a tech background, along with their unusual affinity for marketing and PR that typically wouldn't mesh so well with their computer science backgrounds. Fucking weird as shit combination, if you ask me, but at least they're on our side with it.

"Want to fill me in on what you're watching, since this isn't my area of expertise," I say as I come to stand next to Payton.

"I built the system to alert me even at a first breach attempt and it's the only reason we know this is happening at all instead of it being something covert or insidious that we find out about later. I had the best white hat hackers work to find weaknesses and shore up our systems for just this type of attack, so it's holding right now. Our tech department is working on finding breach points and rebuff attacks, but we've never encountered something of this magnitude. It's hard to tell if it will continue until they find some weak spot we are unaware of, or if they will change their tactics to target something else. Right now, it's just a full-frontal attack on every access point, and if it continues, there is bound to be some sort of faltering."

If this weren't such a serious situation, I would make a joke about his phrasing. "It's the same group from last year. Their retribution was stalled, but they're back on their mission, and they're getting more creative." There's no question to my statement, and Payton nods in agreement.

My intuition tells me this is just the beginning. We're quiet for several long minutes as Payton keeps his eyes trained on the screen and I survey the room. The feel of stress and panic in the air is palpable, thick enough to push through and slow down time so each minute feels like an eternity. I walk around the room feeling uneasy. Any skills I have are useless in this context, and my understanding of cyber attacks is so limited I feel like a child. I don't like feeling purposeless. I prowl back to Payton's side, angrier and more restless than I ever remember.

"I fucking hate this. What does this mean, and why now?"

"War has arrived at our doorstep. Now we figure out how we respond." Payton maintains a low volume, but his words burn with an uncharacteristic anger that is better suited to Hayes or myself.

"We respond with brutal force. We end this as soon as we can," Hayes says, coming to stand on the other side of Payton.

Think of the devil and he appears. He must have broken every traffic law to have arrived not long after I did, despite Payton having called him first. His Buckhead mansion is far enough from downtown to have made the trek harrowing for anyone else on the road with him.

"Cyber attacks take a little more finesse than force," Payton says. He drops his arms from their crossed position and stalks toward the screen on the wall he's been staring at. "There. That's the hacker's signature," he says, pointing at a block of code as it travels up the screen. He turns back to the table and addresses the IT personnel. "Route that through our database and find who is behind this attack. It's likely more than just one person, or they're running some sophisticated programs that are unheard of to get this quantity of attempts. Find them." The people he is commanding nod and their fingers fly over their own keyboards.

It really fucking scares me sometimes how much Payton knows. He likes to pretend he's just this creative communications expert—which he is—when in reality he's an evil genius with an eidetic memory and the ability to pick up any skill he tries.

He was taking electronics apart before he was seven, scaring the shit out of our mom, and even electrocuting me once when I was six. I learned to stay the fuck away from his projects really quickly after that. He knew three programming languages by twelve. He crashed our home security system at thirteen just fucking around and rewiring it to play music when set off. He became more nefarious at fifteen when he discovered hacking and started targeting anyone who pissed him off and creatively embarrassed them. At seventeen, he hacked Dad's online money market accounts and managed to siphon off thousands of dollars into offshore accounts before Dad even knew something was missing, just to prove that he could. He finally put his skills to use for good rather than evil and was top of his class at MIT. He built most of the infrastructure our organization is built on and quietly heads up the entire technology sector, as well as our operations, now. We don't even have an official CTO because Payton is happy to tuck that under his portion of the business as the COO. It's unusual, but that's what he likes, and he's not getting any pushback from Hayes or me on that topic.

"I really wish this were anything but a cyber attack," Hayes snarls. "It's much easier to take out a person or entity when they have a physical presence and I can hunt them down like the rats they are." His deep green eyes are narrowed and carry a gleam of malice that would frighten me if this were the first time I'd caught the look on him. But for once, I'm in complete agreement with him.

I turn to Hayes and level him with my own malicious stare. "I think they learned last year that taking out our physical infrastructure was too high stakes and left them vulnerable to discovery. This is something more insidious and lends itself to an enemy that decided we should really be the targets, not mine workers. You need to call Rex."

A muscle ticks in Hayes's jaw as I mention his old friend-turned-rival who was instrumental in helping us ferret out the nasty group that started this crusade against our company.

"You know what he wants. If we call him in now, we're giving him way more than we'll get from the help. We already let him cash in his favor by vouching for him when the FBI was investigating. He got six months of house arrest instead of prison, and he didn't lose his company. That's plenty of repayment."

Octavius Rex, founder and CEO of Rex Omnia, took a huge risk to make sure we had all the documentation he had been collecting on his shady business partners—the bitter losers we took Gage Geological, Kilowen Industries, and Donner Investments from. We've stayed out of contact with him for a year to ensure he wasn't connected to us as the leak that took down the group as they planned a second mine collapse, right here in Georgia, this time.

In return for his help, Rex asked for a seat on the Board of Directors for Olympus International. Bringing in an outsider, a business rival, at that, would be akin to putting an enemy in our house to run rampant. He would know every major play before it happened publicly, be able to influence the path that Olympus takes in all future expansion, know the inner workings of our organization, and block us if he saw fit.

Granted, my brothers and I are also on the board, so there is still plenty of sway we could use to supersede his vote, but it's the principle of the matter that gets under Hayes's skin. He doesn't want an outsider weighing in on our company's future. Especially one we stole a legacy from who may still have plans for his own form of vengeance played out in a long game format.

"I don't think we have much choice, here, Hater," I say, getting under his skin further by using an old nickname he despises. "Call Rex in and see if we can get to the bottom of this before we lose our asses in the market when news of this attack reaches investors for our publicly traded subsidiaries."

"Or worse, they manage to get in and put ransomware in our system so we can't access anything while they plunder and pilfer anything they want. We can't run our business without company email, databases, and financial systems. It would mean the end of any in-progress acquisitions. Do you want to lose out on billions? Because that's what this is looking like it's set to be," Payton says, rejoining us.

"Fuck," Hayes says, admitting defeat as he pulls out his cell and dials a number. He rolls his eyes when the call connects. "I'm not calling to catch up, Rex," he grits out. "Your old friends are back at it. We're fending off a cyber attack on our servers and systems right now. Know anything about that?"

I turn to Payton while Hayes continues his conversation with Rex.

"Do you think it's an inevitability that the attack will be successful?"

Payton turns toward me, assessing. "It's brute force for a cyber attack, but there's a calculation to each attempt, as numerous as they've been. I think whoever is behind this wants us to know we're sitting ducks and they're playing with us. This took a lot of resources—"

"And there are plenty of people who hate us that have the resources to fund something like this," I finish for him. "So why now? What do they stand to gain other than inconveniencing us if it doesn't work, and mining our data and fucking with everything if it does?"

"If I were on the other side of this, I would want access to all of the deals in the pipeline, see who we have our eyes on, what we stand to gain from our ventures, and also where our money is right now that would be easy to pick off."

An ominous groan follows Payton's last words, and we both turn to the table full of IT employees, frantically tapping away on their keyboards.

"They got into Pegasus," Luca says without looking up from his laptop. "The rest of the attempts have stopped now that they're in, so I think this was their main goal and the rest was a distraction."

Payton rushes over to Luca's computer and they confer quietly as Luca continues to type.

"You've got to be fucking kidding me," I say, running a hand through my hair and pulling.

Pegasus is my project under the Olympus umbrella. It's the name of the company creating clean energy engines I'm planning to use on a fleet of charter jets, and was set to go to market in the new year. Proprietary information, design schematics, years of development, marketing plans, and pending contracts were just exposed to a hostile force. Our patents haven't been finalized and filed. If this information hits the open market, or worse, the dark web, our competitors will be clamoring to get their hands on the information and get it to market before we can.

"We've managed to boot them from the system and stabilized the network, but there's no telling how much they got, even in that amount of time." Payton's voice is full of dire warning.

We're fucked.

Six

Zander

Five Years Ago

I'm fucked.

Harlowe is way *more* than I anticipated. More beautiful. More vivacious. More captivating. More enthralling. I sound like a fucking thesaurus as I think about how much *more* she is now. Damn.

Of course she's stunningly beautiful, she's an international supermodel for a reason. But she practically radiates with *life*. Her smiles pierce through any armor I thought I had and spear me right in the goddamn heart. Every. Fucking. Time. And her fucking laugh. Jesus, it makes me smile and my cock sit up and take notice every time I hear it. No one else has managed that. It makes me a little furious, really, but I can't stay mad enough to care about her effortlessly breaking through every wall to do anything about it. Instead, I'm laughing at her bad jokes, listening with rapt attention to her captivating stories of modeling life, and finding every opportunity to get my hands on her.

I thought I knew her body was tight and perfect from her photoshoots, and seeing her in person, but having her in my arms is an entirely different experience that makes me lose my damn mind every time, and it's been less than twenty-four hours, and on a jet at that. I don't have a limit when it comes to how much I want her. I'm liable to become obsessed, given the amount of time I have her at my disposal.

She's absolutely trouble.

As promised, once Harlowe had a glass of champagne, she got a look in her eyes that let me know my time was limited before she would have her way with me. I pulled her into the private bedroom before she could take my cock out right there in the middle of the plane. We have a very discreet flight crew who would have looked the other way and given us privacy if needed, but there's no need to subject them to that. And I'm feeling a little *proprietary* about Harlowe. I don't want to share any part of her with anyone, crew or not.

Once in private, she unfastened the halter neck of her dress, freeing her fucking incredible tits before she pushed me onto the bed. Her eyes stayed on mine as she crawled over me, tits swaying, unbuckled my belt, unfastened my pants, and freed my cock as I raised my hips for her to move my pants down. She kept that eye contact as she licked up my shaft and swirled her sweet tongue over the head of my throbbing cock. I groaned as her hand stroked up to meet her mouth and she played there for a few excruciatingly good minutes. The sounds of her mouth sucking, hands stroking, and humming around me mixed with my own feral groans as she found every sensitive spot and knew just the right amount of pressure I wanted, hard, like she pulled it straight from my head. She finally broke her stare and hollowed out her cheeks to suck me deep into her throat, doing something with her tongue that felt so damn good I lost it. I grabbed her head and fucked into her mouth as she smiled around me like that's what she had hoped for all along. This woman knew exactly what she was doing to me.

It hadn't taken long to learn that Harlowe had her own way of doing things, and she's very aggressive, yet just as easily bent to my will. It's a new dynamic for me, as most women go meek and pliant in the bedroom, happy to follow my lead completely. I like the give and take we're establishing. She's keeping me guessing, making me work for it, challenging me at every step. It feels good and gives me all sorts of ideas for what this trip will be, not just in the bedroom, but in every activity.

She wasn't lying when she said she wanted my eyes rolling back in my head. That's exactly what happened as she took me down her throat. I saw fucking stars when I came in her sweet and talented mouth and she swallowed me dry. We had twenty hours and a couple of stops to refuel to get to know each other on the plane, and her face the first time I made her come is seared in my brain's most beautiful images folder forever. She's a fucking wildcat in bed, and I want to learn every noise she makes and every spot that sets her off. I will know Harlowe Sorenson's body better than she does before this trip is over. It didn't take us long to find ourselves comfortable around one another, our bodies naturally gravitating toward the other.

Right now, she's nestled comfortably in my lap on the transfer boat as we make our way to the private island I booked, and I'm feeling far more relaxed than I expected to as I run my hand up and down her bare arm, actually enjoying the contact rather than going through the motions with the sole intent to seduce her. I didn't think I was one for cuddling, but I definitely like having her lithe body tucked between my legs, her back tightly pressed to my chest, head on my shoulder, my arms around her waist, and her hair tickling my face as the wind whips around us.

I realize I'm not looking for the next thing, but firmly in the present, with the woman in my arms, focused on what's happening right now. For once, I'm not craving the bigger push, the next rush, harder task, or moving the needle on what the goal is, personally, professionally, or otherwise. Is this just the feel of real relaxation experienced for the first time in years, or is this something more?

Is this what contentment feels like?

Could I be slipping into something as mundane as that this easily? I think the fuck not. I carefully pull back any emotions that may have leaked into each caress of my hand on her soft skin, pull apart the feelings that may somehow have entangled themselves right along with Harlowe, and remember what this is—a chance to get my fill of her and be done. It doesn't matter what rules I've broken to get to this point. I won't be breaking any more when the trip is over. No attachments. No repeats. We're on the same page, no matter how good it feels right now.

Just keep fucking telling yourself that, man.

"Where did you grow up?" I ask in her ear over the roar of the boat's engine.

She turns her face to be able to shout her answer back to me. "Atlanta, born and raised. I moved to LA at eighteen to start my modeling career and that's my home base now."

"Are you telling me we grew up in the same city and I managed not to have found you before this?" I ask, tightening my hold on her waist and feeling incredulity settle over me. She was so close and I never even knew it.

"You're like twenty-nine, right?" She waits for me to nod before she continues. "You're five years older than me. It's not like we would have ever been in school together, even if I grew up near you, which isn't likely, Mr. Moneybags," she says playfully. "What makes you think that out of the six million people in the Atlanta metro area, we would have found each other?"

"We were destined to find each other, baby." I deliver the words flippantly, but damn if I don't believe them right down to my soul.

Yeah, I'm fucked.

Seven

Harlowe

"Ugh, this Olympus data breach is ruining your cooking segment coverage. The investigation and the news of their stocks plummeting and how that's affecting the market are the only things the news is running with tonight," Alicia says in a nasally tone that sometimes drives me insane. She called me to talk about my schedule for the rest of the week, since two more segments were bumped as more pressing news stories came through.

I roll my eyes at her lack of empathy. "I think a cyber attack and corporate sabotage is obviously a bigger story right now. If they want to focus on that, it's warranted." I'm not about to fight for fluff piece coverage when there's serious shit happening around us, not even if it's Zander's company stealing my spotlight. "It's just a cookbook and a few recipes I was going to share. I can do that any time." I swirl the dregs in the bottom of a glass of red wine that I've been nursing since I got home from my downtown signing event and Hendricks went to bed. It was enough of a mess today to need a weeknight drink when I would normally save it for the weekend.

"We have to strike while the iron's hot, honey. We can't let the momentum die when you have the Gourmet Network sniffing around looking for a possible new show with you at the helm. It's everything we've been working for, and why this cookbook was so important after the success of your YouTube channel."

Guilt pecks at me, knowing there is a game plan in place for my success, and it requires a hell of a lot of work and tons of appearances to keep my name and face in front of a larger audience. And yet, I can't help but feel like it's all for nothing, and I might as well not even try.

"Let me know if there are additional changes to the schedule. I'll film an episode to upload this week, and I'll post to my socials so at least I'll have new content. My posting schedule has been weak since the book launched. I'm sure my subscribers would like to see new recipes."

"You're bigger than YouTube, you're going to have a major network show!" she says exuberantly, and a little too early for my taste. "I'm working with the publisher and focused on booking you more TV spots. We might be able to reschedule the spots that were bumped from tomorrow to next week, which would still be okay."

"I always appreciate your positivity, Alicia. Thank you."

"Night, honey!" she says, blowing kisses and disconnecting the call.

I turn the phone over in my hand a few times and consider calling Knox. He's really good at cheering me up.

He has this ridiculously positive mindset and is really great with pep talks. It must be the lifetime of football coaches pumping up the team that instilled that quality in him. My fingers hover, ready to hit his contact, when I decide against it. I don't really want to be cheered up by him right now.

Instead, I open Instagram and post a thirst trap selfie of me in a skimpy tank top eating a creamy pasta dish that's featured in my cookbook with a huge ass smile. I write a racy caption about *cacio e pepe* that sounds like the smut I like to read—I mean, *creamy cacio* is just begging to be used sexually—and throw in some body positivity about loving yourself at any size and actually enjoying your food. It's a hard-won lesson I will gladly share with anyone who wants to hear it, and if looking happy while eating pasta with my tits out drives that point home, I'm more than happy to do it.

I do this occasionally to remind myself, and my followers, that not only am I a foodie and a mom, I'm still fun. While I'm now a *former* model, I'll be a catch no matter what size my jeans are or if I eat carbs. Even though it's late for my normal commenting de-mographic, my notifications start ticking up right away, and my DM inbox numbers start increasing. Alicia will be happy with the engagement, even if I don't interact with any of the comments tonight. I sigh and close the app. I don't feel like talking to anyone else after such a wild day.

When I got home and the girls all left, I had to contend with letting down my son, on top of needing some major work done to my car. To say Hendricks was disappointed that he couldn't go to school is an understatement. His full bottom lip pouted out spectacularly, and he gave me these big, storm cloud gray puppy dog eyes that would melt the blackest of hearts. I've never met a four-year-old who loved school so much. I can distinctly remember crying when my mom dropped me off at school and fabricated illnesses to keep myself home with her instead of going to class. Not Hendricks. He's such a good kid, who loves learning, and I hate letting him down.

"Mama? I can't sleep."

I turn to the doorway of the living room to see the tousled hair and sleepy eyes of the brightest part of my life. I set my wine glass on the coffee table and open my arms to him. "I was just thinking about you, and how much I could use one of your Hulk hugs right now. Can you come give me a big squeeze?"

Hendricks smiles and rushes over, blanket trailing from his little fist, and throws himself into my arms. I wrap him up and hold him close, breathing in his warm, sleepy scent, feeling him nuzzle into my neck, and sigh.

These hugs are magic. Just holding my baby boy, my child, makes the problems in my life seem trivial by comparison. I rub his back and hold him quietly, knowing he will talk if he feels like it, and sometimes just needs a hug to sort through his little boy emotions. He's a sensitive kid, observant and smart enough to pick up what's going on around him. I try to keep his world as simple as possible because he deserves to have an uncomplicated life.

My brush with celebrity and the path I'm on now writing cookbooks, posting my video content, interacting with social media, and encouraging body positivity, can be all-consuming. It's a full-time job and more, since I don't farm out my editing or commenting on the different platforms, preferring to do it all myself so my message never gets twisted by someone else. But that work means time away from my boy, or my attention split much of the time. The evenings are for Hendricks alone, and I'm usually pretty good at being present. Tonight, he must be feeling my anxiety and the stress of the day radiating off of me to be having trouble sleeping.

"Do I get to go to school tomorrow?" he asks in his sweet, clear little voice.

I lean back into the deep couch and look at him as his head rolls to my shoulder. "Yes, my love, you do. I'm sorry you had to miss class today, and I will do my best to make sure you never have to miss again, okay?"

He nods and blinks heavily. His soulful gray eyes, fringed by long, dark lashes, are a carbon copy of the ones that looked at me today on the side of the highway. His caramel skin, full lips, and soft brown curls are from me, but those eyes... they will always remind me of the father he's never met. Will never meet, if I can keep him protected from the man who cut me out of his life so efficiently. I can be enough parent for Hendricks on my own. I don't need a man interested in only his success, who refuses to give in to attachments and wants nothing to do with me to screw up the balance I've created for my son.

"I saw that sleepy look. How about I take you to bed and we can cuddle until you fall asleep?" I offer.

Hendricks smiles and hops out of my lap, pulling on my hand to bring me with him. "Can you rub my back, too?"

"Of course, my love." And I do just that, holding him a little tighter, knowing that I'm back on the radar of the one man who could possibly disrupt our lives more than my crazy schedule ever could.

Eight

Harlowe

Five Years Ago

"You keep looking at me like that and we won't make it to dinner," I say, catching Zander's bold gray gaze devouring me while I apply a coconut-flavored lip balm to my lips as I look at my reflection in the mirror across from the bed in our villa.

He looks incredible, lounging on the bed in casual linen shorts and a short-sleeve shirt. His wardrobe changed quickly once we arrived, and I haven't seen the business casual since. I cap the lip balm and return it to the toiletries bag that has been neglected. I haven't been wearing any makeup since we arrived. I haven't needed to. We've been in the water, diving or snorkeling, or here in the villa, fucking or lazing around together as we get to know each other. But the lip balm is a necessity with all the sun, sea, and kissing.

"Maybe I want dessert first," he says, coming up behind me and untying the beautiful sarong from my hips that I received from the island host when we arrived. "And I'm willing to be late for dinner to make sure I get it."

I laugh, because we're the only occupants on this island, and the small restaurant on the other side will stay open and have dinner ready for us whenever we decide to make our way over there.

"Do you find dessert funny, Lowe?" he asks, slipping in the new nickname he adopted yesterday just as easily as he slips his fingers into my bikini bottoms and strokes me.

I sigh at his touch as my eyes flutter. "I think *you're* funny, Zander." I wish that his name had a shorter derivative, and there was something I could call him that would be just mine, the way he so easily found one for me. It's so intimate. I'll have to work on that.

He's pulling on the strings of my bikini bottoms now, slowly untying one side, then the other, rather than dragging them down my legs, which would be easier. But in the three days we've been here, I've discovered Zander doesn't do easy. He does his way, and that is usually hard. My bikini falls to the floor and Zander kneels behind me, his hands skimming up my legs and parting them wider, so I'm forced to hop out a few steps to accommodate where he wants to be. His breath is hot against my ass as he traces his lips across the swell of each cheek. I'm wet just from the anticipation of what I know will happen, a shiver running through my body.

"Look at this sweet cunt dripping for me. Such a needy little thing. Bend over and put your hands flat on the mirror. I want you to watch as I eat out this greedy pussy from behind until you come all over my face."

I close my eyes and shudder at his words, but I do as he says, bending at the hips and placing my hands on the mirror in front of me. My pussy squeezes tight at the sight of our reflection, him kneeling behind me, catching his intense gaze over the swell of my heart-shaped ass.

"Such a good girl. And Harlowe," he says, getting my attention again. "Keep your eyes on me. You need to watch me, honey. And you better fucking scream my name when you come."

"Make me," I taunt, knowing full well he is capable of delivering on any promise he makes when it comes to my pleasure.

"You better brace yourself, little Wildcat," he growls.

That should have been enough warning. I should know by now the force he is capable of. But when Zander spears his tongue into my pussy, I yelp and try to pull away. Not because it's bad, but because it's too damn good, and I'm too sensitive. We've had sex countless times since we arrived, and it somehow keeps getting better. But my body is hypersensitive, and he's aware of it, for better or worse.

Zander laps at my entrance, fucking his tongue in and out. I didn't know a tongue could do *that* and it would feel like... fuuuuck. My hips buck away again, completely out of my control. Zander swiftly traps my thighs with one strong arm, keeping me in place before moving his tongue to my clit, flattening and swirling it tightly over my sensitive nub. Now I'm moaning, my fingers clawing against the mirror without finding any purchase.

"You taste so fucking good," he growls, his words humming against me and making me shiver.

Zander slides two fingers inside of me, releasing me from the onslaught of his damn talented tongue, and I suck in a breath while I can. He leisurely strokes those thick fingers in and out and I relax into the familiar sensation, moaning with how good it feels. I feel my release start to build from that perfect pressure he is using.

My eyes fly open as he bites one of my ass cheeks hard enough that I'll probably have a mark. At the same time, the fingers that are around my thighs strum at my clit with brutal efficiency, knowing exactly how much pressure I need. I make a strangled noise caught somewhere between a yelp and a moan as the pleasure and the pain mix, and I catch his eye in the mirror where he is looking over my hip, his gray eyes locked on my face in the mirror.

"You weren't watching me, Lowe. Your eyes were closed. Only good girls who follow my orders get to come. Bad girls get their asses marked. I'll pull these slick fingers out and spank it red, next time."

"Bastard," I barely manage to rasp.

He hasn't stopped the delicious circling of his fingers on my clit while his others pump inside of me just right. He's curling into my G-spot with each thrust. When he hears the catch in my voice, he thrusts a little harder, ramming the base of his knuckles against the entrance of my pussy in a way that threatens to have my eyes rolling back in ecstasy, but he wants me looking at him, so I manage just a flutter of my lashes before I return my hazy gaze to him.

"So fucking responsive. Look at you, dripping down my arm, making a mess of me, baby. But I want all of this sweet juice on my face. You're going to come for me, fill my mouth with you, got it?"

"Zander," I moan, letting my head fall down between my outstretched arms that are shaking from bracing against the mirror.

"That's right, you're going to scream my name when you come. I can feel you getting close. I'm greedy for your orgasms. I want them all." His words are a growl as he presses his mouth back against my pussy, his fingers sliding out and his tongue moving to my entrance as he continues to circle my clit, faster and harder now.

My hips buck into him, and he takes it, his hands and mouth working so well together I have no idea what is going on despite being able to see it all. I just know I can feel a toe-curling orgasm building at the base of my spine, stiffening my body and freezing the breath in my lungs as he continues his work on my pussy. When it finally washes over me, I scream his name, my hips bucking against his face, my legs shaking, and a feeling of utter relief coursing through me. I barely manage to keep my eyes open while Zander maintains eye contact with me in the mirror, somehow, from his spot between my legs where he has just annihilated me.

A moment later, he stands and sweeps me up into his arms, walking me across the room to the bed. He lays me out, kissing me while I can still taste myself on his face. He leaves my mouth and positions me just so—arms above my head, legs spread wide—while I come down from the orgasm he tore from my body, and stay docile, languid. For now.

"Such a fucking gorgeous picture of perfection."

I roll my head and see him removing his shirt and shorts. I stretch and roll to my side so I can take him in better.

"You're not so bad yourself," I return.

Zander is hot as hell and incredibly fit. The definition of tall, dark, and handsome could have a picture of Zander and need no other explanation. Tanned skin, even features, stunning storm cloud gray eyes framed by thick, dark lashes, and at least six-foot-three, so he's tall enough for me to wear heels and not tower over him. His shoulders are broad, chest and abs sculpted, back defined, and legs strong. But he's not bulky like a guy who spends all of his time in the gym to get that physique. He's the kind of fit that is built by his hobbies and activities. We've been swimming and diving and running around for days and the man doesn't stop. He's a force of nature that is just waiting to see what he can accomplish next.

And from the look on his face now, I'm next.

I roll to my knees and sit up, pulling the hem of my tank top up and over my head and tossing it on the floor at Zander's feet.

"Did I say you could move from where I put you?" he asks, arms crossed over his chest, cock straining in front of him.

"Did I say I would be your little fuck doll you could position *just so* to be compliant and take your cock when you wanted?" I volley back, slipping the ties of my bikini top off to free my breasts, which feel heavy and in need of his hands. "If you want this," I purr, gesturing at my body, "crawl to me, like a good boy."

I sit on the edge of the bed and widen my legs invitingly. Two can play at this little game. If he wanted to demand I keep my eyes on him while he ate me out from behind, he can get on his fucking knees again and crawl for me now.

"Fuck," Zander growls.

He looks torn for a moment between wanting to maintain control and wanting to relinquish it to get what I'm offering. But eventually, he realizes it's all just a game, and his smile returns as he drops to his knees for me. He maintains direct eye contact, those gray eyes challenging me with each movement of his powerful body as he manages to slink across the floor like a jungle cat until he's in front of me.

"That's it, Zand, just like that," I tell him appreciatively, as his hands slide up my legs and he rises.

"You like me on my knees at your feet, ready to worship you, Lowe?" His words are a sexy taunt mere inches from my mouth as he bends over me.

"I like you anywhere with me, but that will do. Now, are you going to fuck me, or are we going to dinner?"

He palms my breasts, pressing them together, and I arch into his touch. "You're a little brat."

I shrug, unfazed, and smile coyly at him. "I've been called worse."

His hands still. "I'll kill anyone who says anything worse." He's suddenly more serious than he's been since we arrived on the island. "No one has the right to speak badly of someone this… fucking… amazing," he says, placing kisses on each of my nipples in turn as he speaks. His focus returning to sex means he wasn't *that* serious about his comment.

Besides, I don't think it's worth the total buzzkill to go into the endless times the opposite has been true, so instead, I wrap a leg around his hip and roll us so I'm straddling his hips. I'm now within reach of the bowl of condoms we keep on the nightstands flanking the bed for easy access, and I grab one, opening it and easily slipping it on him.

"I think I'd like to ride you before dinner. Watching you crawl to me got my horse kink going," I joke, and we both laugh.

"That would be called pony play, which is why I know you don't actually have that kink," Zander says, grabbing the base of his cock and holding it upright for me. "But, fuck yes, you can ride me anytime."

I scoot up until he's notched at my opening and inch down until the head is inside me, my head rolling back at the delicious way I have to stretch to accommodate his girth. I have to lift and adjust several times before he is able to press in.

"That's a good girl. You can take me," Zander says, his hands heavy on my hips, pressing my body down on him as I whimper. "Your body was made for my cock. Just a little more, baby." Finally, he's all the way inside of me and I pant in relief. "Fuck, you feel so good, Lowe."

He's certainly the biggest man I've slept with, and it takes a moment to adjust each time, but damn, does he fill me perfectly, and hit every spot just right. It doesn't matter if I bounce up and down like I'm recreating a porno or if I rock my hips back and forth, it always feels good, and he always gets me off, which hasn't been true for those other men.

I start rocking my hips and place my hands on Zander's thighs behind me for balance. He takes the opportunity this presents and palms my breasts, taking his sweet time to weigh each round globe in his hands. He runs his fingers across my skin and rolls my nipples in his fingers, pulling each tight bud once they are straining at his touch, eliciting gasps from me. I feel the sensation zing through my body—a lightning bolt sent straight to my pussy—and my orgasm hits me out of nowhere, startling us both at the intensity as I clamp down on him and shout in ecstasy.

"Fuck," I swear, folding forward as the waves rush over me and I continue to scream my release as Zander pinches my nipples. "Too much," I finally beg, covering his hands with my own and forcing them away as my orgasm abates. I'm sweating, my chest heaving, and he has a delighted smile on his face like he just got a new toy.

"That's fun," he says in awe, sitting up and pulling me tighter to his body, hands possessive and roaming. "Your nipples are an on button for your clit." He bends his head and his lips meet my neck, kissing along my skin until he finds a spot on my neck that has me shivering in his arms and my pussy clenching him again in little aftershocks.

"I'm not some machine you can turn on or off at will, you psycho," I say on a breathy exhale, but there isn't much rebuke in my tone. I didn't even know that about my body. I've had my boobs played with, of course, and my nipples, too, but it's never felt like *that*.

Zander continues kissing along my skin and moving me in his lap, finding all of my erogenous spots, capturing my moans with his mouth, and proving he's in control of this session no matter who is on top.

I've never been this responsive with anyone else before. There's something about the draw Zander has on me, the physical connection we obviously have together, that has our bodies so in tune. And he's more than aware of it. Like right now, as his talented fingers work their way back to my breasts and stroke over my nipples, until they are tight peaks he can pluck, and set me off again. I buck wildly against him as the release surges through me, leaving me panting from the power of it. He holds me tightly through the waves, thrusting his hips into me as it continues. My fingers thread through his hair and wrap around his strong shoulders, finding my own way to stay grounded.

"You feel so fucking good," he rasps into my neck. "I love when you come for me. Three now. How many more can I get from you, Lowe? I want your pussy clenching my cock until you're a shaking mess, begging to stop."

"I'm not above begging, but it's for more," I gasp, wanting to even the playing field, just a little bit.

But he's keeping score, and he's winning. Through the frenzied lust we've felt and our mutual desire for each other, Zander is taking the time to learn my body. He's getting to know every sound I make and cataloging how I move so he'll know what I like and what will set me off even faster the next time our bodies come together.

This is more than casual, more than a typical fuckboy wanting a willing plaything on a fancy vacation. I was happy to be the willing plaything, but now, well, it's already feeling different. Better. I've been Zander's sole focus each day. My pleasure, his priority. My challenges, his game. That's not feeling casual.

Maybe... oh God, do I even let myself think it now? Maybe he wants more than casual *with me*? Before I can even let my thoughts trail down that rocky road that will obviously lead to disappointment, I cut myself off.

I know the score. No attachments. That's Zander Olsen to a T. It doesn't matter if he looks at me right now like he wants to memorize every curve of my body, or his kisses demand ever more from my mouth, and his body fits better with mine each time we come together. The next orgasm hits me with the same force as the thought that when these two weeks are up, so are we.

I just have to keep reminding myself of that.

Nine

Zander

Days later, we are still reeling from the breach into our servers and hackers getting access to Pegasus, along with other sensitive company information. We have been working longer hours than usual, doing top-to-bottom sweeps to ensure nothing else was collected from the attack, but the damage was done. What they did get into was enough.

We lost deals immediately. The Rosenthall deal was dead as soon as the news broke about the breach because our credibility and the security the project needs were undermined. Acquiring Rosenthall would have given us the manufacturing capacities needed to produce the Pegasus project at scale. Now, we have to see if there is any use in following through with a plan that has been leaked to the highest bidder on the dark web.

I know it would be worthless for the team running Pegasus to file patents on plans that are in the hands of our competitors and they're scrambling to change the manufacturing timelines to try to beat others to market. If that can't happen, they'll be looking for how they can alter intrinsic portions of the current process, but what we have taken years to achieve, and it won't be replaced overnight.

And now we have to deal with having Octavius Rex integrating himself into the Olympus architecture after calling him in to help with the breach.

"You three look like shit," Rex says when he enters our conference room and sees all three of us waiting for him.

"We didn't ask you here for your opinions on our appearances, Rex," Hayes says, impatiently waving him in.

"But it still bears saying, because I enjoy it when you smug fuckers look down. Grant me my small victories when life has been so unfair to me," he replies with mock humility, making himself comfortable across the table from Hayes. They were close friends through business school, and a few years after, until we decided to buy out his father's company and strip him of the legacy he was set to take over. That sort of kills a friendship in its tracks. Now, they're begrudging allies when necessary, at best.

"Tell us what you know about the cyber attack," Payton says, diving right in. Dark circles rest under his eyes from the long hours he's been pulling, and his temper is more volatile than usual, for valid reasons. He feels personally responsible for this breach since it was his system that failed.

"I heard you were unlucky enough to be targeted, and the hackers stole some pretty important details for an up-and-coming project. Weren't you just interviewed in

Forbes about the engine plans, Zander?" he says, looking my way with a glint of mischief in his eyes.

"Among other things, it was one of the topics that came up," I say, staying neutral until I know what he is insinuating.

"Well, it does seem particularly interesting that the article came out the same day you got hacked." Rex leans back in his chair and steeples his fingers. "Correlation or causation?"

"Bad timing and some determined group of assholes," I respond. There's no way that my interview would have spurred a cyber attack from our enemies in that quick of a time frame. This had to be in the works way before the article came out. The Pegasus project wasn't secret, but how we're managing to produce the results that would set us apart from other clean energy engines was.

Rex tips his head back and forth, weighing my words. "I *may* have heard something that leads me to believe the article was the catalyst, if not the cause. You remember Andreas Donovan, CEO of Donner Investments?"

I nod and make a motion for him to continue. Rex likes to draw things out, and I'm not feeling the most patient at the moment.

"He has a son, Archer, who is making quite the name for himself in the tech world. I guess he didn't want to go into finance after dear old dad lost his company to Olympus and watched you burn it to the ground."

"Get to the point, Rex," Hayes says, sounding bored and irritated. Not a good combination from my eldest brother, since it's likely to turn him into a vindictive asshole just for sport.

"Archer is a software developer and coder, and if what I heard is correct, likes to dabble in breaking and entering of the cyber variety to steal trade secrets and wreak havoc for funsies."

"Some punk kid went to all that trouble to hack into our system, went through every precaution we had, just for *fun*?" Payton repeats slowly. His face is a mask of indifference, but I can hear the underlying rage.

It actually seems like something Payton himself would have done when he was younger. From his tone, it doesn't sound like he appreciates the idea when the shoe is on the other foot. His usual shit-stirring attitude is markedly missing, and Rex doesn't even realize what he is walking into by delivering this information now. While Payton may be the most genial, golden retriever type of the three of us, we're all cut from the same cloth, and he's fully capable of the ruthlessness Hayes is normally tasked with.

"I've heard a rumor he's developed some sort of program called Achilles that runs multi-faceted assaults on servers looking for specific weak points with high-value targets as the end-point. I don't know all the details; it goes over my head, but sounds a lot like what you experienced. He probably had a backer wanting something from the effort. As far as I'm aware, he's kind of a hacker for hire and takes jobs that interest him enough. I'm sure getting back at the people that not only ruined his father's company but also sent him to prison would be enough incentive to take on your firewalls and cyber protections."

I scrutinize Rex as he leans back in his chair. He's playing it cool, but I can see there's an undercurrent of fear running beneath his placid surface. Maybe he came across this information from another sensitive source that, if revealed, could potentially put his life at risk once again. I'd be hesitant to give up the details if that were the case, as well.

"This explains his signature," Payton says under his breath, and we all look at him for an explanation. "His digital signature on the code he ran to get into our system?" When we look at him blankly, he continues. "Our digital forensics identified his signature from the code used and ran it through our database of attack signatures. He included a clever illusion to a bow and arrow in the code, because, *Archer*."

"You can positively identify him as the culprit for this attack?" Hayes asks, cracking his knuckles and looking like he's ready to pull the kid out of whatever hole he's hiding in so he can personally deliver the ass-kicking he deserves.

"Not exactly. I can identify it against other attacks, but there is no clear indication that Archer Donovan is the hacker, since this particular signature belongs to a hacker who hasn't been caught and identified." Payton's explanation makes sense, but it doesn't seem to stop Hayes from planning all the ways he will be making Archer pay for his alleged crimes.

"If you want my two cents on this situation, I'll give it to you," Rex says, like we're not all fuming around the table. "A competitor likely saw your article and hired someone with Archer's skill set to break into your network and steal the plans for Pegasus so they could get a jump on you. Do I have solid evidence that it was Archer who facilitated the breach, or know who would have hired him? No, I don't. All I can say is this theory fits what I know of both Archer Donovan and the rest of the group I was partnered with."

We need more than a theory to go on. "We didn't ask you here for conjecture, Rex. We wanted your insider information," I reply, flattening my hands on the table and staring at his smug face.

Rex holds up his hands in a shrug. "I'm no longer a part of the inner circle, so you can't blame me for not knowing exactly what's going on. It's not like I have another thumb drive for you to use to take down your enemies. I only had one shot at that. Now I've been kicked out of the boys' club for not being thrown in prison with the main three for my part in what they had planned last year."

I shake my head, knowing it's futile to ask for more information he won't be able to provide. "Fine. This at least gives us a jumping-off point. Thanks for your time."

"Is this a good time to bring up that you owe me now?" Rex says, crossing his ankle over a knee. "That board position is looking real comfy right now and I have some extra time on my hands."

"Fuck off, Rex," all three of us say at once.

Ten

Zander

By the time I'm finally ready to leave the Olympus International Tower, it's well after dark. I ask Weiss to send Javi into my office as soon as I leave my last meeting and then tell her to finish up for the evening since she's been here longer than I have. She just gives me a knowing look and a backward wave as she exits my office. I can't believe I still haven't melted that woman's iceberg exterior.

I have an idea that's been percolating in my subconscious all day, despite everything else that is going on. Probably not a good one, given the day of negotiations that didn't go my way. I had to fight with Hayes to up our offer for a deal that would replace Rosenthall, and I'm annoyed as fuck after dealing with that shifty bastard Rex only providing the barest information. Besides that, Payton's incessant need to hash out how we are going to fight back after we learned of the connection to Archer Donovan left me feeling drained.

Despite the work piling up and the team scrambling to pivot, I can't stop thinking about running into Harlowe, of all people. Why would we be thrown back together like that? To have seen her photos on the Atlanta Haute List moments before the world conspired against me, literally crashing us into each other, just so we would be in the same place at the same time? Not fucking normal.

Neither is my irrational obsession with her all week, despite my insistence that I wouldn't think about her again, and I couldn't possibly have any attachments to her this long after. I'm still obsessing about the time we spent together and how that could have changed my life as I know it, now that I've seen the photos of her son.

To make matters worse, I gave into my curiosity and looked up her Foulmouthed Foodie Instagram account, only to catch the fucking thirst trap she posted the same night I saw her. Holy shit, did that one grab me by the balls. Her glorious, feline smile as she took a bite of some delicious, creamy-looking pasta dish, her tits looking even more fucking delectable, slightly out of focus, just below the forkful of food. Her caption was the kicker, my cock growing harder with every salaciously dirty word that tripped across my feed, saying *creamy cacio is her favorite*, and ending with loving yourself at every size.

It was a reminder that, yes, her body is different, and goddamn does it look so fucking good I could spend another two weeks eating her up and learning every new curve and how it fits against me. I fisted my cock right then and came so quick and violently it felt like lightning snapped down my spine with the force of the ropes of cum that shot out of me. I don't know the last time I jacked off to a photo on the internet, one that was safe to post to a social media feed, at that.

I need to see Harlowe. I have to talk to her. It's a thought that has never crossed my mind about any woman who has been in my bed, and that breaks the rules, but so does possibly having a connection with her that stuck around longer than I did.

I retreat to my office and pace behind my desk. There's way too much at stake and going on in my professional world and the stress from my personal life is only adding to the mix, given the fucking bombshell that I'm pretty damn sure I have a kid and Harlowe doesn't want me to know anything about him.

"You wanted to see me?" Javi says as he enters my office without a knock. Thank fuck that didn't take long.

"I need whatever information you have on her," I say, hand outstretched for good measure.

Javi takes a seat across from me and pulls out his phone. "I'm going to take a flying leap and assume you mean Harlowe Sorenson." He taps his phone screen and scrolls a bit.

"Of course, that's who I mean. I give you the credit you deserve for your intelligence and aptitude to connect the dots. No need to rub it in," I gripe.

"Touchy about this one, are we? Sending a photo of her insurance documents and her contact card now. Don't say I never do anything for you. I follow your crazy ass out of perfectly good planes and give you contact information

I'm pretty sure you normally wouldn't want." He gives me a knowing look.

My phone vibrates on my desk and I immediately snatch it up. "Thanks," I say, already saving the contact. "Have you sent her your insurance info yet?"

Javi rubs the back of his neck. "We've had a lot going on the last couple of days. It sort of slipped my mind. I should send it right now." He swipes his screen open again and starts tapping.

"Don't bother. Send it to me instead." Possibilities are rushing through my mind, concocting scenarios and evaluating risks. If I see Harlowe, I need an excuse. This could be it.

Javi pauses and looks at me hard before shaking his head in deference. "Okay, but can I also offer some words of unsolicited advice?" When I don't stop him, he continues. "Maybe don't show up unexpectedly. Give her the heads up I know you yourself would want. Connect with her and create a rapport before you spring your obnoxiously big ego on her after however long it's been. You seem to have a history, and that alone is unusual for you."

I cock my head and consider his words for a moment and finally nod. He's intuitive, catching on to far more than I've said. He knows my normal patterns with women, and yet he's read into the quick interaction from Monday that there was something very *not normal* about the situation with Harlowe. I hate that he's that perceptive when it comes to my personal life, but that's why he's my SVP. It doesn't mean I'll actually take his advice, but I appreciate it nonetheless.

I point a finger at him. "You think on the next level and have my back, even when I'm not looking for it."

Javi gives me a crooked grin and stands from the chair. "I think that's one of a handful of true compliments you've given me, and with that, I'm out of here before you ruin it by saying something shitty. Good night, man. Be careful." His backward wave as he strides through the door is enough to get me to crack a smile.

The smile fades when I realize once again I'm about to break one of my steadfast rules: don't contact anyone you've already fucked. That's how things get messy. That's when attachments form and expectations spring up. I'm not relationship material, and I never let anyone consider the idea because I'm out of their life too fast. But if I keep after Harlowe like this, whether or not she wants it, there will be a problem. I know this for a fact.

Harlowe was trouble from the start, and we both knew it.

And yet, here I am, going against my better judgment. I grab my suit jacket and leave the building without another thought to my own rules.

I'm already pulling up the message from Javi with her insurance card as I slide into my sleek, vapor gray Karma SC2 electric car, knowing I'm crossing so many lines by typing it into my GPS and starting the drive to her home. I know there's a process I should take, a better road to conversations with her about the kid who could very well be mine, but the only path I've ever taken has been the hard one I found for myself. I'm treading on unknown terrain with baggage that wants to take me down, but I'm starting the trek, anyway. I've scaled actual mountains. How hard can this be?

Harlowe lives a ways from downtown, but still in Atlanta proper, and it's strange rolling through the very suburban neighborhood when I normally stick to the highrises of downtown. I know I can't just walk up to the door and expect her to let me in for a chat, so I pillage more of her information from Javi's message and dial her number.

I'm surprised she answers an unknown number, even one with a local area code.

"Hello?" Her husky rasp floods me with a sense of nostalgia that shouldn't exist, and it takes me a moment to reply.

"Hey." I swallow. "Lowe, it's me." My voice is low and casual, not disclosing the internal turmoil as my brain screams warnings about how bad this could be. My heart is pounding a rapid staccato beat in my chest, expecting her to hang up on me. The adrenaline rush of the situation keeps me on the line, feeling each roar of my spiked pulse like a drug. *Rush. Rush. Rush. Mine. Mine. Mine.* She gets me so fucking high, and I've only heard her voice. Seeing her will send me to the fucking moon. I won't need to jump out of another plane for years if I keep this up.

Her sharp intake of breath is clear through the line before she slowly says, "Zander?"

"I'm at your house. I have Javi's insurance card for you." I use the last-minute excuse I created for what brought me to her home after dark. I clench my jaw, knowing she won't buy it any more than I can sell it, and that's saying something, given I have built a world-class business based on how I can sell a vision.

She chuckles softly, but the sound holds no mirth. She's laughing *at* me. Fuck.

"Your audacity knows no bounds. Javier could have sent me a photo of his insurance card like he said he would, yet here you are, skulking outside my house, using it as an excuse to be there because you think you have the right to everyone else's time and attention, you pompous ass."

She saw right through me and fucking called me out like I'm nothing. I tip my head back against the seat and close my eyes. I don't want to fight with her, not when there's so much on the line. "You're right," I grit out, leaving it at that. She doesn't need to know how on the money she is.

"Oh, wow! Well, that's new. I didn't know you could ever admit defeat," she says, the warmth of her voice soothing despite the words that needle at me. "Why are you here, Zander?"

I scrub my hand across my face, feeling the rasp of beard and grit from a day in the trenches of business. "I need a drink," I say, more to myself than to her.

She sighs. "There are bars strewn all across this city and you chose to come all the way out here to get a drink from me." She's quiet for a beat, and I'm readying for the disappointment when she turns me away. "Get your ass inside and be quiet about it. And do not, under any circumstances, make me regret letting you in."

I'm out of the car before the call ends. There's a lightness to my step that shouldn't be there with the weight of responsibility and the shattering of rules put in place to protect me and those around me. I rap my knuckles against her door, stilling in anticipation, and she opens it a moment later. Warm light spills out onto the dark porch as she's revealed in a blue and white striped pajama set that, while not skimpy by any means, hugs her curves and looks adorable on her. Her face is bare of makeup, dark hair tumbling over her shoulders and calling for my hands to twist in the long tresses.

Just seeing her calms some of the manic energy in me. I'm able to take a full breath for what feels like the first time since I saw her last. She stays silent, wariness in her expression as she looks at me on the threshold of more than just her home.

I'm bathed in her presence, memories of nights spent with her barreling straight to the forefront of my mind like a good bourbon on an empty stomach. The thoughts tangle around my limbs and trip me as I hesitate on the doorstep. Every instinct in me says to gather her in my arms and crush her against me, to take those full lips with mine and kiss the hell out of her. To touch her the way I know she likes. But, while I'm acting irrationally and against my better judgment, I'm not my baser instincts, and I know better than to rush into her space and take what isn't offered.

Who the fuck am I to want her this badly after walking away? I made my decision, knowing full well it was the best option. I shouldn't want her still, after having had my fill of her. But there is something more than our explosive chemistry and memories holding us together, and that's what is driving me to be this out of control of myself. If I can just get some answers from her, maybe I can stop this madness and get back to what I do best—no attachments.

"Are you going to stand there all night, or are you coming in?" she finally asks, cocking her hip and placing a hand on it. My eyes are drawn to where her hand rests, the new fullness calling to my hands, asking me to sink my fingers into her lush curves and pull her tight against me.

I blink the thought away. Being around her and not putting my hands on her is going to be a nearly insurmountable task. Good thing I like a challenge.

I follow her inside without a word, softly shutting the door behind me. She pads over the warm-toned hardwood, her bare feet peeking out from under the cuffs of her pajama pants, her ass jiggling through the stretchy material, and I have to will myself not to grow hard at the tantalizing sight. We pass a comfortable-looking living room and make our way into a spacious kitchen that has been done in the home's modern-meets-traditional style.

"I have a bottle of merlot open, and I may have some gin and tonic around, but this bar ain't stocked with much else." She pulls open the fridge and eyes the contents, arranged to perfection with carefully labeled containers holding a host of ingredients, and fresh produce stocked in the crisper drawers. "I have sparkling water, milk, and juice boxes, too." She turns back to me and shrugs a shoulder, not apologizing for her lack of drink options. A heavy pour of bourbon is what I really need.

"The wine is fine." I settle myself at a stool along the island, the thick marble veined in a deep blue-green that reminds me of the Indian Ocean we swam in together and I can't help but trace it with a finger while she pulls out a wine glass. There's one glass sitting in the sink, so I know she opened the wine for herself. At least there's not a second glass in that sink, so she wasn't drinking with the fucking jock she's seeing.

Rage fills my blood at the thought of him and the feeling of—what the fuck is this? *Jealousy*? I look up when she sets the wine in front of me. I smooth my thoughts away to contemplate later and let a smile touch my lips. It's my disarming expression, but her face hardens when she sees it.

"Are you going to tell me why I'm playing bartender to you tonight, or should I guess at your nefarious intentions?"

She leans on the island across from me, the undone first few buttons of her pajama top gaping with the movement and showing me the swell of her tits. It's hard to drag my gaze back to her face when memories of her incredible body and how responsive she is under my touch surface in my mind. On Monday, her nipples grew hard when she saw me, so even if she hates me now, her body remembers and may not feel the same way. Mine fucking knows what it wants, my cock twitching at the very sight of her.

"I was dealing with a lot of shit at work today. You may have heard about the cyber attack on Olympus?"

She nods warily. "Who hasn't?"

"The attack was to get into a project that isn't ready and the hackers stole proprietary information that is likely already sold to our competitors. It means years of work down the drain if we can't push production and get our product out before anyone else. It's also tanked a bunch of our subsidiary stocks and we're losing millions due to investors thinking we've had all of our data mined, so it's been a stressful few days."

"Oh, I see. You're actually taking this bartender thing seriously and plan to spill your woes all over my kitchen." She rolls her eyes and arches a brow before continuing. "Let me be clear. I don't care. I don't care what's going on for you, professionally or personally. It doesn't concern me and I'm not being paid to pretend otherwise. So what really brought you *here* tonight?"

I can't stop thinking about you. "What do you think threw us together again earlier this week?" I say instead of the thoughts that bang around my head.

"Uh, traffic?" she says, her beautiful face twisting in confusion. "Wrong place, wrong time," she continues sardonically.

I take a sip of the wine—it's good, and a far cry from the tropical cocktails she enjoyed in the Maldives with me—and wave a hand through her explanation. "I saw you on the Atlanta Haute List just before Javi hit you. There's a reason you were thrust back into my life twice in the span of a morning. I think you know why," I say, hoping her thoughts run parallel to mine.

"Please enlighten me," she says with another roll of her eyes. "I thought it was bad traffic navigation on your friend's part. As for why you saw something about me, I never asked to be the focus of a local gossip blog, but you should know they don't exactly take our feelings into account before writing about us."

So she has read about me, too. She crosses her arms and cocks a hip, striking a pose worthy of being photographed when she's just in her pajamas in her kitchen, dark hair tumbling down her back, calling me out on bullshit I didn't even realize I was stepping in.

I skip the preamble, going for the real reason I'm here, hedging my bets that I may get more out of her this way. "You have a kid now. One who could conveniently coincide with a trip we took years ago, and you never mentioned him to me. All I have are questions, Lowe. You hold all the answers."

My fingers grip the stem of the wine glass tightly while my words are looser than I would normally hold them, knowing she doesn't want to play games any more than I want to. I realize I misjudged the situation when her posture changes, straightening up and closing off. How can I know her body so well, yet not know the right thing to say to her now at all?

She plants her hands on the island and stares me down. "My son is of no concern to you."

"You think not?" The words come out quick and incredulous. *Entitled.*

She stiffens and I wonder why I'm making it my concern when clearly she doesn't want to share it with me. But I can't let it go. Not when I saw the similarities for myself. I rub a hand across my face and feel what little patience I have waning.

"He has my eyes, Harlowe. I can see that from a grainy cell phone photo published on a gossip site. It could be a coincidence. Who knows if you found another gray-eyed man to fuck right after me, but I'm thinking that's not the case." The words are sandpaper in my throat, tearing up from a locked-down vault and exiting before I can carefully filter them out.

I know as soon as I speak that I hate the idea of another man touching her and fathering a child with her. I hate that I could be wrong when I don't even know if I want to be right. I hate that I want to move around the island and bend her over it, making more gray-eyed babies with her. *Fucking hell, get a hold of yourself, Olsen!*

"You better drink that wine faster; you're overstaying your welcome." She says the cold words with a hot fury as she unwinds her arms from the protective stance along her waist and paces down the length of the island before returning with a look of righteous indignation animating her striking features. My Wildcat is still in there, vicious and beautiful, willing to claw and fight, to challenge me like the valkyrie she could so easily be. "You think you can waltz into my home, demanding to know about me and my life after *five years*?" She laughs bitterly before returning her fiery gaze to me. "You discarded me like a used cum towel. Why now? Why couldn't you have cared back then, when it actually mattered?"

"You knew what you were getting into when you boarded that jet. I laid it out clear as day, and you agreed. It was just an all-expenses-paid vacation where we would fuck like bunnies and have a really good time in paradise. It would be over when we got back. I never lied to you or told you I would be good relationship material. I'm not."

I'm standing and moving toward her as my words froth at our feet, white-capped waves rushing onto a desolate shore and leaving the foam of memories behind. I don't intend to touch her, but suddenly, I have her in my arms, her hands on my chest and face tipped up to meet my eyes, a look of surprise widening her gaze.

"What are you doing?" she asks hotly, her furious breaths pressing her chest against mine, fingers unconsciously curling into my shirt like she wants to keep me close. Do it, little Wildcat. Claw me, bite me, fuck me up and keep me here.

My hands roam along the too-familiar planes of her body, one coming to rest at the small of her back, just above the swell of her amazing ass, the other tangling in her hair at the nape of her neck and pulling until I get a sound from her I'm sure she doesn't want me to hear. It feels so natural. So right.

Fuck, what am I doing? I shake my head slowly. I can only answer her honestly, no matter how convoluted it is.

"Reminding you of what we enjoyed, as per our agreement," I growl, my eyes trained on her lips.

My body moves unhurriedly into hers as my brain disengages from rational thought. She makes no move to step away, her body warm and pliable against mine, eyelashes fluttering. I kiss the surprised O of her mouth before I can stop myself. It's a brush of lips, butterfly soft, that has hers parting against mine. I sweep my tongue against hers, still soft, still tentative. She tastes like red wine, dark chocolate, and something drugging that is altogether her that I will never be able to get enough of.

My fingers clench, tugging her hair, and a little whimper rises in her throat. I keep the kiss gentle when I want to haul her up onto the counter and pillage her lips. I take my fill of her mouth slowly. The intoxicating taste of her that hasn't changed in five years sends my head buzzing with adrenaline, my veins pulsing with the rush I crave so badly. *Mine. Mine. Mine.* I move my lips to flutter along her jaw, feeling her neck roll to give me access, and am seconds from biting just under her earlobe where I know she's sensitive when she freezes in my arms.

Cold clarity washes over me. I remove my lips from her skin and my hand from her hair, pulling back immediately. But I can't bring myself to let go of her hip, where my fingers dig into the plush softness like I need an anchor to keep myself attached to her. The steel rod of my cock is pressed tightly against her hips and has a mind of its own that very much wants this to continue.

I shouldn't have done that, and I damn sure shouldn't have come here tonight. This was a mistake I couldn't stop myself from making. My thoughts refocus, disengaging from the very physical reaction I have to her. I have to stop this, stop thinking it's okay to touch her now, when I know better. I have to kill this piece of me that wants anything more than I should.

"We had a physical connection. You weren't offered a place in my life other than for the duration of a trip." The words ground me in reality, not the fantasy land I thought I could get away with exploring again, even just for a few minutes.

She untangles herself from my grasping hands and puts more space between us, her molten chocolate eyes flashing. "What the fuck is this?" she hisses. "Are you trying to rub my face in how I misjudged you? Why would you kiss me like you want me, while telling me I mean nothing to you and you never offered me more than what I got? Just to, what, make me even more aware of what wasn't on the table to begin with?"

I rake a hand through my hair and look around, not sure why I'm acting without thinking, doing the exact opposite of what I know I should. I shouldn't even be here. I should have told my brothers my suspicions and let them subpoena a paternity test and kept out of a fifty-mile radius from the gravitational pull she has on me. Where's the fucking restraint I usually have in spades?

"I didn't mean for that to happen." My voice is gritty with self-loathing. I hate not knowing the motivations that push me to be so fucking impulsive, to overstep boundaries I put in place for this very reason. How could I lapse like this?

It's Harlowe. She's the antithesis of my rules, and everything my desires want, but my self-preservation knows isn't good for me.

"It was a mistake to let you in tonight, and it was a mistake to get mixed up with you in the first place." She's backing away from me, her eyes narrowing. The fury of her words feels like a punch to the gut, my lungs constricting with the reality that I brought this on myself.

"You're willing to call your child a mistake to bite back when you feel insecure about misreading what was offered?" The words are meant to cut her back, but I instantly hate myself for saying them when I catch the flicker of hurt cross her face that is quickly replaced by resolute indignation.

"How can you be such a shallow asshole?" She holds up a hand to keep me from responding to the rhetorical question. "No, I shouldn't even ask, it's just in your selfish nature. You didn't give a shit about me before you saw a headline that was enticing enough clickbait to get you interested for some reason. Please, just go back to forgetting I existed. It was easier that way."

"I can't fucking forget about you," I say, my words coming out harsh, yet the most honest of anything I could have said tonight.

I run my hand against my stubble in irritation, frustrated that this went ass up when I had every intention of being civil. She pushes my buttons so easily. Instead of remaining in control, I slip into bad habits and strike first before anyone can get the upper hand on me. Only, this isn't the place or the time to be acting on those well-honed skills.

"This isn't what I wanted when I came here. I had no intention of fucking up your night or fighting with you."

She's backed away from me as far as she can, her arms returned to the defensive position across her chest as she stares me down. "I've spent years getting past the blip in my timeline where you reside and I don't owe you space or my time now." Her voice is brittle.

The brokenness in the words tells me just how hard she's worked to put me behind her. I should have stayed there and let her have her peace. I don't deserve to be in her present or her future after how I fucked up her past.

"Should have quit while I was ahead." I reach for the full wine glass across the island and set it in the sink next to hers, wishing this had gone differently and I could have sipped it while talking to her like a reasonable man. I don't wait for a reply as I cross the kitchen and see myself out as she remains frozen in place.

This is exactly why I don't do repeats or attachments. There's not a chance of the vacillating drama to contend with if you just steer clear of seeing the person you fucked ever again. And hell, why would you care what happens in their life after? Feeling something other than intense pleasure or sexual satisfaction is overrated. Why did I decide to follow through with the urge to contact her, to see how she had changed over the years, or if I could still fit into her life with the kid that could possibly be mine?

It. Doesn't. Fucking. Matter.

Back to not caring, removing attachments, and continuing on with what I do best.

I slam my car and pull up Instagram, opening my DMs, and furiously scrolling through the messages from countless beautiful women. I settle on a gorgeous model in town for a shoot who messaged me this morning, and send her a casual *Are you up* before continuing my scrolling. It takes less than a minute to get a reply with an invite to a party she's at full of heart emojis. Bingo.

I'll fuck my way past this sudden attack of conscious and the shitty masochistic walk down memory lane I took myself on. I'll be back to myself tomorrow and Harlowe will be firmly removed to the past where she belongs, kid or not.

Eleven

Zander

Five Years Ago

"Do you see that reef out there? I'll race you to it."

I look over at Harlowe, who once again looks incredible in a cobalt blue bikini with a scoop top that lovingly holds her tits in perfect presentation for me to admire. She's shading her eyes and judging the distance seriously. I feel a smile tugging at my lips as I consider her latest challenge. Yesterday, it was who could find the most abalone and coming face-to-face with a reef shark that she stared down and waited for it to move on while her lungs nearly gave out. The woman is fearless.

"What makes you think you can beat me in an open-water swim that's at least two hundred meters?"

"Ten years on a swim team and a whole lot of confidence," she replies, turning to me and dropping her hand from her gorgeous face, sun-kissed and perfect in every way. "Why, worried you'll be beaten by a woman?"

I pull her against me. "I like your confidence. It doesn't bother me to potentially lose to you with all that swagger. But I'd like a fair wager. So what do I get if I beat you?"

"I'll titty fuck you. It's a lot of work for something that's all about your pleasure instead of mine, so it's a fitting prize." Her answer comes without hesitation, which makes me wonder if she already had it prepared before she made her first comment about the bet.

My gaze instantly drops to her tits, pressed invitingly against my chest, and it is a wonderful visual to consider fucking her there. I push a finger down into her plush cleavage, slick with sweat and her coconut sunscreen, and imagine my cock following the same path. I'd rather do something that gets her off, but if that's what she's putting on the table, I won't argue. I pull my slick finger out and nod.

"And what would you like if you win?"

She grins widely. "I want you to draw me a bath, complete with flowers, bubbles, candles, the whole nine yards. I want you to take it with me and massage my shoulders for at least ten minutes before it devolves into fucking. Because it inevitably will, but I want that guaranteed pampering and shoulder rub first."

Fuck. That sounds like couple shit. But it also sounds like something I'd like to do now more than anything. I tilt my head, evaluating if that would be going too far, if it would break too many rules. "Deal," I say before I can overthink it. I've already broken all of my rules for her. What's one more?

Her smile is brighter than the light reflecting off the Indian Ocean around us. "Good. See you at the reef."

And just like that, she's racing down the beach and into the water, her long legs churning up sand and splashing through the water. I immediately pursue her and plunge into the warm ocean hot on her heels. It's been a minute since I've had to swim with any sort of competition in mind, but the form is ingrained in me and I slice through the waves, letting my strokes pull me along as my strong kicks stabilize my body against the rolling waves. The saltwater burns my eyes, but I have no choice but to keep them open to see if I'm on course, and if Harlowe is anywhere close by. I see a splash ahead and realize she's far enough out that I may not catch her. That damn Wildcat knew what she was doing and baited me. No wonder she was confident enough to challenge me and make a bet out of it. I double down anyway, putting more strength into each stroke and working to close the gap.

My max effort isn't quite enough. Harlowe is treading water when I reach the reef, and she's barely out of breath. "I like my baths on the hot side. Those plumeria flowers the housekeepers keep putting on our bed would be amazing in the bathwater. They smell so good," she says when I swim up next to her.

"You're a shark," I accuse, blinking saltwater out of my eyes.

She laughs, the sound a bit scratchy from the ocean, but still drilling straight to my cock and getting me to smile despite feeling a little bitter over her now obvious deviousness.

"I never said otherwise. I told you I swam competitively and was confident. You could have taken it for the heads up it was, but you underestimated me."

"If I did, even unconsciously, I certainly learned my lesson. I will make you the best bath you've ever had tonight. You'll be so relaxed you'll sleep like a baby."

"Mmm, that sounds good, but I've been sleeping fine. Maybe it's because I've been woken up at dawn more often than not by you impatient to start the day with something sure to get the heart rate up."

"If I do recall, you're just as likely to be the one to wake me up. Just yesterday, your mouth was on me before my eyes were even open." I start lazily swimming back toward the beach, and Harlowe follows.

"Only because your giant dick pressing into my ass woke me up first. I had to do something about it." She smirks as she side-strokes next to me.

"So you put it in your mouth? Hey, I'm not complaining," I say when she gives me an exasperated look. "It was an incredible way to wake up. Fuck, I'm getting hard just thinking about your sweet mouth on me."

I swallow a mouthful of seawater as a wave hits me in the face while I'm thinking about her waking me up with her incredible brand of head that makes my eyes roll back every time she goes down on me. I cough and sputter, remembering we're still a hundred meters or more from shore and I shouldn't be thinking about fucking Harlowe's mouth while survival is on the line.

Harlowe laughs and mutters, "serves you right," before she starts swimming toward shore with her powerful strokes. I can see how she beat me. Her long, lean body is built for swimming, the water seeming to bend around her as she cuts through it. Fuck, she's sexy. Another wave hits me in the face and I realize I better get my shit together before I drown unintentionally.

After dinner, I send Harlowe to relax while I work on her prize. I go all out, collecting every flower I can find to fill the huge bathtub in our villa so Harlowe can have the luxurious, relaxing, sexy bath she requested as payment for winning her bet—rigged as it was. Bath oil and bubbles were part of the toiletries set included on the table next to the tub, so in they went, as well. I don't remember the last time I took a bath, but joining her for this one doesn't sound like a bad option. I make sure there are several condoms within easy reach on the table before I leave the bathroom in search of Harlowe to let her know it's ready.

She's stretched out on her side, her head propped on one hand while reading one of the romance novels she brought with her in a cushioned nook on the little deck overlooking the darkening water off the back of the bedroom portion of the villa. The ocean is beginning to churn, the sky a mass of clouds streaking across the horizon with an approaching storm.

Harlowe is oblivious to the weather and looks sexy as hell in a loose slip of a dress that hits her high on her thighs, the breeze lifting the hem and showing me there's likely nothing else underneath as the sun sets along the horizon behind the deep gray clouds. I give myself a moment to appreciate her like that, completely relaxed, unguarded, and not putting on a show for my benefit.

I know she's been playing a role. I never asked her to, but I'd be stupid to assume she would agree to this trip without some level of expectation, especially for what I asked of her. She likely thinks she needs to be a certain type of character to satisfy me. She has no idea that all I wanted was to get to know the woman behind the photos, the one who captivated me so much I had to break my own rules for her. I just wanted to know who she was off-set, out of the images that grabbed me by the balls and made me chase her. To know her like this.

I couldn't tell her that and risk her thinking I wanted anything more than just this trip. I can't promise her more. I can't promise her me, not off of this island, in the real world where business comes first and she would get the leftovers. Not when she deserves something so much better.

But tonight, I can offer her this piece of me that no one else has, or will ever have. She gets the real me, the whole me. The me that is in over my head and absolutely fucking crazy about her.

"Your bath awaits, my goddess divine," I say, bowing low to her at the doorway to the deck.

She smiles at me over her book. "Your goddess divine, huh? Really laying it on thick tonight."

"I've been humbled by your athletic prowess in the sea. How else should I address you, my queen?"

"Oh, I could get used to this," she says, humor bubbling through her words. She sets her book down and rises from the cushion-strewn nook, stretches, and walks to me. "Remember, it's ten minutes of shoulder rubs before the fucking." Her eyes narrow into a look of pure feline seduction, and I feel my balls tighten in response.

"Yes, my great and mighty deity of power and grace, I'm your willing and humble servant," I say, dipping my head in reverence as she passes, making her laugh loudly.

"You're too much. I definitely like your crass, demanding ways more than whatever this is. What would you call it, anyway?" She stops and turns toward me, waiting for my answer.

I straighten up, considering her question seriously, because I could just as easily stay in this role, worshiping her forever. "Acolyte is probably a good term."

"Drop the acolyte act. I want my Zander back."

My Zander. Fuck, I want to be hers so badly.

She grabs the neck of my shirt and pulls me to her, crushing our mouths together, and I react instinctively.

My arms wrap her against me exactly as I have come to enjoy the last week, one hand low on her back, the other along the column of her neck, my thumb and forefinger angling her jaw for my mouth to claim hers. She moans into my mouth, her body going soft where mine goes hard, and I thrill at the responsiveness she has to my touch.

"Don't start something I can't finish for at least ten minutes." I nip at her bottom lip and take her hand to walk her through the villa.

"It's part of losing the bet. You have to control yourself," she says playfully.

"No, Wildcat," I chastise. "It's you that will have to control yourself."

With that, I lead her around the corner to the bathroom and she gasps at the sight of the tub, full of bubbles and flowers, candles glowing around the edges of the windows and along the floor, illuminating the darkening bathroom. A soft rain begins to patter against the windows, creating a soothing soundtrack for our evening.

I turn to her and run my hands down her sides until I get to the hem of her thin dress and slowly raise it up and over her head. She lifts her arms for me while keeping her eyes locked on mine, and I was right, she's completely bare underneath.

"Fuck, Lowe," I growl, working on my control despite what I just said about it being her needing it. "You look so fucking good every time I see you like this. I want to worship you." I blink and lift my eyes away from her body which makes me want to drop to my knees and do as I promised. But I have to pay up first.

She's smiling like she can read the very real struggle I'm experiencing on my face. I reach behind my head and pull my shirt off by the collar, catching her expression shifting to interest as I shuck off my clothes to step up behind her and trail my fingers along all of the exposed skin I have access to like this.

"Your hair will get in the way. Tie it up," I order.

She gathers her long, wavy hair into her hands and pulls it up, twisting it around and tucking it into a knot at the top of her head. "Better?" She smiles.

"Now, do you want me to get in with you, or do you want me to rub your shoulders from out here."

"In," she says on a shaky exhale. "In the tub with me," she repeats, stronger this time.

So, into the nearly too-hot water I step and hold out a hand for her. She takes it, stepping in, turning, and together, like we've done it a million times before, we sink into the tub, her hips fitting snugly between my legs, her back against my chest. We fit perfectly in every way. It's no surprise that a giant bathtub is no exception.

Harlowe lets out a low moan of appreciation and sinks back against me heavily, the hot water instantly soothing her muscles. I'm already sweating from the temperature and hard from her little sounds, but this is as much my punishment for losing as it is her prize and I'll endure it silently so she can enjoy herself.

I begin kneading her neck and shoulders, and she purrs out her appreciation. That's right, my vicious little Wildcat can purr, and the sound stirs up an unholy need in me.

"Fuck," I breathe against her ear. "Keep making those noises baby, keep telling me what you like with your body. I love knowing that what I'm doing makes you feel this good." My voice is low and full of my need. Her shaky exhale is all the answer I need.

I continue to slide my thumbs along her slender muscles, working on instinct and what I have gleaned about what she likes from our trip so far. Her body grows heavier against me and the continued sounds of satisfaction that punctuate the quiet of the bathroom give me every indication of where she wants me to touch her now, much as she does any other time my hands are on her. I work out any knots I find, smoothing the tension from her shoulders and enjoying the feel of her becoming even more relaxed under my hands. The rain on the windows has steadily increased as the storm grows closer, lightning flashing in the distance.

When I've rubbed her shoulders for a fair amount of time, I start moving elsewhere. I know she's sensitive just below her ears, so I make sure to massage up each side of her neck with slow, deep strokes. She shivers, goosebumps rising along the skin of her shoulders. I know she likes it when I touch her just below her collarbones, so I let my fingers brush along the front of her chest, stretching her back against me tighter.

Her head falls against my shoulder and her breaths come out in shallow pants next to my ear, her dusky nipples now peeking through the bubbles, giving me even more incentive to touch her everywhere. I trace my hands down each of her sleek shoulders, kneading and working until my hands are under the waterline, and I graze the sides of her tits with my fingertips as I work down the full length of her arms and begin to come back up. I feel her tense in anticipation, subtly shifting herself so I'll have to graze her tits again. I still my hands at her elbows instead, and she makes a huff of impatience.

"Do you want your shoulder massage to include more now?" I ask, my voice a low caress next to her face that is still on my shoulder, so close to mine.

"Yes," she pleads, the word simple, yet holding so much yearning. A flash of lightning strikes closer to our villa, followed by a boom of thunder several seconds later, adding to Lowe's plea for more.

"This is all for you. Tell me exactly what you want." My voice is silky, hands barely moving along her arms again, fingers drawing small circles on her skin under the water.

"Touch me everywhere you know I like it. You know my body, Zander. I want to be yours. I want you to touch me like you own me," she begs, half mad with a desire that almost surprises me. Almost, but it doesn't, because I feel that same burning need for her.

"You're already mine, Lowe. All mine," I growl, grasping the graceful column of her throat, feeling her racing pulse under my fingers as I turn her face toward mine so I can claim that plush mouth that just said the most dangerous thing she could to me. Because I do want to own her. I want her to be mine. I want to have her be my forever, maybe even love her. My other hand gives her tits the attention she was seeking, kneading and stroking in time with my tongue against hers, rolling one nipple before lavishing the other with the same attention.

Her body is writhing against mine, angling, looking for more of my touch. I continue my path as I draw lazy circles around the undersides of her breasts, along her ribs, down her taut stomach, and finally to her sweet little pussy that she bucks up into my hand once it's within reach.

"Needy girl. Let me take my time enjoying all of you. You're mine, after all, and I'm quite indulgent. I like to visit all of my favorite parts, and unfortunately for you, that is everything on this exquisite body, so there is a lot I have to lavish with attention even if your cunt wants my fingers more than say, your hip bone." I keep my voice low and sensual as she growls when I move my fingers over to her thigh. She bucks again and I tsk at her. "There's my Wildcat." I bite her neck to keep her still, but she's writhing now. I lick up to her ear. "Beg me, if you want it that badly."

It has been torture for me not to bury my cock inside of her while she's been this pliant and sexy, this beautiful and relaxed, making the most incredible noises while I massaged her soft skin as steam rose off of it. I want to hear her say she needs me just as badly, and she's as wild as I am for her now.

"Please, Zander, I need your fingers. No, I need you. I need you inside of me. I need you to fuck me. God, I think I'll die if I don't have your cock inside of me now. Please, Zander. Please fuck me," she whimpers, her hands on my thighs, trying to reach between us, but I'm holding her too tightly for her to slip her greedy hands behind her back to grasp me.

Everything she says is fucking music to my ears. She's so perfect. I groan with it, my fingers gripping her thigh tightly with the need to sink my cock inside of her body the way she wants me to.

"You're so pretty when you beg, baby. Of course, I'll give you what you want. On your knees and wait like a good girl with your hands on the edge of the tub."

I let her go a little reluctantly so she can obey. Harlowe rises out of the protective cage of my body onto her knees and I miss the feel of her against me instantly. I'm rewarded by the sight of her, rising like a goddess from the bubbles and steam, flowers clinging to her like they, too, can't stand to be parted from her perfection.

I groan again at the sight and file it away as another of those most beautiful images I've seen. Her perfect profile and the curve of her neck are caught in the flash of lightning as she looks over her shoulder at me, her sun-kissed caramel skin glowing in the candlelight, reflecting off droplets of water and iridescent bubbles. The boom of thunder rattles the windows as the storm swirls over the villa now, mirroring our own frantic needs and desires.

I have to tear my gaze away to get myself out of the water, blinking and reminding myself she's real and won't disappear if I look away while I reach for a condom on the little table next to the bathtub, ripping the foil and slipping it on my cock. I kneel behind her, angling myself to enter her from behind like this. She's so tight, her knees only able to spread so wide by the sides of the tub, but I press in inch by tight inch until the tip is tightly wedged inside her little pussy.

"Hold on to those edges or we'll both go in face first and drown, got it? I can't be gentle. Not with how much I want you. Not with how much you need me." She makes the most delicious sounds of relief and pleasure that I slam home roughly, sloshing water around us and over the edge of the tub onto the floor with a splash. "I'm going to fucking ruin you, Lowe. You're mine."

We both groan and the feral need to really make her mine, to possess her, has me gripping her hips, hard, and pumping into her, pulling out to the tip, over and over again. What started as being completely for her has transformed into taking my own pleasure, but Harlowe is screaming yes, her back bowing, hips pressing back into the way I'm brutally fucking her. She'll have marks on her hips from my fingers tomorrow, but I'm out of my mind with need and she doesn't seem to care.

Water is going everywhere, sloshing over the sides of the tub with every fast pump of my hips, candles hissing out around us, smoke adding to the curling plumes of steam filling the bathroom around us. The storm outside matches our intensity in every way, flashes of lightning nearly constant, thunder shaking the very foundation of the villa and making my heart skip.

Her body feels custom-made for mine, every plush curve molding to my hard planes, her pussy taking my hard, deep thrusts as our groans and sounds become animalistic, primal. I'm out of my mind with the feel of her, but I'm lucid enough to want her to feel this good, to come apart around me and drive me further over the cliff of becoming completely lost to her. I slow enough to move the fingers of one hand to circle her clit, and the other hand up higher to her tits, playing with her straining nipples as I keep her pressed to me. I continue my driving assault into her cunt, feeling the trembling of her body, on edge. I pump my hips up hard, pull back, drive up harder.

"Zander!" Her choked gasp is my only warning. Her face lights up with the crack of lightning that burns outside the windows as her pussy clamps down on my cock, her orgasm detonates, and she shatters with the boom of thunder that follows, her internal walls spasming around me in the most explosive release she's had yet. I fight the tight hold and force myself in again and again.

"You're mine." The guttural growl is a foreign sound to my own ears while I bury my cock in deep, pressing my hips tight to hers as my release follows shortly after while I clutch her against me. Our breathing stays ragged, harsh as the howling wind and cracking of the very sky over our heads that knows we just broke every rule there is.

I'm utterly, madly, stupidly in love with this woman.

And even as I'm still heady with relief in the post-orgasmic glow, I know I'll have to cut out my bloody pulp of a heart when I walk away from her at the end of these two weeks. There's no way I can realistically take whatever we are creating here in our little vacation bubble back into my life back home. No matter how deeply she is now embedded in my heart, or how entwined my fucking soul is with hers, my first focus will always be business.

There is no room for a beautiful, vivacious, and all-consuming woman like Harlowe in what is leftover after work wrings me dry with all I have vowed to give of myself to the mistress of industry. Harlowe deserves more than coming in second to that. She deserves more than I could ever fucking give her, even if, selfishly, right this moment, I want to keep her all for myself.

I know I will have to let her go, and I'll have to crush her so resolutely there will be nothing left to come back to if I give in to my weakness.

Twelve

Harlowe

"Put on a pretty dress, do up your hair, and get yourself ready. I'm taking you out to the best restaurant in town. I know the chef. Her food is incredible."

I smile as I let Knox into the house, his deep voice ringing through the open living room. Before he rang the bell, I was chopping vegetables for the dinner I invited him to. He likes to joke that eating in my kitchen is better than any restaurant he could take me to. I head back to the kitchen to finish my preparations.

"Knox!" Hendricks yells, jumping up from the Legos he was assembling on the floor. He runs and launches himself at Knox, who catches him under the arms and swings him up into the air.

"Hey, little man! Are you being good for your mama?" Knox walks to the couch and plops down with Hendricks in his arms and I watch as he interacts with my beautiful son. It turns out he's great with kids. He comes from a big family and has twelve nieces and nephews.

Knox continues to surprise me the more I get to know him. I never expected to date an athlete, always assuming they were too focused on their sport, one-dimensional, or at worst, major players flaunting big-time contract money. Knox hasn't been like that. He's humble, focused but still present, and he's been incredibly attentive. We haven't been dating long, but I felt comfortable enough bringing him into Hendricks's life after we went on a handful of perfectly fine dates and I felt safe enough with him, and my kid has preened under the attention of a strong male figure.

I bite my lip, feeling a little guilt for my role as a single parent, raising a little boy without a father around. I let my lip slide out of my teeth and scowl at the cutting board under my hands. It wasn't my choice to do this alone. I never would have chosen to do this on my own. But I wasn't given the option from the very beginning, and there was no way in hell I would have begged for it from the man who cut off all contact with me immediately after unknowingly knocking me up. Well, for my son, I would have begged, if I had the chance, but I wasn't even given one.

I knew without a doubt that Zander Olsen did not want to be a father. He was very good at preventing the outcome. Except once. And that was all it took to change my entire life and create a new one. So, why is he trying to find out more about Hendricks now? What would have changed for him to come around, not remotely interested in fatherhood, just needing the confirmation of his progeny? Would he stop trying to worm his way into my life if I told him the truth, or would he want more? It's the more that has me worried.

"Harley, get your cute butt over here and see what the little man has built. I swear, he is the most inventive kid I know, and that's saying somethin' because I have lots of nieces and nephews."

I cringe, my fingers flexing against the cutting board, and release the knife and poor sweet potato I had been absently slicing into ever smaller pieces. I've had many nicknames over the years, and Knox has latched on to one of my least favorites. It doesn't suit me, but it also isn't worth fighting over, since it's just a nickname. I make my way over to the couch, where I lean against the arm and gaze over Knox's big body, making my deep couch cushions look tiny, and Hendricks kneeling next to him, little boy face animated as he tells Knox about his Lego creation.

"It has a rocket back here and these wheels help it roll real fast. This propeller makes it fly, and these wings steady it in the air," Hendricks explains, pointing at the multi-colored bricks and plastic pieces patchworked together into the semblance of a vehicle.

"He built a—" Knox pauses and consults Hendricks, "hey, little man, what did you say this was called? I want to make sure I tell your mom the correct name."

Hendricks looks up with a smile, his eyes shining under the attention. "It's a quadmantulator," he says, making up a term I've never heard before. "Quad, because it does four things. It flies, it drives, it hovers, and it rolls, see," he says, tossing his creation along the couch with a burst of noise he's decided should accompany it. The wings break off as it hits the arm of the couch and he huffs. "I'm still testing it out. I gotta fix what keeps breaking." He picks up the pieces and returns to the floor where his Lego pieces are carefully grouped together, not by color or shape, but by some other sorting method he favors. He is meticulous, though it just appears messy. My little mad scientist in the making.

"I'm impressed that he knew quad means four, and he listed four different actions his machine can do," Knox says, looping a big arm around my hips and scooping me from the edge of the couch to his lap.

I'm tall at five feet nine inches and sporting mama cushioning, so I'm not the thin model I once was, but in Knox's lap, I feel small. I blink rapidly as I think of another man who made me feel light and graceful and fit against me so perfectly that we became extensions of the other instead of two distinct people. I tilt my head against Knox's shoulder to avoid him seeing any distress that may be evident on my face. I can't be thinking of Zander now, when Knox is holding me, showing me what true attentiveness can look like after years of going through life alone, raising a son whose father had no clue he existed, and wanted to stay that way.

"I'm making turkey burgers and sweet potato wedges," I say, lifting my head to look at Knox's profile.

While he's become a part of my life, I've hesitated to really let him in. True, we have something warm, but it's not an all-out burning fire of lust that propels us to keep seeing each other. It's warm like a friendship, a camaraderie, and while I find him attractive, and I enjoy his company, I haven't felt that spark I know is possible between two people.

A spark I felt with Zander that turned into a roaring wildfire only to have it smothered out immediately. Knowing how easy it is to crush hopes, I feel I'm holding back even now, when he's been nothing but amazing. I haven't been able to open up about Hendricks's father, or most of my life before him.

Knox knows me as the foodie girl with a YouTube channel and a new cookbook, not the model who flew around the world for high-profile shoots, eating only carrot sticks and subsisting on iced coffee. He knows me for sharing thirst traps and body positivity on social media, but not the hard-won truce I've made with my body after years of eating disorders and low self-esteem. There are dark places and skeletons in my closet that I haven't been able to share with him, no matter how dependable he's been, because, deep down, I know he could crush me, too.

After Hendricks is in bed and the dishes from dinner are cleaned up, Knox pulls my feet into his lap on the couch and rubs my instep. "You okay, Harley?" he asks softly, his eyes on the muted TV screen streaming The Office, giving me some space to answer without being too direct.

I sink down into the couch cushion with the tingle of pleasure that rolls its way up my leg from his hands. "Everything's fine," I answer automatically. "Just feeling the nonstop press schedule, I guess."

"I was getting a little worried that you hadn't called me to come over in weeks, not since before your car accident. You sure it's just your schedule? Nothing else?"

This is one thing I both adore and hate about Knox. He asks the questions that others would politely ignore. He checks in. His perception and persistence are some of the reasons I finally agreed to go out with him a couple of months ago, after we ran into each other at the stadium where I was treated to a VIP experience, thanks to Callie's husband. We had met previously at a gala, so we were familiar. When he saw me outside of the locker room after the game, he'd insisted he should take me out, saying he'd been watching my channel and wanted someone else to cook for me, for once, but since he couldn't, he'd pick a restaurant and really go all out. Callie had prodded me in the back, nodding with big eyes when I turned to look at her for help, so I reluctantly agreed. True to his word, Knox had picked a delicious restaurant in a trendy neighborhood and had talked my ear off and had me going in turn. So I agreed to see him again, and that turned into what we have now, a very casual, comfortable relationship of sorts where I don't call him my boyfriend, but he's everything that could be.

Except... well, he's never once made a move on me. We make out a little, but he's never even felt me up, or gotten so carried away by passion that he's tried to take it further. At first I thought he was being a gentleman. Or maybe he wasn't that interested in me. And yet, he keeps calling, wanting to see me, showing his interest. It's a little confusing and definitely not something I have any experience with, as I was either pawed relentlessly by a handsy date, or I knew exactly what I was getting myself into when I let a relationship progress physically.

So, what's Knox's deal? Am I not attractive, or have I lost that spark now that I'm a mom?

"Do you want to stay the night?" I ask, rather than answering his own question that got my head spinning needlessly.

His fingers still on my foot and a brief look of discomfort flits across his brow before it's smoothed out, and he turns to look at me with his trademark wide smile.

"I think me staying over would upset your routine with Hendricks in the morning. This is new, and making sure I don't mess anything up with the little man is my highest priority. Let's take it slow." He pulls me by the knees so I'm stretched out flat on my back and he turns to hover over me. My heart rate quickens as his eyes stray to my mouth, then lower. "I'd love to spend the night with you, but I can wait."

My stomach dips with the rejection. He may have just given me the nicest rejection I could have hoped for, but he still told me no while saying all the right words. I tilt my head to the side and study him. His shoulders are set with a tension his easy smile masks, and his touch is warm, but almost clinical where he holds the backs of my knees. There is no soft brush of a thumb along my bare skin, no tentative slide up my thigh like I would expect. His body language doesn't seem to match his words.

No. I have to stop analyzing his every move and word. I'm just looking for reasons to not trust his ability to be patient and take it slow like he said.

He's different from the guys I've been with before, and that's good. He's dependable. That's new for me. So, if he wants to wait, to not get physical or take our relationship to that next obvious level, I can accept it. It's the least I can do for someone so nice and caring, for someone who actually wants to be with me. It's the bare minimum I should expect and accept.

I nod at him and smile softly. "Thank you."

He chuckles. "What are you thanking me for?"

"Being a gentleman, I guess, and for prioritizing my son over sleeping with me," I admit. It feels far too vulnerable to say it out loud, to really bring sex into the conversation for the first time without just hinting at the prospect. *Real mature of me to not even be able to talk about sex with the man I just asked to stay the night.*

Knox grabs my hands and pulls me into a sitting position. His thumbs gently rub across my knuckles. "Your relationship with Hendricks will always be a priority. Don't settle for any man who doesn't respect that." His sincerity just about breaks me down completely.

Before I can start ugly crying in front of him, I pull my hands away and swiftly swipe under my eyes for any excess moisture, and stand. "Okay, you've officially made me a total mom mess, so I should say goodnight and take my sappy self to bed."

"Get some rest and kill that talk show tomorrow," he says, following me off the couch, again showing me how much attention he pays to my schedule and life. "You can call me whenever you want. You know I'll always make time for you. My schedule is just practice, training sessions, and games. Nothing too important," he jokes, kissing my forehead.

I walk him out and wave goodbye from the porch when he drives away in his entirely too practical SUV. The man doesn't even have an ostentatious car.

And so my unfortunate celibacy continues.

As usual, when I'm feeling a little overwhelmed, I take control the only way I know how. I pull out my phone and open Instagram, posting a photo of me, head tipped to the side, taking a bite of a Korean Bulgogi taco as it falls apart on my face. It's another recipe from *At Home with Harlowe* and a super fucking hot titty shot that I look way too good in. It's another obvious thirst trap, but I write a caption that says *it's okay if we fall apart, tacos fall apart and we still love them—even if our bulgogi tacos wanna recreate a bukake video, we'll slurp that shit up to the last drop, we ain't wasting the good stuff.* I hit post and close the app before I can even see the engagement numbers. I didn't do it for anyone but me. I like the way I look in the photo, I enjoy writing a bit indecently for the audience I've built, and those are good enough reasons to post it, even if it helps with other things in the process.

Thirteen

Harlowe

Five Years Ago

Something shifted between us in the bathtub. It was seismic, and we both felt it, but didn't talk about it. Not last night when he scooped my still trembling body out of the water, plumeria flowers clinging to my skin, wrapped me in a fluffy towel, and carried me to bed. He dried us both off before we crawled naked between the covers, into each other's arms, legs entwined like we couldn't stand to have even an inch of our bodies apart. Not this morning when he woke me up with his head between my legs, eating me out with a slow and deliberate sweetness that brought me to awareness, then had my back bowing, fingers clawing at his hair as I came against his mouth.

We don't say anything at all as we tentatively feel out the other in this new space we entered when I asked him to touch me like he owned me and he responded that he already did. We're not talking about it now as we feed each other pieces of fruit with our fingers for breakfast on the deck with the ocean breeze ruffling our hair and cooling the heat in his searing gray gaze. We probably won't talk about it at all, because what changed was what we both want from this trip, no matter what he said about it going into the vacation. The bridge to casual, no attachments, no repeats, was absolutely scorched last night, with no hopes of returning that way.

"Do you like lobster?" Zander finally asks, pulling my attention away from this new connection—this *attachment*—between us, and back to him in the flesh. *God, he's beautiful.*

I smile, knowing he wants me to go on pretending that everything is back to the way it was before, and I can do that. I can play this role, no matter what it means, or even if it breaks a little bit of me to do it.

"Of course. I'm sure it's incredible, caught fresh here, just like all the fish and seafood we've had."

"We can catch it, if you want. You up for a little adventure, Lowe?"

And my challenging Zander is back, here to see if I'm willing to meet him on his latest quest for adventure.

I scoff. "Like I would turn down the opportunity to catch my own dinner? Show me where and how and I'll catch enough for the both of us. Give me a kitchen and I could cook it, too, and your mouth would water." Confident. Brazen. I'm the Wildcat he has taken to calling me who taunts him, challenges him, and is his equal in all his playful pursuits. Right back into the role I will play for him.

Zander's storm cloud gray eyes are more than interested, relief flitting through those fathomless depths that I'm willing to play along. "You like to cook?"

"That's like saying you like to make money when you mention you're in business. I'm brilliant in the kitchen. If I wasn't modeling, I would absolutely make a run at being a chef."

"I'm intrigued. I have always been told not to trust a skinny chef. It seems like a model would be the last person I would think of as a good cook."

I keep the fun smile fixed on my face. He absolutely does not want to hear about the last six years of disordered eating, of hating my body for not being what casting directors were looking for on shoots or campaigns or catwalks. He doesn't want to hear that I cooked wonderful meals and only let myself eat a bite of each dish and threw the rest away for fear of the caloric density and what it would do to my figure.

"Just because I'm a model, and I can't eat as much as I'd like, doesn't mean I can't cook. Let me sweet talk the chef at the restaurant. I'll make my way into that kitchen and we'll see what he has to say about my skills, and you can see for yourself, Zander, that I can blow your mind with another taste of my remarkable talents."

"Well, consider this challenge fucking accepted. I'm ready for you to blow my mind yet again, little Wildcat."

Before I can do that, we have to catch the damn lobster.

Zander and I take a boat out to a reef and he gives me the briefest crash course in spotting lobster among the rocks and reefs, how to use a tickle stick to herd them out of their hiding spots, to grab them with my hands. Then it's just putting on a mask, snorkel, and gloves, and we're in the water on our hunt. It takes no time at all for my competitive streak to get going and of course, I'm looking for the juiciest creature to win some imaginary contest against Zander.

Once I figure out what I'm looking for, the task becomes fun as I push the spiny lobsters out of hiding, hunting for a perfectly sized catch in between breaths. Finally, I make my selection, grabbing the lobster and swimming for the boat just as Zander comes up with his own catch.

"Look at you, a natural, as usual," he says, tossing his tickle stick and lobster into the back of the boat. He fluidly hauls his beautiful body up onto the small deck at the rear of the boat and turns to help me in next.

I push my mask and snorkel off and wipe water out of my face. "That was fun. I got an extra lobster for something I have planned."

He looks over his shoulder and spots the second lobster I found on an earlier dive and whistles. "Overachiever," he laughs.

"Shall we go back to the island and I'll really wow you with my overachiever abilities? We have hours before dinner. I'm sure we can figure out a way to fill them." I walk my fingers up Zander's bare chest until my hand is flat against it and I'm looking up at his lips, saltwater still clinging to his skin, reflecting the sunlight like jewels.

He closes the distance and captures my lips, his tongue slipping into my mouth and twisting with mine. He tastes like salt and heat and storms and I'm pulled right back into the feeling of belonging to him, of being his, that I forget to play. I just am. My arms wrap around his shoulders, fingers winding up into his wet hair and digging in, keeping him close, here, mine.

He answers in kind, fingers threading into my own salt-slicked waves and pulling tight, making me moan into his mouth. I feel him harden against my thighs and my core clenches in need, wanting to have him inside of me right now. His chest rumbles against me, an answering groan of longing, and I know neither of us wants to stop whatever we've started, though a small boat full of lobster isn't the easiest place to act on our desires.

"Back to the villa?" I ask, barely pulling my mouth from his.

"Back to the villa," he agrees.

We return to the island and drop the lobster off at the restaurant with a promise from the chef that I can use his kitchen, and he's quite intrigued by my challenge of a *wok off*. We walk hand-in-hand to our side of the island, shoulders bumping, talking about the rainbows of fish, the coral, and current from our dive. I offer to stow the snorkel gear while Zander heads inside.

When I walk up the stairs into the villa, I hear the shower and wander into the bathroom, where I let out a sigh of appreciation at the sight that greets me of Zander's powerful body under the spray of the shower-heads. I don't even stop to take off my bikini. I just open the glass door and join him under the spray of warm water, untying the strings as I go and letting the skimpy pieces fall to the floor at our feet.

"I hoped you'd find me in here."

He pulls me to him immediately, his lips on mine, his hands on my skin feeling hotter than the water that sluices over our bodies. He drags his teeth along my neck and I shiver, feeling my body going molten, heavy. This is exactly where I need to be.

I wrap my arms around his toned shoulders, my hands finding his back, anchoring myself against him and let out a sigh of pleasure as something clicks into place. I blink in brilliant awareness, then the shock subsides to the feel of Zander around me, his lips on mine, our bodies together.

This moment in Zander's arms, in the middle of the Indian Ocean, feels more like home than anything has since I left my mom's house in Atlanta at eighteen to start my career in modeling. I've led a nomadic life since then, traveling the world for jobs, and not feeling settled in any one place. This place, specifically, isn't home, but this person, this man, feels like he is. And I had missed him in the moments that we were apart. I pull away from his lips and stare at his face in wonder, and he gives me a questioning look.

"I missed you. Isn't that stupid?" I say, a little embarrassed to speak the vulnerable, errant thought out loud. It had been minutes. That's all it took for me to feel needy for him, to want his touch and crave his eyes on me. To feel this sense of homecoming now.

"No. I missed you, too."

His admission, whispered against the shell of my ear as he palms my breast, is unexpected, so unlike his rules and no attachments mentality I wonder if I misheard him, but I couldn't have. His fingers between my legs thankfully stop the thoughts I know will only get me into trouble and instead, I'm focused on the feel of him slipping two thick fingers inside.

"That's my girl, nice and wet for me already. I'm going to fuck you with my fingers until your legs are shaking. Will you be a good girl and come for me?"

I let out a shaky whimper of need as he pumps his fingers harder, his thumb finding my clit and taking up a lazy circling path that is in stark contrast to the movement his other fingers are making, pressing in hard against the sensitive spot inside me. My eyes close and my head tips back. Zander's mouth closes over my nipple and his teeth graze the sensitive bud while he licks after the slight sting. I feel the orgasm building, Zander working up the tension and stealing my breath as he continues to pump his fingers. His tongue flicks over my sensitive nipple again just as he crooks his fingers and pushes hard and I shatter, my cry breaking free as my pussy clenches and my knees sag. Zander catches me, pinning me to the wall and letting me ride his hand until my pussy releases his fingers, until I can open my eyes and stand on my own again.

"Zander," I say, pulling him closer, needing him inside of me, a need so great it's unintelligible. "I need you, please," I whisper, my fingers in his hair, on his face, my lips on his skin.

"Tell me what you want, what you need." He brushes water off my face with his thumb, his eyes bright, intense as he stares into my face. "Or you have to tell me to stop, because I'm going to fuck you and make you mine, and I won't be able to let you go, Lowe. This is it. You're mine, baby."

I feel my eyes prick and my chest squeezes at his words. I want that, so badly, but this is a line he's drawing. We've already crossed it, but he's giving me an out. He's telling me there's still a chance we can walk away unscathed, unaffected, no matter how much we would be lying to ourselves. This is us dropping the roles and being our authentic selves, letting us feel the things we've been dancing around, no matter how fucking bad it's going to feel when we have to leave them behind at the end of the trip. I think a tear slips free from my eye, but it mixes instantly with the spray from the shower.

"I want you, Zander. All of you. I want every piece of you. Give me everything. I want you to belong to me as much as I belong to you."

"Pretty words, Lowe, such pretty fucking words," he whispers, his eyes screwing up tightly. When he opens them, his storm cloud eyes look like a fire has been lit behind them, smoke and ash swirling and rising in those depths, and I know it's the restraint, the no attachments, and the rules he lives by to keep himself walled off burning to the ground that feeds those twin fires.

His head lowers, and he captures my mouth with his, the kiss searing hot, carrying the fire from his eyes and igniting me in turn. I burn for him, flames licking through me, catching on the dry kindling of feeling rootless and having finally found my home in him. Embers spark and burn out all the memories of not being good enough, knowing he's choosing me now. Flames catch in the darkest parts of me where I feel I will never amount to anything, giving me twin flames to light up those places and I feel a glimmer of hope for the first time that I can have a purpose beyond being a pretty face. A wildfire catches, warming me from the inside out with the knowledge that I can belong to someone like Zander Olsen.

Zander fists his cock in one hand and I lift my leg to his hip as he notches it at my center and pushes in, keeping his eyes trained on mine with each slow inch of him filling me.

"You're mine. Say it for me, baby," he commands, voice rough, low, and broken, like the fire that is burning in his eyes is raging through the rest of him, too, and he's struggling, needing my reassurance that he'll come out the other side whole, better.

"I'm yours, Zander," I respond, wrapping my arms around his shoulders and threading my fingers in his hair, pulling until his eyes meet mine. "And you are mine. You are all fucking mine."

Zander's smile is all male pleasure, possession, and need, so when his hands grip my thighs tightly and he backs me roughly into the wall, I'm ready for the punishing fucking I know he is so capable of. But instead, he takes his time, shallows out his thrusts and angles his hips so he hits a new part of me that feels even more incredible than I expected. He hooks my ankles behind his back and grips my ass, squeezing and kneading while he kisses me sweetly and as slowly as he fucks me.

No, that's not it, he's... *he's making love* to me.

Zander Olsen is making love. *To me.* A dam of emotion bursts open inside of me with the orgasm that blooms and swells and rips a sob from my throat as I crest and overflow. I cling to him as he continues to move so gently, so sweetly, with me wrapped around him, the waves of my release continuing to roll through me as tears of relief track down my face as my love for him stokes the fire burning in me, raging hotter, higher, lighting up every dark place and making it golden and bright and lovely.

"You feel so fucking good like this. I'll never be the same. Fuck, Lowe, I'm ruined, you own me. Your pussy is everything. I want to live inside of you. I want you forever, just like this. Just us. Lowe, you're mine. All mine, forever, baby."

He wants me, not the role I'm playing. He wants to keep me, even after the trip. He wants this to be real. And just like that, I'm irrevocably lost to this man. I softly cup his face in my hands and kiss his lips that speak such filthy, lovely, sweet, and deliciously dangerous words that set me on fire and make me think of forever with him. He kisses me back with the same hunger and longing, the same need and desire that is fueling me.

The next time I come, it's with our foreheads touching, my eyes locked on his, his groan and my whimpers mixing as he is pulled over the edge with me into a soaring release. It's the most intense, soul-searing experience that will stick with me long after the shower washes away the evidence that there was no condom easily at hand just this once.

Fourteen

The Atlanta Haute List

Celebrity Chef Taking Down Fort Knox, Or Digging Out Of Billionaire's Shadow?

Our new favorite couple, Atlanta cookbook author and former model, Harlowe Sorenson, and her beau, professional athlete, Knox Contraire, look to be getting comfy. Reports of Knox's late-night visits to Sorenson's home are just the tip of the iceberg when it comes to these two. They were spotted getting cozy at Napoletana Pizza last week, and our insiders feel confident that things are moving along nicely. Now that they are regulars on the Haute list, we decided to give them a deeper look.

Knox hasn't been linked to any notable names throughout his football career, but it's not surprising he would latch onto former top model and current social media sensation, Harlowe, who is one of the sexiest, yet also most relatable, celebrities in our city. He's an up-and-coming athlete destined for success, and she's switching gears and continuing to make a name for herself no matter what she's up to. They could be the next power couple, conquering several industries at once and cementing themselves in our hearts forever.

So, what's Sorenson's story? Harlowe is an Atlanta native who has remained unattached since she was last linked, although briefly, to the youngest of our illustrious Atlanta billionaire brothers, Zander Olsen. Thaaaat's right, Hauties, our favorite billionaires are making it into all of our stories these days. We've been digging up dirt all around the Olympus foundation, linking the brothers to the who's-who of Hollywood and business alike, and we stumbled upon some news from before the Haute List was born.

It turns out that Harlowe was listed on a flight manifest to the Maldives five years ago with Zander, returning two weeks later and not being linked to him since. That fits Olsen's modus operandi with beautiful women—wine and dine them, then release them before anything can be made of the connection. Though, two weeks is about thirteen days longer than most women get at Olsen's side, so it has us scratching our heads at what could have happened in those two weeks in paradise.

Just know we see you, Zander and Harlowe, and we can't help but wonder at the timing and make connections between the illusive son carefully guarded from the world by Sorenson. No posts to social media containing a full photo, no candid paparazzi shots with the little one in tow, and only our in-the-know Hauties' submissions of blurry shots from brief outings to go off of, but we can still see a *possible* resemblance to one of Atlanta's, and the entire business world's, top billionaires. Could this be the start of our generation's very own Watergate, ahem, ZaddyGate? Hashtag it now, we're calling it first. We'll let you be the judge, and of course we'll keep digging. For all the Haute gossip, click Like and Subscribe!

Fifteen

Zander

"Fuck, what now?" I growl, pushing away the tablet Payton thrusts into my hands as soon as I walk out of the elevator. I read the headline and scan the article, noting quickly what is insinuated in bold font on a crisp website that most of Atlanta will read today and speculate about nonstop.

"Why the hell didn't you tell us about this, Zand? Is it true?" Payton asks, his long strides matching mine as I barrel down the hallway, looking for the privacy of my office to rage in. That fucking blog needs to be scraped from the internet already. We have the money and resources to do it, so why is it still up?

"Is what true? It's a fucking gossip site that likes to make connections where there aren't any," I say, putting as much confidence in my voice as I can.

It's a question I have resolutely decided not to care about as I fuck my way through my social DMs in an attempt to get back to the normal me. A me I can't fucking find when Harlowe insists on posting the thirstiest photos imaginable. I should be immune to her and yet

I'm stopped in my scrolling every fucking time by the expressions on her face, her glorious tits, whatever goddamn recipe she is showing off, and reading her words that sound like the filthiest of food porn that gets me hard and has me stroking my cock and coming in my hand like a horny teen. I should block this account, too, which would be for the best. Yet I haven't, because I'm a masochist using the flimsy pretense of following her to potentially find out about her kid for myself.

"Is it possible you have a child?" Payton's voice is low, spoken only for me to hear knowing there are far too many eyes and ears trained on us as we move through the busy office space toward the executive office wing. "We know you fucked her, went to the Maldives with her, spent way more time with her than you ever do. Could you have gotten this girl pregnant?"

He calls her a girl when she's the sexiest goddamn woman he would be lucky to even meet. I carefully keep my eyes ahead, not answering his question or meeting his inquisitive ocean blue gaze that is steadfast and fixed on me, looking for any signs of weakness he can exploit. I shove through my office door hoping he'll be shaken off, but he follows through and nearly runs into me when I see Hayes has already made himself comfortable on the black leather sofa facing the door, his phone in hand.

"Is *this* why Harlowe was coming around the office after your trip? Maybe she was trying to tell you that she was left with more than sand in her panties from your trip?" Hayes asks, fire burning through his deep green stare as he holds up the phone, showing the same Haute List story. My brothers and their demanding eyes are going to be the death of me today. "Should I congratulate you on the birth of my nephew now, or after the paternity test?"

I stay silent while I move to my chair behind my desk, grasping for the smallest piece of control I can muster, even if it's just the act of being at my desk and in a position that normally makes me feel powerful.

Payton closes the door and leans back against it, the tablet lit in his hand while he scrolls. "Gossip site or not, the Atlanta Haute List had correct information about the flight manifest when we know she accompanied you to the Maldives. So why don't we know about this mistake?"

"I don't make mistakes," I growl, my head lowering slightly, ready for the challenge these assholes are no doubt going to throw at me. The question sends me right back to the last conversation I had with Harlowe. She said it was a mistake to get mixed up with me, and it fucking hurt. If we did create a child from that trip, he's no mistake. I don't care if it wasn't the intention or something I ever considered. If he's my child, my son, he will never be a mistake.

"You made a mistake by not following up with one of your longest-running..." Payton pauses, glancing up quickly while searching for the right word to call my trip with Harlowe, "hookups, I guess. You just did your typical Zander move and cut off all contact with her and had absolutely no idea you may have had a bigger souvenir from that trip to paradise than a killer tan and a wet dick."

"Oh, give him a break, Pay, the man doesn't do repeats. He just uses a woman for a day or a weekend, and we clean up the mess if they want to stay longer. How many times have you or I shown up at his penthouse, NDA in hand, to find a disgruntled date that didn't want to leave despite Zander's clear instructions?" Hayes says far too casually to match the hard set of his face.

"True, we've had our share of chasing off the clingers who didn't get that Zand wouldn't want to sleep with them again after their value, as something to conquer had been diminished when they opened their legs to him." Payton strolls away from the door and settles his long frame into a chair across from my desk. "The biggest surprise here may be that he spent more than one night with a single woman, not that he may have a kid because of it."

I could crack a tooth with the ferocity of my jaw clenching. They're not wrong, but it feels far more irritating to hear them discuss my motivations and hookup history with such bluntness. It's beginning to sound like I may have fucked up.

"What pisses me off the most is his fucking conquer the mountain mentality that sent him careening after his next conquest after creating a major liability. What do we know about the woman? She's a former supermodel and she's making a name for herself with a cookbook and YouTube channel, but is she going to shake him down? How much money is she going to want, and why hasn't she made her appearance before now, looking for it? She didn't sign an NDA, so what's she waiting for?" Hayes asks Payton, deliberately ignoring me.

"Shut the fuck up, both of you. She refuses to even say if this is my kid. There's no way." The slight catch to my voice at the end of the sentence gives away my lack of confidence in the words. I cross my arms and lean back in the chair, creating some distance from their accusations.

"There's no way, or there's a chance and you're just an idiot for being sloppy?" Hayes probes, leaning his big arms on his knees and peering at me with an intensity that I want to punch away.

"Did you raw dog her the whole trip, or did a condom break? Did you forget, even once, to wrap it up? What are the chances here? Give us the truth because we need to know if there is even the slightest possibility you may have a child, whether or not you know about it," Payton says, mirroring Hayes in his position and making me want to fly out of my chair under their scrutiny. "We need the information if we're going to get ahead of this and help you figure it out."

The softening of his voice is what finally buckles me, and I blow out a breath I didn't realize I was holding and drop my arms to the desk. "It was only once, and I didn't think anything of it. I don't forget things like that. It's second nature to grab a condom, but we were in the shower and it just progressed faster than either of us realized. It was just the one time."

Harlowe's sun-kissed caramel skin had been glowing from our afternoon under the tropical sun, the scent of her coconut sunscreen thick in the shower enclosure when she stepped in after me. Her body had molded against mine, her long, burnished brown sea salt waves falling down her back as the water washed over us both. She'd said she missed me, and I knew I would never be the same because I had missed her too. I slipped into her wet heat bare and made love to a woman for the first time in my life, knowing it would change me forever. When we both came, I looked into her eyes and lost myself to her completely. It was a dangerous game we both ended up losing, in the end.

"Zander, this is serious," Hayes says, his voice bringing me back to the present.

The pungent fragrance of plumeria and coconuts is such a visceral memory, it feels like a punch to the face when my eyes refocus in my office. I also realize I've become uncomfortably hard, my cock straining in my pants under the desk. Fucking hell. From a single memory, Harlowe has me this twisted up. She will be the death of me, if not my brothers, at this point.

"I'm quite aware of the seriousness of the situation. I haven't spoken to her in years. Until," I pause, remembering her face and the small changes to her physique that only enhanced her allure when I saw her weeks ago on the side of the highway, and then the feel of her against me when

I stopped by her house that week. "Javi rear-ended her in traffic a couple of weeks ago. It was a total coincidence and the first time I've seen her since the Maldives trip, and she didn't say anything about a kid to me." I don't mention my late-night visit.

Payton drops his tablet into his lap and palms his face with an exasperated sigh. "Did you talk about anything else besides the fender-bender that day? Did you happen to think maybe it's no coincidence this story has leaked and they are making connections after so many years? She could have leaked it herself as a way to put pressure on you."

"Or the Atlanta Haute List is just another stupid gossip blog intent on coming up with the juiciest clickbait story, regardless of the facts," I retort, anger deepening my voice as my hands grip the desk until my knuckles whiten.

"Gossip or not, they got access to our flight manifests and were able to link you two from the right time period. That takes an insider here and some searching. I don't like what that implies about our employees and how easily our private information is getting out," Hayes says, his anger rising to meet mine.

He's always been incredibly private and comes down hard on anyone who steps out of line trand shares company or personal information. He had his own struggles with the Atlanta Haute List when he met his now-wife, Paige. They were hounded from the beginning, every public step they took ended up on the Haute List, all the on-and-off portions of their relationship splashed on the internet, and several employees were let go in the process. It doesn't surprise me in the least that his main concern is privacy and potential company leaks.

"Fuck!" I exclaim, my hands shooting out and stopping my brothers from continuing in this vein. "It doesn't matter how it got out. I don't know if the kid is mine, and Harlowe isn't telling me anything about him. She's the only one who can confirm who the father is, and she wants nothing to do with me."

"We can have a paternity test subpoenaed from her," Payton offers gently.

I shoot daggers his way and wish I could toss him out the window. "For fuck's sake, you don't know her like I do. Sending a team of lawyers after her is just going to raise her defenses and make her howl her rage to anyone who will listen. That's a lot of ears right now that she has a new cookbook out and is appearing on local and national news segments and morning shows, and has stories splashed across the internet." It's stupid to admit I have been digging into Harlowe since she crashed back into my life, but it's the truth and may help us out. "We don't need to demand a paternity test if she's not even asking for the connection. We would have heard from her by now if she was trying to get into my bank account. Leave her the fuck alone," I growl, surprised by the intensity of my rage as I stare my older brothers down. I don't want them harassing Harlowe. Or going anywhere near her.

Payton steeples his hands in front of his face, his blue eyes blazing with an intensity that can only mean he's scheming. "Or we can turn this around in our favor. The public loves a good romance. They love seeing a bad boy reform for the right woman. Both would do wonders at taking the heat off Olympus while we clean up the cyber attack mess and the Pegasus issue."

My throat constricts and my mouth goes dry. *No.*

"Are you seriously suggesting what I think you are, Pay?" Hayes asks, squeezing his temples between a thumb and forefinger. "There's no fucking way he would do it."

"Think of the headlines," Payton says, holding his hands out in front of him to highlight an invisible marquee. "*Fuckboy billionaire breaks with one-night-stand tradition to become a family man.* It would push public perception up faster than our stocks dipped in the first few weeks after the cyber attack. It would take the heat off the company at large, and you know we need that. It's taking forever for our stock prices to come back up after we sent the all-clear that our data was safe outside of the Pegasus project."

"This is ludicrous. You can't force me to claim a child that I have no proof is even mine and force a relationship with a woman I haven't spoken to in five years just for public perception." My heart is beating wildly against my ribs at the very prospect. That's far more than attachment. It's life-changing.

"You want to play at being CEO, but you balk at the prospect of putting your reputation as a sex-crazed fuck-boy on the backburner when it's what could save the company." Hayes scoffs and shakes his head. "All you would be doing is making a show of the attempt at reconnecting with Harlowe and the kid. We're not asking you to fuck her out of pity. We know you wouldn't do that since she has no value to you, being a conquest well in your past," he says, both challenging and poking fun at me.

"Olympus needs you to man the fuck up and take some goddamn responsibility for once in your personal life. You made the choice to fuck without a condom and this is the consequence, just coming at you a delayed five years later. Our company's reputation is still at rock-bottom and you figuring out your role as a parent would show your ability to take responsibility for your actions, and a softer side of the company leadership." Payton leans back in his chair, confident in his ability to push me into a corner there's no fighting my way out of.

I cast a glare from him to Hayes and point my finger his way, looking for any way out. "Why can't we leak the news about Hater popping out kids with his hot debutante wife? That would show a softer side of the leadership, and the media already loves them, so it would be easy to focus on that."

Hayes stiffens, but quickly relaxes, with a small smile softening his hard expression as he likely thinks of his wife who is about three months pregnant. "We're working on that, but we can't announce anything yet, so stop deflecting from what's asked of you now. If you have a child, you need to be more than a sperm donor. You're a fucking Olsen, act like it. Own your mistakes and stop being a coward."

Fuck. He's hitting below the belt, cutting off the legs of any other possibility I can latch onto. The worst part is he's right. I am being a coward. But there's a bigger obstacle in place than just my own hesitance to accept the mantle they want to saddle me with.

"Harlowe wants nothing to do with me," I grit out.

"Change her mind, idiot." Hayes's look is withering. "You're the hotshot CEO who can close any deal. Consider this the challenge of a lifetime. Make it work or prepare to watch the company you love so much be picked apart and crumble at your feet."

Sixteen

Harlowe

Five Years Ago

"Is this really our last day in paradise?" I ask, as we walk hand-in-hand along the beach back to the villa after our final incredible dinner.

It was bittersweet and extra special to have Chef and the staff at the little restaurant that has fed us so well these past weeks all come out to wish us well. They have been so kind and taken great care of us and even let me into their kitchen whenever I felt like whipping something up to impress Zander. One playful *wok off* with the Michelin-starred chef was all it took to gain access to his sacred space as well as earn his blessing to win my man through his stomach as well as his cock. It didn't hurt that he liked my lobster ceviche, as well. We've exchanged contact details, and I hope to keep in touch with them.

"It doesn't feel like it's been two weeks, right? It feels like it's been two days and two years at the same time. I don't know how time can work like that sometimes," Zander says, sounding relaxed. He raises our clasped hands over my head and pulls me into his side without letting my hand go, so he has his arm around me now as well.

"I wish we could stay here like this forever," I say, feeling wistful and nostalgic, knowing that things will inevitably change when we get back home. They have to, just for the sake of normalcy and leaving this delicious slice of paradise and vacation mode for the real world.

God, it will be torture to not sleep in the same bed as Zander. To not wake up next to him. To not have his hands on me or see his gorgeous gray eyes drinking me in every time I turn around. At the very least, we'll have to figure out how we'll work long-distance with us living on opposite coasts, and my modeling work taking me all over the world without a real set schedule while he works Monday through Friday seven to seven or something hideous like that.

Should I try to find a job that is more stable and less nomadic? Would he be willing to move, or to travel with me? Should I move back to Atlanta? These are just the surface level questions that pertain to our physical geography, though. What about the deeper questions like, what are we? Are we an official couple? It sure feels like that, saying we belong to each other, that I am his and he is mine, and using words like forever.

It's a far cry from the no attachments condition and nothing more after the trip that was promised when he invited me to come with him two weeks ago. Those bridges were burned, and those lines crossed too thoroughly to imagine ourselves able to go back to that reality now. I have given in completely. Stopped playing my role. Let him see me fully and unconditionally, and embraced everything he has given me in return.

We spend our last night in paradise slowly making love, the moonlight spilling in through the open windows gilding our bodies in pale light as we whisper secrets and make promises that neither of us is sure we can keep. The sound of the ocean joins our soft moans and the whimpers Zander wrings from me, creating a soundtrack that will forever haunt my memories and remain the most evocative of symphonies. We play with each other, but not in the roles we took when we arrived. Our fingers lace, and our lips twist, chasing one another across the huge bed as I giggle and he growls. We're relaxed and silly and serious all at once.

He expertly navigates my body, knowing every spot, knowing everything I could want, and delivering before I can think to ask for it. He turns me, positions me, holds me, and applies the right amount of pressure to all the right places, so it's one orgasm after another bowing my back and keeping me clutching at him. My pleasure continues until I'm sweating, limp, and tear-streaked in his arms, begging him for just one more, because I don't want him to stop, even if I don't think I can physically bear it. I don't know what changes tomorrow holds, and I want all the pleasure he can give me, just in case I have to go without for an extended period of time.

"You're insatiable," he murmurs into my neck as his hips still against mine. "You're shaking. I'm going to break you if I make you come again."

"Please, Zander," I whisper, voice hoarse from crying out so many times. "I just want you so damn much."

He places soft kisses across my face, stilling when his lips are hovering directly over mine. "How can I say no to that when I want you just as badly? One more. Then you're going to sleep. We have to be up early."

He stops talking and starts kissing me again. He adjusts our bodies, raising my hips just so, dipping his so he hits me just right on his next stroke, and his skilled fingers begin to lazily circle my overstimulated clit with the softest of caresses, and immediately the orgasm begins to build.

Zander's kiss grows harder as he feels my body tensing, trembling, my gasps caught by his mouth. I don't know how his movements can feel so unrushed, lazy even, yet stoke such a fire in me, each slow thrust, in and out, hitting me in every perfect spot to light me up and set me off. Or the way he kisses me with an unhurried grace, the way his tongue can sweep against mine and take exactly what he wants and leave me begging for more.

I didn't think it was possible for someone to know my body this well, to love it this well, this thoroughly, to give it everything it needs, and so much more. Zander is showing me care, affection, and love, even if he can't say the word. I don't expect him to. I won't make him. This is more than enough for me. More than I ever expected from him. I am satisfied.

I gather the sheets in my fingers, twisting and pulling as that delicious tug starts low in my belly, my muscles growing taught and my lungs freezing as I hold my breath before the orgasm breaks and I lose my fucking mind once again for this man.

This man who once told me no attachments and I had agreed. This man who I once thought was solely a fuckboy with no capacity for caring, but I now know is capable of so much affection and care, it is absolutely staggering. This man who holds me like I'm precious. Who calls me his. Who puts finger-sized bruises on my hips and thighs from the times I need him to fuck me hard, but holds me gently in the comedown and worships me like he wants to keep me forever.

I feel the sheets tear under my fingers, holes ripping straight through the thousand thread count like it's tissue paper. My voice breaks on the choked sob that is ripped from me as the release barrels through me.

Still, Zander thrusts into my raw, well-used pussy, but his movements are growing erratic, no longer controlled and slow, his hands now gripping my hips as he swells and finds his own release while my muscles clench and pull at him. He growls a feral sound full of manly satisfaction, head thrown back and hips locked tight against mine, the sight one of stark male beauty, the moonlight shining off his sweat-slicked skin, his muscled body tight, trembling, and finally, he collapses over me, panting with effort. I'm more in love with him in this moment than I thought possible.

I wrap my arms and legs around him, pulling him against my own sweaty body and hold him as he comes down from the high. I pepper soft kisses against his face and run my hands soothingly along his back as it rises and falls under my touch, the beat of his heart against my own chest gradually slowing.

"Thank you," I whisper, feeling my raw throat protest, and know my pussy isn't the only thing that is feeling the effects of two weeks of sex with Zander Olsen. The man has fully lived up to the rumors. He is truly a legend, an absolute god. Any title that has been bestowed on him is well-deserved, but the one most-fitting is *mine*. I'm sure we'll shock everyone when it becomes known that he's off the market and will be leaving his one-and-done ways behind.

"You're so perfect," he says, nuzzling into my neck and huffing a sigh of contentment.

"Shower, then sleep?" I ask, tracing my fingertips through the sweat on his back.

"Yeah, we more than earned it."

He pulls out of me and I miss the feeling of him filling me up immediately. I follow him out of bed to the bathroom and watch as he disposes of the condom. He's been so diligent, so safe.

I feel a momentary twinge of panic, thinking of my empty birth control packet in my toiletries bag on the bathroom vanity. I thought I'd grabbed a full pack, but instead grabbed the used one and ran out a few days ago. I'll switch back as soon as I get home and it will be fine. Missing a few pills won't be that big of a deal. We only had that one time in the shower when he fucked me bare, when I realized I was completely in love with him, anyway. Otherwise, he's had a condom at the ready and we've been protected. I'm clean, and if he's that good about protection, I'm pretty sure he is. It won't hurt to get checked at home, though, just to be sure.

Zander is back in his business casual on the private jet, a silver-gray shirt that does wild things to his eyes, and black slacks this time. He puts me in a spot next to him when we board, holding my hand and making sure I'm comfortable. He strokes my arm and we chat, but I can tell we both feel the strain of leaving the easy island vacation behind and what that will mean for us. There is a tension underlying everything, and it's hard to ignore. I find myself slipping back into the playful role for him just to relieve some of it, and he seems to appreciate the gesture, but doesn't fully commit to his side of role-playing that requires him to banter back, to say something wholly inappropriate or suggestive.

About ten hours into the twenty-hour flight, something changes. He moves to a table toward the back of the jet where he pulls out his laptop and cell and starts working, growing quiet, distant, or barking orders on calls that seem to take hours, and I feel like I would be intruding on his workday if I sit near him. I pull out a romance novel to read, turn on my own phone, and catch up on emails, texts, social media, anything to keep me distracted. He stays at it, the crease on his brow growing deeper, and I feel him slipping away from me.

But I'm probably just being paranoid. Maybe this is work mode Zander, and I should get used to him being so focused. He is the CEO of a multi-billion-dollar empire. That must come with a heavy workload and a lot of responsibility. There's no way the company he runs got where it is without a lot of sacrifices and countless hours of work on his part. He has a business to run and I can be okay with that. I settle back into my seat with that realization, feeling a little more at peace.

The flight crew sets out dinner for us in the small dining area and retreats to their galley space without Zander looking up from his laptop. I look at my phone, which I've been mindlessly scrolling through out of boredom. Zander has been working for close to eight hours. I smile and get up, sauntering over to his work area, sliding into the seat next to him, and placing a hand on his chest as I smile up at him.

"It's been a full workday. Care to join me for dinner? You haven't taken a break at all and you have to be starving. You barely ate breakfast and skipped lunch completely."

"It's fine. I can eat while I work. Have them bring me dinner over here," he says dismissively, barely looking at me.

I school my features and try not to let the cool tone hurt me. "They've already laid everything out in the dining area. Just take a break. You only need a few minutes to eat," I say with a smile and more patience than I normally would give to someone who spoke to me with such shortness.

"I have too much to catch up on. This is important. I don't have time to waste, Harlowe."

I pull back at his harsh tone, his use of my full name that smacks of strangeness after hearing him call me his preferred nicknames, and the insinuation that *I* am not worth his time now.

"It's just dinner, Zander. I'm not asking you to put your laptop away and pay attention to me for the remainder of our flight or anything. The least you could do is have dinner with me for ten minutes if this is how you want to spend the next few hours." My own voice is hot to his cold, my temper rising at the feeling of being brushed off and ignored so completely for hours on end after having had his undivided attention for two weeks straight.

"It's just ten minutes to you, but I'm working on a deal that could make my company millions, so I'm sorry if my priorities offend your sensibilities. I'll take my dinner over here. I don't care what you do. Don't make more of this than it is. It'll be easier when we get back and go our separate ways."

I drop my hand from his arm and pull away like he's slapped me. I feel my mouth working to form words, to make sounds, but nothing comes out, and I'm fighting like hell to keep the sharp prick of tears behind my eyes from manifesting into true waterworks.

"I see," I finally manage. I swallow hard against the tears and force my emotions down, wanting to be sure I have read this correctly before I react. "Your work is important, I get that. I'll communicate your wishes to the crew. But Zander," I start, having to clench my trembling hands together to get my anger, fear, and sadness under control enough to finish. "We're going to see each other again. When you say we go our separate ways, you mean until we figure out what to do next, right?"

I look up at him as his fingers halt over his keyboard, feeling hope surge in my chest, tentative and new, but built on the back of what we discovered over our two weeks together. This new love, because that is absolutely what it is. This belonging. This owning. This mine and yours and together and forever. That promise of forever is what I hold on to tightest of all right now, when it sounds like he is dismissing me from his life instead of welcoming me into it like I thought he would.

"There is no next for us." Cold. Final. Heart-wrenching and so devastating, I feel like the jet just took a nose-dive, and I lost my stomach somewhere in the freefall.

"What do you mean?" I ask, voice shaking. "I don't understand." How did I read this so wrong? I know he's pulled back today, but not to this level. We made promises. We made *forever* promises.

He sighs in impatience and pushes the laptop away from him so he can grip the table until his knuckles whiten. His eyes close and a muscle in his jaw flexes once, twice, then stills. When his eyes open again, there is a cold light like dawn on a battlefield that blazes at me and I draw back from that intensity, so unlike the warmth and desire I have come to expect. This light is frozen and looks ready to punish and push me away, and I don't like what it could precede.

"I told you there would be nothing more after the trip when I invited you to come with me. You agreed to no attachments. It was two weeks of no cares in the world, and I more than delivered on my end of the bargain. Now you have to honor it. When we land, we go our separate ways. There won't be any repeats. There is nothing after. There is no us once we step off this jet."

Cold clarity cracks over my head and spreads like an icy flood down my spine, sending tingles through my veins and rushing along my skin. He is trying to go back to that? He thinks he can reach back to what he initially said and that will be it. I'll have to admit he's right, I did agree. I knew the score when I joined him and I'll have to live with it when I leave. But he's dead wrong, because we burned those bridges together, cans of gasoline and torches in hand, and we can't go back that way no matter how much he thinks he can. Anger simmers in my veins and it feels a hell of a lot better than the hurt, the betrayal and fucking heartbreak that wants to drown me in utter devastation, so I cling to it.

"You psycho motherfucker," I seethe. "What was this? Was it all a lie? You made me yours, Zander." My voice cracks on the admission.

I close my eyes to avoid him seeing just how painful this is for me, how much it hurts that he could be pulling back now, that he could be saying he doesn't want me after all. I'm not important. I'm nothing more than the pretty face he chose to fuck for two weeks. Turns out that's all I'm good for, after all, being pretty. He's extinguishing those lights, taking back the fire and flame he gave me to light the black places in my soul, and returning me to darkness. I open my eyes and feel tears slip down my cheeks.

"You didn't just fuck me. You claimed a piece of my soul and *you gave yourself to me*." I place my hand on my chest and can nearly feel the gaping wound where my heart should be, where the piece of him should be that he has stolen back. "That's not casual. That's not anything like no attachments. You tied strings to us that wrapped us together in promises of forever. You made love to me and it was slow and sweet. You came inside of me and said you were ruined, that you wanted this, you wanted me, forever. You gave into this and I don't care what you are saying now, I know you felt it, too. You can't deny this, Zander. I won't let you. You are mine. You want forever with me."

My words are angry, heartfelt, full of emotion and everything he has made me feel since I realized I was falling for him and he was right there with me. Tears are streaming down my cheeks now and I don't stop them. If he wants to see what his rules and casual, no attachments will do to me, I'll let him.

Zander's storm cloud eyes brighten with what looks like pain and misery, briefly showing me the swirling eddies of ash and smoke of those very rules he had burned to the ground for me before he slams down a shutter of cold indifference over them and a flat gray wasteland is all that stares back at me. He fully turns toward me, his laptop and work forgotten, at least momentarily, and I secretly hope I have managed to pull him back to me, that he will admit he was wrong and he does want forever after all, that we can make this work. My hope is dashed as soon as he begins to speak and his flat eyes match his flat, hard tone.

"Listen to me carefully, Lowe, because I will only say this once. You got a very different version of me on this trip. A version that doesn't exist in real life. That man can't leave this jet, so forget about him. Forget anything he told you and don't expect me to be him. I'm not capable of being what you're looking for now, outside of that very specific instance in that very specific place. I can't be what you need or want and you deserve better, so forget about me. And know I'll do my fucking best to forget about you. Forever is a lie."

A quiet sob wrenches free from the tight hold I'm using to keep myself together. But my pride keeps me from utterly losing my shit in front of him. So, I use whatever grace I can muster, rise from the seat beside him, and head to the bathroom. In privacy, I give into the silent, gut-wrenching sobs that wrack my whole body, sending tears trailing down my cheeks, and snot coating my face. It takes me a long time before I'm able to pull myself together, and longer to get my puffy eyes and red face under control. When I leave the bathroom, I find a seat with my back to Zander, put earbuds in, and try my fucking best to forget that he is behind me, forgetting all about me before I'm even gone.

When we land in LA, I'm back in a role. This one the beautiful, aloof model who enjoyed a fabulous tropical vacation with a billionaire and expects nothing from him now that it's done. It may be harder to play than I would have imagined going into the trip, but I somehow manage. I follow Zander off the jet, and he hands me into the waiting car without so much as a kiss on my cheek before he heads back onto the jet so he can return to Atlanta. He doesn't even turn to look at me once.

Just like that, the trip is over, and Zander Olsen has left my life forever.

Seventeen

Harlowe

"Harlowe! Who is your baby daddy?"

"Is Zander Olsen Hendricks's father?"

"Why hasn't Zander ever been seen with your son?"

"Harlowe, are you that greedy you wouldn't even share custody?"

"Why wouldn't you want a billionaire in your life?"

"What does Knox think? Does he want to fill the shoes of an Olsen brother?"

"Who is the father?"

The questions have been non-stop and come from every direction. I've been asked in comments sections on my latest cooking videos, on my social media posts, in my direct message inboxes, from strangers on the street and paparazzi alike as I dropped Hendricks off at school, shielding him with my jacket and body to avoid any photos being taken. I'm going to have to arrange for someone else to do school drop-off and pick-up for my son if this continues so there aren't photos of my child plastered all over the internet. Everyone is suddenly very interested to know about my sex life from five years ago and why I'm a single mother, and won't give me even a moment of privacy to gather my thoughts or figure out my next move.

The front door opening startles me from scouring the comments of my latest YouTube video, my defenses high after all the unwanted attention.

"If you're walking into my house without an invitation, you're about to get stabbed," I call out, clutching a large kitchen knife in my hand and tentatively peeking around the wall to the entryway.

"I tried calling you, but your phone must be broken. No other reason not to answer your mom's calls, yes, Lolo?" returns a familiar voice with a slight lilting accent that thirty years in the United States hasn't managed to remove.

I lower the knife as a flood of relief courses through me and feel the first genuine smile in a week split my face. "Well, look what the cat dragged in!"

I quickly set the knife down before I cross the kitchen to greet my mom. I lean down to embrace her shorter frame and inhale her familiar perfume of exotic spices.

"What are you doing here? I thought you were in Singapore visiting Auntie June, Auntie Nancy, and the cousins." I take the bag from her hand and lead her into the living room to sit down.

"I know you need me and still you didn't call. Family first, Lolo. When have we ever weathered a storm on our own when there is absolutely no need to? You're lucky the aunties and cousins didn't come with me for an intervention." She settles herself on the couch and opens her arms to me. I gratefully nestle into her side. There's something so comforting about having your mom show up when you need her most. I could cry in relief now that she's here, even if there is nothing she can do to stop the flood of press and accusations.

"When the storm involves the media, a billionaire, and revolves around who I've had sex with, I figured I would leave you out of the mix."

She pats my hair and then pushes my head abruptly off her shoulder.

"Hey," I say, mock indignation flashing as I sit up.

"You talk cock," she says, slipping in a *Singlish* phrase for nonsense that pulls from the phrases of her past life in Singapore she must have picked up again from her recent visit. "We have to stand by one another, even if it means I have to know about who you take to bed. It's not that unusual. You think I don't know you have sex? How'd you get my grandbaby if not from sleeping with a man?"

"Mom, I will never feel comfortable talking about sex with you. Not after your scared straight campaign to keep me out of trouble in high school."

I shudder, thinking of the blown-up photos of the reproductive tract, graphic illustrations of women in labor, and even regret-filled articles supposedly written by teen mothers she stuck to the refrigerator weekly from the time I turned thirteen. I knew exactly how babies were made and had intimate knowledge of anatomy and the horrors of childbirth. I wanted nothing to do with boys until I graduated and moved to Los Angeles to pursue modeling. At least I knew what to expect once I did have sex.

"You know I just wanted to protect you. Your father would have done worse things to make sure you knew the risks. And he would have been the most excited when you came back here growing that darling little boy in your belly," Mom says, her voice resolute and reassuring.

My father died when I was twelve. He was a six-foot-five-inch Nordic giant, the kind of man wrought from Vikings. He was from Denmark originally, an architect by trade—a real white-collar job for someone so insistent on working with his hands and laboring every chance he got. He could build anything you imagined from metal, fabricating everything from custom-built bird cages to impressive iron sculptures that live on in palaces and hotels across the world even now.

He met my mother at a hotel in Singapore where she worked as the head desk clerk. She came from humble Malaysian roots, growing up rather poor in the affluent metropolis of Singapore, yet from the way she tells it, the strapping Dane who walked into the lobby looking for his meeting with the company head in order to build a new decorative iron sculpture immediately treated her like royalty. They were married six months later, and he moved her to Georgia, where the architectural firm he worked for was based. She's been in Atlanta ever since, even after he was hurt on a job site and succumbed to his injuries.

"You didn't seem to care who Hendricks's father was back then. You never even asked," I muse. Mom had opened her home, the one I now occupy, to me and my swelling belly, no questions asked. She seemed to know I needed this baby to be mine alone, and she never so much as questioned how her twenty-four-year-old daughter found herself with child and retired from an exploding modeling career.

"There are some things that don't need answers, only intentions. You were intent on bringing a life into this world and providing for it the best you knew how. I was intent on making sure you were supported. Simple as that."

I pull back and give her a wry smile. "Enough with your Earth mama good vibes. Where's the Singaporean nosy nana in you? Did you show up today knowing I'll have to start making statements and naming names?" Maybe Alicia put her up to this. She was particularly interested and got me to admit that Zander is, in fact, Hendricks's father in a call we had about this just yesterday.

Mom slides a side-eyed glance my way and tries to hide her mischievous smile. "You have to do what is best for you and Hendricks. But you also have a reckoning coming your way. Whatever you decide to do will have consequences, whether you keep the father's identity a secret, or tell the world. I am here to be on your side." She looks at me fully and slides a gentle finger along my cheekbone. "And give you a break. Have you been sleeping at all? If these under-eye bags get any bigger, they'll take up more space than what's available in an overhead bin of an airplane."

I let out a bark of laughter and bat her hand away. "You're horrible, but I love you."

"I brought back some Korean beauty eye patches from this trip. You could use them."

"I'm not above your bribery with good beauty products." I kiss her cheek and hop up from the couch. "I'm testing out some recipes for pad see ew and green papaya salad. Come help me chop veggies and make yourself useful if you plan on staying. The Mama suite is always made up for you, but you have to earn your keep."

"Take my bags in there and I'll make sure you're not making traditional food too Western. You have to make your recipes modern for your cookbooks, but I need tradition and spice, Lolo." She rises primly from the couch and follows me out of the living room. "Those Bulgogi tacos you posted were too spicy for your own good, but not the right kind of spice. Dirty girl, I looked up that bukkake reference and had to wash my phone after."

I cackle like a hyena and take her bag into the room that was once my childhood bedroom. It was strange to take over the primary bedroom when she let me buy the house from her so I could raise Hendricks right where I grew up. She moved into a smaller townhouse nearby and spends much of her time traveling. She is financially secure thanks to my father's life insurance and frugal ways that allowed him to sock away much of his earnings that kept her in the manner she had grown accustomed to, being a stay-at-home mom and housewife. That translates into travel funds now.

I sit for a moment on the plush bed and stare around at the neutral decor with large green plants giving color to the modern space. My whole house has a lush green vibe, much influenced by Mom's life living in Singapore. She has a style of her own, and I picked up on that from a young age.

Growing up with immigrant parents and of mixed race in the South was...interesting. I was teased for my uptilted eyes and the strange lunches Mom packed for me when I was young, and then for my towering height in middle school when I shot up before all the boys hit puberty.

I hated everything that made me different. My height, my coloring, my eyes, my parents who had over a foot of height difference between them, my mom, who was often thought to be a mail-order bride, my heritage, even my name which was bastardized for sport by cruel kids, and turned into Harlot Score-nson to humiliate me. Being different made me a target, and I carried so much shame for just being me. I was never comfortable in my own skin and couldn't embrace the things that made me unique.

Modeling didn't change that, so much as highlighted the differences as selling points. I was ethnic enough to fit many campaigns, to be the diversity inclusion to an all-white roster, and to lend an exotic edge to an otherwise homogeneous look. It also worked against me when I couldn't fit a pigeon-holed casting call. I also couldn't put a toe out of line for fear of being too brazen, too scandalous, and not bookable. Heaven forbid a brand would think I was too slutty, too wild, or too loud for their target audience. I made myself meek, quiet, just the right kind of model, and played the role they wanted as often as I could, and that meant I could never just be *me*.

I sigh deeply and pull myself up from the bed. I pick up a framed photo of Hendricks as a baby and cradle it in my hand. No use thinking about the past, even when it has lasting repercussions like little shock waves that startle you out of complacency to be reminded of the severity of the situation. Like having a child fathered by a person of interest.

What people are focusing on and the media has so wrong, as usual, is the motive behind keeping Hendricks to myself. Zander cut off all contact with me. How was I supposed to tell him he had a son when he didn't even want to hear from me? I did my best to talk to him and let him know. All I managed to do was get my number blocked by Zander and myself banned from Olympus International Tower. That's not at all how I thought it would end, after the way we met.

I set the picture frame gently back on the nightstand and leave the room, hoping I can leave the memories that cling to me, the frustration that prickles even now, years after I have accepted my fate and moved forward, but maybe not completely on.

But now I have to turn around and trudge upstream into the past and perhaps make Zander care about something that happened years ago. Make him care about a kid he never wanted that connects us together when he has made it quite clear there is no future for us.

I return to the kitchen, where Mom has dutifully chopped the veggies for me and set up my bowls of spices. She helps me test the recipes and makes adjustments with me, insisting on a higher spice level while I want to caramelize the noodles more.

I get her to snap a cute photo of me slurping up the pad see ew noodles, midriff bared in a crop top, that I post to Instagram with a caption about what else I can slurp and is tasty. My posts are getting thirstier by the day and my audience is eating it up. Mom says my phone is going to burst into flames if I keep going this route, but my engagement is through the roof and Alicia is thrilled with the insights, so I'm not stopping anytime soon.

Eighteen

Harlowe

Five Years Ago

"I'm late," I say, walking into Paloma's room of our shared apartment, my hands shaking.

"For what? I didn't think you had a shoot planned for another few days. Did you book something last minute and not tell me? Do you need me to drive you? LA traffic is bad, so hopefully they'll be cool waiting," Paloma says, immediately grabbing her phone and pulling up her GPS app, ready to input an address for directions. Ever the problem solver. Ever my best friend, ready to save my ass without even knowing my latest dilemma. I grab her arm, stopping her from grabbing her purse.

"No. Paloma, I'm *late*. My period."

"What do you mean? You're on the pill, right? Maybe you messed up the timing and it'll show up later today or something."

"It's not a few hours late. I was supposed to start two weeks ago. I'm *late* late."

"How..." she asks, guiding me over to her bed and sitting me down. "How are you late?"

I run a hand through my hair, greasy because I haven't washed it in days from pure apathy. I haven't felt like doing much of anything but cry and mope since I got home from the Maldives. I haven't *felt* much at all, actually. I don't know if I prefer that to the soul-crushing pain of realizing Zander lied to me and ripped out my heart in the aftermath of his revelation that he could be a completely different person from the man I fell in love with and suddenly want nothing to do with me once my usefulness was expended. A fresh wave of grief and anger rises up in my gut, and I shut my eyes against the tears it brings with it. I have a new problem to deal with, and I don't think I can handle both at the same time.

"I missed a few pills on my trip, like four or five, total, and I got right back on a new pack when I got home. But, well, there was one time we didn't use a condom, and I guess one time is all it takes, really, and now I'm late. Oh my God, Paloma, what if I'm—" Paloma puts up a hand and stops me from continuing.

"*Ay, Dios*. Stop, don't say it out loud or put anything into the universe you don't want to be true. It's fine. Let's just be calm and do what we have to in order to be sure. I'll go get you some tests to be completely sure and we'll figure this out together, okay? It could just be birth control weirdness. Maybe starting a new pack later than you should have threw off your cycle. That kind of thing happens all the time. It could totally be what's going on right now. It's going to be fine."

"Okay, yeah, that could be it," I agree, grasping at anything that sounds even remotely plausible.

Paloma pulls me into a tight hug before she releases me and smiles in what she must assume is a reassuring manner, though it just looks like she's planning to commit murder, and the someone most likely to be her victim is named Zander Olsen. I told her everything as soon as I got home. If I was angry about everything, Paloma was furious. She wanted to fly to Atlanta right then, march into the Olympus International Tower, and throw Zander out of the highest window she could find. She's felt all the emotions right along with me. I know she's been worried about me as I mope around the apartment, my tan fading, unable to sleep because I got used to being in Zander's arms, and now I feel too lonely to fall into a sleep deep enough to be restful.

"I'll go to the store just down the street. It won't even take ten minutes, and then we can sort this out. I'll grab mango sorbet while I'm there, and we can laugh and celebrate when we realize it was all a mix-up after. Sit tight, I'll be right back." She kisses my head and prepares to leave the apartment on her mission. "Maybe shower and wash your hair while I'm gone. You stink."

"Thanks a lot." I roll my eyes, but know she's right. I won't listen either way.

I'm still grateful for her optimism and level-headedness when I'm so utterly losing my mind right now. Thinking I could be left with one more reminder that Zander wants nothing to do with me would be devastating. I won't even be able to tell him if I am pregnant. He blocked me on social media, and I'm pretty sure he blocked my number because it doesn't even ring and goes to voicemail every time I call him, and he hasn't returned a single text. There's not a single way I can get a hold of him short of seeing him in person, and I highly doubt that would happen without great pains being taken to arrange it, given how unlikely we are to cross paths. I know Zander orchestrated the few times we did run into each other prior to our trip, so that was purely because he wanted it to happen.

As promised, Paloma returns about ten minutes later, a bag swinging off her arm full of pregnancy tests and a pint of mango sorbet that she chucks in the freezer for later before she grips my arm and steers me into her bathroom.

"I read the directions while I was waiting in line. All you have to do is pee on the stick and wait. The kind I got tells you pregnant or not in the little window, so you don't have to decipher any codes or lines."

I open the plastic shopping bag and see she brought home a bunch of tests. I quickly count. "Six tests?"

"I wanted to make sure we had extras in case you wanted to get verification. You don't have to use all of them, obviously, but you know, just in case."

My hands shake as I take out one of the tests, open the innocuous box, and pull out the test that doesn't look like it could ruin my life. I look at Paloma and she nods.

"I'll wait outside. Let me know when you're finished peeing and we can wait for the results together."

She steps out of the bathroom and I'm left alone with the plastic stick that could damn me to hell or tell me I'm being a dumb fucking baby who made a mess of her birth control in addition to falling for an asshole. I pee on the stick and set it on the vanity, resolutely not looking at it as I wash my hands and open the door for Paloma. We sit on the edge of the bathtub, shoulders touching as the silence grows around us.

"I set a timer when I heard the toilet flush," she tells me, showing me her phone that is counting down the minutes.

"Paloma, what... what if it is," I begin, but she shakes her head, stopping me. Her silky sable hair tumbles over our touching shoulders, blending with my lank sunkissed brown waves that would have been so pretty after the time I spent in the sun if I washed it. She was right again. I should have showered.

"We're not putting anything into the universe until we know for sure. No what-ifs. We will speak in absolutes only when we know." Her timer beeps and we look at each other for a moment before she turns it off.

I stand from the bathtub and take the two steps to the sink where in bold letters the clear window of the plastic test reads PREGNANT. I stumble back and Paloma catches me, seeing the results and shushing the wailing noise I realize is coming from me.

"We can take another, just to be sure. These things can be faulty. That's why I bought a bunch. Here, sit down." She directs me back to the edge of the bathtub as hysteria rises in me and I start to shake violently.

"I can't be pregnant. I can't! Paloma, I just started booking big jobs. Givenchy made me the face of their perfume. I've only shot two campaigns with them. They won't want a pregnant model. I can't be on Sports Illustrated pregnant. I was barely fit enough when they asked me to be on the cover this time around. This will ruin my career before it really gets started, and I'm only twenty-four. I'm too young to have a baby." Tears streak down my cheeks, and I'm back to feeling again, but it's panic and fear instead of heartbreak and sadness. I sob openly, holding my knees and barely able to breathe.

Paloma is kneeling in front of me, hands on my shoulders, staring into my face. "This isn't the end of everything, Lolo, even if you are pregnant. We can be certain first, so let's take more tests."

So I do, and all six of the tests scream PREGNANT at us, and Paloma can no longer deny the truth. I'm definitely pregnant.

"My career is over," I moan, face down on my bed, where we've moved from the bathroom and the incriminating pregnancy tests screaming my failure to take a little bitty pill properly at me. Paloma lies next to me, rubbing my back. I'm no longer sobbing, but I can't stop the tears from leaking into the pillows.

"You have choices," she says, hesitantly. "It's really early. You could take a pill and erase everything. Zander would be gone from your life and you wouldn't have to think about that lying asshole ever again. You wouldn't have to sacrifice your career or give up what you have worked so hard for. You could keep your contracts and continue shooting and traveling and go on as if nothing even happened."

I roll over onto my back and stare at the ceiling while the tears slide down into my hair now. The picture she paints is the easy one. It's the logical one and would give me the most freedom. It provides the most security and allows me to keep my life exactly as it is with everything I have worked to achieve. It's what I know I should do.

But I would lose something that was made during a tiny moment in time, a blip in the vastness of the universe, where two people let down their walls and fell in love in the middle of the ocean. It would erase the proof that Zander and I had existed in the same space and time and he had given himself to me, and I had let myself belong to him, even if it was fleeting. It would remove the possibility that he had seen the real me and wanted that woman, flaws and all. I would lose the one small thread still connecting me to Zander forever, the only attachment he couldn't possibly deny.

With that thought, my future solidifies in front of me. I will give up everything to protect the life we created against all odds. I will sacrifice my career, turn my back on what

I have worked for, and raise the little piece of him that Zander left with me when he couldn't be man enough to give me the forever he promised. This will be my forever, and it will be enough. I will be enough.

I turn to look at Paloma, seeing her concern, and feel a tender love and appreciation well up in me. "I'm keeping the baby. Looks like I brought you home a beautiful souvenir after all."

Three weeks later, I'm in Atlanta doing what I imagined when I wondered how I would even tell Zander if it came down to it. I look up at the sleek metal and glass skyscraper of Olympus International Tower and take a deep breath as I push into the polished lobby.

I tried calling, but the damn receptionists wouldn't put me through, saying the CEO wouldn't take calls from anyone who wasn't on his approved list. That sounded like bullshit, but here I am, feeling desperate and needing to tell Zander that not only did I come home thinking he was a lying asshole, but, oh yeah, surprise, we're pregnant and I'm having your baby!

I don't expect anything from him, I just want him to know. It's the decent thing to do. To give him the choice to be a part of his child's life or, like with me, forget that it exists entirely. I place a protective hand over my flat belly that won't show the evidence of this life for a while yet and send up a plea to anything listening that Zander isn't that cruel, but even I can't put it past him, now.

I walk up to the impressively large matte black counter in the lobby and smile. I'm in Prada business wear and look like I belong in this building, another role I can pull off expertly, so the receptionist smiles back politely, ready to be of service.

"Hello, Layla," I say, reading her nametag. "I'm hoping you can help me. I'm an old friend and business associate of Zander Olsen's in town for the day, but I just got a new phone and no longer have his number to reach his direct line so we can connect. Would you please be a dear and let him know I'm here?" Disarming, slightly embarrassed to be asking for help, bringing her in as the one person who can be the savior. Piece of cake.

Layla's smile drops and her cheeks grow red. "I'm sorry, I'm only allowed to contact the administrative staff for the C-suite. I can't just call any of the Olsens outright."

I wave a hand like it's nothing, when I want to grab her phone myself and start mashing buttons. "That would be fine. Would you mind reaching out to Zander's admin? I would love to catch him before he leaves for the day, if possible."

She nods, seeming relieved by my understanding attitude.

I tamp down my impatience and frustration. I just want to get this over with. I don't expect Zander to change his mind when he finds out, but, well, he *might*. I know there is a decent man in there somewhere, no matter what a dick he became when we boarded that jet and returned home.

I look over at the bank of elevators and notice that the people getting on them are using passes to make them rise. Fuck. Even if I managed to get into an elevator, I wouldn't be able to go anywhere without one of those, so I can't just bluster my way onto one and go to the highest floor. I need a way in, and it's at Zander's, or his admin's, blessing.

Layla sets down her phone and looks over at me with a frown. "I'm sorry, Mr. Olsen–Zander–" she clarifies, since three Olsen brothers run this company, "isn't expecting any visitors, and is very busy and can't make any room in his schedule to see an old friend."

"It really is important that I speak to him, as this is the only day I'm in town. Can you please try again and let his admin know to tell him that it's Harlowe Sorenson to see him?" I don't know if that will help or hurt my cause, but it's all I can try at this point.

"I'll try," Layla says, sounding a little annoyed with me now that I'm becoming more insistent and making her attempt the call again. I'm sure the admin she's speaking to is a real ball-buster, used to talking down to anyone below the top floor of the building, and a lowly receptionist trying to get an unexpected visitor clearance to see the CEO is going to get a brutal dismissal.

I step away from the desk to give the girl a chance to say whatever she needs to as I feign disinterest. When she looks my way again, I smile and make my way toward the desk.

"Any luck?" I ask.

"She said to have a seat and she would see what she could do."

"Thank you for your help," I say, feeling trepidation, since it's not a pass to the top floor or Zander striding down here when he heard my name and taking me in his arms and telling me he was so fucking wrong to push me away. I sit in the lobby and count the minutes as I wait. I watch as employees begin to leave around five, and the building starts to empty out. Layla the receptionist shuts down her desk at five-thirty and I'm still waiting. I grab her arm before she can slink out of the lobby completely.

"Hey, what's the deal?" I ask, blocking her exit.

"I don't know, his admin never called back. I'm off the clock now, so it's not my problem anymore."

I'm furious as she darts around me and leaves. I turn back to the bank of elevators and march over to them, beginning to push the button and hoping a door will miraculously open and I can get somewhere on one. An elevator door opens then, and a huge man steps out and I take a step back out of habit.

I know at a glance that this has to be one of Zander's brothers. They have the same dark hair, similar jawlines and builds, though his is definitely the gym-made kind, and his eyes are a piercing dark green. He doesn't look friendly as he eyes me up and down.

"Are you Harlowe Sorenson?" His voice is a deep baritone that registers as vaguely familiar because it sounds a bit like Zander's, and there is a pang of longing that hits me from that little bit of home in the tone. I nod in acknowledgment. It's quickly shut down when he indicates I step into the elevator with him.

"I'm Hayes Olsen. If you would follow me, please."

Every instinct in me is screaming not to go anywhere with him. He feels like certain death, and I don't know why. He's handsome enough, he's a successful businessman and Zander's brother, but there is something unsettling about him, like he handles the unsavory aspects of the business, or he's the one they turn to when they need to get their hands dirty, and he enjoys it a little too much. I swallow as I realize I could be one of those unsavory aspects of business now that I'm on the wrong side of Zander's one-and-done conquests. I've heard from model friends about being thrown out of his penthouse by one of the brothers with an NDA in hand.

Despite every part of me that thinks this could be a bad idea, it could also be my only way to see Zander now. I step into the elevator and Hayes lets the door slide shut. I feel my hands start to shake. He slides a card over a reader and hits a button on the panel, but it's not one of the top-floor numbers, and I know I won't be taken to see Zander after all. I deflate a little, but try to change tactics.

"Does Zander always send his brothers to collect his friends when they stop by to see him?" I ask, a friendly note masking the fear I feel. I'm performing any role I can to get through this.

"Zander doesn't have female friends," Hayes says without humor as the elevator starts to rise with surprising speed.

I roll my eyes. "No, he has women he fucks and then is done with them," I murmur.

I can feel Hayes's head turn to me and I'm sure he's appraising me. I look over and meet his scary green stare. It's deep and is, in fact, taking my measure. I will myself to quit being a little bitch and stop shaking. Instead, I grasp the anger of being dismissed, underestimated, and counted out and use it to give me a bit more of a backbone now, when I need it most. I stand up straighter and lift my chin, rising to my full height and more in my four-inch Louboutin heels. I can stare him dead in the eye, though he may have an inch or two on me.

"I was one of those women. I can tell you think I'm a problem, but I don't intend to be. I just need to talk to Zander. Give me five minutes with him. That's all I need. Then I'll sign whatever you want and be out of your hair." Honest, to the point. I'm a good girl you can trust, is what I'm trying to tell him. Not a problem in the least.

"That's not how this works. That's not how Zander works."

"You don't understand. This is important. I just need to speak with Zander directly. I tried calling, texting, social media, but everything has been blocked. I tried calling here and got nowhere. This is my only option. I wouldn't be here otherwise. I want nothing to do with him," I promise, even if there is still a part of me that would like something to do with him, hurt and all.

The elevator stops and the doors open to a floor that appears vacant of employees and leads directly into a conference room that is lit and has a stack of papers on the table. Hayes extends his arm for me to exit the elevator ahead of him.

"Please, I'm begging you. I just need to speak to Zander. Two minutes even. I can be brief. I don't need much time. I'll leave as soon as I speak to him." I'm walking backward, resorting to pleading as I enter the conference room, Hayes following me, his face looking impassive, stoic, unimpressed. He really was a good option to send, as intimidating as he is and as unwilling to be swayed as he seems to be.

"I'm sorry you had to experience the worst of my youngest brother's qualities, Ms. Sorenson. I really am. I make no excuses for why he is the way he is. Zander is a compulsive womanizer. His actions are deplorable more often than not, and he makes no excuses for his own behavior, reveling in the fact that he only spends one night with a woman before he loses interest in them. I know that can be hard when he sells you a story of how special you are to get you into bed." He pulls out the chair in front of the stack of papers for me to sit.

"Two. Weeks." I sit on the edge of the chair and fume that I have to be here at all when I just want to talk to Zander.

"Excuse me?" he says, taking his own seat next to me.

"We were in the Maldives for two weeks. Yes, he said a lot of pretty things and made a lot of promises that now feel like chewing broken glass to think about, but that's beside the point. I need to speak to him about another matter altogether."

Hayes shows genuine interest for the first time, his green gaze sharpening and taking my measure again, as if I surprised him. "Well, it seems you've already had more time with Zander than he's allowed with anyone else, so consider yourself lucky. Or unlucky, as it is. I think he's an insufferable asshole, so I apologize that you had to spend that much time alone with him. I really don't envy you."

Despite the situation, I bark out a laugh, and get what I imagine is a rare smile from Hayes, as well. "He admitted to being an entirely different person on the trip, so I think I was shown someone other than who you're used to," I admit. "Maybe he treated me better. I guess I'll never know, now. But I do need to talk to him. I have to tell him something incredibly important. Then I swear I'm done with him for good. You will never see or hear from me again if that's what he wants."

He shakes his head almost sadly and lets out a deep breath. "Listen, Ms. Sorenson, you seem smarter than most, so I'm going to level with you and just lay this out. We're here to have you sign this non-disclosure agreement and come to an understanding where my brother is concerned. He wants nothing to do with you, as hard as that is to hear, and would prefer not to deal with the aftermath of his hookups. He won't be speaking with you today or at any time in the future. I get the lovely job of explaining that Zander is a complete moron, we can both agree he is an idiot who needs to learn how to treat women, and then I will escort you out once you understand that under no circumstances are you to contact him or come here again."

"You can't be serious," I say, taken aback by his bluntness. "I *have* to speak with him. It's imperative," I insist.

"We are prepared to offer you a million dollars to make it easier to stay away from Zander, as well as Olympus International. Part of the NDA here stipulates the length of time and—"

"I don't want your fucking money," I blurt, cutting him off, outraged that he thinks I'm here looking for a handout, like I'm some whore that needs payment for services rendered. "I'm not signing anything. I have no intention of saying anything to anyone. All I came here to do was speak to Zander. I have something incredibly important and time-sensitive I need to tell him. I don't need money and I'm not looking for him to date me or anything otherwise. You are unbelievable and this is so fucked."

"You will sign the NDA," he says, looking bored with my outburst, but his eyes are sharp, cunning, and I know I should be scared. Instead, it pisses me off that he thinks he can order me around.

"No, actually, I won't. That document would only be legally binding if both parties agreed to sign it retroactively. I do not agree. So you and Zander and your whole family can fuck right off." I scatter the stack of papers across the table and floor as I stand and stalk out of the conference room. I asked my manager casually about NDAs when I got back from my trip, wondering why Zander hadn't made me sign one before we left. It was quite illuminating and turned out to be helpful now.

I stab the button for the elevator and hope like hell the car will go down without needing a special pass. I feel, rather than hear, Hayes come up behind me and turn to see him lean on the conference room doorframe, nearly blocking the entire opening with his impressively large frame. He really does have a scary aura, or whatever it is that hangs around him, especially as he turns his cold green eyes on me.

"Ms. Sorenson, I don't recommend fucking with my family, if that's your intention in not signing the NDA. If you so much as drag our name or our business into any of your bullshit, you'll feel the wrath we're capable of. We don't tolerate those who wish to make enemies of us, so I don't advise it for you. It won't end well."

I keep my back straight and stare him down right back. I don't care how big or intimidating he is, I won't let him threaten me after what Zander did. "I don't recommend fucking with *me*, Mr. Olsen. You can tell Zander that yourself. I don't want anything to do with any of you, or your fucking company, so don't worry about me or what I'll be doing. Stay away from me and we won't have a problem." The elevator dings and the doors open, providing an escape route away from Zander's scary-ass big brother.

Thankfully, the doors close and the car descends as it should, and I ride down in a shaky silence, my lip wobbling with the effort it takes to hold on to my fierceness and pride. To keep my facade of warrior strength that I'll be taking with me against any foe.

I'll need this strength and power to raise a child on my own, to protect them from the world, and to shield them from men like Zander and a family as powerful as the Olsens. Once I'm out of the building, I let myself fall apart, tears coming in an endless stream that has people on the street looking at me like I'm crazy. I'll have to do this completely on my own, without Zander so much as knowing that he'll have a child in this world, raised in the very same city, even.

I will be moving home to live with my mom once my current contracts are complete. I can't continue modeling after I have this baby, not without a family and help in place in LA, and not when it will put me in the public eye and potentially at risk of Zander and his family learning about his child.

I'm making a choice right this moment to make sure that Zander Olsen never gets wind of this baby, because if what Hayes said was true, they could see this as a retaliatory act on their family. Any mention of Zander being the father of my child could be construed as dragging the Olsen name into my bullshit. They could try to take the baby from me, and then I'll have absolutely nothing left of my forever with Zander. So I will guard my child from that possibility, and that means pulling away from the life and career I thought I wanted so badly.

Nineteen

Zander

I punch in Harlowe's number, my fingers drumming on my desk as I wait for it to connect. Instead, it goes straight to voicemail.

"You have reached me. If you know, you know, so do the thing." Her voicemail message brings a slight grin to my face with the absurdity of it, but the raspy voice is unmistakable.

"Lowe, it's me. I need to talk to you." I pause and glance around the pristine interior of my office, forming some kind of plan or message, or something that can give me direction. "Just call me." I rattle off my personal number and end the call, feeling stupid and out of my element. I hate this.

"Fuck," I breathe, dragging a hand across my face. Why couldn't she have just picked up so I could ask her right then if he's my kid or not? "Fuck!" I say with more intensity. I don't want to feel helpless, waiting on some woman to change my life forever or put me out of this wretched misery of not knowing for sure. If Payton's right and I can use this to save the Olympus image, I'll need to reestablish control and direct this how I want it to go.

I pull up Instagram to see if she's been active on socials, even if her phone is going straight to voicemail, and see her latest thirst trap that feels set just for me. Fucking noodles again. Her caramel skin is more on display than usual, her midriff showing above high-rise leggings along with one bare shoulder that her cropped shirt is falling off of. She makes a face I know only too well as she hollows out her cheeks, slurping up noodles from chopsticks held above a wok. It takes me straight back to when she sucked my cock just like that, taking me down her throat, making me come faster than I wanted, sending bolts of lightning up and down my spine. The dirty caption that must be meant for me? Something about fucking *slurping*. I can *hear her sounds*. I exit the app like it's on fire, throwing my phone on the desk and bending at the waist, pushing my now pulsing, rock-hard cock down and groaning at the friction of even that motion because I can't fucking do anything about it here at work.

"Goddammit!" I roar to my empty office.

I'm still pacing angrily around my office half an hour later when Weiss knocks softly and cracks the door.

"I just wanted to remind you of your lunch meeting in fifteen minutes. The Henderson project is on the docket, as is the restructuring of Milagro Inc. It's just you with Javier and the directors leading the teams. Hayes and Payton won't be in attendance."

Finally. I could use the familiarity of doing what I do best to take my mind off of Harlowe. Milagro is being incorporated into our mining operations and will need top-down restructuring, something I can do in my sleep, so it's just the project I need to refocus on what is important. If I'm not pushing the constant growth of Olympus, I'm at risk of being outpaced, outmatched, and outplayed by some other company looking to exploit any weakness they can find with us.

"You have the files for me to review?"

Weiss rolls her eyes and hands me a stack of folders. "You doubt my efficiency one more time and I'm calling in sick. I'll let you deal with an admin from the pool downstairs for a day and you'll be groveling at my feet to come back and make everything run smoothly again," she says dryly.

"Have I given you a raise lately? You deserve it," I tell her, knowing she's probably already scheduled the meeting herself with HR and accounting for her annual raise. She doesn't deem me fit for an answer as she leaves my office. This is one woman I need on my team and by my side in business.

My gut twists and a phantom thought escapes my locked vault, telling me there is another who may prove to be an even better asset, and possibly partner. If I can just convince her to answer me.

The meeting with Milagro Inc. went exactly how it should have, but finding Payton waiting for me in my office when I finish has the black clouds sailing right back into my clearing skies.

"What?" I ask, sliding into my chair and pulling a folder toward me to rifle through the contents.

"Any news on the daddy front?" he asks. "It's been a week, and all I've seen are gossip blogs hounding Harlowe and making assumptions about her kid's parentage. I thought you were going to do the right thing. Man up and take responsibility."

"I've been a little busy here, running our multi-billion dollar international company, dealing with the continued fall out of our stocks and image hitting rock bottom, and leading our constant expansion," I say, lack of patience clipping my tone.

Payton throws his hands up in the air and rolls his eyes. "Oh, the big CEO is so busy," he mocks. "You have a fucking kid. I don't care if you just found out, it's time you owned it. At the very least be certain. Get Harlowe to admit it or get a paternity test. But you need to make that connection now before the media speculation gets worse."

My frustrations boils over and I stand, leaning onto my desk and leveling Payton with a *fuck off and die* stare. "How would you feel if you were a model I'd fucked and sent on her merry way while I cut off all contact and made it impossible for her to tell me she was pregnant? Would you be happy to hear from me, now?"

Payton shudders. "Gross. Please don't ever make me consider what it would be like to fuck you."

"Grow up, you know what I mean," I say, scrubbing my hands down my face and resettling into my chair. "She hates me. There's no way she's letting me in now." From her refusal to take my calls and the glacial response I've received in person, it doesn't look like I'll have an in anytime soon.

"I hear you, even if I don't like what you're saying." Payton sighs and leans back in his chair. "We can have the legal department handle this quickly and efficiently, if you want. They can force a paternity test, and you can sue for parental rights. It wouldn't be pretty, but you'd get in."

"That's the last thing I want to do. Fuck, man. I don't want to force Harlowe to do anything, especially not sue her for rights to her kid. If she doesn't want me in the kid's life, that's her choice."

Payton tilts his head and stares at me like I've just sprouted tentacles. "Did you just say something entirely too human and, for once, not egocentric?"

I contemplate throwing my Mont Blanc pen at him, but I like it too much. "I'm trying to reach out. I've left her messages," I admit instead. "Let me do this my way before you get lawsuit happy. You of all people should want to avoid a domestic legal battle that would just be more bad press for Olympus."

"For once, I'm not thinking about Olympus here. I just want you to do what's right and honorable, no matter what it costs us."

"I think hell just iced over," I say, staring in shock at Payton, who has always put the company image, the bottom line, and what we're capable of ahead of everything else. "This day is too fucking weird. Get out of my office so I can finish up for the day without you wreaking more havoc."

"Use the patented Zander charm to win her over. You've had no trouble getting a woman to fall for you in the past. Why wouldn't it work now?"

"Maybe because she saw what that got her the first time around," I quip, returning to my stack of paperwork. I may jest, but the comment is far too real, and I'd rather not dig into that too deeply.

"Just do whatever you have to in order to get on a united front with her. Having gossip sites hyperbolizing about a potential relationship you once had, or coming up with possible reasons Harlowe has kept the kid from you all these years, doesn't look good. It'll get uglier the longer you wait. At the very least, take it and play up a happy co-parenting rhetoric that will get the speculation off what is really happening." Payton stands and walks to my office door. "And don't wait. Turn the narrative now or you'll never wrestle it back." He pats the doorframe as he leaves and I'm left with his parting words and a hazy plan taking shape.

My mind is too far gone down the Harlowe rabbit hole to be of any use at work, so when the clock has inched closer to a decent quitting time, I'm already headed down the elevator to the garage. I slide into my car and palm my phone like I may have missed a call from Harlowe in the time it took me to get down here.

"Fuck it," I mutter, starting the drive to her house, hoping she'll be home mid-afternoon and not out doing who knows what. It's important enough to have this conversation in person, and I want to have it now, so that's what I'm going to do.

I've been thinking of ways to get Harlowe to see my side, treating the situation like any other business acquisition. I'm looking for the cracks in my opponent's armor to use as handholds while I scale their defenses and present a perfectly planned solution just when they need it the most. I can go in, guns blazing, demanding that I meet the child I somehow fucked into existence, yet had no idea was a walking, talking little person until just a month ago. I can appeal to her need for stability and promise her the boy will have the best of everything, college paid for, a trust in his name, and maybe even financial security for her.

I shake my head at the stupid track my thoughts are going down. She would have been banging down my door, wanting financial assistance, if that was her endgame. Instead, she's been cagey about the boy's parentage even after he pinged my radar, not once looking for a hand-out. So, what does she want, and how can I use that desire to my advantage? The answer comes to me slowly, a mist-shrouded cityscape revealed as tendrils of fog roll away, exposing the very real brick and mortar colossus that was always there, yet undetectable until you reached its edges.

Oh, fuck me. I can't. Not *that*. Despite my internal protests, I know with certainty what route I need to take, and it fucking kills me to admit that Payton had the right idea, and I knew it all along.

What pissed her off the most after our trip, despite knowing the score going into it? What has she brought up more than once at this point about the situation that fucked with her head? She wanted a fucking *relationship*. She wanted that happily ever after I never promised, but she could see so clearly. She wanted the forever, even I felt could have been ours, that had me running for the hills and blocking every chase route she could have attempted because it was too *real*.

So, how do I unfuck the situation I carefully removed myself from and let swirl down the drain? One. Fucking. Step. At a time.

"Goddammit, I have to get my woman back."

When Harlowe pulls into her driveway, about fifteen minutes after I arrive, I'm ready to start this process. Ready to get through the cracks in her defenses and work my way into her life. She walks back down the driveway to stare at my car with fists on her hips, challenging me to make my move while I have a chance. Her face registers recognition, disbelief, and finally, resolution as I climb from the sleek electric car and walk up to meet her.

I'm mesmerized by the valkyrie that meets me in the driveway, dark eyes flashing in calculation. Her hair is in a messy bun on her head, no makeup on her stunning, flushed face, her body clad in tight workout clothes still stained with the sweat from her trip to the gym. Her body looks even more incredible like this and it takes everything I have not to walk right up to her, grab that amazing ass, and haul her up my body. She didn't even try and still managed to have the advantage here, setting me back with her raw beauty and powerful presence that has me wanting to bow at her feet and beg her forgiveness.

"I tried calling." My voice vibrates with promise and expectation. "I left you messages, but your voicemail box is full now, and you didn't answer my texts," I say, hands slightly raised in front of me like I'm approaching a skittish feral cat. She could bolt at any second before I can deploy the Trojan horse I'm hoping gets me into her guarded citadel of a life.

She smirks, the smile cruel. "How does it feel to be on the other side of the line when all you want is to have your calls and texts answered by someone and you can't reach them?" She rolls her eyes and crosses her arms over her ample chest, covering the sports bra that is peeking out from under a light jacket. "I'm surprised you kept my number this time around after blocking me years ago. And since when does not answering a text or call mean you should just stop by?"

"I need to talk to you, Lowe. You owe me that, at the very least."

She stalks toward me, anger narrowing her eyes like I'm the only thing she sees and she wants to destroy me.

"I owe you?" she repeats. "No." She shakes her head and her look hardens. "I don't owe you shit, and I never asked for anything from you," she says for good measure, stabbing a finger into my chest. "When it was me trying to talk to you, you decided I wasn't worth your time or energy, I wasn't worth knowing. You cut me out of your life faster than you buy and sell businesses. It doesn't matter what came of me after you had your fill." She pushes her palms against my chest and shoves futilely with a frustrated wail before backing up a step when I don't budge. "Why do you get to show up and demand an audience with me and get the outcome you want, now?" The words burst from her, a broken dam that can't hold back the frustration, the uncertainty, the fear and loneliness she must have experienced after I cut her off.

My chest grows tight where her hands just were, shame walking cold fingers down my spine as it finally hits me what my *rules* have done to her. Possibly to countless other women. Selfishness has always felt so noble and good when I saw it through the lens of my own happiness and conquests.

"You don't understand. I had to make the break," I say, my words tense and strained with the horror of the wreckage I've left in my wake for years.

I knew I couldn't let anything remain between us after the trip. It was agony, watching what that did to her, what I did to her, and having to keep a straight face, to lie to her and tell her she meant nothing to me. All I wanted was to scoop her into my lap, bury my face in her neck, and tell her we did have a forever because I would be hers until I took my last breath. But it was the truth when I told her the man she wanted didn't exist outside of that island and I wasn't good enough for her.

She laughs bitterly. "I understand just fine. You wanted to use me. You needed company so you wouldn't get bored in paradise. You wanted a willing body to stick your cock in. You didn't want anything other than a distraction from your life that was far more important than a relationship or a person. You may have sold me a beautiful lie, but I realized the truth of who you were fast enough. You became a completely different person on the flight home. No need to tell me what I do or don't understand. I'm not stupid."

We're circling each other, predators evaluating weaknesses and looking for the right moment to make a killing blow. This isn't going how I planned, and I have to get it back on track or this will have all been for nothing.

"I never said you were stupid, and I never lied to you. You don't know me at all. And from how crazy you're acting now, I may have dodged a bullet back then by doing what was necessary," I fire back, spitting the words out like rapidly thrown knives to pierce her back as my self-perception crumbles around me. I realize my error of letting my anger lead as her eyes go wide. Fuck. That wasn't the tactic I should have taken.

"Dodged a bullet?" she hisses. "You're calling me crazy because I don't like that you showed up at my house after five years, demanding I listen to you? Insisting that I owe you my time and you deserve my consideration when you blocked my number and sent your brother to escort me out of your office building when I tried to talk to you?" she scoffs. "Maybe I would have listened had you manned up and talked to me after that trip, but no, you cut me off and waited all these years to try to explain yourself. You're still just an entitled rich boy who has no idea what it takes to be a man."

She raises a hand between us, palm out to stop any rebuttals. I catch it in mine and step into her space, feeling her heat, both her anger that sparks and pops like a wildfire, and the feel of her body as it stumbles into mine. She yanks to pull away, but I don't release her. I want to crush her against me, feel her body mold to mine, and crash my mouth down on hers, no matter how angry we are.

"You know exactly how much of a man I am," I growl, low and dangerous, sensual heat pouring from us both even as she fights to keep her composure.

She sneers at me, not taking the bait. "Yes, I know what kind of man you are." She gives me a cruel smile, eyes narrowing. "You're a man who walls himself off from connection, who refuses to take responsibility, and runs as fast as he can from something good because it got under his skin."

I growl in frustration and tip my head back, absently pulling her closer to me with a crushing insistence. When I lower my head and fix my eyes on her, I see a heat in her molten chocolate pools that makes me shiver in anticipation. This is the fighter I know. This is the walking temptation that puts fire in my blood.

"Finally, little Wildcat, something you got right," I seethe, stepping even closer.

We're chest to chest and she's not moving away and my hands are on her waist now, holding her to me. She tips her head back to meet my eyes, her hands on my chest, gripping my shirt tightly instead of pushing me away as she breathes just as heavily.

"You did get under my skin," I grit out. "You burrowed so deep it took years to pull you out, bit by bit. Do you know how often I still look around when I hear a laugh that sounds like yours, searching for you? Every time I smell coconuts, I think of your damn sunscreen and the feel of your skin under my fingers." I close my eyes and feel a muscle in my jaw tic as I lean my face into hers, my nose against her cheek as my lips find her ear, and inhale her scent deeply. "You weren't supposed to stick with me.

You were a short-term investment, but you had long-term consequences," I bite out quietly, anger coursing through the words in a shocking cascade of confession I never expected to reveal, not to her, or myself.

I pull back to watch as she schools the shock that widens her eyes and tries not to let me see. "I'm nobody's short-term anything, Zander," she spits right back at me, holding onto her own righteous anger. "I'm a *forever* investment, and my life isn't yours to play with." She twists free from my grip and steps back, out of my heat and the closeness that melded our bodies together. "It's time for you to leave. There's nothing for you here. No one you need to worry your pretty little head about."

"Harlowe, he's my son." I hear the catch in my voice as I acknowledge what has to be the truth, speaking the words low and with a fair amount of pleading for her to give me this. "Let me be a part of his life and let me into yours. I'll take care of everything, make sure he's always provided for." I make a dive off the course I set, going to what feels comfortable when I'm negotiating, and that's upping the stakes to get the other party to agree to my terms.

She pauses to turn around slowly from her walk back up the drive. She levels me with the most serious *I will fuck you up if you come for my child* stare.

"He's not your son. He's mine, and I can provide for him just fine on my own. He doesn't have a father, just a sperm donor that I made a mistake of letting close to me. You don't have to concern yourself with me or Hendricks.

Don't worry, I don't want anything from you, not your money, not your acknowledgment, and certainly not you wanting to play father now when it's convenient for you." The exhaustion and trepidation that coats her words gives them a low, sticky quality that will be impossible to wash clean. I can see the fire in her has gone out, and instead of feeling victorious, it takes it out of me, as well. Neither of us wants to be fighting in her driveway.

"I'm not done with you, Harlowe." My words are a heated declaration rather than a threat. I will make her see reason, let me in and work with me, not against me. I follow her up the cracked concrete driveway until all that separates us is the threshold of the garage, the door hanging above us, a guillotine poised to sever all the threads weaving us together again.

She blinks quickly, her thick lashes sweeping over the dark circles below her warm chocolate eyes telling me how tired of this she is. "You're five years too late, Zander."

My heart clenches with her words and I feel the anger flood out of me, leaving just my desperation behind. My brain finally catches up, and I remember what my whole purpose was for coming here before I got caught up in fighting with her.

"It's the right time to try again, Lowe. Differently this time. You and me. Not just for a weekend, or a few weeks. You and I both know we're perfect together," I say, reaching out a hand and letting my thumb skim her cheek. "I'll be the man you need me to be. You're all mine, Lowe.

Forever, remember?" I say, going for broke, pulling out the most painful memory from the vault, the one that burns as I rip it free and throw it at her feet. It's my heart that she stole and I had to cut out when I boarded the jet to come home. The very heart I locked away and vowed never to need again. Yet here it is, still beating solely for her, bruised and bloody as it may be.

I watch the shine of tears form in her eyes as she clicks the remote in her hand, sending the garage door trundling slowly down between us.

"You told me forever was a lie, Zander. You were never mine to have."

I see the hitch of a sob part her lips when I have to lower my arm to avoid the door, and catch a stray tear streaking down her cheek as it obscures her face, erasing her body, and finally cuts us off completely.

"I'll be here when you're ready," I say to the closed door, hoping she's still just on the other side, listening.

That woman. She's infuriating. She's infatuating. She could be my most epic downfall.

It takes me several moments after her garage is shut to get my feet to move away. It takes longer to admit that she may have won this battle, but the war is still mine to win.

<h1 style="text-align:center">Twenty</h1>

<h1 style="text-align:center">Harlowe</h1>

"Mama, do I have a daddy?"

My breath catches in my throat, as cold, hard fear blurs my vision. I gratefully pull into my driveway and jerkily throw the extra nice rental vehicle I was somehow upgraded to at no cost to me into park and blink back threatening tears. My baby, my four-year-old child, the one I wanted to shield from the horrors of the world a little longer, just asked me the one question I never wanted to hear from him.

And on the day Zander fucking Olsen showed up to tell me he's not done with me. That he finally wants to try again, like he didn't put five years of hell between us when he blocked me. His soft touch at the end of our argument nearly erased the pain and hurt we were exchanging. It almost crumbled my defenses and had me sinking to my knees in relief.

But I couldn't do it. Not right then. And I'm proud that I could stick up for myself and demand better than whatever Zander is willing to give. There is no way the billionaire fuckboy has reformed and would be stable enough to bring into our lives now. Putting my heart on the line is one thing, but I have Hendricks to think about above all else. I look into the rearview mirror at his sweet face and gorgeous gray eyes that ground me back in the present.

"Why do you ask, love bug?" My voice is calm, but I can hear the strain in the words and just hope Hendricks misses it.

"I heard Miss Sharon and Miss Stephanie say my name at school, but they weren't talking to me. They were talking about my daddy. I didn't know I had a daddy, but they said I did. They said," he pauses, rolling a Hot Wheels car along his thigh, his brow scrunched up in contemplation. "They said he had powers and money. Is my daddy a superhero, like Black Panther or Batman?"

More like Iron Man, I think. A billionaire businessman fuckboy sounds closer to Zander. Besides, Tony Stark happily reveals that he is Iron Man. Zander would totally bask in his glory if he were capable of creating a superhero persona. I'm going to have to talk to his teachers if they're gossiping in front of my kid.

"Is he?" Hendricks asks again, forcing me to stop imagining a fictional Zander in hot superhero armor and return to the very real boy in the backseat. The weight on my shoulders eases a little, knowing he is more interested in knowing if his father is a superhero than who his father actually is.

I turn in my seat and face him. He looks up and smiles his bright, innocent smile. How much do I tell him? How much will he understand? What is the right answer for his little boy mind that is far too advanced for some of his emotions? I sigh.

"Everyone has a father, but not everyone gets to know them as a daddy. You have me, and we're a team." I hope that satisfies his inquisitiveness.

"But does my father have superpowers? It would be so cool if he could fly or shoot bad guys with rockets, pew pew!" He stretches his fist up and blasts imaginary foes from his car seat.

I smile, wondering if it would be easier to just say his father is a superhero busy fighting crime, so he can't be a part of our lives. Finally, I just go with the truth, knowing at some point he will know it regardless. "He is as normal as you and me, my love. No superpowers that I know of."

"Are you sure? Most superheroes hide their powers and only show 'em when they're wearing a mask. Maybe he didn't show you his powers. I bet he would show me. I would keep his secret." Hendricks returns his attention to his toy cars, muttering rocket noises to himself as he enacts a chase across his legs.

Hendricks is right. Zander showed me exactly what he wanted to, and then shut me out when it got too real. Or maybe I saw what I wanted, a promise of something more with a well-known fuckboy, when it was me being delusional thinking I could be the one to change his ways. I fell into the same trap so many women do, thinking I could change the man, turn him into something more dependable and worthy of my efforts and attention. I was shortsighted enough to believe the attention he gave me was an indication of his intentions for after the trip. The writing was always on the wall; I just chose not to read it for what it was. Not until it was too late.

I climb out of the car and unbuckle Hendricks from his car seat. His baby fat is nearly gone, slowly morphing his body into that of a lean child. "I'm pretty sure he's just a normal guy, no superpowers, but if he did, I know you would hold his secret safe in your big heart, because you are trustworthy and good, my little man."

"You're good, too, Mama. He should have told you about his powers, so you could tell me and we could keep the secret together." He wraps his arms around my neck and hugs me fiercely, as if he knows that I need it so much right now.

I smile and kiss his golden cheek and bury my nose in his soft curls as I hold him in my arms. He still smells like my baby, even as he slowly outgrows my arms. When will he be big enough to know the story of how he came to be? When will I feel comfortable telling him about his father and why that man isn't a part of his life? Will I even get the chance to choose the time, or has it been picked for me, forcing me to break into the past and pull it into the light, pale and squirming in my hands?

"Can we watch Iron Man? Or Cars? I wanna have a movie night and eat snacks on the couch with you," he says, detailing our weekend ritual despite it being a week-night.

"Of course," I reply, not able to deny him the small pleasure.

My phone vibrates in my bag, and I shift Hendricks to my hip so I can retrieve it. I finally turned it back on consistently after a week, hoping that was enough time to avoid the constant barrage of questions from everyone who has my number. It has stayed relatively silent and lulled me into a false sense of security that my life would right itself. When my fingers finally pull the sleek phone from my bag, it's Knox's face and number on the screen. I prop the phone between my shoulder and face, answering with a quick hello.

"Hey," he says, his deep voice rumbling in my ear. "You and the little man wanna hang tonight?"

I glance at Hendricks, clinging to my body as I haul him into the house and finally manage to set him down. "I told Hendricks we would watch movies together tonight. I'll have to ask if he wants company," I say.

Mom greets us and takes Hendricks's hand. "Why don't we go into the kitchen for a snack? Mama is on the phone," she says, giving me a wink. I cringe and palm my forehead.

"Oh, and my mom is here. She's been helping me out with everything that's been going on, so you would have to meet her," I hedge, not sure I even want that. Knox and I haven't gotten serious. He feels more like a friend I kiss sometimes, and though he's now a part of Hendricks's life, would it make it too real to introduce him to my mom?

"You know, I'm great with moms. I don't mind meeting yours if you want me to. I'm also totally okay hanging at home and letting y'all have some family time. I just thought..." he trails off, his voice uncertain.

"What's up?" I ask, heart jumping into my throat, wondering what the issue is.

"I thought you might want to talk about the press stuff that's going around. It's hard having your life speculated about so publicly. If you need me, I'm here." His low voice sends shivers along my spine, lifting my spirits just a tiny bit.

"Knox, listen, I'm sorry I haven't talked to you about any of this—"

He cuts me off. "No need to be sorry. This is your life, and you get to decide who knows your history. Well, unless you're a celebrity and gossip columns get ahold of information to tear into. That ain't right, but it's the world we live in. I know there's a lot of my life I don't want people freely talking about, so I can only imagine how bad this feels."

I slide down the wall of the entryway until my feet are stretched out in front of me on the floor and sigh. "There are some skeletons I never wanted to let out of the closet."

He chuckles. "You and me both."

I tilt my head to the side and my mind starts up a conjecture of ideas. "What would you have buried that people could have a field day with in the media? You are squeaky clean and so perfect. Did you hit someone too hard at football camp?"

He stops chuckling, "Let's just say there's plenty and nobody's perfect."

"Let me list your good qualities and refute that statement," I say, smiling as I get a chance to focus on someone else. "You do charity work on the regular. I mean, how many foundations and programs have you worked with this year alone? Seven? You spend just as much time volunteering your time as you do at practice, and they all love you. You are a shining example of promoting teamwork, and have received awards from every team you've played on for being the moral support and glue that holds the team together. You are a role model for tons of people, you are super straightforward and honest, and you've been really kind to me and Hendricks," I say, ticking off the statements on my fingers.

He laughs, but it's not the deep, full-body sound I'm used to. "Thank you for seeing the good in me, Harley."

"What's wrong?" I ask, attuned to his change in mood. "Did I say something?"

"It's just..." he begins, but stops himself, clears his throat, and takes a moment.

"Why don't you come over tonight after Hendricks goes to bed and we can catch up? You're right. I owe you an explanation."

"I have to go. I'll call you later. Keep your head up and don't let the gossip get to you."

Before I can stop him, he's ended the call and I'm left holding the phone in confusion. Was it something I said?

"My grandson said he can have ice cream and cookies. Should I be the good nana and give him the junk food, or would that spoil his appetite if you have something planned for dinner?" Mom asks, finding me still sitting on the floor in the garage entry. "Oh, Lolo. Why are you on the floor?"

I look up at her and grimace. She sits next to me, stretching out her legs with a groan that belies her age, but not her health. She's spry and exercises more than I do.

"The guy I'm friendly with just ended a weird conversation abruptly. Something I said about skeletons in the closet spooked him, I think. It just feels like a shitty way to end an already bad day."

"Are you talking about the argument you had with that sharply dressed man in your driveway earlier?"

I slowly roll my head against the wall to look at her. "Were you eavesdropping on me, Mom?"

She avoids my stare and smiles crookedly. "No need to eavesdrop. I think the neighbors heard you shouting at each other. I was just watching to see if you needed backup, but you had him covered just fine, my little tiger. Want to talk about it?"

"How much did you hear, exactly?" I swear to God, if the neighbors start ratting me out to the gossip rags, I'm going to burn down their houses. Try being nosy without your lace curtains to peel back, Mrs. Brady!

"Most of it. Is he—?" She waves her hand toward the living room, where I hear the strains of a Marvel movie beginning.

I hang my head in defeat. If she could put that much together, it's no stretch to think everyone else will, too. "Yes," I admit quietly. "That was Zander Olsen. Have you heard of him?"

"Of course I have. I'm not living under a rock. I live in the same city and I follow your career and what's written about you, good and bad."

"You do?" The shocked tone in my voice makes her scowl, the little lines by her eyes deepening.

"I started a long time ago, so I'd know where you were modeling. Then it just became a habit to keep tabs on what was said about you in case I needed to burn someone's house down." *Ahh, so that's where I get it from.*

"He would never have known about Hendricks if that dumb gossip site, The Atlanta Haute List, hadn't linked us," I gripe, tossing my keys from hand to hand with a jingle.

"You wouldn't have told him, eventually?"

"Not if I could help it. He didn't want anything to do with me after our trip. Why would he want to know about his child?" I say, pulling my legs under me to stand and holding out a hand for Mom.

She takes the offered help and rises, following me into the house and to my sanctuary, the kitchen.

"How do you know what he would want if you didn't give him all the information? We hardly know how we will react to new situations. We can't begin to untangle anyone else's actions."

I pull items from the fridge and pantry so I can create Hendricks's favorite snack board for movie watching. "I did what I thought was best."

"You were angry, Lolo. I could feel your anger for months when you came home. And so sad. Your sadness filled this home and pushed out any hope for a better outcome than what you had settled on." She puts a bag of popcorn into the microwave as I arrange goldfish crackers and grapes into a pattern on a wooden tray with peanut butter cups and blue M&M's. Hendricks refuses to eat the other colors, even though they all taste like chocolate to me.

"Are you saying I should have shown up, Hendricks in my arms, and demanded he see his son? I'm pretty sure I would have been arrested and Hendricks taken from me." My voice drops low and I feel the cold trickle of fear that has followed me around since I brought my son into this world of what the Olsen family could do to me or Hendricks.

"It seems like he's interested now. What's stopping you from letting him know his boy?"

"You don't understand what kind of man Zander Olsen is," I say in warning.

"Is he a bad man? Did he hurt you, or try to take your life away? No, he gave you a beautiful son who is so sweet and pure."

"He's a liar, and he only cares about himself."

"Then why was he outside demanding to know his son? A man who only cares about himself wouldn't have shown up today. He wouldn't have made the effort to come up against you. You're an Amazon warrior. You terrify men."

"Hey!" I protest. She gives me a knowing look and I feel my indignation deflate.

"You're intimidating. You're tall and beautiful, with a sharp tongue and a fast mind. Men don't stand a chance when you decide to break them down." She pulls the popcorn out of the microwave and empties it into a bowl before she continues in a softer tone. "That man didn't crumble, Lolo. He took your viciousness and still asked for what he wanted. That tells me he's thinking of something more than himself. He's thinking of his future, and what he's contributed to this life that will succeed him. That's more than many single moms can ask for."

"Great. It was easy enough to ignore when it was just Alicia, but if you're team Zander now, what am I supposed to do?" My manager had worn me down and gotten the truth out of me, as well. She's been fully on board with a plan to push me back into Zander's orbit, thinking it will be good for my book sales and the possibility of a cooking show.

"Does Alicia want a son-in-law? Because I do, and you won't even introduce me to the man you're *friendly with*, as you say."

"Whoa," I say, holding up a hand to stop her. "We're not talking marriage here, just introducing him to Hendricks. Slow down, Mom, you're getting way ahead of yourself."

"I'm not getting any younger, and neither are you. Thirty this year and not married. Old maid," she says, grabbing the snack board and the popcorn bowl before moving into the living room to sit with Hendricks.

"Cold-hearted old lady," I murmur in affection.

I look at the bags of snacks, wrappers, and crumbs left on the island, which gets awesome natural light in the afternoons, perfect for shooting photos of my recipes for my socials and videos. Today, I could grab a photo of this for another impromptu post. I unzip my jacket and grab my phone before I can think twice. I bend over backward onto the island, lying among the snack bags and decadent treats with one arm above my head, tank top straining to keep my ample tits contained, and snap a selfie of me facing into a slant of sunshine cutting across the marble and snack debris.

I stand back up and brush crumbs off my shoulders while I check the photo, which definitely caught the intended image I'd hoped for. My ordinary brown eyes look like rich chocolate pools, my skin like burnished caramel glowing in the sunshine as golden-wrapped peanut butter cups, orange goldfish crackers, green and red grapes, and colorful M&M's are haloed around me in a foodie dream. I open Instagram and post my latest thirst trap and caption it, *feeling like a snack, who's hungry,* before posting and exiting like the sly she-devil I am.

Twenty-one

The Atlanta Haute List

Bad Day For Billionaires

Zander Olsen was dealt quite the day, with sources revealing he showed up for a showdown at the home of former flame, Harlowe Sorenson, in broad daylight. Reports say a heated argument took place in the driveway of all places, with the two battling toe-to-toe over an unspecified topic. We happen to think there may be some contention regarding the identity of Harlowe's baby daddy, and Zander showing up now gives us all the pretty pieces to start connecting more dots for #ZaddyGate. Does he want to stay anonymous (sorry, buddy, that's not happening), or find a way to fit into the family now that the secret is sort of out, at least enough for us to speculate on?

How does Harlowe's current beau, Knox Contraire, feel about this newest development? He hasn't been linked with Harlowe since before we uncovered the bombshell for ourselves, and he's notoriously hard to get a response from for anything other than his football games. Could this news be driving a wedge between our favorite new couple so soon? Honestly, we don't know who to pick to win in this battle of incredibly attractive, powerful men. We can't help but lean toward an Olsen brother when one is an option, as we are huge fans of that Atlanta-based family.

Besides, there's just something about a perpetual bachelor that makes you root for them to settle down. A ready-made family seems like a good bet to domesticate Zander and give him some stability so he can face his business demons. Wait, who are we kidding? We are team Zaddy Zander, all the way. Sorry, Knox! Remember to hit Like and Subscribe for all the Haute Gossip!

Twenty-two

Harlowe

I need to talk to Knox. He deserves the truth, no matter how badly I want to keep it to myself. And something tells me he has his own truths he needs to get off his chest after our last phone call.

When he rings the doorbell mid-afternoon, I've already worked myself into a bit of a mess, which translates to having stress-baked three completely unnecessary desserts. What I need with chocolate chip cookies, angel food cake with strawberries and fresh whipped cream, and cinnamon streusel coffee cake, I don't know, but my hands needed something to do while I waited after texting Knox and asking him to stop by.

I've also taken tripod photos of myself with chocolate streaked across my cheek, licking whipped cream off my fingers and lips, holding a handful of cake while leaning on the island topless surrounded by the desserts that strategically, and just barely, covered my tits. I posted one to Instagram with a caption that read *sugar and spice and everything nice, that's what good girls are made of, but bad girls will eat you whole* before bolting out of the app and letting Alicia deal with the engagement numbers, which have been astronomical.

She's been positively thrilled, and book sales have continued to increase, so whatever reason I've been drawn to post these damn thirst traps, they're obviously working for me. Yesterday, she said *Food & Wine* Magazine had called me the sexy, foulmouthed Ina Garten in their latest write-up on my book, and I had beamed in pride. Ina Garten is my idol. I just need a bunch of gay friends to host for boozy lunches now.

"Hey," I say, smiling when I open the door and let Knox in.

"Hey," he replies, a nervous smile on his face. "Too early for the little man to be home. Is your mom here?" he asks, shrugging out of his jacket and setting it on the edge of the couch before he settles himself next to where I'm already sitting cross-legged and twisting my hands.

"She's out for the afternoon. It's just us. I thought we could use some time to catch up. There's been a lot going on lately. Do you want anything to eat? I was stress baking today."

He smiles, warmth infusing his face as he raises an eyebrow at me. "I saw that. You really know how to hook your audience. I'm good, though." Knox runs a hand along his buzzed head and blows out a breath as the humor retreats. "Why does this feel so serious and weird? We're cool, Harley. No matter what's going on."

I look down at my hands and still their movement before launching into what has been haunting me. "Zander Olsen is Hendricks's father, and he wants to know his son."

I cringe. The words come out in a rush like I've ripped the tape off of a cracked pipe and it decided to burst. That wasn't what I'd planned to say. I made notes and practiced how to segue from one topic to another while I was baking. I was going to ask about his life lately, talk about how I've missed hanging out, and then gradually lead into the Atlanta Haute List speculation and all the nosy as fuck people that popped up wanting to know my business.

Knox saves me from having to explain. "I thought that might be what you wanted to talk about. You know you don't have to tell me, or anyone else, every little bit of your life, right? It doesn't matter if every gossip site and people you don't know are asking. You don't owe it to anyone if you'd rather keep it to yourself."

"I know that, I do. It's just... you deserve to know, since, well, we're in this," I say, gesturing between us at whatever we are.

I keep telling myself I have a boyfriend, since that's the easiest way to label what Knox and I are trying, no matter how platonic it sometimes feels. Yet, I can't bring myself to call it a relationship when it matters. It's more of a situationship, I guess.

"I think Zander will be coming around here more. I wanted you to know before you saw some headline or read whatever the gossip sites are saying about me, or us."

"Do you have feelings for him?" Knox asks softly. He's staring down at his clasped hands, and he radiates calm, when I expected something more furious. I thought there'd be crazy accusations and demands from him to never see Zander again, because it was too much of a betrayal of our situationship.

"What? No! Of course not! There's no way anyone can develop feelings for a man who chooses not to stick around longer than necessary," I say in a rush, feeling guilt wash over me. He didn't accuse me of anything, yet I feel like I've crossed a line already. I've let Zander too close. Whether or not I intended to, I've enjoyed every one of the small touches he's given me. And he kissed me. It's as good as cheating and I should really come clean to Knox now, no matter what happens.

He holds his hands out in front of him, a gentle smile on his face. "Hey, It's okay if you do. It's okay if you want him even now, no matter your history. He's the father of your child. That's a unique bond you will always share with him, whether you like it or not. There will forever be something tying you together, keeping you in each other's orbits. That's pretty fucking hard to compete with, actually."

How Knox can hit the exact sentiment on the head is astonishing, but also why I gravitated toward him to begin with. I shake my head.

"God, Knox, this isn't how I wanted this conversation to go at all. I just wanted to tell you about Zander. We didn't even date. We spent two weeks together on a trip and then he shut me out of his life completely. It was over before it ever started, but I got Hendricks out of it. It's complicated. I never wanted him to learn about Hendricks after the way we left things, but now Zander knows and he's insisting on getting to know Hendricks."

"As is his right, but only if you allow it. You have raised that little boy for four years all by yourself. You have protected him, nurtured him, and turned him into a cool as fuck kid. There is no denying you can do this on your own." He takes my hand in his, his thumb brushing gently over my knuckles. "But you don't have to do it on your own, not if you don't want to. And if he's here, wanting to make the effort, I think it's worth letting him in."

"What are you saying?" My brows knit together as I study Knox, trying to parse out his thoughts, his motivations.

He's not at all angry or even a little bit jealous. He's taking it way too easily for hearing that his sort of girlfriend's sort of ex is back in the picture and will be close to her. Where is the rage? The *touch her and die* vibes? I know exactly how Zander would react if the roles were reversed, and I feel myself leaning toward his over-the-top alpha bullshit response than this quiet acceptance.

Indignation rises in me, and I feel myself getting worked up. Am I not worth fighting for? I'm a fucking catch and he should care more than this. I'm about to start pushing back when his soft response stops me dead in my tracks.

"I think Zander is a better match for you than I'll ever be," he says, as if he's read my mind.

I blow out a frustrated breath and sit up straighter. "Knox, that isn't—"

He shakes his head and silences my protests. "I haven't exactly been honest about my intentions with you."

I purse my lips in confusion and stare at him as he keeps his gaze down at where he still holds my hand gently in his much bigger palm. My quickly rising anger swirls in me with nowhere to go. I'm not exactly mad at him, I'm mad at a situation I'm creating in my head.

"I think I'm gay."

The breath rushes out of me in a gasp. His admission hangs between us like the dropping bomb it is, and when the words finally click in my head, the explosion leaves me reeling.

"You're... gay?" I ask, looking up into his worried face as my anger morphs into shock and, if I'm being honest, relief courses through me. "So, why are you dating me?"

"Because I didn't want to admit what I secretly knew I was. I wanted to be normal. I wanted my teammates and the fans to see me with you and never question it. Because you're cool as hell and I like spending time with you. There are a million reasons why I wanted to be around you, but it's been me lying to myself, and wasting your time in the process."

"Knox, no, this hasn't been a waste of time," I say in a rush, gathering his other hand in mine and yanking on them both so he'll meet my eyes. "You have been so good to me and Hendricks. You've been patient, kind, and so respectful." I pause and look at him with new eyes, seeing every interaction we've had through the lens of this information. "Though, now I know why you didn't want to sleep with me, and thank fuck because I was developing a complex thinking that I didn't have any sex appeal now that I'm a mom and look different from when I was modeling. Knowing I have the wrong parts to get you off makes me feel a hell of a lot better about it, actually." We both break into laughter, and just like that, the tension that was hanging thick around us mists away.

"Fuck, thank you for making me laugh. This has been weighing on me far too long, and I think I got too worked up about how to tell you and not make you hate me."

"I could never hate you, not for this," I tell him. "You don't get to choose who you're attracted to and love. It's just wonderful that you get to find love at all, and I hope you'll look for it where you actually want to, now."

"Well, I did sort of lead you on and take up the last few months of your free time with a really slow build-up to nothing, so I was prepared for the worst."

I laugh, but I can see why he was worried. We both have things we need to come clean about. And now it's my turn. "Zander kissed me," I say cautiously, feeling an uncharacteristic blush steal up my face until it's hot.

"That man looks like he can kiss the hell out of anyone. Fuck, I bet he'd turn half my teammates if he really put some effort into it. How was it?" Knox looks up shyly, and I glimpse the real him staring out at me from his deep espresso eyes for the first time. He's vulnerable, but doing his best to let me in, and it opens my heart to him even more.

I think back to that first night Zander showed up at my house and had me play bartender for him while he worked through his work crises and whatever reasons had driven him to my doorstep. When he kissed me so gently, then said some of the most vicious words he could, I was left reeling.

"We were fighting. He just showed up at my house asking why we'd been suddenly thrown back together and why I hadn't told him about Hendricks. I told him I didn't owe him any explanations after he cut off all communication and ghosted me. It wasn't like either of us planned for a kiss to happen. One second we were arguing, and the next he had me in his arms, kissing me so fucking softly I didn't even think to stop him. When I called him out on it, he reminded me what hadn't been on the table and why I shouldn't have wanted him after. It was... confusing."

Knox whistles. "He's all up in your head, Harley, damn!"

I close my eyes in pain and lift my hand to stop him. "Okay, if we're going to be gay besties now, you have to stop calling me Harley. I have much better nicknames than a fucking mid-life crisis motorcycle manufacturer or a psychotic clown-loving baddie bitch. Pick anything else."

Knox leans his head back and laughs so hard he shakes the couch. "Why didn't you say something earlier? I wouldn't have called you that if I knew you didn't like it."

"I didn't have the heart when we were kind of dating. Now that you're out with me and I'm not trying to get you in my bed, you're getting everything unfiltered."

"Fine." Knox laughs again. "What would you prefer I called you?"

"My friends call me Lolo. I'd like you to be my friend."

"Friends is good. Since that's out of the way, *Lolo,*" he says, emphasizing the nickname before he continues. "Why is Zander Olsen fucking with your head now after, what, five years? He has the audacity to kiss you and then tell you that you shouldn't expect anything from him? Do I need to crack his head open?" He squeezes his massive fist until his knuckles pop ominously and gives me a look that tells me he would, if I asked him to.

I shake my head, but smile appreciatively. "I think Zander is confused by his own feelings, and it's messing with me," I answer, leaning back into the comfy couch cushion and blowing out a breath. "I don't know how to feel, or what to expect. He's so intense. One second, he's pushing me away, saying he blocked all contact because he never promised more, the next he's showing up wanting to know about Hendricks and, like, woo me, or something."

"Wait, I have to follow this up before you continue. Woo you? Do men know how to woo women in this century? That sounds like a romance novel, but, like, the ones from back in the day when they had Fabio on the cover. All shirtless dudes and fainting women with heaving bosoms."

"What do you know about romance novels, football player?" I ask, narrowing my eyes and wondering if I'm going to get to know the real Knox Contraire, reading habits and all.

He gives me a sheepish grin and rubs the back of his neck. "Truth? My mom loved those damn books. She would come home from the grocery store each week with a new paperback and leave them around the house. Even at a young age, I was interested in the dudes on the covers, so I would pick them up from time to time and read a few chapters, looking for the sex. Whatever was in those books was hot as hell when I was twelve."

"Oh my God, you're not kidding!" I say, leaning forward and grasping his arm. "I loved my mom's V.C. Andrews books when I was in my teens. Those were some messed up stories, though. Locking kids in attics, the brothers falling in love with their sisters. But the new romance authors putting stuff out now?" I purse my lips like I'm eating spicy food and fan my face. "It's even better. No closed-door bullshit. They tell you everything that is going down, from the intimate noises to what is going where and how the characters feel. It's hot."

"I wouldn't be opposed to borrowing some books," Knox says, laughing.

"I have a bunch that are male-male, too," I tell him, raising my eyebrows. "You don't have to read just straight romance to get your kicks anymore."

"No shit?" he says, his eyes widening and a look of genuine interest crossing his face. "They make gay romance novels now?"

I nod enthusiastically. "In whatever flavor you're into, whether it's vanilla or something kinkier. But they're usually love stories at heart, no matter who the characters are or what they're doing. I love them. I'll get you an e-reader and a list of titles you may like to download."

"I think that's the nicest thing someone has ever promised." He puts his hand on his chest and stares at me with true feeling. "You know, I think I like us even better this way. Thank you for making my first time coming out to someone so... easy. It's made the idea of telling my family a little less nauseating."

"Thank you for being your authentic self with me, even though you were scared of telling me. I like us this way, too."

He gives me a shy look before he moves his gaze away. "Will you still be my date to galas and events? I don't think I'm quite ready to come out to the world."

"Knox, I'd do anything for you, short of something that could get me thrown in jail because I have a kid who needs me here. Being your date to a gala would be totally fine."

"Good, because there's one this Saturday I've been asked to speak at, and I'd like you to come with me."

"You've got yourself a date."

Twenty-three

Zander

"What do four-year-olds like?" I muse aloud to Javi when we finish up for the day.

I can't stop thinking about the boy, Hendricks, and what he may be like. I may never know if Harlowe gets her way. It's Friday and business is shutting down for the weekend, despite the PR hell that still looms over Olympus like the plumes of smoke from war campfires. We have teams working overtime to rebound our stock prices and fix the Pegasus mess, but it's slow going, so I've had time to think. Too much time.

"I only know my nieces and nephews, man. I don't know if they're normal or not. I guess they like watching YouTube and anything created to market their favorite cartoons. Are we branching out into children's toys or something?"

I shake my head absently, still wondering if he's a cool little kid, or a total shit. Some kids just are, nothing the parents can do about it. I laugh to myself and feel Javi eyeing me in concern.

"No, we're not adding anything for kids to the Olympus umbrella. I was thinking that some kids are just jerks. I was wondering what mine would be like."

"Little psychos, I bet. Jumping down flights of stairs in towel capes, pretending to fly. Or launching themselves off the slide at max speed and knocking kids over. You're too much of an adrenaline junkie to have a kid be mild-mannered or chill. You deserve a kid that gives you regular heart attacks with their antics to make up for the shit you've put me through."

I laugh and start gathering my things to leave. "You ever think about settling down and having kids?"

"All the time. I want a big family someday. I'm one of five, you know. My *madre* is a firecracker. You ever get a *chancla* thrown at you, or is that just us Latin families?" he asks, wincing with the memory.

"My mother chased me with a fried chicken drumstick once when I broke her favorite Waterford Crystal vase practicing my standing backflip in the dining room. Not a sandal, but it was the closest thing at hand, and she ended up throwing it at me as I ran up the stairs."

"White people are weird, man," he says, shaking his head and preceding me into the elevator. "Are you thinking about kids because of Harlowe?" I look over at him quickly, but his face is open, and he seems to be genuinely curious.

"Yeah. I don't know if I'll be any good with kids. What if he hates me? That is, if Harlowe ever lets me close enough for him to hate me. But I don't know the first thing about kids, and I think I'm going to fuck this up if I do get the chance."

"Be interested in him. Kids want to show you their shit—drawings, toys, dumb dances they do that make no sense. They just want you to give them attention. You don't have to do anything special." He claps me on the back when we exit into the garage. "You'll be a good dad. I even think you'll make a good husband someday, if you ever decide to put the bachelor life behind you."

I bark out a laugh. "You think?" I shake my head as I reach my car. "You have absolutely no grounds to make that assumption. But thank you," I add after a pause. I nod my goodbye and climb into the car.

Put the bachelor life behind me... well, I have to start sometime, and apparently, it's what Olympus needs more than anything right now, so I may as well try. My drive home is short, and I look around my palatial penthouse of gleaming surfaces, white marble floors, surrounded by glass and metal walls that give me a clear view of downtown Atlanta. I shuck off my jacket and tie and settle myself in the pristine living room. Nothing about this space says kids or a family. I dial Harlowe, surprised the call connects after a few rings.

"Hello..." her throaty voice answers, and a shiver travels the length of my spine with that one cautious word.

"What are you doing tonight?" I ask, settling back into the plush leather seat with more confidence than I should have given the recipient of my call. She can see past my booty call language better than anyone, but I'm not really versed in a better tactic.

"Really, Zander? I've already seen you more in the last few weeks than I have in five years. What do you want?"

"You, Lowe."

She sighs heavily and says without much heat, "Liar. You never want what you've already had, so tell me the truth. Why are you so persistent now?"

"I want another chance. I may not have changed enough to make up for what I did to you, but I'm willing to be what I need to be now, and that's a father." I can't promise her I will be perfect, or that I've changed my ways entirely, but I'm telling her the truth; that need may supersede want for the first time in my life.

She's silent for so long I wonder if she's hung up on me, but finally, she responds. "I'm about to film a new recipe for my channel. Hendricks is out with my mom, but they'll be back before dinnertime. It's really boring, just me talking to a camera and resetting a bunch of times when I fuck up. There will be lots of food at the end. You could..." she pauses, blowing out a breath and making me wait like it's Christmas morning and I'm about to tear into a gift, "...come over?"

I'm off the sofa and grabbing my jacket before her words trail off. "Fuck yes. I'm on my way."

The drive feels ridiculously long, and with every second that ticks by feels like I'm losing out on my opportunity.

When I pull up to her house it feels different. I was angry, selfish, and looking for answers the last two times I tried this. Today, I was invited, which changes everything.

Harlowe answers the door wearing a white tank top and blue shorts with a soft bow that ties around her waist, emphasizing the narrow place my hands could rest above the swell of her wide hips and the long legs that seem to go on forever. Her hair is down around her shoulders, darker than it was when I could freely run my fingers through the thick lengths that fell around me when she was on top, riding me. The visual hits me out of nowhere and I nearly groan from the need that flares to life, wanting her again.

But she's all business, waving me inside and padding barefoot back to the kitchen that has been transformed into a mini studio. She has a camera on a tripod with an LCD screen behind the island, another camera angled down above her workstation, and two lights arranged on either side illuminating her workspace, which is neatly set up with bowls of ingredients at hand. She has pots and dishes stacked to the side, out of the frame, and a remote that she picks up and waves at me.

"You have to be quiet when I'm recording, and don't laugh at me or make me laugh. This is serious, Zander, even if you don't think it's as worthwhile as your business ventures because I'm not making millions."

I palm my chest and give her a look of astonishment. "I'm quite aware of the seriousness with which you take your job. I've been catching up on your videos, so I know how you do your thing. I'm a foodie now, you know."

She rolls her eyes. "I don't care what you are. I have to get this last dish filmed and photographed before this video is done. I mean, I'll have eight hours of editing to do after it's filmed. Between the uploading process, the caption writing, and the stills for social media, it will all take even more time. Basically, my weekend is fucked."

I hold up my hands in surrender to her busy schedule and motion for her to get to it, while I take a seat at a barstool at one end of the island, far from her camera set up. I stare at the veined marble and all I can see is the image of her lying in the middle of it, surrounded by snacks, her tits barely contained as the sunlight cut across her, that she posted to Instagram. Her fucking caption about bad girls swallowing you whole fists me in the gut, and I nearly groan with longing again. I look up, wanting to grab her by the chin and fuck her mouth, reminding myself just how good that feels right now.

After several attempts to talk about her dessert dish to her recording camera, she looks over at me and frowns, her brow drawing down in a way that is just adorable when I know she's actually frustrated.

"You're making me nervous," she pouts. "You have your intense gray psycho eyes on like you want to eat me, and I don't usually have an audience when I'm cooking."

"Come here," I say, pushing away from the edge of the island now that I've managed to get control of my cock and motioning her closer.

She narrows her eyes at me, but she does as I say, stopping a foot or so from my stool. I take her hands in mine, feeling her hesitation as her delicate muscles tighten, ready to pull away at the slightest wrong move from me.

"You are amazing to watch. I learned more from a few of your videos than I have my entire adult life cooking for myself. You also made me spit out my coffee laughing at least once, which is saying something, because your jokes are bad, but you're still funny without even trying."

"You have such a way with backhanded compliments," she says with faux sweetness and an acerbic smile. "You try being entertaining for an audience of millions while cooking and trying not to burn the house down or cut off a finger."

I stand and walk her backward around the island, her hands still caught in mine, until she's back on the squishy foam mat in front of her cooking setup. "Why don't you show me how you do it," I say, releasing her hands and hitting record on the small remote she has velcroed to the front of the cabinet, out of sight.

She blinks a few times, taking in my close proximity, then looks at the camera where she catches the red light and sees us standing next to each other on the small LCD screen. I can see when she makes up her mind. It comes in minor adjustments. The squaring of her shoulders and the intake of a deep breath. The smoothing of her hands along the marble and the shift of her hips. She transforms in front of my eyes, losing her nervous energy and radiating confidence, in her element once more and seemingly fine with me joining her here.

I pull at the unbuttoned collar of my white shirt and feel out of place, but I don't move as she begins talking to the camera, repeating her rehearsed lines and glibly indicating me at one point, but otherwise letting me stand near her unobtrusively. This time, she doesn't flub her lines and goes through the motions of the recipe steps with ease. I get lost in the way she weaves a story along the way, listening to her sweet rasp of a voice as I relax against the counter behind me.

"When I visited Singapore with my mom, she took me to the hotel she used to work at," she says, directing her story to the camera while she sprinkles in ingredients, but I'm caught in the spell she's weaving with the few words. "The bakers who made hundreds of desserts daily were so methodical, but each one told me they found pleasure in the steps, considering baking the culinary equivalent of science. Each ingredient must be measured precisely, or unintended consequences could arise and ruin the dessert."

"Or cause a happy accident?" I offer with a smile as I lean my hands on the countertop behind me to keep from touching her as she moves through the steps of her recipe with ease.

She turns and considers me while she stirs the batter in the bowl in front of her. "Sometimes, yes. But most of the time, too much of one ingredient can throw off the balance of the finished product." She turns back to the camera. "The hotel bakers needed to consistently create desserts by the batch. They didn't have room for errors *or* happy accidents."

"Good thing life doesn't have the same rules as a hotel kitchen," I say, moving to lean my forearms on the island so I can be next to her, but it's not enough, so I knock my shoulder into her side for more direct contact. I'm drawn to her whenever I'm in her presence, never getting my fill, and this is no exception.

"Don't distract me, I'm busy creating culinary science," she says. Then, with a wicked gleam lighting her eyes and quick as a flash, she glops a spoonful of batter on my face. She laughs, sounding shocked at herself, but pleased nonetheless. This is the Wildcat I know from the Maldives. She's still in there, and still keeping me on my toes.

I gingerly wipe batter from my eye and feel it drip from my nose with a plop onto the marble. "You're a naughty girl," I growl, my arms quickly encircling her waist to keep her close and rubbing my face against her neck and chest, smearing the batter onto her skin and making her squeal.

"I'm sorry, oh my God, stop," she pleads, laughing and squirming in my arms.

Instead of stopping, I give in to the feel of her and let my mouth trace over her collarbone, and lick up her neck to catch some of the batter I just put there. Harlowe makes a sound of surprise, but the grip she has on my shoulders tightens and her protests weaken. I find that spot on her neck and suck just the way I know will drive her wild and feel her writhe in my arms. Her back arches, body molding against mine, and I keep her there, biting at her neck again as my hand finds her ass, and press her tight against me, grinding against her softness. She makes a whimpering sound that I catch with my mouth as she turns her face to mine and opens to me, her hands in my hair, holding me close as I devour her mouth.

Fuck, she feels so good. She tastes even better than I remember, all honey and coconut, her plush lips soft and insistent against mine as my tongue sweeps against hers and captures a moan. I reach down and hook my hands behind her thighs and haul her up onto the counter without breaking our kiss, pulling her against me with my fingers digging into her ass and groaning into her mouth because she feels like heaven everywhere I touch and I can't get enough.

I can feel her pussy, hot even through our layers of clothing, as I rock against her with the steel hardness of my cock, and I bet she's fucking soaking her panties. I want to slide my hand in to see, part her folds with my fingers and feel how wet she is, then taste her. I pull away from her mouth with the intent of doing just that.

"Zander, please." The breathy plea isn't for more, and it snaps me out of my thoughts of eating her sweet pussy.

When I slowly release her, I'm cautious of the mood shift that just occurred. Having her in my arms felt so natural. Her curves fit against me even more perfectly than I remember, her skin warm and soft under my stubbly face. The taste of her drugging. My cock is rock hard from the brief moments I had her in my arms, my mouth on hers, and all I want is to feel her under me, on top of me, in front of me, again. But I acted without thinking, taking the physical from her without knowing if that's what she wanted. It sure as hell felt like she wanted to be in my arms, kissing me, but what do I know when it comes to Harlowe, now? She stares at me with wide eyes, her body trembling, and I don't know if it's from fear or from holding back.

"Now who's ruining the recipe?" I ask to break the tension, the words vibrating deep with need as I let my feelings infuse into them.

"You're right, I shouldn't have started that." Her own reply is breathless as she hands me a dish towel, and grabs another to clean off the bits of batter from the caramel skin of her chest.

I catch a stray bit of batter she's missed from the top of her cleavage and pop my finger in my mouth, tasting the honey and vanilla she stirred in a few steps prior. It tastes almost as good as she does. She holds my gaze, hand stilled from her task, mesmerized by the moment.

I nod at her camera and smile with evil intent. "I think that was some good footage. It'll whip your audience into a frenzy of speculation and set the internet on fire."

Fuck, it set me on fire. I want to watch the recording back over and over again to see how she reacted to my touch. I want her to put it online right the fuck now and show the world she belongs to me.

She looks at the camera and frowns, using the LCD screen as a mirror to clean off the rest of the batter. "It will probably end up deleted. I can't use that." She slides off the island and stops the recording.

"Don't you want more views? I don't really know how YouTube works, but wouldn't breaking the internet be a good thing for you? Because that's what that little moment would do."

A part of me is desperate to convince her to use it. It's the part of me that is fully on board with breaking every rule, with throwing caution to the wind, and finally giving in to the attachments I've always run from.

It's funny how quickly that part of me could be swayed for the right situation, the right woman, and how desperate I am now for her to be mine. It's been there for five years, simmering under the surface of casual hookups and meaningless sex, knowing that I'd already found the best fucking thing to ever happen to me and I'd let it go, severed it from my life, because I was a fucking coward and couldn't figure out how to make that work in the life I'd created. Now I'm willing to put it ahead of everything else, but I may be too late.

"It would be a hell of a way to announce we're making this work."

She considers my words for a moment, pursing her lips and shaking her head. "This isn't going to work. I need someone solid and dependable. Someone like Knox. You like novelty and would be done with this as soon as the shine wore off. I've already been through that and I can't do it again, Zander."

Her words are a bucket of ice water over my head, dousing me in reality. She'll never trust my ability to change unless I show her. I have to get rid of the fucking football player first. I won't share her, but this isn't my choice to make. I have to convince her I'm the only man she needs in her life, the only man that could complete the family we've created and I've missed out on for years. Before she can get around to telling me to leave, the front door opens and a flurry of noise and activity tornadoes into the house and my heart rate ratchets up with it.

Harlowe turns to me with wide, nervous eyes. "That's Hendricks. Don't make me regret this. You have one chance with him, Zander, don't fuck it up," she whispers.

I feel my hope deflate with her words, while a new anticipation twists my stomach into knots at the prospect of meeting the source of the noise and movement. *Will he like me? Will Harlowe introduce me as his father?*

My brain short circuits and I'm left with just white noise as soon as he rounds the corner to the kitchen, the world slowing down and my vision tunneling so all I see is the boy. He's radiant, dark hair curling softly around his face, gray eyes animated as he heads for Harlowe, holding out toy cars clutched in his fists. He launches himself into her arms, his little voice running a stream of chatter the whole time. She catches him with a practiced ease that makes me oddly jealous, standing up with him wrapped around her, completely absorbed by his story and laughing a full, unguarded laugh at something he says.

The moment is frozen in my brain, a snapshot in time that will stay with me the rest of my life—Harlowe holding her boy, *my son*, lit by production lights, surrounded by the familiar tableau of her kitchen, an indulgent smile just for him—is seared into my retinas and instantly filed away in the most beautiful sights folder of my brain. It instantly replaces Machu Picchu at sunrise and resides next to the hundred other snapshots of her in the Maldives that live there already.

"Hendricks, I want you to meet someone," Harlowe says, setting the boy down and angling her body towards me. "This is my friend, Zander."

I don't even let her *friend* comment get to me because I have the full attention of this little person to contend with, and I need to make the best first impression possible.

"Hi," he says, eyeing me for half a second before he decides I'm worthy of his attention. He holds out his hands.

"This is Optimus Prime and this guy's the Batmobile. Who do you want to be?"

"Batmobile, for sure," I say, with a quick look at Harlowe. She's tense, her hands clasped at her stomach as she watches us. She gives me a small nod when I answer. I notice a well-dressed Asian woman standing unobtrusively on the other side of the island, watching the introduction with a sharp eye. This must be Harlowe's mother. She raises an eyebrow at me when she catches me staring, then inclines her head at Hendricks as if to say *back to him, idiot.*

"Want to build a racetrack for them? I have lots of Legos and blocks, come see." He doesn't wait for me to answer, holding out the Batmobile for me to take, then grabs my free hand. His own little hand is strong as he pulls me into the living room, and I savor the warmth and reassurance of it before he lets go to quickly dump out a plastic tote filled with blocks on the carpet.

So, that was it? I was just accepted by this little kid when he asked to play. Maybe four-year-olds are simpler than I thought they would be to win over. Simple or not, I know my world just got turned upside down and will never be the same. All the complications of life just dimmed, my focus narrowing down to one universal truth that replaces everything: this is my child and I will do anything to make sure he is happy, safe, and has everything his little heart could want, including me and his mother working together, rather than against each other.

Twenty-four

Harlowe

"Don't say a word," I whisper to Mom as she fights the smile that tugs at her lips while staring at me.

My heart is hovering somewhere in the region of my ass as Hendricks leads Zander into the living room to play. It's a sight I never expected to see, and it fills me with equal parts dread at the potential for this to go badly, and elation that my sweet son and his father are meeting for the first time and Zander seems perfectly happy about it.

"I guess you finally let him in. What changed your mind?" she asks, leaning on the island next to me as I stare at the two of them on the rug playing with toys.

Zander looks perfectly at home, his large frame sprawled on the ground creating a track with Hendricks in his charcoal gray slacks and crisp white shirt, sleeves rolled up. It shouldn't look so… normal. Or, damn, have so much sex appeal it hits me with a flood of warmth right in my center. As if my thong wasn't already ruined by whatever that was in the kitchen a few minutes ago, seeing him playing with Hendricks now decimates the thin fabric and threatens to send me to my room with the need to change if this keeps up.

"I don't know," I finally answer, truthfully. "It doesn't seem fair to keep Zander out of Hendricks' life because I don't like how things went with us. It's not really my choice, is it?"

"It will always be your choice. You're his mother. But I'm glad you let him in and are giving him the opportunity to get to know his son." She wraps an arm around my waist and tilts her head on my shoulder.

His son. A feeling of trepidation passes through me with her words. He's always been mine. Now I've exposed him to the man who hurt me the most, and there's a part of me that doesn't trust his motivations now. If he hurts Hendricks... well, Zander will feel the extent of my wrath if he so much as disappoints my boy.

"Hendricks seems pleased. He has a captive audience willing to build racetracks with him."

I shake myself from the thoughts of potential heartbreak and snort out a laugh, because that's saying something. Hendricks has more interest in building things than I have patience or time to indulge, and too often I have to tell him I'm too busy to play on the floor and exercise his robust imagination. Zander is currently connecting blocks into towers and creating a cityscape for Hendricks's track to wind through. He's giving his full attention to the task, asking Hendricks questions about which colors he should make each tower, or how high they should be, and engaging him like they're equals and the job at hand the most important thing he could be doing.

I feel tears prick my eyes and sniffle them back so they don't fall. Deep down, in the recesses of my heart, this is what I'd hoped I would have gotten from the Zander who whisked me around the world on a tropical vacation and made me feel like the only woman who mattered. Before I knew the cruelty he was capable of.

I straighten up, determined not to get lost in my feelings and the what-ifs of a naïve young woman who thought she could change a man. Or be swayed by the jaded, sex-starved woman who wants to get fucked hard by that very same man.

"I have to finish filming this recipe. It shouldn't take too long, and then we'll have my honey cake for dessert."

"Will the handsome gentleman be staying for dinner?" Mom asks, pulling away and looking at the mess of cake batter on the island from earlier.

Making that mess could have gotten us into trouble. I was so close to ripping his clothes off and making him take me right there in the kitchen. God, was that hot. *Nope, focus, don't go there, Harlowe.*

"If he'd like to," I answer hesitantly.

I have a healthy take on an orange chicken dish I made for the channel earlier that's ready to go, and of course there are at least four servings, so it would feed us all. I don't know if Zander even wants to stay. He could be humoring me now by playing with Hendricks, but he might pull back when he gets bored with entertaining a four-year-old and wants to leave. He may have dinner plans for himself, or even a date.

The icy fingers of the thought skate up my back and thread into the hair at the nape of my neck, forcing my head to look back into the living room where Zander is still on the floor. A hot rage follows the path the ice took and burns through me. Would he have come here tonight with the sole intention of meeting Hendricks, take a detour to make out with me in the kitchen, just to leave and fuck another woman? I couldn't put it past him, that's for sure.

Did he touch me like he had earlier just for the camera? His tongue had seared a path along my skin, his breath hot and tempting. He hauled me up onto the counter and pulled me against him as easily as if I'd still been in model shape, not forty pounds heavier. Had it been for show because he thought he was helping me, or because he couldn't keep his hands off of me? How do I know I can trust him now, when I don't know all of his motivations? I have too many questions and not enough privacy to ask them, so I shut down my wayward thoughts.

"Well, I'm going to ask him," Mom says, pushing away from the island and making her way into the living room. She settles on the couch and gets Zander's attention. I watch as they have a quiet conversation I can only catch snippets of over Hendricks's continued stream of chatter.

Zander looks up and catches my eye. He looks curious, and questioning. When I nod yes, a brilliant smile splits his face and erases the small lines of tension from his skin. I suck in a breath at the way that one smile hits me in the gut, twisting the air from my lungs. It's a smile of promise, of joy, but also calculation. I don't trust that smile, no matter how much I want to.

I'm able to finish filming my recipe quickly, taking photos of the finished product once I pull it out of the oven, and cleaning up my production mess while Hendricks commands the attention of his father and grandmother. Dinner is ready shortly after, and I join the group in the living room to let them know.

Zander is on his stomach on the rug, mirroring Hendricks across from him, explaining how an engine works in terms simple enough for a four-year-old to understand. He's pointing out axles on the Hot Wheels car he holds, showing how the engine creates power to turn the wheels, which moves the car. Hendricks has his most serious and concentrated face on as he follows each step of the process, like he will be tasked with reporting back on it. He'll likely be telling me about this very thing for days, the little sponge for information that he is.

"Sorry to interrupt the fun, but dinner is ready. Time to clean up and eat, Hendricks."

"Mo-om," Hendricks whines, looking up at me from the midst of his toy-strewn play area. "We just finished the track. I can't clean it up without testing it out."

"Hmm," I say, considering him. "How about one race to test it out? But just the one. It's bath and bedtime after dinner, and you know we don't leave a mess out when you go to bed just in case Alfred decides to eat your toys."

"Fine," he grumbles, already hunting for his racing vehicle of choice.

"Alfred?" Zander asks as he pushes himself up into a sitting position.

"The robot vacuum. It runs in here overnight and we've had a few Lego-related disasters and meltdowns thanks to Alfred." My explanation sounds so childish, but Zander nods in complete understanding.

"Robot butlers aren't the best at knowing what is a mess and what is a perfectly good track, right, Boss?" he asks.

"Right, Zan Man," Hendricks answers back, having secured his car.

I look between them. "Nicknames?"

"That one is way better than the previous option," Mom supplies for the guys, who are crawling across the rug to the start of their track, which covers a large portion of the space. "Hendricks kept trying to rhyme his name with a silly song, so he had Zander bobander banana fana bo bana before they shortened it."

"Didn't roll off the tongue quite so easily," Zander supplies. "Alright, Boss, this is the race that will cement your status as the best track builder in the world. Let's make it good."

"Three, two, go!" Hendricks calls excitedly, pushing his car down the track with all the noise and engine sounds he believes required. He continues along the track, weaving through block towers and around toy obstacles. When he completes the track, he launches the car off the rug and throws his hands in the air.

Zander rushes over and scoops him up, twirling him around, and making crowd noises as my little boy laughs and squeals. "And that, ladies and gentlemen, was the best race, on the best track, in the best place, we have ever seen," he says in a mock announcer voice before setting Hendricks down.

"Best. Track. Ever!" Hendricks says, jumping up and high-fiving Zander's outstretched palm.

"Absolutely, little dude. Now, how fast do you think we can break it down and put everything away?" Zander asks, like he's issuing a challenge. "I bet I can get all the towers put away before you can clean up the tracks."

"No way, I'm faster," Hendricks says, dropping to the rug and pulling pieces of track up as fast as his little hands allow.

I watch as Zander smiles indulgently, giving him a head start, then he also drops to the rug and grabs fistfuls of blocks to stuff back into their containers, and the race is on.

Hendricks is a good kid, but he isn't normally as inter-ested in the clean-up portion as he is in the mess-making part. I never expected Zander, of all people, to be good with kids, but he's just proved he can not only play with a child, but also incentivize him to clean up without argument. I cross my arms and tilt my head as I watch the two of them now, scrambling around on all fours, Hendricks giggling as Zander blocks him from a section of track by collapsing his body on top of it.

An ache blooms in my chest as all the things I wished I could have play out in front of me, and I still can't fucking trust any part of this, no matter how much I want to.

Twenty-five

Zander

Harlowe's dinner is damn good, but it's no surprise, given her career direction. The conversation is flowing and easy between me and her mother, Lily, and Hendricks seems intent on holding my attention when he isn't taking neat bites of his dinner at his mom's insistence. So why do I feel the draft of an icy wind from Harlowe? She's perfectly civil, but she's avoiding my eyes, and only speaking to me when she has to.

Haven't I shown her I want to be here, with them both? Can't she see I'm trying my best to be the person her kid needs? Why isn't that thawing the frozen tundra of her acceptance of me into her life?

"I'll take care of bath and bedtime. Zander, why don't you help Harlowe clean up?" Lily says, when Hendricks announces he's done with dinner.

"Can you come back to play again, Zan Man?" Hendricks asks, stopping next to my chair on his way around the table. "I had fun with you today."

Fuck. What is this feeling in my chest? It's warm and fuzzy and my brothers would have a field day if they knew how high the words of this four-year-old just got me. It feels like falling out of the sky, the adrenaline rush pushing every last thought out of my head except for yes, that's exactly what I want, to be a part of this boy's life. I look up at Harlowe, a smile freezing on my face when I see the stricken look on hers. She catches me looking and immediately averts her gaze as she gets up, clearing the table with hurried movements.

"I had fun with you too, Boss. You just let your mom know when you want me to stop by and she can call me, okay? I know you're probably pretty busy, but we can try to make our schedules work, because this was the best night I've had in a long time." I look up at Harlowe when I say that, and catch her eyes with mine. I mean it, and I want her to feel the utter sincerity in the sentiment.

Hendricks puts his arms up and captures my attention again. I turn and scoop him up into my chest and let him hug me around the neck. I tentatively wrap my arms around his little body, so fragile and small, taking the affection and reveling in the feeling of something so innocent, so pure, wanting to hold me. Soon, Hendricks is wiggling, and I set him down so he can hug and kiss Harlowe before following Lily to the back of the house.

I stand from the table, gathering dishes and walking them to the kitchen where Harlowe is already loading the dishwasher. I set the stack of plates on the counter and walk up behind her, my hands flattening on either side of the sink, boxing her in with my body, ensuring she knows

I want to be here, making her feel every part of me so she can't escape this time.

"That went better than I hoped," I say quietly, my breath moving the hair around her face from our close-ness. It's still not close enough. I want to be inside of her, our bodies pressed together along every line, every limb entwined.

She sets down the glass she was rinsing in the sink and turns off the water. I feel her take a deep breath before she responds. "Hendricks seems to like you. And you...you're actually really good with him."

Hearing her say that eases some of the tension in me that stems from thinking I'd be a huge fuck up. I wrap one arm around her waist and pull her tight against me. "Of course I am," I say, putting bravado into my tone that belies the nerves I'd experienced when he blew into the house and I was confronted with the consequences of one night and the unintended agony I'd caused in the aftermath. "I'm good at everything I do." That last part is growled just a hair from her ear, and she shivers.

"Zander, stop." Harlowe's words are a quiet plea without the warmth I would have expected from my proximity.

I step away from her, giving her space before she can ask for it. I know I'm treading on thin ice, only here because she allowed me, and despite being desperate to rush in and take everything I want, including her, I have to play this smart.

"What can I do, Lowe?"

She turns, her hand resting at the base of her throat, fingers spread like she's keeping herself from speaking, or holding herself back. A pained expression crosses her face and she looks down for a beat before her eyes meet mine. The pain and struggle I see mirrored in her gorgeous, fathomless chocolate eyes nearly brings me to my knees. What the fuck did I do now to put *that* look there?

"I need to be able to trust you. I can't let you into Hendricks's life on a whim, or for some passing fancy, you have that drives you on your quest to try new things. If you're serious about being here for him, you have to prove it."

She steps toward me, her finger outstretched, accusing me of the very things that have been my rules in the past. I let her come closer and feel my muscles tense and ache as I barely keep from touching her, knowing this is what she needs from me. To listen to her, hear the words she is saying, and take them seriously.

"You can't get bored at playing a father, and you can't fucking pull away from him if you're over the cute bonding moments and life gets real. He deserves someone steadfast and strong enough to be there when it's not fun. He needs a father who will be able to tell him no as often as yes, to make sure he learns balance and restraint. He needs someone who won't walk away when he's throwing a tantrum, or whining, or being a little shit, because he's a *kid*, Zander. He will have his bad days when he's less likable, but he will need you to love him despite it."

Her words convey four years of experience. Hard-won truths she's discovered because she had to. Harlowe never had the option to turn away from the little boy who needs her so much, not even when, as she says, he is less likable. I'm jealous of her experience and the way she knows him. But I fucking brought that on myself. Now I have to live with that truth just as much as the fact that I will never get the last four years of his firsts back. The first smile, first word, and first steps will never be mine. Harlowe got all of those because I couldn't find it in me to break from my rules, not even when I knew I had something special, because it fucking scared me.

I've been a real piece of shit.

And now I'm here because my brothers want me to man up and do the right thing, and bring up the public perception of our company, while I'm at it. I still don't have the best motives, despite my desire to have a relationship with Hendricks, and see where Harlowe and I can find our second chance in the process. No wonder she's being hesitant and untrusting. I've never given her any reason to trust me, only the opposite.

"I can't promise to be perfect," I say, running a hand through my hair and considering the effect my words may have on her. "But I'm here because I want to be a part of that little boy's life more than anything. And I want to be a part of yours. Let's try this, Lowe."

"That's the thing, Zander. This isn't something you can just try." Her eyes are sad, like she's already written off any attempts I could make. "You're either in, or you're not. That's the kind of person Hendricks deserves. That I deserve, too."

I don't know if I can say the words she's looking for, because I don't know what they are, and I'm not sure they would be true. All I can do is give her everything she deserves, and it starts with me turning over a new leaf. I have to figure out how to be a better man.

I reach out and cup the back of her head, pulling her close and kissing her forehead gently before releasing her. "Thank you for letting me in tonight. Thank you for everything. Goodnight, Lowe." Before the worst parts of me can be swayed by the closeness of her body and all I want to do with it, I walk out of that warm, comfortable house, with the beautiful little family I want so fucking badly to be mine.

Twenty-six

Zander

"Hello, little Paige, this is some event," I say, slinging an arm around my sister-in-law's shoulders as I look around the swanky event space of the gala she's hosting for her foundation, The Elysium Garden Project. The foundation is a combination of a community garden and the Big Brothers, Big Sisters program with a business focus. It feeds inner-city communities while teaching business skills, or so that's the idea she and my brother came up with.

"Well, hello to you too, Zander," she says, peering up at me. "Glad you could make it. What, no date? I gave you a plus one if you wanted it. I figured you'd bring one of your models with you." She purses her bright red lips and scans the area as if one will magically materialize.

"Stop touching my wife before I break your arm," Hayes growls, appearing as if summoned by the mere presence of another man too close to his lady. He forces himself between me and Paige, wrapping a possessive arm around her waist, displacing me entirely.

I gracefully side-step away to avoid the very real threat. One wrong word and his big, meaty hand will be around my throat, and I prefer breathing without a collapsed trachea.

"Rub salt in the wound your wife was just inflicting, why don't you, Hater." I turn back to Paige. "No date. There's only one woman I'd want on my arm and she's not too interested at the moment, but I'm working on it," I say with more candor than I've ever used around them. New man, new me, and all that bullshit. I guess I have to live it even when I'm not around Harlowe.

Paige gapes at me before a huge smile lights her face. "Wait, what? You, Mr. No Attachments, have lost your mind over a woman? I love this so much! I need all the details!" She hugs Hayes, and he looks down at her with an affectionate smile that we never see from him in the office. He only glowers at us. Rude.

"What a lovely little family reunion this is," Payton says as he joins our huddle of Olsens in the large and crowded ballroom, saving me from explaining my situation to Paige. "Why are we all over here in a corner? Shouldn't you two be out there schmoozing money from all the people who showed up? That's what this gala is for if I'm not mistaken." He nods his head at Paige and Hayes.

"Thanks for the reminder, Payton. We really should be looking for funding for our second year, which is looking to double the amount of gardens we will be putting in," Paige says, turning big green eyes on him. "But I would rather just celebrate our first year of successfully operating the Elysium Garden Project over here a little longer before I have to ask people to contribute." Paige bites her red lip and scans the room packed with people in formalwear warily. While she is perfectly at home hosting lavish affairs, she doesn't relish being in the spotlight if she can help it.

"Isn't that why we have a guest speaker? He's supposed to tug on the purse strings with whatever speech he'll give during dinner so you don't have to," Hayes says, smoothing a hand over her shoulder and rubbing her neck to ease her worries. She visibly melts into his touch and I find myself jealous that he can have that kind of effect on her.

"Who'd you sucker into that role?" I ask with a laugh at her look of relief instead of giving into my own feelings of what I would give to have Harlowe melting under my own hands. I look around the crowded ballroom that is filled with lavishly set tables decorated with beautiful florals befitting the garden project the gala is benefitting. Hayes and Paige could easily fund the project themselves, but find that philanthropic pursuits are good for others as well, and opened up their second year of the foundation to donors.

"Knox Contraire, from the Atlanta Condors. He's been so wonderful this year, volunteering his time at so many of the garden sites. He's a favorite of the kids and has a way with speeches, so it was a given that he would share his experience helping with the program," Paige says, grinning innocently at me.

I go still, feeling a hot rage seep into my blood. The fucking football player who has had his hands all over Harlowe. Is she going to be here with him? I wouldn't be surprised, since they're dating. Fuck. He's a complication I've conveniently forgotten in my haste to get back into Harlowe's life.

"Isn't that him over there? He's hard to miss at six-six. The dude is huge," Payton supplies, a hint of humor in his tone, and I glare his way to catch where he's looking.

I turn my head and feel the air leave my lungs, but it's not the brick house of a football player I see, it's the stunning vision in black beside him that knocks the breath out of me. Harlowe, looking like a sparkling night-wrapped goddess, stands regal and proud at his side and I take her in like the air I breathe. Her golden skin glows against the inky black of her long dress, a slit cut high up one thigh nearly to her hip, showing off her entire leg. One shoulder is bared, the material gathered over the other in an asymmetrical design, and her waist looks impossibly small, her hips swelling below invitingly so I want to trace my hands everywhere her curves go. Her hair is caught up in some sort of classy low knot with soft wisps around her face and I want to put my fingers into it and pull, messing it up as I bury myself inside of her.

I snap my eyes away. My cock already embarrassingly hard, and I have to turn to adjust myself discreetly to avoid my family discovering just how affected I am by seeing her across the fucking room. I don't know if I can do this, be here with her in this ballroom and not have her with me, my hands on her, or putting her in my lap where she belongs. Fuck.

"Time to find our seats. Looks like y'all saved me from having to make any additional awkward conversations. Thank goodness for three broody, giant men," Paige says, pulling on Hayes's hand when the music quiets and the lights dim. "You're all sitting at our table. Come on." She snags my tux sleeve as she passes and I have to follow after them like a fucking puppy. It's a hell of a lot better than sitting at another table with a bunch of random people, though.

We wind our way to a table near the center and take our seats. I lounge in mine as I quickly scan the place cards and see there is an empty seat next to mine, as well as next to Payton's. Paige sees my look and shakes her head sadly as she tsks at me.

"I told you I gave you plus ones. It's not my fault you both came alone. Read your invitations next time." She shrugs at me. "Our table is going to be on the empty side, unfortunately."

"Is it just us four?" I ask, feeling relief wash over me.

Paige's cheeks redden, but she gets a big smile and seems to glow with excitement as she looks over my shoulder quickly and then back at me. "Nope. We have two more. Knox and his date will be joining us. Have you heard of Harlowe Sorenson? She's a cookbook author and I love her YouTube channel. I've been following it for a few months now since Knox started dating her and told me about it. I can't wait to meet her. Don't mind me if I fangirl. I'll try to keep it together, but no promises."

I fight the urge to palm my face. Of fucking course, fate would do this to me. Paige doesn't do social media and hates the Atlanta Haute List even more than I do, so she's likely not aware of the connection Harlowe and I have. Hayes probably hasn't told her about my situation, with how adamant he's been about me proving Hendricks is mine through a paternity test. Paige is so innocent and has no idea what kind of mess she's inadvertently created just by seating us all at the same table tonight. This could get so fucking ugly. I'm liable to explode in rage if I have to watch Knox touch Harlowe. Paige jumps up from her chair and I know I have to get my shit together for what I'm about to endure.

"Knox, hi, thank you so much for joining us tonight!" Paige says, rushing around the table to shake the giant man's hand.

"Of course, Paige. I'm happy to be here and support the mission of your foundation," Knox says, his low voice smooth and velvety and I hate the sound of it on principle. I hate everything about him. From the way he has a hand on Harlowe's back, to the way he stands beside her, dwarfing her in every way and looking so good next to her. They're a fucking matching pair with his classy all-black tux and her gorgeous black dress. Well, two of us can wear bespoke tuxes, fucker, and I bet I have the better tailor.

I watch as Paige grows a bit starstruck when she faces Harlowe, and it's kind of cute to see my sweet young sister-in-law, who herself is a billionaire, owns the fastest-growing distillery in the South, and sits on the Board of Directors for the largest boutique hotel group in the country, vibrate with excitement and trip over herself at the prospect of meeting Harlowe.

Granted, Harlowe is the fiercest woman I know and exudes confidence and power. She's also a woman I've fucked to tears and is the mother of my beautiful child, a woman that I'm desperate to have a shot with again. Who knew a situation like this would ever play out the way it is?

"Harlowe, oh my goodness, it is so nice to meet you! I'm Paige Fairchild Olsen and I'm a huge fan. I watch all of your videos and I love your cookbook. I've been working through all the recipes since I got it and everything has been amazing. I think my husband would agree, right Hayes?" she says, waving her hand behind her to elicit a response from my brother, who is now rising from his seat at her insistent beckoning.

"You're so sweet. Thank you for saying such nice things. I appreciate it," Harlowe says, genuine warmth on her face as she takes Paige's outstretched hands in her own. Belatedly, she seems to register who is at the table with Paige, glancing around, then taking in the hulking presence of Hayes as he stands behind Paige. "You," she bites out with quiet fury, her eyes narrowing at Hayes.

Paige looks between Hayes and Harlowe, confusion removing the animated joy she was just experiencing. "I'm sorry, I don't understand."

I'm on my feet in a moment and at Harlowe's side, called to action by that fury, facing down my eldest brother with murderous intent as the rest of the table stares at us in shock. There is history in that one word, and from the way Hayes evaded my questioning the first day Harlowe was brought up in the boardroom, I know they had a tense run-in, and if this is her reaction, it wasn't pretty for her.

"Lowe, baby, I'm here," I whisper in her ear, not sure what I want to convey, other than I am on her side. I put a reassuring arm around her waist and feel her stiffen.

She whips her head my way, then back to Hayes. "Excuse me," she bites out, her voice shaking with undisguised rage. She turns away from us and leaves the table. Knox catches her hand and she whispers something to him and he nods, then returns to the table and sits. Fucking coward.

I stride around the table to Hayes, who gently moves Paige behind him, and Payton stands to intercept whatever brawl may be brewing between us. We stand together, a triad of powerful brothers among a sea of black-tie revelers not quite seated for a formal dinner, some aware of our presence, others completely oblivious. We couldn't care less what anyone else thinks of our family squabbles.

"What the fuck happened?" I quietly snarl. "Five years ago."

"I already told you everything," Hayes snaps. "She came to Olympus looking for you and I told her you didn't want to see her. I don't know why she would still be angry."

"There has to be more. She wouldn't be that pissed to see you now if you just wouldn't let her see me," I press, keeping my voice quiet to avoid making a scene for Paige's sake, but I'm radiating with anger. My hands shake with the urge to wrap around his neck and force the truth out of him, all because of one word from Harlowe's lips when she saw my brother. I would bring this entire place down on Hayes's head for her.

Hayes shrugs his big shoulders and looks over at Paige, standing several feet away and studying us with a worried expression. "I may have offered her a lot of money to stay away. But it doesn't matter, she refused."

Payton groans, shoving a hand in his hair, and looks visibly disturbed by that revelation. "Seriously, Hayes? We always keep that as a last resort kind of thing. We never actually offer any of his hookups money. Why did you think to try it on this one?"

My blood boils, my entire body shaking with the effort not to break Hayes's cold face right here as I meet his steely green eyes. He doesn't even look embarrassed. "You treated her like a whore and you're surprised she still hates you? You fucking idiot. She probably came to tell me she was pregnant, which she wouldn't have wanted to tell you, and you offered her money to fucking disappear. Some brother you are." I push away from Hayes, but he grabs my jacket and keeps me close for one last parting shot to my ego.

"You're the fucking asshole who made that the only choice I had in the matter. If you weren't fucking everything once and discarding it like a spoiled child with a broken toy, leaving me and Payton to clean up after you, I may have had an alternative option and would've thought to let her see you. You brought this on yourself."

He shoves me away and returns to the table, pulling out a seat for Paige before taking his own and leaving me to soak in the cold truth of his harsh words.

Payton puts a hand on my shoulder and leans his head into mine, holding me in place as I make to leave. "Don't let him get to you. We've only ever wanted to protect you. You trend toward self-destructive tendencies and we never wanted anything to bite you in the ass later. Hayes did what he thought he had to in the situation. Was it right? No, but we can't change that, now."

"Fuck off," I growl, pushing Payton's hand from my shoulder. It may be the truth, but I don't want him fucking rubbing it in right now. Maybe if I had done things differently, like Hayes said, I wouldn't be fighting with my brothers over how they treated a woman I slept with, because maybe she would be here with me tonight and I wouldn't be jealous of another man who brought her, instead. Fucking hell.

I turn away from the table of my family and the fucking football-playing giant who didn't think it was worth going after his visibly upset date, pushing around people, not caring if I'm being rude. I need to find Harlowe. I need to start changing the past and everything I set into motion that got me to this fucked up spot where I've broken everything that could have been so fucking beautiful.

Twenty-seven

Harlowe

Of course I would run into Zander and his scary asshole brother here. I lean against the wall in the first bathroom I spotted when I exited the ballroom on my escape from that awkward interaction. I knew the gala was for a foundation Knox has been working with this past year; I just hadn't asked which one, or who runs it.

Seeing the green-eyed brother, Hayes, brought back all of those feelings of pain, anger, and fear I had experienced in those weeks and months I spent crawling out of the heartbreak Zander had left me in when we returned from our trip. That terrifying aura of death was still there, though somehow tempered by his sweet wife. How he managed to find someone as seemingly nice as her I can't begin to decipher, but stranger things have happened. Like Zander wanting to get to know Hendricks now, and trying to get back into my life after writing me off so thoroughly.

I wash my hands for something to do, since standing in here is earning me weird looks from the other ladies who come in to do their business or refresh their lipstick. I don't know how I'm going to make it through an entire dinner at the same table with the man who treated me like a common whore and Zander both, while Knox gives his speech. Would it be rude to just stay in here the whole time and hide? Yes, and I'm no coward. I can do this, even if I have to play the role of an unaffected supporter the whole night and pretend nothing weird happened. I can do this.

I straighten and look at myself in the mirror. I look damn fine. Paloma went all out, pulling an incredible dress from her designer contacts and styling me like I'm attending a Hollywood awards show rather than a charity gala, but it feels good to look good and it's nice to not be battling my physical insecurities on top of everything else. It's like armor, and I'll need it to make it through dinner without losing my temper, my mind, or my patience. Or all three, given the family seated at that table that I need to return to.

I push back out into the hall and immediately have to stop before I run into the broad, unyielding chest of someone. I inhale the intoxicating scent of storms and sandalwood as I gasp. Not someone, *Zander*.

"There you are," he says, taking my hand tightly in his and pulling me further down the hall away from the ballroom. "Are you okay? I've been looking everywhere for you."

"I'm fine, Zander, now let me go. We're missing the gala; people will talk," I hiss.

"Let them fucking talk." His tone is unyielding, and all I can do is follow where he leads.

He hustles us through doors and halls, looking this way and that until he finds an unoccupied room that I don't get a good look at before he closes the door and pushes me up against it roughly, one hand tight on my waist and the other on my throat, tipping my chin up as his mouth comes crashing down over mine, stealing my breath in a moment. His lips are firm and insistent and it takes me a second to realize that mine are parting, welcoming his tongue that is teasing along the seam.

He takes that invitation and plunders my mouth, his tongue sliding along mine in just the way he knows drives me wild and I lose it. All the restraint, the anger, the hesitance, and the terror at the thought of getting hurt again shatters as he kisses me. I think of him lying on the floor playing with Hendricks, begging me to be a part of our lives. I think of him following me up my driveway saying he wants a second chance with me, and his voice breaking with the urgency. I think of that first night he followed me around my kitchen and kissed me through his own confusion, like he couldn't stop himself even if he wanted to. My arms wrap around his shoulders, hands claw into his hair, holding him close and taking the kiss as much as he is.

Fuck, I need this, too. It feels so reassuring to be wanted, to know he came after me, that the first thing he wanted to do was kiss the hell out of me. I bite and suck at him, and he groans, hand sliding from my waist to the slit in my dress and caressing the exposed bit of my thigh that shows before hitching my leg over his hip and grinding his impressively hard cock right into my center. I whimper as he trails his hand around my thigh and dips the tip of a finger under the edge of my thong and swirls into the slickness he is creating. He groans as he coats his finger in my heat and rolls his hips again. I moan and push back into him, hunting for that elusive friction, lost in the moment, not at all in my right mind, sure I will regret this if I give myself a second to even consider the situation. But right now, we're all feelings and no thoughts, and damn does Zander Olsen know how to make me feel good.

Zander is the one to slow the kiss, nipping at my bottom lip and pulling away with a hazy look as he stares at my lips. He keeps my leg around his hip, removing his finger from my slick heat, but the feeling of him hard against my core is a testament to whatever restraint he is using not to push his pants down and move my dress and thong aside and bury himself inside of me right now. He brushes his thumb along my bottom lip and dips it into my mouth until I suck it in, feeling it pop free when he slowly pulls it out. I gaze at his lips, willing them to come back, to kiss me again, for his hips to roll into me again, to give me that bit of friction that would feel so good.

"I fucking hate that you're here with another man tonight." His voice is rough, angry, but his touch is still soft where he cups my cheek. "I don't like him touching you, or that you look good next to him, and that he's probably so much better for you than I'll ever be. God,

I want to fucking destroy him." His gray eyes are hard, electricity crackling in the depths.

He tips his head forward and bites at my exposed neck, hard, punishing me for being Knox's date, yet finding that place that makes me shudder and go liquid in his arms, anyway. He rolls his hips into me again, making me whimper. He licks the spot on my neck to soothe the sting and brings his forehead up against mine, his eyes shut tight.

"But the way you just kissed *me*. The way your pussy is wet for *me* right now. That gives me hope." His eyes open and I see the gray smoke and ash of those fires from so long ago of the hope he is speaking of that once flared so brightly in me, too. "Hope is a very dangerous thing for a man like me. It will make me do all kinds of crazy shit."

I finally find my voice after the whirlwind of running into him and the kiss. "What kind of crazy shit? Are you going to go psycho on me?" I arch an eyebrow at him, looking to lighten the mood and get myself out of what is starting to feel like too intimate of a situation.

"I'm going to win your heart, little Wildcat. I'll even earn it, this time." He places a gentle kiss on my lips to seal that promise. "Now, are you okay? Hayes is an asshole on a good day and I'm sure you met him on one of his worst."

I stare at him, wondering at the changes I'm seeing. He came after me because I was upset, and he kissed the hell out of me first as a very welcome distraction. What. The. Actual. Fuck. I pull my leg down from his hip and he releases me, giving me a few inches of personal space to stand and straighten my dress. That slit really came in handy, and he's right, I'm soaked for him.

"I'm fine, Zander. I was just startled to see your brother. I've only met him once and you're right, it wasn't under the best circumstances, so forgive me if I didn't have the best reaction just now."

Zander looks away and runs a hand through his dark hair, rumpled from my own hands that were pulling him close to me, and it just makes him more attractive. When he returns those eyes—my son's eyes—to me, they're haunted.

"Whatever happened between you and Hayes was my fault. I'm sorry. He wouldn't have done what he did if I hadn't established my shitty patterns with women that led him to treat you as badly as he did. I brought this on us both and, fuck, Lowe, I'm so sorry."

Zander owning up for his part in something he wasn't directly involved in? Again, what the fuck? I just stare at him in disbelief, not sure I could speak if I tried.

"I didn't even know you showed up at Olympus until recently, but why would I? It wasn't in my nature to want to know back then. He wouldn't have told me. My brothers thought they were cleaning up my messes like they always did. I didn't want to know what they were doing on my behalf."

"I thought as much," I say, looking down. "You didn't want anything to do with me once you walked me off that jet and put me in a car." I swallow hard, thinking of him returning to the plane without once looking back at me. The crushing reality of knowing it was likely the last time I would ever see him.

"I'm so sorry," he says, cupping my face and looking into my eyes. He's so earnest and full of yearning I can feel my resolve cracking.

I shake my head, pulling out of his hands. "This isn't the place to be having this conversation. We're supposed to be out there at a table together supporting a charity, not hiding in a room hashing out five-year-old wounds. We can talk about this later."

When Zander starts to pull me back into his arms, ready to protest, I smile at him and press a soft hand to his chest.

"I'm listening now. Give me time to absorb it all. I have a date out in a ballroom giving a very nice speech that he worked hard on. The proper thing would be for me to be out there to listen to him speak now, not getting felt up and making out with someone else in a—" I finally look around Zander's broad shoulders and catch the buttery soft light spilling from lamps on small tables at groups of chairs clustered around a room that is paneled in rich wood tones, with a crackling fireplace at one end, "—a study of some sort."

Zander's face grows dark with rage and I smooth a wrinkle from his forehead with my thumb. He catches my hand and presses his face into my palm, calming at the touch. "I really fucking hate him, Lowe, but I know this is your choice. As much as I want to make it for you, I'll just have to prove I'm the better man for you."

"Fine. I'll tolerate your asshole brother, and you can tolerate Knox. We'll both be miserable together. If you're lucky, I may even find your leg and play footsie with you under the table." I give him a wicked smile, and the one he returns is just as devilish.

"Goddamn, I love your smart mouth. Challenge fucking accepted, Wildcat."

Twenty-eight

Zander

"Where's your head been? I can't believe what you just let slide in the meeting. How dare you not talk them down from walking away when you had the chance," Hayes growls at me.

Things have been strained between us since the gala last weekend. It's been a tense week of work, more so than normal with the big grumpy baby holding a grudge against me for upsetting Paige at the gala she worked so hard to plan and put on. It was as much his fault as mine, and I'm not helping matters with my own feelings toward him for what he did to Harlowe.

I'll never get that instant defensive posturing she took and the outrage that entered her tone when she saw him out of my head. Knowing what put her on the defensive in the first place is enough to make me crack a molar from the strain of grinding my teeth not to deck him every time I think of it now.

I turn to glare at Hayes as we leave the conference room we have spent the better part of the day in. We're negotiating the purchase of another manufacturing company to replace the Rosenthall deal we lost due to the cyber attack. The Pegasus engines will never get off the ground if we don't increase our capabilities in this industry, and our timeline is extra tight.

"I'm playing the long game, Hater. They'll come around in the next meeting. Kanisarek needs a bailout, and we're the only option with deep enough pockets to make a worthwhile offer."

"So why did they dismiss ours and end negotiations just now? We need this, Zander."

"Just trust me. They want this deal as much as we do. They will come crawling back to us accepting the offer in a few days. We won't have to capitulate or sweeten the deal any more than we have, and we'll be able to make any demands we want."

I turn to meet Hayes's angry green gaze, like his eyes have Hulk rage, and I stifle a laugh at his expression. I learned all about Hendricks's favorite Marvel characters while we built tracks and now I'm thinking in those terms at work. Is that how fatherhood works? I play with my kid one time and now I'm changed forever? I think I'm good with that.

"What's so fucking funny?" he snarls as we enter the executive boardroom to reconvene with our team and run a quick analysis.

"Your fucking face is funny."

"Get serious, Zander." The big grump takes a seat at the table, continuing to glare at me.

I sit across from him and smile, because I know it'll drive him crazy. I finally look away and address the assembled team. "Listen up. The clock is ticking on Kanisarek. They will be reopening negotiations tomorrow, or within forty-eight hours, max. We need to have everything ready to go for a much quicker timeline than anticipated, because we're going to demand a shorter close time since they walked away. I want Pegasus ready to go as soon as we have Kanisarek under our umbrella. Any questions?"

"You're that confident they'll change their tune?" Luca asks, his tone cool, matching his icy stare. That motherfucker has sociopath vibes, but Payton vouches for him being semi-normal, so there's nothing I can do but deal with his penchant for cold affectation.

"That question doesn't warrant an answer, given what I've just said. Anyone else?" I look around and catch Payton's appraising look. I nod my head in his direction.

"I'll have the team start working on the press releases and get legal rewriting the contract."

"Finally, someone who is thinking proactively. Good. You all know what to do. Make it happen and don't be surprised if they reach out even sooner than expected. They're salivating for this deal, no matter what they said today."

When the teams have broken off and everyone but my brothers and the executive team has left, I rap my knuckles on the conference table, waiting for one of them to challenge me. It doesn't take long.

"You're insane if you think Kanisarek is coming back and will be looking for anything less than what they originally asked for," Hayes growls, flattening his hands on the table and standing. "You shouldn't have let them walk out today."

"No, you're just shortsighted and focused on the pretense. They don't want to let us go, but they think walking away will make us up our offer, which we made sure is over market value. They're playing on our recent misfortunes and hoping we're licking our wounds enough over the cyber attack to make concessions we otherwise wouldn't. They miscalculated. I have no intention of upping anything and I won't have my hand forced."

"Sometimes we have to work through a deal. We do it all the time. What makes you think this one will be any different?" Diego asks from Haye's left. His normally perfectly styled dark hair is a bit out of place from running his hands through it when he got stressed during our negotiations, and his navy suit is looking rumpled. Our entire team is feeling the strain of rushing to get this deal in place before our schematics and plans end up hitting the market before we can make it happen ourselves.

"Kanisarek has been in a steady decline for the last two years, taking in less profits and bleeding out in quality issues. They have a solid manufacturing stream, but they keep trying to diversify into areas that haven't suited their structure and abilities, like electronics. They're frustrated and ready for someone to come in and take over, removing the temptation to try another new thing that fails. They've separated those areas in this deal, but we'll still get what we want in the end." This explanation isn't new. We've all read the same documents, but sometimes it takes pointing out the obvious for the group to see that the simplest answer is often the only one you need to pay attention to.

"Fine, we'll trust your hunch on this," Hayes says, pushing away from the table and grabbing his jacket from his chair. "I have a pregnant wife to get home to, and even in her emotional state, she's far more interesting than you fuckers."

"Speaking of kids," Payton says, halting Hayes with an outstretched hand and turning to me. "What do we know about the potential little Maldives souvenir? It was interesting seeing you and Harlowe together at the gala this past weekend, but no news on the paternity front."

I lean back in my chair and face my brothers. I take a deep breath, and when I blow it out, I feel a smile turning up the corners of my mouth. "He's all mine." The statement is far weightier than the words would seem. I'm claiming Hendricks, fatherhood, and everything that comes with it. For once, that doesn't scare me. It makes me fucking proud. Over the moon.

Payton lets out a low whistle and Hayes tilts his head, reading me more effectively than I'd like him to. Payton strides around the table, a grin on his face as he throws an arm around my shoulders. "Congratulations, I guess? Do you want to make sure, or are you as confident in this as you are about the Kanisarek deal?"

"He looks just like me. And he's obsessed with Legos," I answer confidently, taking the hug and beaming.

"Lots of kids like Legos, that doesn't mean he's yours," Javi says in a practical tone that has me shooting daggers his way. He's supposed to be on my side, not working against me.

"I was obsessed with Legos and building cities. I played with him last week. It was uncanny. He even thinks it out and plans the way I do. That's not normal for a four-year-old I didn't have a hand in raising. It's nature versus nurture type shit."

"No, I'm with Javi on this. It could be a total coincidence that you liked to play with the same toys as a kid. I'm going to need more than that to believe it," Hayes says, shrugging into his jacket. "Get a damn paternity test already and either make it official in a way that only DNA can, or know for sure you don't owe them anything."

I sink back deeper into my chair, hating that my brother can't see what I have. Meeting Hendricks in person, talking with him, playing with him, watching him with Harlowe and Lily—it set something in me on fire. I now have a purpose beyond myself, beyond my own aspirations and professional achievements. I have a person who will look up to me, expect me to set a proper example and be there for him when life is anything but easy. I know without a doubt that he is mine. I know Hayes just wants me to be sure that the little boy with soft brown curls and stormy gray eyes that mirror mine is truly my progeny in case something goes horribly wrong between me and Harlowe.

"No," I say simply. "There's no need. That kid is mine, Legos or not. It's not even about money or owing them anything. I could never force a test on them." I don't even want to ask Harlowe about it. I trust that the defensiveness she has shown in keeping me from Hendricks is as much of an admission as any test. She wouldn't be worried about me getting close to the boy if I had no connection to him.

"You actually can force this. It's not hard to loop in legal," Luca says, straightening his already perfect tie and rising from the conference table. "Hiring someone to dig into her past would be just as simple. Make sure you have enough dirt for a case should this go wrong and you end up fighting for custody."

"Damn, that's dark, even for you, American Psycho," Javi says, calling Luca the name we reserve for when he's being his most calculating and cruel.

I bristle and lean toward Luca, leveling him with a glare. "Watch your fucking mouth. That's the mother of my child you're talking about. Stay the fuck away from her."

"Everyone is thinking the same thing, you're all just too chicken shit to say it out loud," Luca responds as he leaves the conference room, looking as unruffled as his cool tone implies.

Payton shoots me an apologetic look before following after his SVP. "We have filters that keep intrusive thoughts like that safely inside our heads. We've talked about this," Payton says, ready to discuss what is appropriate in the workplace and what needs to be kept to himself.

"And that's a great reminder to never get on Luca's bad side," Javi says, shaking his head and standing.

"I feel sorry for whatever woman finally tries to settle down with him. He'll have a file a foot thick on her before she's even agreed to their first date," Diego adds.

I shake my head, letting go of the rage that filled me a moment before. He's not worth the effort. "He'll probably find someone with as icy a demeanor and even weirder kinks. I bet he's into electrostimulation or wax play. He needs heat to thaw that iceberg of a personality," I add, because it's way more fun to discuss someone else's issues than have mine be the focus of the conversation.

Hayes pauses in the doorway. "Get the paternity test, Zand. Just to be sure."

"He's mine, so shut the fuck up about it, Hater." Now I'll just have to figure out how to convince my brothers to believe it as much as I do. Fuck.

Twenty-nine

Harlowe

"Harlowe, I have the best news for you. Are you sitting down?" Alicia asks over the phone as soon as I answer.

"I'm driving Hendricks to school, so technically, I'm sitting in the car." I glance in the rearview mirror and see Hendricks is busy with his toys and isn't paying any attention to the conversation playing over the car speakers.

"That's good enough, but do not crash your car so soon after getting it repaired." She barely pauses for any sort of response from me before continuing on in an excited rush. "You're on the freaking New York Times Bestseller list. With a cookbook! That's the kind of thing people like Martha Stewart and Ina Garten do, and look at you, right up there with half of your Mount Rushmore of cooking icons."

"Shut up," I say on a forced exhale as the news hits me square in the stomach. "My book? It's a bestseller?" This doesn't feel real. I must be dreaming, or I didn't hear her correctly.

"Yes! Your amazing cookbook, the one we have worked on for years. *At Home With Harlowe: A Foulmouthed*

Foodie's Guide To Eating Well is a mother-effing bestseller. You did it, babe!"

She lets out an excited squeal and I can't help joining her. "I can't believe it. I never expected to see my book rank highly, let alone get onto a bestseller list. This is insane."

"It is so well deserved. You did this. Your recipes, your personality, the way you can connect with an audience. It all came together to make something truly special, and I'm so proud of you," she says, gushing more than usual and being my biggest hype woman, in addition to my normally very focused manager.

"Thank you. Oh, my God, this is surreal!" My voice wobbles with the effort to not burst into happy tears. I was too afraid to hope for my book to be a bestseller out of fear that the opposite would happen, that I wouldn't sell a single copy and my dreams would be fruitless, left smashed sadly under the feet of uninterested people.

"But that's not even the best part. The Gourmet Network called and they want to shoot a pilot for a new cooking show based on *At Home With Harlowe*! They love the Foulmouthed Foodie social media side of things with your thirst traps and want to do something a little racier to hit a new demographic for their streaming service. Like spice it up in the kitchen or something. We have time to pitch ideas, but they absolutely love you."

My heart leaps even more as I learn that the authentic, strong, brazen parts of me that I have completely embraced and shared with the world are what have attracted this new opportunity my way. It doesn't feel possible, real even, that the parts of me that I once hid and shied away from are now making my dreams come true. "I think I'm going to throw up. Not in my wildest dreams did I even expect this."

"This is an incredible accomplishment, sweetie, and you deserve to revel in it. Please go out and celebrate. I wish I was there because I would absolutely take you out and treat you to everything your little heart desires to really make sure you mark this momentous occasion. Oh, I have another call. Love you, babe. I'm so proud of you!"

Alicia ends the call and leaves me dazed as I pull up to Hendricks's school without remembering how I got there. The drop-off is quick because Hendricks is always excited to go to school, so I am quickly left with my thoughts and feelings. Enough people are buying my little cookbook to make me a bestseller. Not only that, The Gourmet Network wants to shoot a pilot for a new show *with me*. What is this life? It's better than any dream I could have had for this book release and my future, and I want to follow Alicia's advice, because she's never steered me wrong. She said to celebrate, and that's just what I plan to do.

Mom was happy to watch Hendricks and Paloma was down to celebrate with me, but Callie couldn't make it, so just the two of us are at some place downtown that Callie recommended when I called to tell her the good news. We're enjoying delicious overpriced cocktails and nibbling on several of the appetizers now.

"How many books do you have to sell to make you a bestseller?" Paloma asks, taking a sip of her purple-tinted concoction with a pretty orchid adorning the rim.

I swirl the straw in my own cocktail, a pink drink with a plumeria flower on the side. "I have no idea, but I would assume a lot. Alicia didn't tell me the number, only that I'd made the list."

"That's incredible. And an option for your own cooking show! God, Lolo, that's so cool. I knew you'd do well because you have so much talent and your food is amazing, but it's one of those things you can't really expect and just have to hope for the best with, you know?"

I do know. It's exactly how I feel. I pluck the flower out of my drink and twirl it in my fingers close to my nose, inhaling the heady floral scent. "The last time I saw plumerias was in the Maldives." The *with Zander* part of the statement is left unspoken. I tuck the bloom into my hair by my ear, remembering when the flowers were stuck to my skin after the bath that changed my life and had me falling in love with a liar.

"How are you feeling about Zander coming back around and wanting to be a part of your life?" Well, I guess it won't stay unspoken on her end.

"He wants to be a part of Hendricks's life," I amend.

"Babe, you're usually so good about not lying to yourself. You're making me take your place tonight? Fine, tough love best friend it is." She downs the rest of her drink and levels me with her hazel eyes. "That man is after you like a hound on a fox, and if you want to tell yourself this bland little story that he's just wanting to get to know your son, that's doing the situation a disservice. He. Wants. You," she says, flourishing her empty glass.

"He's had me. He doesn't do repeats. Whatever has brought him back into my life is motivated by Hendricks, and maybe seeing me, kissing me, touching me, is just a ploy on his part to make sure I allow it to happen. There's no way he wants anything serious enough to actually try to have a relationship with me beyond that. It's not in his nature."

It's hard to trust Zander's motives now when he's shown me how effective he is at promising forever and then yanking it away when I give in completely. Even last week at the gala when I gave in to that kiss with him that felt so damn good and he promised to earn my heart, I still wasn't sure if it was because he saw me there with Knox and was jealous, or if he really meant it.

"Do you actually know that, though? He has a one-track history when it comes to dating. Maybe he wants to try something different."

Her defense of Zander is a surprise. She's normally very much in the anti-Zander camp, given what went down between us. Maybe telling her Knox and I decided to just be friends instead of dating gave her the idea that I want something more with Zander. Which...I may be warming up to. Like, a lot. Seeing him with Hendricks broke down so many of the walls I have up against him. It may have melted the ice, but it's still hard to trust him with my heart after he shredded it once before.

"I think you mean his *nonexistent* dating history," I say before taking a drink to remedy the flustered feeling that is rising in my chest. I ground myself in reality rather than give in to a fantasy daydream that may or may not be manifesting in my head. "You can't count hookups as dating, no matter how many of them he has."

Paloma scoffs and signals for the waiter to refill our drinks. "Didn't he say he wanted a second chance with you? That he wants to try this? That's huge from a confirmed fuckboy." I'm beginning to see the downside of sharing everything with her. She has no issue using the information against me when it suits her. I glare at her, but it lacks my usual force.

"That's the thing. I don't want to try something with him without knowing he'd be committing fully to it. I let him meet Hendricks. He's now inextricably connected to me and my son, and if we did try out a relationship and he decided it wasn't for him, I would still have to see him, interact with him, watch him with Hendricks, whether I wanted that or not. It would absolutely crush me to see him and know he was going home to fuck another woman.

Why would I even give myself the opportunity to feel like that?"

Saying the thoughts out loud hurts more than I thought it would, but they deserve to be spoken, as this is the reason I'm holding myself back from him now. I know the devastation he's more than capable of, even after seeming so sincere.

"For the very real chance it could lead somewhere even better than you could imagine. I know I've said some shitty things about him in the past, because what he did was shitty, but I also believe in second chances and people realizing the error of their ways. Or, I will if that's what this is. You're seriously hot, talented, smart, funny, and a total catch. I'm surprised you don't have even more men falling at your feet asking for a chance with you. It doesn't shock me in the least that Zander is trying to get your attention again now."

"The timing is the hardest part to believe. Zander could have come around at any point in the last five years, yet it took seeing a story about me with another guy and my kid for him to reappear wanting answers and second chances. What's his motivation? Is it that he has a kid, or that I was seen with someone else?"

Paloma studies me as she drags a finger through the sugar on the rim of her empty glass. "Well, you're not with anyone now. And most guys wouldn't come within a ten-mile radius of any potential children, yet there he was when it was made public. That speaks volumes to me."

Our server appears with our drinks and gives me a minute to think about Paloma's reasoning. The fact that Zander chose to come back into my life *after* learning about the possibility he had a kid is telling. She may have a point.

"Are you on Alicia and Mom's side now?" I ask, taking a grateful sip of my pink paradise in a glass.

"Do they want you to see what happens with Zander?" she asks, lifting her drink and sipping.

"Definitely. Mom has slightly higher stakes, but they're strongly team Zander."

"What did you want the most when you got back from your trip with him?" she asks, leveling me with a look that lets me know she's about to dish out some especially tough love, and I'm not going to enjoy this part.

"I wanted him to talk to me instead of ghosting me."

"That's not all, and you know it. You wanted a *relationship* with him. You wanted to be the one who changed him for good, no matter what he told you about his intentions. He's offering that now, isn't he?"

"I don't know what he's offering, really. I'm not even sure he knows. It's such a foreign concept for him I wouldn't be surprised if he's completely winging it just to see if he can."

"Why are you such a cynic all of a sudden? Normally, you'd be willing to give someone the benefit of the doubt and would take it at face value. Is it because he broke your heart before?"

"This is Zander, I'm allowed to be cynical about him," I say, catching the note of defensiveness lacing my tone.

She tsks and shakes her head at me. "I was there, remember? I held you when you were falling apart. I know you were heartbroken. You wanted something more with the man and were devastated when you couldn't get a hold of him after your holiday, and then even more so when you found out you were pregnant. It took a while for you to be okay not having him in your life, and I think that happened because you were mad and wanted to prove you could do it on your own to spite him."

"Okay, I'm a spiteful wretch who doesn't trust the guy now."

I drain what remains in my glass and feel the warmth of the alcohol seeping into my blood and radiating out from my stomach. I don't have the heart to fight with her or continue lying to myself on this. I'm usually truthful to a fault, but it's hard on this one topic tonight. I don't think I have the fight in me at all when it comes to Zander.

She's right. I wanted this effort from him so badly five years ago. I wanted him to say everything he's saying now, just back then. I've had five years to harden my heart against him, but it doesn't change what I wanted to hear all along, or that it lights up a part of my heart to have him saying it even now.

"Fine, you know it all bitch. I'll give him a chance. And hey, maybe I'll even get something fun out of it. I could finally get fucked properly for the first time in forever before it all comes crashing down on my head."

"That's my girl. Get that good dick, no matter what it costs." Paloma grins at me, and I burst into tipsy giggles.

"God, what I would do for that right now," I admit on a groan. My phone vibrates next to my hand on the table and I look down out of habit. Zander's name flashes across the screen. "Damn, if it isn't trouble calling. It's like he knew I was talking about fucking him with this timing."

"Well, you better answer when the dick is making itself available like that. And I'll support you, no matter what you decide to do. I could still carve his eyes out for how he treated you, even if he fucks you like a champ. This is your life, Lolo. If you really want Zander, even a little bit, give him a chance and see what he's like off that island, in the real world, now."

Thirty

Zander

"Were your ears burning?" Harlowe's greeting when she answers my call is so unexpected it makes me chuckle softly. The din of a crowd can be heard over the line, and I instantly wonder where she is, and who she's out with. Is she on a date? No, she wouldn't have answered my call so easily. She could be with friends.

"Why? Are you entertaining your friends with stories about my cock?" I ask, fishing for the information I crave and leaning back in the smooth leather seat of the Karma where I decided to call her before leaving the tower. I enjoy the rasp of her voice, and, if I'm being honest, the idea that she's talking about me. I was planning to ask if she's free tonight, but that can wait if I've been on her mind. I want to know the details.

"Not exactly," she says, her voice lowering. "But if you want me to kiss and tell, I can share that you liked having a finger up your ass when I sucked you off."

I sit up straighter. "That is patently false information, and you know it," I say, a prickle of unease going through me at the thought of her sharing something like that with the wrong person. A nasty gossip site like the Atlanta Haute List would share even the most untrue of accusations about me just because they enjoy highlighting my family for some reason.

"I'm kidding, Zander, relax. I wasn't telling anyone about the weird things you like in the bedroom. And who knows what could have changed in the last five years? Maybe you *do* like your ass played with now. I won't judge you for it."

I hear the clink of a glass and wonder if she's drinking, and that's why she's in this rare playful mood that reminds me so much of the woman I pursued with a passion just to turn away when I was done with her. But that's the thing I've come to realize. I was never done with Harlowe Sorenson, and I don't think I ever will be.

"What are you doing right now?"

"Enjoying a ladies' night out. We're somewhere downtown. Brick and Barley, I think? Something pretentious and overpriced for the craft cocktails and food we ordered. We're celebrating my cookbook being a bestseller and getting a cooking show option. But hey, the drinks are strong and the food is decent." I hear an unintelligible sound from Harlowe's end of the conversation. "And the company is amazing. That's Paloma, by the way. She's the company and she wants you to know she's awesome."

I hear laughter, and I wonder how long they've been at this. I tap the restaurant name into my phone to see where it's located. Not far from the tower. I type out a quick text to Javi and return my attention to Harlowe. "Want even better company?"

"Sure, why the hell not? The more the merrier," she says, sounding as relaxed as I've heard her since she crashed back into my life. Thank fuck for whatever cocktails she's been enjoying to have loosened her up this much.

I hear a protest over the line and bet Paloma isn't as on board with having her ladies' night crashed. But that's what Javi's for. He'll wingman for me and not think twice about it. I saw the way he looked at Paloma when he rear-ended Harlowe last month. *Was it just last month?* It feels like a lifetime ago already. It won't be a hardship for him to talk to Harlowe's pretty yet prickly friend, who is likely not a fan of mine if she's been around for a while. I wouldn't like me either, if I were in her position.

"I'll be there in ten. Enjoy another cocktail on me. I want to treat you ladies for your celebration."

"Don't mind if we do. We're getting the bibimbap bowl and the flank steak sliders if you're paying. Hear that, Paloma, Zander has our tab. Get whatever you want." Harlowe pauses, listening to Paloma. "She says she doesn't mind you joining us. She's ordering dessert, too."

I laugh. "Fine, just leave room on the table for my drink when I get there."

The drive doesn't take long, and I hand my car off to the valet as I scan the sky full of dark clouds threatening rain, and maybe even a thunderstorm. Javi meets me at the door to the restaurant and sends me a questioning look. Like me, he's removed his tie, but coming from work, we're still in our jackets and slacks. Not a bad look for this restaurant, which is a pretentious place known for strong drinks and an Asian fusion menu, according to the web search I did while on the phone with Harlowe.

"Feeling like overpriced drinks and small portions? This isn't usually your type of place. I happen to loathe it." Javi looks from me to the name of the restaurant printed on a grain sack outside the entrance.

"You might not love the place, but you'll definitely like the company," I promise.

"Which of your Instagram groupies are we meeting tonight?" he asks, sounding intrigued.

"Not a groupie, and you've met them, kind of."

Javi looks at me curiously, but doesn't hazard a guess.

I scan the restaurant when we enter, ignoring the line of people waiting for tables. I spot Harlowe across the restaurant like my eyes are drawn to her and motion with my chin at Javi to follow.

"Oh," he says in understanding when he catches the direction of my gaze. "Yeah, this won't be bad at all."

I slide into the empty seat next to Harlowe, resting my arm on the back of her chair and enjoying the surprised smile she gives me in response to our arrival. She looks incredible. She's wearing a strappy tank top that shows off her shoulders and most of her upper back, a flirty ruffle down the center that draws my eyes to her cleavage, sending visceral memories of what her nipples look and taste like sling-shotting around my brain.

She has a plumeria flower tucked behind her ear closest to me, the scent intoxicating and sending me straight back to when I was in paradise with her. I think of when plumerias were decorating her body last and bite back a groan of longing that's so fierce, I have to turn my head and clear my throat before I can return my attention to Harlowe.

"Hello, bestseller and future cooking show host. Congratulations," I say, trailing my fingers along the exposed skin of her back. She shivers in response and leans into my touch. She's definitely a few drinks in.

"Thanks," she says, her cheeks rosy. "This is Paloma," she says, gesturing to her friend across the table. "I see you brought the bad driver with you. Paloma, this is Javier. And you know of Zander, but you get to officially meet him now." Harlowe finishes the introductions.

"My driving record would indicate otherwise, and again, I'm so sorry for the accident. I hope everything is back in order now," Javi says smoothly, settling into the open chair next to Paloma, who eyes him warily.

"It's true, he's usually a better driver than that, but I-85 gets the best of us all at some point. I hope you liked the rental."

I've made sure all of her repairs were done to my exacting standards and she didn't have to pay for any of it. I tear my attention from Harlowe and nod at her friend and the spread on the table.

"Did you order everything on the menu? I'm serious about it being my treat. You deserve it." I again look at Harlowe when I finish.

"We ordered plenty, don't you worry, Daddy Warbucks," Paloma says with humor.

Javi laughs and turns to her. "That's a new one. What else do you call him?"

Paloma grins, but it looks mean. "Sperm donor. Asshole. Conceited jerk. Hit it and quit it. Johnny Bravo."

"I understand all but the last one," Javi says, clearly not interested in having my back in this situation. "Care to elaborate?"

"He's a big, dumb, caricature of a narcissistic womanizer who is obsessed with himself and can't make a relationship work out." She crosses her arms and stares at me as she explains.

"Harsh, much?" It's to be expected, though. "Feel better after getting that off your chest?" I ask, holding back the anger that would like to fire off my own insults. "And you're the overprotective friend who has Harlowe's best interests in mind." I hold out a hand when I see her bristle and prepare to retort. "I more than deserve it."

At my acceptance, her prepared vitriol dies before she even gets started, and she looks confused. Javi turns to her then, and smiles his disarming, blinding white grin that promises fun.

"I have plenty of stories I could tell you that would more than reinforce your ideas of him." As he captures

Paloma's attention like the wingman I knew he'd be, I turn my own to Harlowe.

"Congratulations, Lowe," I say again. My voice is so quiet it's nearly drowned out by the noise in the restaurant, but she leans closer to me to hear better. "I'm so proud of you. I'm glad you're celebrating this victory."

She smiles and looks up at me with her sweet brown eyes all liquid soft. "Thank you."

I lazily drag my fingertips along her spine and watch the reaction it causes. Goosebumps rise on her skin, and her nipples grow hard against the black silk of her top, making me more than aware that she's not wearing a bra. I can look right down the front of her shirt from my vantage point and it does nothing to stem the desire for her that is coursing through me. I fight back a groan and look away from her incredible tits.

"You look beautiful." I bring my hand up to cup her cheek and run my fingertips along the flower at her ear. "This brings back some very good memories."

She melts into my hand, sighing as I trace my thumb along her skin, her eyes closing. "It made me think of you, too."

"Where's Hendricks tonight?" I don't know if it's the right question to ask, but I want to know. "I miss him. He's a really cute kid."

Harlowe's eyes flutter open and she stares at me a moment before smiling softly. "He's with my mom for the night."

She's mellow and soft, and I like her in this state almost as much as I like the wildcat fighter she can be when angry. It reminds me of the soft moments we had when I lost myself in her, when I made her come so many times she cried and still begged for more, not wanting it to end. When I promised her forever and told her I was ruined. I wasn't lying about that. I would be hers forever, even if I couldn't bring myself to honor my promises when we left our vacation. A part of me has remained attached to her all this time, waiting, wanting, needing her, locked away in the vault where I threw it after carving it out of my chest. Now I've dragged it out, slapped it back on my chest, told it to beat again, and hope it will repair the rest of me that's broken.

"He's asked about you every day since you came over. He likes you."

"I told you I would come over any time he asked. You didn't say anything."

"I wasn't sure how to feel about it. I promise I'll let you know the next time."

"What about you? What have you been thinking about, when you think of me?" I ask, hoping we're on the same page. Hoping we can get there if she's not. I continue to trace my thumb along her cheek and she lets me, which feels like a huge fucking win in itself. I feel like we turned a corner after that kiss at the gala.

"I didn't delete the footage from when you came over while I was making the honey cake. Those few minutes you were in the frame with me were... insanely hot. We're hot together. I've watched it back countless times. Thought about it in bed a few times, too."

She blinks, breaking the spell she's wrapped around us, and looks up at me from under dark lashes, her eyes luminous and full of heat. I realize I've leaned in even closer as she spoke quietly, drawn in by her voice, eating up the magic of her words.

"I wanted to taste you so bad right then, Lowe. I could feel how hot your pussy was when I pulled you against me. I bet you would have been sweeter than the batter I licked off your neck. But you stopped me. Would you stop me tonight if I wanted to bury my face between your legs and drown in your sweetness?"

She shivers, but looks down, and I feel like I've lost her by being too bold, by telling her how badly I want her instead of how badly I want to be the man she needs. I should be working harder to gain her trust instead of acting like the stupid fuckboy who is only capable of breaking her heart that she thinks I am.

"If you take me home tonight, you can see for yourself." Her eyes are clear when she meets mine, challenge illuminating those dark depths that hold my whole world.

My heart leaps, but I slow my instant desire to scoop her into my arms and run for the fucking doors right this instant before she can change her mind. I move my hand down to the column of her throat and turn her face so she's fully looking at me, making sure she knows I'm dead serious with what I'm about to say.

"If I take you home with me, I'm not letting you go this time. You'll be mine. Whatever that means in *this* world, in real life. No vacation bullshit." My voice is low, hoarse.

I'm terrified out of my mind with what this declaration means for the both of us. How will I back it up? How can I be the man she needs when Olympus has already claimed so much of me? But I'll figure it out. I'm willing to do whatever I need to in order to make her mine now.

"Promise?" her voice shakes and I see the hesitation in her eyes, the challenging mask slipping and showing me the scared woman who knows how easily I can hurt her, how simple it is for me to sell her a lie and change in the very next moment. Yet she's still asking for it.

"I promise. I won't hurt you again, Lowe. I'm so sorry for before. I know that words will never make up for what I did to you. I'll show you now that I mean to be better, to do better by you and Hendricks. I'll be the man you need and want."

She blinks, and a tear slips down her cheek. I do what I wanted to so badly on the jet when I had to break her heart, and catch it with my thumb, licking it off, tasting her ocean of sadness, her need.

"Hey!" Female hands clap in my face and we both jump. "Excuse me, you two. I don't want to see tears from my best friend when we're supposed to be celebrating.

Whatever deep conversation y'all are having over there has to stop."

Harlowe and I pull apart and look up quickly at the interruption as she dabs slim fingers I can vividly imagine sliding diamond rings onto under her eyes, swiping at the moisture on her cheeks. The spell that captivated us is broken and the loud bar comes back into focus, reminding me that we're in public, surrounded by people, and were not, in fact, alone having this very heartfelt conversation.

"It's fine, Paloma," Harlowe says, placating her friend with a quick, watery smile. "I'm fine, it's all good."

"I'll make it up to you later," I promise in her ear before I return my attention to the table, loaded with plates of food and cocktails. "Let's celebrate your book being a bestseller and getting a show, as is only proper." I pick up the closest drink, a pink cocktail with one of those flowers that's tucked behind her ear, and hold it up. "To bestsellers, fresh starts, and forever."

Harlowe looks at me quickly, then across the table at Javi and Paloma. I keep my eyes trained on her, glass raised until she picks up her own cocktail and clinks it against mine hesitantly. "To bestsellers."

"To bestsellers," the others echo, clinking glasses and smiling at her while avoiding the rest of my awkward toast.

I sip the hideous cocktail and set it down, slipping the plumeria flower into a pocket for later. I rest my hand on Harlowe's thigh and realize she's wearing some leather-type leggings that hug her thighs and I look down quickly, only to bite back a groan as my hand involuntarily squeezes tighter at the sight. Whatever the material is feels like a second skin, buttery soft and warm, black as night, and stretched tight over her thick thighs that are pressed together on the seat. I want to peel the pants off her and have those thighs wrapped around my head tight like she's squeezing my fingers, keeping my hand trapped in place. I rub my thumb on her outer thigh and leave my hand where it is as I try to focus on the table conversation, the other people here with us, when all I can think of is the heat coming from Harlowe's pussy, mere inches from my fingers.

"Javi was just saying he wants a big family. What about you, Zander," Paloma asks, hazel eyes sharp as she draws me into the conversation with a landmine of a question that's sure to weigh my intentions as only a protective best friend can.

I shoot Javi a withering glare and he shrugs apologetically, but also gives me a look that more than says *you brought this on yourself, cabrón.* Well, fuck. How do I answer that when it's only recently that I've even considered the possibility of having a family at all? I look down at Harlowe and see the guarded look of hope she is working so hard to hide peeking from her gorgeous eyes.

This is it. Go for fucking broke. Lay it all out. Commit to the man I want to be or get the fuck out of here right now. She deserves my fucking best, and if I can't give it to her now, with an answer to a simple enough question, I don't fucking deserve a second chance with her at all.

"I want whatever Harlowe wants," I say for her to hear, but loud enough for Paloma and Javi to catch. Paloma lets out a small gasp while Javi chokes on his drink. "How many babies do you want, Lowe? Girls? Boys? A whole baseball team? Just the one? I'll give you anything you fucking want." Javi starts coughing in earnest now and Paloma whacks him on his back until he stops.

"Zander," Harlowe says slowly, eyes wide, looking spooked by my declaration. Okay, maybe it was a bit much. I should have just stopped at whatever she wanted. It was a good enough answer, but it wasn't the answer I wanted to give.

"Are you feeling okay, bro?" Javi asks, reaching across the table like he's going to feel my forehead. I bat his hand away, keeping my eyes on Harlowe.

"I'm serious. We made such a beautiful little boy. He's amazing. I want as many babies as you want." I'm high with the feeling of saying this out loud now, of accepting the truth, of knowing that deep down it's what I want so fucking badly, but only if it can be with her.

"Zander, do I need to take you home? Was there something in that cocktail?" Javi says, leaning over and pulling the glass toward him to sniff it. "I think you're scaring her. Dial it back. This isn't like you," he says quietly when he's closer to me. His face is concerned, probably thinking I've lost my mind to be saying what I am. He's never seen me like this. Hell, neither have I. I catch Paloma staring at me, with a hint of a disbelieving smile turning up her mouth that goaded me into this spot. I smile and let her see the truth. What I'm saying sounds crazy because I'm crazy about Harlowe.

I refocus on Harlowe's face and see what Javi does, undisguised fear. But if I know this woman at all, I know she's afraid to want what I'm saying, not that I'm saying it. I give her a reassuring smile. "I guess we have a lot to talk about before we start talking about babies, right, Lowe?"

She starts laughing and drops her face into her hands. "Oh, my God, Zander, you're such a psycho," she says behind her fingers, which instantly eases the tension around the table. Javi resettles in his seat. Paloma shakes her head and sends Harlowe a glance to check in, and seemingly satisfied, sips her purple cocktail.

"Well, that certainly turned the mood of the night. Thanks for that lovely conversation starter, Paloma," Harlowe says, giving her friend a withering look across the table.

"I think you crying over whatever he was saying to you before I asked him the question was the downer, but hey, feel free to blame me for asking what we all wanted to know anyway," she replies with enough sass to give me a good look into their friendship. They're close, probably share everything, and she's protective of Harlowe. Good. Can't have too many friends like that when you have assholes like me out there ready to break the hearts of good women.

"Paloma!" Harlowe says, gripping the table and giving her friend a stern look before shaking her head. "I think I've had enough celebrating for the night. I should get home."

I give her a look, wondering if she plans to go home alone, or if she'll let me take her home with me. She doesn't look at me, but a moment later, her hand comes to rest on my thigh, and slowly begins to slide up. With me, it is.

"You can't be the pooper on your own party," Paloma says, pouting across the table at Harlowe. "Your mom said she would watch Hendricks all night if you wanted and you still want to call it now? Boo, you're no fun."

"There's a great bar down the street with an exotic liquor selection I could show you if you want to keep it going. Unless you're set on these pink and purple cocktails, then I guess I can tolerate another round or two if you promise to share more embarrassing stories about these two," Javi offers with perfect timing. I send him a secret look of thanks whether he did it on my behalf or not.

"I *could* go for a good scotch after all of these sugary drinks," Paloma says, considering Javi's offer. "Fine, let's go be fun and Harlowe can go *home*." She gives Harlowe a look as if she knows exactly what that means and where her hand is right now. "Zander, can I trust you to make sure she makes it *home* safely? We took a car service here to avoid having to drive back after."

"Yes, Paloma, I'll take her *home*," I answer honestly, and smile wickedly so she knows exactly what I have planned.

Harlowe huffs out a laugh at the exchange. "Stop it, you two," she says playfully. "You're worse than my kid."

"Our kid," I correct her, and kiss her on the forehead before I rise from the table and hold a hand out to her.

"*Ay, Dios,*" Javi and Paloma say together, and burst out laughing at the timing.

Harlowe and I stare at each other. She raises an eyebrow at me and I just shake my head. Something tells me I made the right call in who my wingman was for the evening and those two will be quite happy about their situation now. I put my hand on the small of her back and look at our friends.

"You two be safe. Have fun. Don't do anything I wouldn't do." I wink at Javi, who just shakes his head back, but the smile on his face tells me everything.

Thirty-one

Harlowe

A light rain starts to fall just as we prepare to exit the restaurant hand-in-hand, my stomach knotting in anticipation.

"Stay here so you don't get soaked. Only I should be doing that, not the fucking weather," Zander says, voice low and sensual as he gives me a panty-melting grin before he ducks out the door quickly and runs to the valet stand.

Raindrops cling to his hair when he returns, and I brush a stray drop from his jaw. He catches my hand and holds it there, staring at me so intently, his eyes shimmering with the heat of a summer storm so I can't look away. I think he's going to kiss me right there, but just as he shifts his body and starts to lean down, his unusual car pulls up and his attention is drawn away. He shakes his head, still not taking his eyes off me, but ushers me out of the restaurant and into the car.

He lives downtown, so the drive is short and quiet as we vibrate in anticipation of what the night holds for us. The ride up the elevator of his high-rise building is full of longing glances and a tension that builds the closer we get to the top floor. I'm trembling with the nearness of him, with the promise of what's to come, and the possibilities of what this all means. His fingers keep up a slow caress along the open back of my tank, but he stays silent until the elevator comes to a stop at a marble vestibule that opens to the door of his penthouse. He leads me with a hand at the small of my back across the space and unlocks the door, letting me walk in ahead of him.

Zander's home is insane, as expected. It's modern, full of sharp edges, lots of glass and metal. It's a child-proofing nightmare to my mama's eyes. He doesn't let me fully inspect the palatial space before he's in front of me, pulling me into his body, his hand on my throat in that sexy, commanding way of his, angling my chin up to his face.

"Do you want this as badly as I do, Lowe?" he growls, mouth close to mine.

"Yes," I breathe, feeling the heat pool between my legs with the low urgency in his tone.

"Do you want me, as shitty as I was to you?" He lets my chin drop and smooths the hair away from my face gently, like he can smooth away the past hurts.

I blink and look down at his chest. "As much as I hated you for what you did, there was always a part of me that wanted you. That always will." I look up at him. "But it will be so hard to trust you." I shake my head, feeling my hair slide over my bare shoulders, hissing against the silk of my top. "I believed in what you told me before and it broke me when you took that away so easily, like it was nothing.

Like I was nothing. But, fuck, I want to believe you now, so badly."

"How do I show you this is real, when I've never done this before? It's all new to me. I'm going in blind here. I don't know the right things to say or do to make you trust me."

"But you do want to do this, right?" I clarify.

"Yes, I want to do this. I would fucking walk through fire for you, Lowe. I want to do everything *this* means. Be a father to our son. Be the man you need. Share a forever with you. I want you to be mine so fucking badly, Lowe. Say the words, baby."

I've waited five years to hear him say those words and mean them. I close my eyes and rest my forehead against his shoulder, breathing in the scent of storms and sandalwood of his cologne. He drops his hands to my lower back and holds me tightly as I process, as I think about how to place my trust in someone who can so effectively shatter it. I don't think there's any way to know but to try, to believe, and hope for the best. I pull my head back and look up at him again, patiently waiting for me when I remember him to be one to take what he wanted immediately.

"I'm yours, Zander." And with those three simple words, his face becomes absolutely radiant, like lightning has cracked open the sky.

"You're not seeing that fucking football player any-more," he growls, hands roaming possessively low and gripping my ass tightly. "I won't be sharing you, so make arrangements right the fuck now, if you need to."

I laugh softly. "I'm not with Knox anymore. He and I decided we were better friends than anything. Turns out, I'm not really his type."

Zander's face darkens with rage. "You're incredible. What the fuck is wrong with him?" he asks, glowering. "Has he taken too many hits to the head or something? Did he not see your out-of-this-world ass? These fucking amazing tits? These thighs I want wrapped around me immediately? You're a goddess; there's no comparison to your beauty. I'm fucking rock hard just touching you."

I laugh harder at his defense of me. "Relax. When I say I'm not his type, I mean you're more his type. Knox is gay. He just came out to me, so you're sworn to secrecy as the only other person who knows. He said I could tell you, if I needed to, after he saw how you acted at the gala. He was impressed with your defense of me, to say the least. You may have a six-foot-six admirer now."

I walk my fingers up his chest and smile, thinking of the way Knox looked when we talked about it on the way home from the gala last weekend. He is seriously on Team Zander with Mom and Alicia.

I feel Zander's muscles ease against me. "In that case, I'm fucking you tonight."

His hands slide behind my thighs and pick me up like I'm not forty pounds heavier than the last time he did this, wrapping my legs around his hips and holding my ass as he carries me through the penthouse to his bedroom. He sets me down on a huge platform bed with a white duvet and just looks at me for a moment with those mercurial eyes of his.

"What?" I ask, feeling self-conscious. Maybe it's my not-quite-toned arms, the bit of my belly with the stretch marks showing where my tank is riding up, or the squish of my thighs pressing together where I used to have a gap.

"You're so beautiful. I've thought about your body so many times. I can't wait to get you naked again."

"Zander, my body has changed." I wrap my arms around my middle, feeling self-conscious, despite years of therapy to get past my hang-ups and being a warrior for body positivity now. "I don't look the same, and I don't want you to be disappointed."

He kneels at my feet, staring up at me as he begins to unbuckle my four-inch heels one at a time, rubbing the instep of each foot, before lifting my leg and placing a kiss on my ankle. "There is not a single way your body could disappoint me. I know your body has changed and every change I've seen has made me that much crazier about you. Your fucking thirst traps on Instagram have been my undoing. Fuck, I've been going insane seeing those and not being able to get my hands on you."

He stays on his knees in front of me as he runs his hands from my ankles to my knees and pushes them apart with a quick movement that leaves me breathless. He moves his hands to my inner thighs and slowly caresses up to the apex of my hips, where he grabs me roughly, and I whimper, feeling my need begin to outpace my self-consciousness. He rubs his thumbs softly along the seam of my pussy, still fully covered by my leggings and thong underneath, but pulsing with hot need for him already.

"I love this new softness to you. It's made me insane to have had even a tiny touch of it here or there against me and not have my fill."

He tucks his fingers into the waistband of my leggings and thong, pulling them down. I lean back on my hands and lift my hips for him as he peels the tight material down my legs with a slow reverence that leaves me speechless. He kisses his way back up my legs until he reaches the edge of my tank, his hands slowly raising the silky material along my skin in a sensual caress of its own as I raise my arms and he pulls it off, leaving me completely bare before him.

He stands and unbuttons his shirt, tossing it on the floor behind him, and I get to drink him in as he toes off his shoes, works on his belt and slacks, stripping down to his boxer briefs. The last five years have been good to him, filling him out, giving him the good kind of bulk that lends power instead of paunch, and he's still exquisite in every way.

He stands staring at me for so long that I give him a look before he can make me feel self-conscious again. "Now what?"

"I've thought about having you back in my bed for so long, it doesn't feel real seeing you here now. I'm just taking a second to sear it into my memory as the moment my fantasies became real again."

My eyes prick with the pretty words, but I know the truth. I shoot him an accusing look. "Liar. You didn't think twice about me after that trip. You made sure of it. No repeats was your motto. No attachments. Be real with me so I can trust you."

He kneels before me again and takes my hands, lacing our fingers. "On the outside, yes, but deep down, there was always a part of me that wanted this right here. I only do no attachments because it wouldn't be fair to give anyone what's left after what I devote to work. My first priority has always been Olympus. Going in early, staying late. Living and breathing deals is second nature. What does that leave for a relationship? Fuck, I'm scared of what that's going to do to you. You deserve better, and I knew it then. I know it now, but I still want this more than anything. So I'm making changes, starting today, but it's going to be an adjustment. Be patient with me as I fight my way through it to give you what you deserve."

"Is that really the reason you didn't want a relationship with me?" I ask, the information sinking in slowly. "Because of work? Not that I wasn't good enough? It wasn't because you didn't want me?" My voice sounds small and I hate the waver in it.

He gives me an incredulous look and brings a hand up to cup my cheek. "You thought you weren't good enough and I didn't want you? You have to be joking. I wanted you more than anything in the world. I fucking fell in love with you, Lowe. The same night you fell in love with me, in the bathtub, with these damn flowers all over us," he says, turning and grabbing his discarded pants, pulling a plumeria blossom out of his pocket, and holding it out to me.

I take it with trembling fingers. "What... I didn't know..." I fumble over my words, but he goes on, saving me from my inability to speak after that proclamation that just blew my mind.

"I couldn't do that love justice. As much as I wanted that forever we promised each other, it wouldn't work in the world I'd created back home, where Olympus came first and everything else a distant second. *You* couldn't come second to anything. You deserved to be first. You deserved to be my queen, and if I couldn't give you that, I didn't fucking deserve you at all. So instead of giving you the scraps of what was leftover, I broke your heart and tore mine out completely, locked it up, and let it fester away, all while being the fuckboy who doesn't do attachments until I saw you again last month and realized I'd fucked it all up. When I found out about Hendricks..." he pauses and shakes his head, looking down at his hands where he grips my thighs like he can't find the words. He looks up, his eyes endless wells of brokenness. "Everything else in my world narrowed. I realized there's something more important than Olympus, more important than work. I wanted to know this kid we made, more than anything.

This kid that you raised all by yourself because I was a selfish bastard who gave you no other choice."

He wipes tears from my cheeks with his thumbs and cups my face in his big hands, staring at me with a look so intense it makes me squirm under the attention.

"You have your psycho eyes on right now. They look like quicksilver and maybe you're going to lock me in a closet and keep me as a pet," I say to diffuse the intensity and the revelation that has burst like the clouds outside, rain now pelting the windows of the penthouse in earnest.

He laughs and drops his hands. "I deserve that. I'm being creepy. I do want to lock you up and keep you forever."

He looks down and makes a noise that is all male, his big hands going to my waist, making me feel small under his touch. His thumbs trace the undersides of my breasts, brushing over my nipples, making me arch into the contact.

"Don't scare me while you touch me like that," I joke, my words becoming a sigh as he rolls my nipples until they're hard peaks.

"You're a very dangerous woman, Lowe. You make me want to do and say all sorts of things that would scare the shit out of us both."

"Like what?" I ask, breathless as his touch roams my skin, his lips and tongue joining between words. It's been so long since I've been touched like this, every nerve ending is craving the attention, needing, and wanting. I lean back on my elbows, shivering under his skilled touch that still knows my body so well as he travels lower.

"I was serious earlier—about babies. How many do you want?" I look down at him as he reaches the apex of my thighs, kneeling on the ground as my legs hang over the edge of the bed, the question asked against my sensitive folds. I thought he was kidding, but, maybe incredulously, he was being honest. He holds my gaze as his tongue parts me and he laps against my center, licking all the way to my clit and we both shudder with the contact, him groaning and me whimpering.

"More," I answer, to both his question and his action. More of his gray-eyed babies and more of his damn skilled tongue.

"Sweeter than I even remembered. Still so responsive and fucking dripping for me. Such a good girl." He slips a finger inside of me. "Just one more?" he asks, stroking too gently to get me there and smiling wickedly because he knows it.

"Another," I pant, my hips rolling, looking for more friction from him.

"Two more." He slips a second finger inside and strokes against my spot with the speed and pressure he knows I like best. My head rolls and I pant. He breathes against my clit but doesn't give me what he knows I want, playing with me.

I grab his hair and pull hard. "More," I demand, throwing my own head back and rocking my hips against his hand, chasing what I need.

"Fine, more babies it is." He stops talking and drops his mouth to my clit, doing something sinful with his lips and tongue at the same time he presses hard against the spot inside, sending me over the edge. I lose my mind, my hips bucking up against his face, and my screams echoing around the large room. He strokes me as my release continues, letting me ride his face and fingers until I'm spent and breathless, delirious with the heady relief that only he can provide.

Tears have tracked down my cheeks again. It's been so long since someone has touched me, made me come, I've forgotten how good it can feel, and I'm surprised that Zander remembers my body so well to elicit this kind of response so easily.

He stands and removes his boxer-briefs in a fluid movement and I marvel at the electric beauty of him, the impressive length and girth he strokes now as he looks down at me sprawled at the end of his bed, feeling satisfied and still wanting more.

"You make me crazy with how good you taste, Lowe. The sounds you make are heaven. You feel so good, everywhere I touch. How do you get better every time I have my hands on you? I can't get enough." He roughly yanks open a drawer on his nightstand and pulls out a condom, ripping the foil and rolling it down his cock. "Tell me when we can start making more babies and I can fill you with my cum again."

I scoot away from him and up the bed. "You're talking a lot about babies tonight. Give it some time. Let's see how you do with Hendricks first. And with me. Now come fuck me, it's been too long for me and I don't remember what it's like."

He kneels on the bed and crawls up my body, his eyes intense as he takes in every bit of me. "How long has it been, Lowe?" He pulls my arms above me and holds my wrists together in one of his fists. The possessive, jealous note in his tone is an obvious double standard given his own fuckboy ways and the myriad of women he has taken to bed.

"You were the last, Zander," I whisper as he hovers above me, with his face so close to mine we're breathing the same air.

His face goes even more possessive, though a tender look passes through his storm cloud eyes, filling them with a mercurial gleam in the moonlit room. He lets go of my wrists to stroke my cheek. "You've always been mine, even when you hated me."

He notches himself at my entrance and pushes in agonizingly slow. My pussy is wet, but still having to stretch to fit him and I moan, arching my back at the near intrusion. He pulls out a bit and can slide in easier this time, and we both groan in satisfaction. I place my hand on Zander's face and stare into his eyes, which look so much like my beautiful son's. He deserves to know my reasons.

"It's why I had the baby. I wouldn't erase that one little piece of you I was able to keep when you shut me out. I didn't want to lose my forever with you, even if I couldn't have *you*."

"Fuck, Lowe." He drops his face to my neck, his arms encircling my back and pulling me tight to his body. "You have me now, forever."

He rises to his knees and pulls me up with him, so I'm straddling his lap, and kisses me like he's starving. Like I'm air and he's drowning. Like he can't get enough of me. This isn't just a joining of our bodies after years apart, I realize, it's a homecoming. Zander still feels like *home*, and being in his arms, our bodies fitting tightly together, has the same feeling of home I felt years ago with him in the Maldives. I blink in recognition and look into his eyes, seeing that same spark of awareness, that same kindling of home that flares brightly for him as well. I kiss him again, never wanting this feeling to end.

I can feel the elusive orgasm building slowly as my hips rock, his hands moving me just right. I push a hand into his hair, the other grips his back, nails sinking into the muscle and holding tight as I ride him hard, pushing the spiraling tension to a breaking point, my whimpers caught by his kisses. I tip my head back, hair tumbling behind me, breathing hard, loving how he feels, and how we move together.

He lowers his mouth to my neck, nipping and sucking at the sensitive spot below my ear, sending a jolt of electricity through me that pushes me over the edge. I scream in ecstasy, lightning flashing behind my eyelids as the storm breaks outside the floor-to-ceiling windows of the penthouse. A boom of thunder rattles the panes of glass, joining in my cries of pure delirium as Zander keeps our bodies moving throughout my release. Rain pelts the glass in torrents now, turning the room darker, shadows swimming around us.

I start to laugh as my trembling muscles finally release me from the deluge of bliss he wrung from my body. I collapse against him, curling into his arms, and let him hold me as I get my breathing under control. "Now I remember what fucking you is like. Holy hell, Zander."

"I'm not done with you, Lowe," he growls. "Get on your knees and give me that delectable ass so I can watch my cock destroy your pussy from behind."

I shiver in anticipation and look up, catching the commanding look on his face, and smile back at him. "Make me," I purr, running a nail down his cheek. Another crack of lightning flashes, lighting up his smoldering gray eyes that take my challenge.

"There's the little Wildcat I remember." With a swift movement, he picks me up and roughly turns me in his arms, pinning my back to his front and clasping his hand around my throat, squeezing gently as I gasp, sending my heart racing and pulling a smile up at the corners of my mouth. Thunder booms, sending the beat of his heart skipping against my back.

"This smart mouth has always been my fucking favorite," he growls against my face. "You miss it a little rougher, baby? You want me to punish this pretty little cunt that's been waiting so patiently for my cock?" He moves the hand he has banded around my waist to grip between my legs. "I'll make you take every inch of me and see what that mouth says after I teach you a lesson."

He lets go of my throat and I take a deep breath that turns into a squeak as he bends me over and pushes my chest into the bed, keeping one heavy hand on my hip. He knocks my knees wider with his leg and pushes into me roughly. I groan, hands fisting the duvet, back arching as I push back against him, meeting the punishing thrusts he's started.

"That's it?" I goad. "I thought you were going to teach me a lesson about my smart mouth."

A loud thwack sounds as his palm connects with my ass and I let out a yowl of pain, trying to jump forward, but he holds me in place.

"Shut the fuck up and take that cock like a good girl."

My body clenches around him, my eyes rolling in bliss even as I whimper, and he smooths his palm over the raw spot on my cheek. He continues the punishing rhythm that has him bottoming out, his hips connecting with my ass on each thrust that rocks my entire body.

"Look at your cunt, taking my cock so well," he grunts out as he slams into me. "You look so pretty." *Thrust.* "Stretching around me." *Thrust.* "Dripping for me." *Thrust.* "Put those pretty fingers to work." *Thrust.* "Touch yourself." *Thrust.* "So you can come apart." *Thrust.* "While I ruin you." *Thrust.*

I moan and unclench one hand from the death grip I have on the duvet that is keeping me from being thrust across the bed and inch my arm under my body, finding my clit and circling. He pushes my hips lower, widening my knees, and drives into me from a new angle, hitting that sensitive spot every time he bottoms out, and I start to see stars as my body tightens around him. I begin to shake, my knees trembling with the effort to keep me upright, and damn does it feel good to take all of him like this. I make a sound I can only call mewling while my pussy spasms, locking up tight around Zander's cock, the breath freezing in my lungs for a heartbeat before the orgasm tears through me, and I scream loud enough I'm sure the neighbors three floors down can hear me.

Another flash of lightning and boom of thunder shakes the room, joining me in my cry of release, and I think that the storm is as relieved as I am that Zander is back in my life and I'm in his bed. I bite down on the duvet as the waves keep washing over me, Zander relentless in his pursuit of my pleasure. With a groan, he buries himself deep and comes, his fingers digging into my hips hard enough to bruise.

He collapses onto my back, tracing kisses across my shoulder, wrapping his arms around me, lacing our fingers together, and squishing me into the mattress in the most divine way, like he knows I want to be entangled in him even now.

"How's that smart mouth now? Throat a little hoarse from screaming? I don't know what was louder, you or the storm."

"Me. Definitely me," I groan, voice scratchy from the effort as I snuggle harder into him. "Why do I keep falling in love with you during lightning storms?" The thought slips out before I can catch it, and he wraps me up tighter, as if he likes hearing those soft words I'm barely able to breathe now as the storm rages outside the penthouse windows.

"It's because we're electric, baby. We'll always set the sky on fire when we give in to each other. Now maybe you'll know I'll love you until the atmosphere can no longer muster the energy to crack the sky open with light and heat and sound to match how I feel. I'm going to love you forever, Lowe, and every time you see lightning, you're going to know the absolute power of my love for you."

Thirty-two

The Atlanta Haute List

Knox Sidelined As Billionaire Proves He Can Do Repeats After All

Our favorite playboy billionaire, Zander Olsen, has finally found a woman he wants more than once, and it's none other than social media sensation, Harlowe Sorenson. The two were seen getting extra cozy at an Atlanta restaurant, Brick and Barley, last night while out with friends, celebrating with cocktails and some longing glances. They couldn't keep their hands off each other in a PDA-filled evening that ended with the pair leaving together in the rain, despite arriving separately *SWOON*. We guess all of that tension finally built up to a boiling point. We do love the explosive chemistry the pair seem to have, and the photos. Y'all. We can feel the pining these two have for one another just from looking at the submissions our Hauties in the know rushed to send in.

While Zander is a notorious player known for a steady stream of one-night stands, we have been speculating about the potential for a relationship between these two since they were initially linked. A flight manifest for a two-week vacation the pair took five years ago was our only clue as to their previous history, but it gave us just enough to build a case for #Zaddygate. There was little to go on other than tension-filled public arguments that we can only expect centered around Harlowe's carefully guarded son, whose father has always been a mystery. Is he Olsen's? Did Olsen even know about the boy? Zaddy Zander really rings a bell for us, but we want the real answers!

The pair appearing cozy now makes us think they reconciled whatever issues may have separated them five years ago after their brief fling (though it was long by Olsen's standards). If Zander is Harlowe's baby daddy, this would make for a very happy family reunion indeed.

However, we can't simply overlook Harlowe's most recent flame, Atlanta Condors tight end, Knox Contraire. They were seen together just a week ago at the Elysium Garden Project fundraiser gala, hosted by Hayes and Paige Olsen, Zander's brother and sister-in-law. Reports from that evening mention quite the commotion, with the Olsen brothers having a very public argument after Harlowe went running out of the room, with Zander following shortly after. The two returned together after a suspiciously long time to rejoin their shared table (awkward, much?). Could this be when things started to turn in favor of Olsen, and Contraire was losing his girl? Was their split amicable, or does he have some less than pleasant feelings about being pushed out of Harlowe's life, and ahem, bed, by the bad boy billionaire? All is quiet on that front, but you know we'll be on the hunt for more clues for our Hauties. Click Like and Subscribe for all the haute gossip!

Thirty-three

Zander

"Kanisarek came back just like you said," Hayes snarls when I walk into the boardroom. "They called last night after you left and started renegotiating. They didn't even wait a full day."

"I told you they were hungry and needed us." I slide into a chair opposite him and take the coffee Weiss hands me with the contracts for the deal that is now back on the table.

"Why didn't you answer my calls? We could have used you to close the deal right then. That's how eager they were. Instead, we had to push it off and now they're asking for more," he says with a cold inflection that's even harder than usual.

Fuck. This is the sacrifice Olympus demands of me. If it's not first in my life, it commands even more. But Harlowe deserved my undivided attention last night, so I turned my phone off. She deserves everything and more. "I had more important matters to attend to."

Hayes levels me with a look that could melt steel. "What the fuck was more important than this deal that would get your fucking engines in the skies on your stupid jets before our damn competition after this nightmare of a cyber attack?" he asks, quiet and deadly, just as Payton enters and looks between us.

"Oh, this will be good. Please, Zander, explain now that I'm here to witness Hayes beat the shit out of you for costing us a few million," Payton says, putting his elbows on the conference room table and propping his chin on his hand as his vivid blue eyes bounce between Hayes and me. The fucking meddler at his middle child best.

"I was celebrating my future wife's success. She hit the bestseller list with her cookbook and was offered a cooking show," I say, seriousness keeping my tone warm and even, pride in every word.

"Harlowe? Your future wife?" Payton laughs, slapping his hands on the table. "I saw the Atlanta Haute List story that you took her home last night. I know we suggested you play nice for the company image, but I didn't expect you to take it this far. Is fucking her so good you asked her to marry you, even being a repeat?"

"She's the best I've ever had. I haven't asked her yet, but I'm marrying her as soon as she'll let me, so get used to the idea."

I'm not ashamed to admit it. I love the idea. Now that I have her back, I don't want to let her go. I didn't even want to take her home last night. I wanted to keep fucking her in my bed, keep her next to me all night, and wake up with her in my arms this morning and every morning after, but she wanted to be home when Hendricks woke up.

Hayes is looking at me like I've sprouted extra heads. "Do you have a syphilis fever or something? What the fuck is wrong with you? Marriage? You? Is it the kid? You don't do attachments or repeats. How did marriage even enter your vocabulary? Please enlighten me, because this isn't you."

They'll never understand unless I lay it all out for them. This is the start of the changes I have to make to ensure that Harlowe gets the very best of me, not what's left over. I need to lay bare the ugly parts of myself to my brothers so I can be the father Hendricks needs, not just an accidental sperm donor who misses out on my child's entire life, all because I've put business first.

"I should've changed five years ago when I fell in love with her the first time. I fucked it up. I missed out on keeping the best thing to ever happen to me. I missed watching her carry our child and getting to know my kid." My voice cracks with emotion and I run my hands through my hair as I turn pleading eyes on Hayes. "I fucking envy what you get to have now. You get to experience your wife carrying your baby, watching her grow, feeling that protectiveness, knowing you made something with her while I was empty, heartless. The woman I loved was alone and scared, doing it all by herself because I was selfish and cruel. I lost out on *that*."

Hayes's face softens as it always does when he thinks about Paige. "Okay, I get it. But we still have Kanisarek to deal with. We needed you available to work on the deal last night."

I point a finger at him, anger fueling me now that appealing to his new, softer side has failed. "And Harlowe needed me celebrating her accomplishments. Some things will be changing, starting now. Harlowe will be my first priority. If she says jump, I'm asking how high. She tells me to leave work, I'm out the door. She wants something, she gets it. If a deal is on the line and Harlowe needs me, I'm going to her. That's going to be my new normal, and we're going to have to figure it out. I'll get this deal settled today and we won't have to bend an inch. I told you they would come crawling back, and they did. Just trust me to make this happen, but know going forward that when I leave work for the evening, I'm going home to my kid and the woman I love, and I don't want to hear shit about work, got it?"

Payton starts clapping slowly, a big ass grin on his face. "Bravo, Zand. I thought Hayes would be the one to renounce his workaholic ways for his wife and kid first, but you beating him to it is really something. Seriously, I didn't see this coming with your fuckboy ways and all. It's going to take me a while to wrap my head around the idea of you as a family man and in a committed relationship."

Hayes shakes his head slowly, like he doesn't know what to make of me, but finally, he nods once with a look of respect. "I guess we could all use a little more of those changes. Now, make the Kanisarek deal happen, and don't make me write any more zeros on those checks than I have to."

That's as good of an acceptance as I'll get from them, and I take it. For us, it's as good as gold and a promise they will respect my new boundaries, even if they don't understand how I got to this point so quickly. I keep my face neutral, but I feel a fierce pride and warmth toward my brothers in this moment for their approval, begrudging or not. I nod back and that's the end of it.

"Call in the team and get Kanisarek on the line. We'll start by offering less. Remember, they walked away from the table first. It's good we made them wait overnight. If they want our original offer, they're throwing in their subsidiaries, too. We'll get their electronics capabilities, which is our end-game, anyway."

"They never had that on the table. We know they were intentionally splitting heavy manufacturing from electronics to make this deal," Payton says, fingers tapping swiftly on his phone, sending out messages to the team.

"If we want to get Pegasus off the ground, this is the only way. We can have manufacturing up and running within the week and at scale with their capabilities. That's even faster than the Rosenthall deal would have been, and only because of the electronics. We targeted them due to the subsidiaries and this possibility." I level my brothers with my most confident glare.

"This is going to cost us. There is no way they are throwing in another portion of their business without getting more from us." Hayes cracks his knuckles and looks lethal. So much for our brotherly bonding over our expanding families.

"I said trust me, Hater. They've played into our hands exactly as I told you they would, haven't they? I can see the bigger picture. Dream with me, here."

"Well, you did it, and I'm still not sure how they left with smiles on their faces despite losing their fucking asses," Payton says, leaning back in his chair after the Kanisarek group has left the conference room following hours-long negotiations. "Normally that kind of deal would result in the kind of mine collapse and cyber attack-style retribution we've seen from Rex's friends."

"It wasn't a hostile takeover and we're not scrapping the whole outfit. They got a more than fair price, and we got what we wanted. I'd call that a decent deal," I respond, rubbing my temples with my thumb and forefinger. I'm ready to see Harlowe, to decide where we're sleeping tonight, to start planning for our future.

"And you got them to take the original offer, no extra zeros. I'm impressed, and our bottom line thanks you. Maybe Harlowe is our golden good luck charm if you getting to fuck her again had you feeling that confident and charismatic in there today to win them over so completely." Hayes claps me on the shoulder as he stands, ready to leave the conference room.

"You're only saying nice things because your finance department didn't have to bend over and take it up the ass to make the deal happen after all," I say with a smirk. He pushes my shoulder roughly.

"Shithead," he grumbles as he turns and heads for his office to finish the day on whatever numbers call to him. I push out of my seat, intent on finishing up early, if possible. I want to see Hendricks when he gets home from school. I have some ideas for a new track to build for his cars.

"I wouldn't start celebrating too fast," Payton says ominously, halting our steps before we can leave the conference room and sending a feeling of dread into the pit of my stomach with the pinched expression on his face. "Looks like our competition is finally revealing itself. Something looking a fuck ton like the Pegasus engine was just announced by Nephele Industries as the latest clean energy jet engine slated for production early this year. Patent pending." He looks up and meets my eyes.

Shit. "The next fucking words out of your mouth better be that legal worked through whatever hurdles they needed to and had this handled so it's a non-issue," I say slowly, knowing in my gut I'm not going to like the answer.

Payton shares a look with Hayes, who is frozen in place next to me, nearly vibrating in anger, then back to me.

"The research and development team couldn't get enough changed from the proprietary information that was stolen in the breach. *You* didn't want us to patent something that is in the hands of who the fuck knows and is being developed as we speak."

I lean down and grip the edge of the conference room table until my knuckles whiten, working to keep my breathing even as my heart beats erratically in my chest. "Obviously Nephele Industries thought it was fucking worth patenting the stolen plans. Why didn't we fucking patent it immediately, so at least we could have been working on an alternative in the meantime while the patent was pending on the original?" My words are clipped, cold, but my blood is boiling with the rage that's surging in me.

I straighten and pace along the bank of windows down the length of the conference room. I feel like putting my fist through each pane of glass, reaching into the gray day outside, and screaming my frustration into the clouds. Instead, I just glare at the rain that has lingered after the storm that screamed with Harlowe last night. I stop my pacing, pushing my hands into my hair the way she did, and try to focus on her. She deserves the best of me, not this hotheaded, angry maelstrom intent on blaming others. It takes a few minutes until my breathing is under control enough to face my brothers again and not want to take a swing at them both. I turn and approach a wary Payton. Hayes remains silent but looks prepared to throttle me if I make a move to get physical.

"Let's get the team on this now. Have legal pull that patent and scour it top to bottom to see if there are any changes from Pegasus. If there are, we file our own patent. We'll keep working to make the changes we need to in the meantime and once we have a viable option, we take that to the patent stage. I should have made the call to begin with, and it's my fault we're in this position now."

Payton whistles. "What did getting that pussy back do to you last night? First, you're setting new rules for your work-life balance, and now, you're accepting blame for a fuck up?"

"No fucking kidding. She fucked the stupid right out of him. He could be turning into a... a decent human being now," Hayes says, tilting his head and studying me.

"She'd have your balls for saying that. She doesn't want me decent, she likes me depraved," I shoot back, feeling a bit of humor flicker to life again. "Now stop messing around. I only have a few hours before I need to see my family. Let's make the most of them."

Thirty-four

Harlowe

"I need details, all of them. From the minute you left the restaurant. Tell me now or I'll keep this coffee to myself, and you look like you need it more than I do." Paloma holds the large iced coffee hostage as I slide into the table she and Callie are already occupying at our favorite café, a super cute Tiffany blue, unicorn-themed place, exploding with flowers.

"She needs details, but I need to be caught up. Paloma won't tell me anything other than Zander and that guy who hit your car showed up at the restaurant last night and you left with Zander. It's not fair that I miss everything because Myles had an event and I couldn't celebrate with you," Callie says, big blue eyes turned toward me as she pouts. "Congratulations on the bestselling book! I'm so proud of you, babe! I got you a cupcake." She slides a chocolate peanut butter cupcake, my favorite, toward me and reaches over to hug my shoulders.

I hug her back. "Thank you! It's surreal. I don't even know what that means, other than my publisher is happy and Alicia has been texting like crazy. Give me that coffee or I'll cut you." I snag the iced caramel macchiato from Paloma's now relaxed hand and she protests.

"You get two sips, then you're spilling all the details. Was it just the night, or are you going to try something?" Paloma insists, poking me in the side as I take big gulps of the sweet coffee.

I swat at her hands to make her stop. I seriously need caffeine. I was up way too late with Zander, but I don't regret one minute of the night we shared. My body is deliciously sore, my hips bruised, my lips swollen, skin still feeling his hands, and he promised to come over as soon as work is over. I felt like a giddy teen when he dropped me off at home, walking me to the door, and making out with me, delaying the goodbye until I was pulling away and closing the door in his face with a laugh.

I turn toward Callie just to spite Paloma. "How was the event with Myles? Was it for the team?"

Callie smiles. "Yeah, some owner's dinner for sponsors, but nothing big. I was there as arm candy for Myles, really. I think Paloma is going to lose her mind, so you better answer her questions." She giggles and sips her lavender latte while eyeing our friend over the rim of her cup.

I laugh when I turn back to Paloma who has torn apart the croissant in her hands and looks like she wishes it was me. "Relax, I'll tell you everything."

I look around us to ensure there aren't any prying eyes or big ears listening in. We're tucked in a corner and it's mid-morning on a weekday, so it's fairly empty, despite the café being an Instagramable hot spot that attracts people seeking aesthetically pleasing pastries and lattes any time of the week. Good. After seeing the Atlanta Haute List this morning, I think I have to be more careful or be prepared for even more stories to come out about us. It's inevitable, really, but I want to be in charge of when that happens, rather than letting the gossip blog dictate the timing.

"He fucked me like I was his sole reason for living. It was so good. Better than I remembered. I must have come a dozen times throughout the night and he didn't want me to leave, but I wanted to be at home when Hendricks woke up. My abs are sore from coming so hard. Best workout I've had in a while. If we keep this up, I'll have a toned midsection again in no time."

Callie gasps and grabs my hands, a huge smile lighting up her face. "I'm so happy you finally broke that long dry spell, and it was so good! I'm swooning." She lets go of my hands to wrap her arms around her middle and shimmies her shoulders in excitement. She's a fierce romantic and wants everyone to be happy, any possible red flags be damned.

"What about all the baby stuff he was saying at dinner? Was he serious? That was totally unexpected, especially given his history. I thought maybe he was just trying to get you into bed," Paloma says, her hazel eyes narrowing. She may have wanted me to get the good dick, but she will always remember what I went through at his hands and wants to keep me from experiencing that again.

"He's serious. About us, *and* babies. He brought it up again and wanted to know how many more I wanted and when we could start on them. He wants this to be… real." I feel warmth spread in my chest from the memory, remembering the look on Zander's face as he wrung pleasure from my body, pushing for the type of commitment I'd long ago lost hope of ever getting from him.

Callie squeals quietly. "Oh my gosh, that's so amazing! You already made the cutest kid. Can you even imagine more? Ugh, I die. My ovaries are exploding as we speak." She slumps in her seat, dramatically clutching her flat lower belly. She has two boys of her own but suffers constant baby fever and can't resist a tiny little human.

My hand slips to my own belly and I remember how it swelled with Hendricks, how his kicks felt, and the fierce love it inspired in me. Despite the fear I had when I found out, I loved being pregnant. By some mercy, I didn't suffer the morning sickness or horrors many women do—maybe because I'd already been dealt such a shitty hand—and it was actually *easy* to carry my son, and I cherished every day I grew him within me. Her fever may be catching. I feel those same butterflies in my stomach ache to bring another little piece of Zander into this world so I can love even more of him. But all in good time.

"An actual relationship would be a nice start before we add more to the family," I laugh. I have to stay grounded when Zander is so intent on flying high into the clouds and taking me with him. He dreams big when I just want stability, consistency, and him.

"Okay, so what happens next? Do you go on dates? Does he move in with you, or you with him? How do you tell Hendricks?" Paloma asks, ever practical.

I scowl at her as I take a bite of my cupcake and chew, giving myself a reprieve from answering her questions that I don't have answers to. I wash the sweet treat down with my coffee and run my hand through my hair while she practically burns holes in my forehead with her eyes.

"Zander's coming over after work today. We'll tell Hendricks when it feels right. He's going to know something's up. He's a perceptive kid and the only man I've brought home prior has been Knox. If Zander is coming around and loving up on me, which I'm sure he is going to do because he can't seem to keep his hands off of me, Hendricks will notice. He'll ask questions. I mean, he was already asking me if he has a dad."

"And you're just going to say yes to all of this and let him sweep you up in it?" Paloma asks, brushing her sheet of smooth sable hair over her shoulder and leaning back in her chair.

"If I want to, then yeah, I will," I tell her, arching a brow in her direction. "What's with the attitude? You were on board with giving him a second chance last night. Why shouldn't I want this now, when Zander is willing to give me the commitment, the relationship, and be the father Hendricks needs?" I lean forward, challenging her right to dictate what I do with my life. She has only so much say—protective best friend or not.

She shakes her head and looks down. "I'm sorry. I'm just struggling to believe that this is the same man who promised you forever then flipped a switch and left you a sobbing mess after that trip five years ago, and couldn't be bothered to give you the time of day to learn you were pregnant afterward." She reaches across the table and takes my hand in hers. "It scared me, the way he left you so broken the last time, Lolo. You've become so strong and resilient since then. I don't want to see him come back and tear that all down again."

"I love that you want to protect me and not see me get hurt again. That was...the worst." I squeeze her hand and she returns it, her hazel eyes softening. "I know there are no guarantees that this time will be different, or that life will treat us fairly, or we will get the outcome we want or even deserve. This could blow up in my face. But it could also be so damn beautiful and turn out exactly the way we need it to. Let's hope for that future, the beautiful one. If I'm willing to take that risk, you, as my best friend, need to support and trust me as I do."

Paloma's eyes shine brightly and she blinks rapidly, a tear slipping down as she looks away. She lets my hand go and swipes at her cheeks quickly. "*Ay, Dios.* You're going to ruin my mascara. This is Tom Ford, bitch. It's expensive and I don't want to reapply a second time today."

Callie starts fanning at her own eyes and we all burst into giggles. "I have hope for your beautiful future with Zaddy Zander and your super cute family," she says, sounding a little choked up but happy. "I wish I could design your wedding gown, but I don't think there's going to be time. I feel like you're going to move fast now that you've gotten to this part. I don't think either of you is going to want to wait."

I laugh and look at Callie with wide eyes. "No one has said anything about getting married yet, Cal," I say, my tone hushed as I look around us again.

She waves away my explanation. "I saw the way he looked at you on the side of the highway. Your single days are numbered. You'll be a wifey soon, and I'll welcome you to the club with open arms."

I raise a brow at her. "What do you mean? We barely exchanged words that day and you were only there for a few of them at that." I'd thought she was struck dumb by Zander's presence, as most women are when he shows up. I hadn't thought twice about her notice and definitely hadn't thought Zander was looking at me in any kind of way that she would have remembered.

"He looked at you like he was starving and you were the only thing he wanted. He played it cool, but it was there. He was Affected, with a capital A."

Paloma nods in begrudging agreement. "She's not entirely exaggerating. He did have this look, like he couldn't believe his eyes that he was seeing you that day. And last night, it was almost disgusting how much he wanted you, how enamored he was with you. He had puppy dog eyes and couldn't take them off you. His hands, too."

Callie grins and taps her feet in excitement. "See, I'm calling it. Quickie wedding and a baby by the end of the year."

I feel my face burn hot in a rare blush. I turn my discomfort on Paloma instead of replying to Callie. "How did your night with Javier end? You look a little tired yourself. Did you get the good dick, too?"

Paloma's wide smile and sweeping of her hair off her shoulder is a harold of the story we're about to hear. "Well, I didn't want to upstage your reunion story, which I felt was far more pressing, but yes, I did indeed get myself a new Latin lover. Javi knows his way around South of the border." She gives us a smug smile that has Callie and I erupting into screams that do draw the attention of other café patrons now. We all start laughing, then huddle close over the table to hear all about her evening in detail.

"Mama, when is Zan Man coming over again? He said he'd build tracks with me but it's been forever. Can you call him? You know how, right? You can make a play date?"

I kneel down and look at Hendricks as I take his coat and backpack when we get into the house after school. "You really liked him, didn't you, my love?"

"Yeah, he was fun. Don't tell Knox, but I think Zan Man is cooler. He knew how an engine works and made the best towers."

I laugh and ruffle his dark curls. "Your secret is safe with me. I'll ask him to come play with you. I would like Zander to come over more often, too. He's very special to me. I like him a lot. Would that be okay with you?"

Hendricks raises his beautiful gray eyes to me and smiles. "Zan Man has eyes like me. We match. That's why you like him."

I blink back the sudden sting of tears and cup his precious little cheek. I wonder at his smart little brain that catches so much for someone so young. I take a deep breath and let it out slowly.

"You're right. You do match. You have his eyes, and you're also super smart, just like him. That's because Zander is your father."

Hendricks dances in place, growing restless with the conversation. "He can stay here with us if he wants. And if we have a sleepover, you can make chocolate chip pancakes for breakfast and he won't want to leave. Then he can be my daddy and tell me if he has powers, like Miss Sharon and Miss Stephanie said."

I laugh and grab Hendricks into my arms, kissing his soft golden cheeks one after the other, until he is giggling. I love his easy acceptance of something I've agonized over his whole life. For Hendricks, it's simple. He's more interested in knowing if Zander is a superhero, and doesn't quite understand what it means to have a father. We'll get there.

"Zander doesn't have any special powers, but you sure do. You make me happier than anyone and give the best Hulk hugs. Ready for one?"

Hendricks opens his arms wide and growls before capturing me in a tight embrace. Then he's wriggling to get out of my arms and heads for the living room and his toys. I stand and put his things away before heading into the kitchen, where I start dinner prep. I'm going all out with a lasagna recipe I've perfected, and I'm making a homemade sauce, so it's going to take a while.

Thirty-five

Zander

Walking up to Harlowe's door tonight feels like I'm beginning again. Not just walking away from who I was in the past, but piling up all the shitty pieces—the fuckboy who slips into DMs, the guy who was afraid of attachments, the douche who didn't do repeats, the hothead who wants to blame others, the man who would rather break the heart of the woman he loves than change his life for her—and setting them all on fire so I can never become that person again.

Each step toward her house feels lighter as I let them go and look forward to the man I want to be. A man of my word. A man who shows up, who sticks around, who has some fucking integrity and knows what's important in this world. I know, now. God, I fucking know.

I set my bag down and ring the bell, shifting the bouquet in my hands as I wait for the door to open. It's about time I do this the right way. No *you up* calls or texts in the middle of the night. No showing up and expecting to be let in with selfish intent. I'm bringing the fucking romance, because that is what my little Wildcat deserves. The best of me, and the best in this life.

"Hi, sorry I'm a mess. I've been cooking for hours," Harlowe says, opening the door. "Oh!" She covers her mouth when she sees the giant bouquet of tropical flowers.

I made sure it was full of flowers we saw in the Maldives; orchids, plumerias, birds of paradise, and more I can't even name. They're pretty, but she puts them all to shame with how fucking gorgeous she is. Her cheeks are flushed, caramel skin glowing. Her dark hair is wavy and loose around her shoulders and I want to thread my fingers into the soft locks right at the nape of her neck and pull it tight as I drive my cock deep inside of her and fill her with my cum, making more of our pretty little babies.

"Hey, Lowe," my voice is a low purr that pours in from the dark. "You look amazing. These are for you." I hold out the flowers.

She takes them as she steps back from the door and lets me in, shaking her head and smiling radiantly. "Flowers and compliments? What is this, a date?"

I pick up my bag and follow her in, shutting the door behind me. "Fuck yes, it is. I'm going to date you every chance I get. Each day I get with you is going to be special. I squandered the last five years I could've had you in my arms. There's no way in hell I'm wasting another one thinking it's ordinary if I get to have you in it."

"Language," she admonishes quietly, nodding her head toward the living room. "We have little ears listening, and he's a sponge that happens to like repeating what he hears."

She leads us toward the kitchen, and I feel like an asshole. Of course, the first thing I do is wrong. I look into the living room as we pass and see Hendricks on the floor in the middle of a pile of Legos and toys, thankfully absorbed in his creations and oblivious to us.

"I'm already messing up this father thing. I'm sorry, Lowe." I keep my voice quiet but I can't keep the note of panic from creeping into it. I can close multi-million-dollar deals, speak to international business associates with authority, and schmooze literal kings and heads of state with ease, but I don't know what to do with a four-year-old kid.

She laughs. "Don't look so horrified. I slip up occasionally, too. You'll get used to it. I don't expect you to jump right in and know what to do." I feel a bit of relief wash over me, but I'm going to do better. No swearing when my kid can hear.

Harlowe bends down and opens a cabinet, pulling out a vase for the bouquet. I set my bag down by the island before I come up behind her as she fills it with water and circle my arms around her waist.

"It smells amazing in here, but you smell even better." I run my nose along her neck, inhaling her coconut and floral scent, and she shivers against me. "Fuck, I missed you today," I whisper, quiet enough so Hendricks is sure not to hear. My hands slip under the hem of her shirt, finding her soft skin and stroking gently. She sighs and leans back against me.

The oven timer goes off, the beeping startling us both and we jump apart like scolded teens. I laugh and she spins to turn it off, grabbing oven mitts off the counter.

"You should say hi to Hendricks before we get carried away in here. He was asking about you today. I told him you would be coming over more and I really like you." She pulls a bubbling dish of lasagna out of the oven and sets it on the island to cool. She turns back to me and arches an eyebrow. "The observant little nugget said it was because you two have matching eyes and that's why I like you." She looks up at me with a rare shy look and I want to take her chin in my hand and kiss it off her face. "I... told him you're his father." She looks at me, seeking approval, and I do take her face now, holding her with the reverence she deserves for this act of benevolence.

"Thank you, baby. That means everything to me."

She turns her face into my hand and kisses my palm before she pulls away and smiles. "He wants to have a sleepover now and thinks if I make you chocolate chip pancakes you'll never leave."

I feel a smile taking over my face and bet it looks cocky as hell. "He's right. You feed me and I'm sticking around for good." I pull her back into my arms and kiss her hard, taking a handful of her delicious ass in the exchange for good measure before I set her back on her feet and turn toward the living room. "Hey, Boss, I heard you were asking about me."

"Zan man!" Hendricks shouts, leaping up from his toys and sprinting across the room.

He launches his little body into my outstretched arms. I catch him, bringing him close, and hug him tight like this is our normal greeting, not the second time we have seen each other. I close my eyes and bury my nose in Hendricks's curls, breathing in the smell of my son and cataloging it away for later. This is the same greeting Harlowe received the last time I was here, the one I was so jealous of. Fuck, it feels good to have the boy in my arms, welcoming me in the same way, and I feel the unfamiliar sting of tears hit me. Am I going to break down over this?

"I missed you, buddy," I say as I sit down with Hendricks still in my arms, not ready to let him go. "I'm sorry I couldn't come to play earlier; I was busy at work. I changed my schedule so that won't happen too much anymore, and I'll have lots of time to play now. Sound good?"

Hendricks nods, his eyes sparkling. "Mama says our eyes match and I'm smart like you because you're my daddy." He holds his hand up to his mouth and leans toward my ear. "Can you tell me if you have powers like a superhero? I'll keep your secrets, I promise."

Hearing him call me daddy does something stupid to me inside that I have to laugh to cover as I look at his eager face. "My only power is negotiating business deals, and while that's super handy for work, I can't fight crime, and I don't have any special abilities like Thor or Iron Man. But maybe I have the power to make your mama fall in love with me. Do you think I can do that?"

I look over my shoulder toward the kitchen and catch Harlowe looking away from us quickly, pretending to be busy with the vegetable dish she's preparing. Hendricks sits up taller and looks with me.

"I can help. Mama loves me, so it'll be easy. Is that your bag? Are we having a sleepover tonight?"

He bounces on my knees in excitement and my chest goes molten, my pulse surging in a way that feels better than anything I've felt in a long time. This kid can take me higher than skydiving, just like his mama can. I may give up chasing the adrenaline rush with these two permanently in my life now.

"Yeah, buddy, I'm staying forever. Now, why don't we put some work in on these tracks and towers before dinner so we can get a run in?"

Hendricks insists on sitting on my lap to eat, wanting Harlowe next to us. It's not exactly easy to eat around a squirming four-year-old, but I can't deny him. While I wait for him to finish eating before I begin, I hold Harlowe's hand on the table, and when Hendricks places his little hand on top of the pile, Harlowe snaps a photo with her phone. When I give her a questioning look, she turns her phone around and shows me an Instagram post on her Foulmouthed Foodie page of all three of our hands together in focus with the lasagna in the background that she captioned *Family Dinner feels good, even if it took five years to get it on the table.*

My chest expands with pride that she would claim me so publicly, and I want to pull out my own phone and share that everywhere, as well. I want to delete every photo I have and make that the only one on my feed, my profile picture, my everything. I've already closed my DMs to anyone I'm not following, scrubbed out all the thots and models and women who had dropped into them over the years, and removed the temptations that don't even get a rise out of me anymore. Not when I can look over at Harlowe and see my whole world in her eyes.

After dinner, Harlowe lets me help with bath and bedtime, bringing me into their nightly routine and showing me what I've been missing all these years. My heart aches with a fierceness at each new piece I get to experience, and when Hendricks looks up at me from his bed, his eyes that do indeed match mine, already looking sleepy, and tells me he loves me, I fucking shatter. I kiss his forehead and walk out of the room to wait for Harlowe to finish up with him.

I know he's four and doesn't understand the magnitude of the words that are just a part of his normal nightly routine that ends with saying he loves his mom, and tonight he loves me because I helped put him to bed. But it breaks down any last vestige of the man I was before I knew he existed. That person is decimated. Struck by lightning and burned to cinders and ash, scattered away on the wind, leaving someone new behind.

"Oh, Zander," Harlowe says when she softly closes the door and finds me leaning against the wall in the hall. I let Harlowe lead me into her bedroom with silent tears sliding unchecked down my face. She closes the door and turns back to me, concern etching her gorgeous features.

I grip her face with an urgency in my shaking hands, making her look at me, at the raw emotion that is gripping my soul, forcing her to be in this place of newness with me.

"I don't want to live another day without you in it. I fucking love you, Lowe, and I love that little boy we made, and I can't get enough of either of you."

She makes a choked sound and her eyes shine with tears. "That's a lot to commit to so quickly. You don't have to jump in this fast. You can feel it out. I'm okay with that." She rubs her hands up my arms, letting me have an out, giving me space to work up to the man she needs me to be.

"When have you ever known me to work up to anything? I go hard and fast after anything I want. I happen to be looking at what I want more than anything in the whole world."

I let go of her face and reach into my pocket to pull out the ring that's been burning against my skin since I put it there before I got out of the car earlier. I drop to my knees because she deserves me worshiping at her feet, and she gasps, leaning down over me, starting to shake when she realizes the direction this is taking.

"Marry me, Lowe. I'll wait for whenever you're ready, but please, be my forever. Be my wife, the mother of my babies, the love of my fucking life. I'm serious. I can't live another day without you by my side, making me the happiest man in the world."

Harlowe collapses into my lap, letting me hold her close as she sobs on my shoulder, her arms around me just as tightly. She is nodding against me and I feel my chest swell with a feeling of utter elation. I stand and spin her around in my arms once, kissing her tear-stained face when she's on her feet again. I slide my hand along her arm until I get to her fingers and bring them down between us, sliding the flawless, five-carat emerald-cut diamond set in platinum onto the third finger of her left hand. The main stone is set off with a diamond halo, the split band studded with even more diamonds, so everything sparkles almost as much as Harlowe does as she smiles up at me now.

"You do move fast," she says wetly, but there is humor in her tone. I brush tears off her cheeks with my thumbs, letting one trail down over her bottom lip, pushing it into her mouth and over her tongue. I let her suck her tears off before I remove my thumb with a pop and drag it down her throat as she shivers under my touch.

"I should have done this five years ago, so no, it's the slowest damn thing I've done in my life. Take everything off but my ring and let me fill you with my cum. We'll see just how fast we can make another baby," I say, my hands sliding down her back until I cup her ass and pull her against me so she can feel how I'm hardening for her.

Her eyes narrow with feline coyness. "If you want me naked, you're going to have to undress me yourself."

"There's my little Wildcat coming out to play. How quiet do we have to be with our kid down the hall? Because you're fucking loud when you come and if I have to stuff your panties in your mouth to keep you quiet, I need to keep those close by." I slip my fingers under the hem of her shirt and lift it up and over her head as she raises her arms.

"I turned his white noise machine on and he's a sound sleeper, plus we're on the other side of the house. Fuck me as hard as you want," she says, her fingers making quick work of the buttons on my shirt and tugging it off my shoulders.

I push the cups of the lace bra away from her incredible tits and get my hands onto the supple flesh below, rolling her dusky nipples in my fingers. "What if I wanted to make love to you instead? You're still going to scream either way. Would you like that as much as me ruining your pretty little pussy?"

I toss her bra aside and slide my hands down her stomach to her jeans, popping the button and inching the zipper down. She's already made quick work of my pants, leaving them at my ankles as I toe off my shoes. She shimmies out of her jeans and panties while I remove the rest of my clothes. I guess we both got anxious and stopped worrying about who took off what pieces of clothing.

"You can do whatever you want to me. I just need that incredible cock inside of me very, very soon," she says, looking down at where it's straining between us. She reaches out and strokes me, the diamond on her finger looking incredible as it moves up and down my shaft.

Her hand feels so good, but I can smell her arousal from here, and when I look down, her thighs are already slick with it. "Your dinner was delicious, but I want dessert now. I need you to ride my face and drown me in that sweet cunt." Her eyes go wide as I take her hand and lead her to the bed, lying down and guiding her over me to straddle my shoulders. "Hold on to the headboard and let me feast, Lowe."

"Zander, this is too much. You won't be able to breathe. Let me just lie down," she says, hovering over my chin as I breathe in her sweet aroma deeply and feel my cock harden to a steel rod. Fuck she smells good.

"Did I say I wanted to breathe? I said I wanted to drown in you. That means I want to eat out this sweet pussy and have you dripping down my face. Now sit and ride my face. The only words out of your mouth need to be my name, harder, and more." I hook my arms under her thighs and grab her hips, supporting her and keeping her tight to my face as I lick along her seam and take in my first taste of her tonight. "Fuuuuuck," I growl, the sound rumbling against her sensitive skin and eliciting a shiver through her whole body.

I flatten my tongue and swirl at her clit and she tentatively rocks her hips with the motion. I hum my approval and lap at her again before I drive my tongue inside and hear her sharp inhale and the moan that gets me. I fuck her with my tongue, letting her grind against my face as she finds a rhythm with her hips she likes.

"More," she encourages, and I growl against her again.

I keep at her, moving to her clit and nipping the sensitive bundle with my teeth and getting a whimper, but she bears down harder on me and I smile at that. I suck on her clit and her thighs start to shake, her hips rocking with more force, and she goes rigid, her moans turning to shouts of pleasure. Her taste floods my mouth and I lap it up, letting her ride my face like the good girl she is.

I flip her onto her back before her waves have even finished and kiss her while she still coats my face. She kisses me back languidly, soft and sated with her release. "Best dessert I've ever had," I tell her, kissing down her neck to her chest.

"I still want your cock in me," she says, a smile turning up the corners of her mouth as she pushes up onto her elbows, following my path of kisses down her body.

When I've made it to her hips, I flip her over and raise her hips so the heart shape of her ass is invitingly spread for me, pussy on display, glistening and still dripping. "You want my cock in this needy little cunt?" I push a finger inside of her, feeling her inner muscles suck me in, wrapping me in her velvety heat. I pull it out and push in a second with it.

Harlowe stretches her arms out over her head on the bed and pushes her hips back against my fingers. I add a third finger and she gasps.

"Yes, I want you inside of me now. I want you filling me up so deeply I'll never get you out."

"I'm going to cum so deep inside of you, and so often, you'll have my seed leaking down your thighs all the time. Is that what you want, baby?"

I twist my fingers and withdraw them from her pussy, which was starting to tremble, and she mewls. I don't leave her empty for long as I notch myself at her entrance and push in, filling her as far as I can. She gasps, still not able to take me in all in one go.

"Fucking take my cock like a good girl. You're made for this." I rub my palm up her spine and she pushes back into me, relaxing around my girth, letting me slide in more.

"God, I love how you feel," she moans, rocking back against me and wiggling her hips, making her ass jiggle in a way that has my eyes nearly rolling back in my head with need. I'm about to lose my load from that little motion alone. I grip her hips hard to still her movements and give myself a chance against her wiles.

"Lowe, goddamn, I'm obsessed with you. There is no comparison. You ruined me for anyone else a long time ago, but this is too much." I look down and watch as I stretch her pussy, the way she greedily sucks me back in, how good our bodies look together. "Fuck, baby, look at you taking me so well." I roll her hips to the side and flip her over, moving her knees up to her shoulders, pushing my body tight to hers so I can look into her eyes as I drive in deep. She grabs my shoulders and holds me just as close.

"Oh, God, yes," she moans, head tipped back as I hit her spot and rub her clit with my hips on each stroke.

"That's right, I'll be your God tonight and you'll be my Goddess every day. I'll worship you with my cock and my very fucking life."

I rock my hips as her thighs begin to shake under me, her face flushed and delirious with lust as her muscles begin a butterfly soft trembling around my cock. I drop my mouth to her nipples, swirling my tongue around first one peaked bud until it's straining, then the other. I suck one tight peak into my mouth, grazing my teeth along the sensitive flesh as I release it.

She gasps, eyes closing tight as her pussy clamps down on me, her orgasm barreling through her and wringing me tight as she screams her pleasure. Her nails rake down my shoulders and I take the pain to keep me grounded, but it ends up mixing with the pleasure and sends me tumbling with her over the edge. I pump my hips tight into her and explode, my release feeling cataclysmic and unending as her orgasm continues to squeeze me, her name ripped from my throat on a groan. Lightning flashes along my spine, my heart thundering in my chest as my pulse keeps up its staccato beat of *Mine! Mine! Mine!* when it comes to Lowe.

I gather her into my arms and roll to my side, staying inside of her and letting my cum spill around us both. I'll bathe her myself later, but for now, she can wear it like my ring.

"We're going to need a bigger house for all the babies I want with you," I purr into her hair.

She sighs happily against my chest, and I can feel her cheek turning up with a smile. "I'll let you find us a big house with more rooms as long as I can have a gorgeous kitchen with pretty natural light for my food photography."

"Challenge accepted, little Wildcat. I'll get you the biggest kitchen I can that's good for taking photos of your food and thirst traps and all the rooms for our babies," I promise.

She snorts out a laugh. "I caught the man my traps were set for. I won't need to post them anymore."

"Baby, you can post whatever the fuck you want to. I'll be the first one liking that shit and bending you over whatever surface is closest when I find you to show you how much I appreciate it. It's your brand and I fucking love it. Don't change a thing about yourself, just keep embracing everything that makes you, you."

"Oh, Zander," she says softly, her hands coming to my face and tipping her forehead against mine before she kisses me gently. "I love you."

My heart fucking aches with how much I love hearing her say those words to me. I never thought I'd get the chance to actually hear them from her after I intentionally broke her heart, and I'll never be fully worthy of that love, but I'll damn sure try to do her love justice now and every day she'll let me.

"I love you so fucking much. Now and forever, Lowe."

Epilogue

Harlowe

Six months later

"That's a wrap on The Foulmouthed Foodie at Home!" Renee, the director, says from the dining room where the monitors are set up. "Congratulations, Harlowe, that was perfect! We couldn't have asked for a better final day of shooting."

The crew begins moving and talking at once, noise and chaos erupting around us after the methodical quiet that had taken over during production. Each person here has become like family in the few weeks they have taken over our home, letting me cook for them, staying late around our long white oak dining table sharing stories, and generally working as a well-oiled machine during long days of shooting. I'll be sad to see them go, but it will be nice to not have production equipment everywhere and gaffer tape stuck to my floors around cables.

I look around the kitchen of the gorgeous home Zander and I moved into four months ago. The lighting in here is beautiful and my food photography and videos have never looked better. My selfies and thirst traps, too. Zander often helps with those now, getting better angles than I can on occasion and always reaping the rewards of being the first to like the post and then fucking me right in the same spot to make sure I know he approves. It turns out he's been my biggest admirer all along, and even if he wasn't engaging with the posts, he was definitely seeing them.

"You were so good, my love. Now you get to play." I set Hendricks down with a kiss and let him run off to his playroom, where he's bound to make a huge mess and be entertained for hours now that he's free from being a part of shooting. Zander rubs my lower back and grins as his eyes track how fast Hendricks escapes. The novelty of being in my cooking videos wore off quickly for our son, and he was itching to leave shortly after realizing that there was a lot of repeating shots and not a lot of action.

I wanted both of my guys to be in this episode, which will actually be the first to air on the Gourmet Network. It will introduce my family to the world, and ground my audience in who I am at my core, and what I believe in. The sexy, foulmouthed part of me is still very much the root of the show, but I want the world to see the softer, family-oriented side as well, and to know the two can coexist in this body and show.

Renee slings an arm around my waist, and I hug her back. "The execs have been so happy with the dailies we have been sending them. This is going to be such a great show. You're a breath of fresh air and so different from anything we have had on the network before. The viewers are going to eat it up."

I laugh at her food pun. "I fucking hope so. This is who I am. They can take it or leave it for all I care."

She points at me. "That's it right there. That's what we need more of on this network and why you got this opportunity to be one of the new shows on the streaming platform. That way you could really let the foulmouthed thing flow." She drops her arm and steps back as she pulls the headset off her neck. "We'll break everything down and get out of your beautiful little family's hair, and Bee will send over the details for the wrap party. We want to celebrate with you before we all leave Atlanta."

"Celebrating with sparkling water and mocktails for me, of course," I say, rubbing the small bump under the tight blue dress I'm wearing, my diamond rings sparkling as they catch the production lights with the movement. The dress highlights the bump, which is the point, as I'm just four months pregnant and only now starting to round out, so it was either put it on display or look bloated.

The house was actually a pregnancy present as soon as Zander and I found out. It was an entirely different experience this time around, with Zander buying the tests and anxiously pacing the bathroom tiles as the timer ticked down the minutes. It was pure joy for both of us when the tests shouted PREGNANT at us. Watching him drop to his knees at my feet, burying his face against my thighs as he cried happy tears, was one of the sweetest things I've ever experienced. My heart was so full of love, adoration, and happiness that I thought I would burst from it. Like with Hendricks, this pregnancy has been easy and I've loved every moment of it. Zander is even more ravenous for my body each day as it grows his baby. I have a feeling he's going to want to keep me pregnant until I tell him I'm done having his beautiful children.

"Mocktails, of course," Renee says, laughing. She reaches up and kisses my cheek. "I'm sure we'll be back here next year filming another season and will get to see that gorgeous baby on the outside and I'll spoil it rotten. If it's a girl, you can name her after me." Someone calls her name and she winks at me before walking off to speak with a production assistant wrapping up cables.

Zander laughs and shakes his head as she goes. We've been having this conversation nightly, dreaming up what our future child will be like and imagining her on the other side. We're having a little girl, and we've decided to call her Hana. Zander picked her name, following the naming structure of Hendricks's and my own starting with an H. I told him we don't have to name all of our babies like that, but I figured I could indulge him for this one, since I did get to pick the first all by myself. I won't tell Renee any of this. We're keeping the gender and name to ourselves for now.

"Are you ready for tonight?" Zander asks, his lips brushing the shell of my ear as his arms wrap around me from behind.

I sigh and lean into him. "I'm looking forward to seeing Paige and the baby. Your brother, not as much, but that's always going to be the case."

We're going to his brother and sister-in-law's house to meet their brand new baby girl, Madelyn James, who was born a few days ago. Well, I guess they're my in-laws, now, too. Zander and I were married last month in a small ceremony in the back garden of our pretty home, and his whole family was invited. I begrudgingly forgave his asshole brother, Hayes, when Paige dragged him over to apologize. That little twenty-two-year-old Southern belle certainly has her man whipped, because he bent to her will as soon as she turned a disappointed look on him when she heard the story of our first encounter five years ago. I won't be underestimating her anytime soon, and I think I'll like having her as a sister-in-law and friend.

"Don't worry, I rarely look forward to seeing Hayes, and I work with him. Payton will be there, too, and he's a great buffer. Or he'll stir the pot. You never know with him."

I turn my head and give Zander a look when he brings up his middle brother. "We need to set him up with someone already. He can't be the only one of you not attached now. You're married and a father with another on the way. Hayes is married and has a child now, too. Payton is single and practically lives at the office by the sound of things. What's his deal?"

"Oh, no. I'm not getting mixed up in that. Wipe that scheming look off your face, wife. You don't have single friends now that Javi and Paloma are practically living together. Leave him alone. He'll figure his shit out when he's ready." Zander kisses me, but I can't stop where my thoughts have gone. I love when he calls me wife and I want everyone to feel this way.

"Don't you want him to experience how happy you are?" I smile wickedly, thinking I've trapped him.

Zander grins and spins me in his arms to kiss away the smile from my lips. "Payton is busy hunting down a hacker at the moment. He doesn't have time for dating or finding love. I think he's more committed to Olympus than any of us."

"Fine," I pout. "I still think his single days are numbered. If even *you* could end up married and a doting father, there's hope for any confirmed bachelor."

Zander chuckles and pulls me closer, tipping his forehead against mine. "That's only because I needed to get out of my own way. It was always you, Lowe. We were meant for each other. I should have gone with my instincts and what I knew in my soul was right and never let you go, but I was stupid and wasted five good years. If Payton can find even half of what you and I have and not mess it up in the process, he'll be so fucking lucky."

"We're so lucky." I nuzzle against his neck and bite his earlobe.

"'That we are, little Wildcat, and I'll never forget that you gave me a second chance to experience this happiness. I love you, Lowe."

"I love you, Zander."

"Now, say your goodbyes. I'm taking you to bed while they finish tearing this all down and I'm stuffing your panties in your mouth to keep you quiet. You can't bite my ear like that and not expect to get your ass marked and have me stretching that pussy as you take me deep."

I shiver and back away from him with a look of bratty defiance before turning to the remaining crew members. "Thank you all so much for making my dreams come true," I say to the busy group of people.

I give hugs and say individual farewells as Zander looks on, his stormy gaze feeling heavy on my back the whole time. He's been incredibly supportive of this whole endeavor. He's also been home so much more than I expected. He leaves early every morning, but he's home for dinner each evening. His phone is turned off before he walks in the door, and he makes sure he has time to play with Hendricks before bath and bedtime, then he dotes on me. Foot massages, bubble baths, long and sensual lovemaking, or hard and fast fucking. Our lives feel so complete, and it's because Zander is in it. When the last piece of equipment has been packed up and each crew member has left, I turn and find Zander leaning against the island, arms crossed over his chest, in the blissfully silent and empty kitchen.

"I told you I was going to fuck you while they packed up, yet you stayed down here and watched them down to the last box. Am I not interesting enough now?" he growls, the tone low and full of sensual threat.

"I just missed seeing my kitchen like this," I say, laying my upper body on the marble island and caressing the cool surface lovingly. I straighten and turn, raising my dress to my hips, pulling myself up on the island, and spreading my legs. "And I knew you would still want to fuck me, even if I made you wait. Now, husband, get on your knees and worship me."

"Fucking hell, Lowe," he groans, rounding the island and dropping to his knees in front of me. "So pretty and wet for me. I bet you were dripping the whole time you were saying your goodbyes and wishing you were full of my cock instead."

He pulls my legs over his shoulders as I smile at him. He pushes the thin material of my thong to the side and buries his mouth against my hot center, his tongue licking against my slickness and making my back arch as I moan. He laps at me, making deep, satisfied sounds that rumble against me, sending small tremors quaking through me already. This is Zander in his element, making my pleasure his priority, finding every spot and place I want to be touched before I can even ask for it. I moan as his fingers slide inside just as I was going to beg for them, pumping and curling as his tongue swirls along my clit in a perfect rhythm.

I push my fingers into his hair and tug, rolling my hips against his face as I feel the orgasm building low in my belly. He presses just so, nipping at my clit and quickly sucking against it until I break. A hoarse shout works its way from my throat as I hold him close and ride his face and hand. "Oh, fuck, yes, Zander!"

He lets me come down slowly, easing me through my climax with gentle strokes and licks until I can uncurl my fingers from his hair and relax my legs from his shoulders. He withdraws his fingers, sucking them clean before he's standing and gathering me in his arms. He holds me close and carries me out of the kitchen, passing Hendricks's playroom and making sure he's content playing before we continue to our room. He sets me down on our bed and gently strips me out of my clothes and removes his own, so careful with me despite how I'll ask him to fuck me and how he'll oblige. His tenderness is something I'm having to get used to, but it's just as beautiful as the feral parts of him I already knew I loved.

"Hard," I say, when he's free of his pants and I've crawled up the bed.

His gray eyes light up and he stalks toward me, grabbing my ankle and pulling, causing me to slide back down the bed toward him. "Don't think you're getting away with being a brat earlier. I told you what I wanted."

He rolls me onto my knees, keeping my hips up and chest lowered, and notches against my opening, plunging into me deep. I moan and smile, loving that he knows just how to treat me. We both groan as he pulls out slowly until just the tip remains, then slams back in.

"If you're teaching me a lesson about obedience, I'm only learning that you give me what I want when I'm a brat," I say between gasps.

He changes his angle and rocks his hips, hitting a new spot that sends tingles along my spine. "You're my brat and I'll give you anything you want. Now shut up and let me fuck the hell out of you like we both want." He grips my waist hard and pulls me tight against him as he crashes his hips into my ass with a jarring force that sends lightning bolts dancing along my skin and lighting me up.

I hold on and let him set the bruising pace, his angle hitting that perfect spot on each deep thrust. My thighs shake with effort, my body tensing, and my inner muscles squeezing, but Zander continues his quest. I bite my lip and push back against him, feeling the edge so close. When I come apart, his name screamed into the mattress, my body exploding around him, Zander is there to hold me up, catch me as I come down, and finally, fall apart with me. Falling apart is the easiest thing to do now, with him by my side. I know he'll always put me back together. I've come to realize that forever was never actually a lie, it was a promise. And it turns out Zander keeps those better than most.

This concludes The Southern Thirst Trap, but the Southern Gods Series continues! If you enjoyed this book, I would be grateful if you could leave a review on the platform(s) of your choice. Reviews are so valuable to authors, and each one helps share our stories with others! If you enjoyed seeing the other Olsens in this book and want to know more about them, you can read their stories! Hayes and Paige's story is told in books one and two, The Bourbon Bride and The Bourbon Bargain. Payton's story is told in book 3, The Southern Submission. Check out a sneak peek in the next chapter!

If you enjoyed Knox in this story and want to know more about him, check out Reckless On Ice, which is his love story and the start of the Gods Of The Ice MM hockey romance series!

Hugs,
Adrian

The Southern Submission Sneak Peek

Payton

"Fucking finally!"

I turn toward the husky, feminine voice of my sister-in-law and give her a teasing smile.

"Harlowe," I acknowledge. "What's the deal? I'm not late."

She reaches for the bright pink box with the oversized white bow I'm carrying, places it on a table behind her, and wraps me in a quick hug. Her growing baby bump presses uncomfortably against me.

"You're supposed to be the buffer but you've failed. Get your ass in there and buff. There's only so much Paige and Zander can do to make Hayes and me play nice for very long. I need more allies," she grumbles, releasing me from her grasp.

I laugh. They have bad blood and it doesn't matter how many apologies Paige forces out of Hayes, or how long they're family, the two may never be friends. They begrudgingly ended their years-long feud following her reconciliation with my younger brother six months ago. Since then, they have managed to tolerate each other without coming to blows. It started as a slight Hayes served Harlowe five years ago when he tried to pay her off to stay away from Zander, treating her like one of the hundreds of other women he'd slept with who'd taken the same. That didn't go over well and it still stings Harlowe's considerable pride.

"You could always fight it out. See which lion wins. My money's on you," I joke. She narrows dark eyes on me, looking very much like a lioness ready to attack and I put up my hands to warn off her claws. "Okay, fine, relax."

Harlowe drags me deeper into the Buckhead mansion Hayes and Paige live in. Soon, the squawking cries of my newborn niece, Madelyn, can be heard. Paige is reclining with the tiny baby in her arms, looking tired but happy. Harlowe and Zander's son, Hendricks, is next to her, peering at the baby with interest. Hayes hovers nearby, watching his wife and newborn intently as if they'll need something in the next second. Zander sits on the other end of the sofa watching his son with a smile.

Zander missed out on the first four years of Hendricks's life because he didn't know he had a son. Once he found out about his kid, he became the most enthusiastic father and loves that little boy with a fervor I haven't seen from him since he discovered sky diving.

This little scene of domestic bliss is a touching sight. Both my brothers now have wives and children, settling into a new era where our company, Olympus International, is no longer the prime directive in our lives. It's still my number one priority, and I'll continue that way. I have no intention of settling down or letting myself fall prey to whatever's in the water they're drinking. There's no chance of that happening because I don't date. At most, I have play partners who let me take out my desires and urges, and that more than satisfies any need I have for companionship and sex. But...I have to admit, seeing my brothers like this looks good. I'm happy for them.

"Hi!" Paige calls with a smile. "Come hold Maddie. She's waiting to meet her other favorite uncle."

My eyes grow wide as I tentatively sit next to Paige, holding out my hands for the pink-wrapped bundle she hands me. The little thing inside has dark hair and a tiny, squashed face that blinks at me sleepily and cries as I take her in my arms. I've never held a baby before, she feels fragile. Her cries grow louder as I hold her close.

"I'm doing this wrong. She doesn't like me." I try to give her back to Paige as the bundle squirms.

"She cries at everything right now. Let her get used to you. My arms need a break and yours are strong from all that swimming you do. Stand up and walk around, she likes that," Paige instructs. I do as the Southern belle tells me, rising carefully and walking the length of the room while my older brother keeps staring like the brooding, protective father he is.

"I'm not going to drop her, Hater, you can stop eyeing me like that," I tell him. I use his childhood nickname, making him grimace.

I laugh and feel the tiny baby settle in my arms, her cries growing quieter as I pace. I catch sight of Cerberus, Hayes's hulking black Cane Corso guard dog, watching me with shrewd whiskey-colored eyes from his bed in the corner. He's not a typical dog that'll love on you or happily take treats from guests. He's only a snuggly pet for Paige. With the rest of us, he's a menacing presence protecting his people, and apparently, I'm holding his newest charge and could be here to hurt them.

"Hey, tell your demon spawn I'm not a threat," I say, looking over my shoulder at Paige, who has more sway with the dog than Hayes does.

"Cerberus, Uncle Payton is our friend. We love him, okay, big guy? I have yummy treats if you behave yourself," she coos in a baby voice that instantly has the big dog's stubby tail wagging. He lowers his head to his paws and lets out a chuff of air as he finally relaxes his bulky shoulders. That dog is too fucking smart and scary. I relax a little now that he's not looking like he wants to jump over the couch and take me down just for holding Madelyn.

"You look so natural holding a baby," Harlowe says in a sing-song voice. She's draped in Zander's lap, looking over at Paige for confirmation. Paige nods when I catch her eye, looking a little too dreamy herself. "When will you start dating seriously so you can have a family of your own? Don't you want this for yourself?"

"She's right, Payton. You look good holding my little baby. It's making my heart burst with happiness. Hayes, you better get over here and hold me before I cry. My hormones are all over the place," Paige says, dabbing at her eyes.

"Oh, no you don't," I warn, ready to hand the baby back right now and get the hell out of this trap my sisters-in-law are setting for me. "You're both hormonal and crazy if you think I'm in need of a wife and babies."

"It's like what Jane Austen wrote in Pride and Prejudice," Paige says. "*It is a truth universally acknowledged, that a single man in possession of a good fortune, must be in want of a wife.*"

I scowl at them both.

"I know the sweetest woman you should meet," Harlowe says with a calculating look as if this was her plan all along. "She's hot as shit. She's a friend from my old modeling days, so I think you'll like her. Consider it a favor to me, since she's new to Atlanta and needs a tour guide. You're just the man to do it because I'm too busy."

I look around the room. Paige is beaming up at me, fully on board with this idea, Hayes is smirking, and Zander is openly laughing as he listens to his wife bait her trap. Fuck no. I'm stuck here holding a baby without an easy escape.

What fresh hell is this? At least Hendricks is ignoring the conversation, rolling his Hot Wheels cars along the couch between Paige and Zander, oblivious to the snare being set.

"I respectfully pass. I'm sure she's wonderful, but I don't want to be set up with one of your friends. Or with anyone, for that matter."

Maddie makes a gurgling noise in my arms, drawing my attention to her tiny face and wondering if I did something to upset her. Is she on Harlowe's side, too? *Women*. They can't all be against me.

Harlowe gives me a disbelieving look and fishes her phone from her purse. She quickly opens it and pulls up a stunning redhead's Instagram account, flashing the phone toward me.

"This is Rachel. She's adorable, funny as hell, and loves the water, like you. You should really meet her before you make that decision." She swipes through the photos and videos for me to see what I'm turning down as I rock back and forth in front of her with the baby in my arms.

Harlowe's not wrong. Rachel is hot and fit, and from her carefully curated Insta feed, looks like a lot of fun. But I'm not looking for the relationship Harlowe wants to saddle me.

"I believe you, I'm just not interested. Don't waste your time trying to set me up." Jesus, my hands are getting sweaty at the thought of being tied down to one of Harlowe's friends when all I want is to work to my heart's content and focus on my job.

Hayes lets out a bark of a laugh seeing my discomfort and stands not wanting me to hold his child anymore. He relieves me of my burden, holding the tiny baby in his huge arms like it's nothing.

"This is fucking great. You're in for it now. Glad her sights are set on you and I can finally relax," he says in a low voice with his back to the sofa. I raise an eyebrow at him but turn and smile in challenge at Harlowe, ready for whatever she thinks she can throw at me. I settle on a chair across from her as Hayes moves around the room soothing the fussing baby.

"Okay, maybe not a model, then," Harlowe says, intent on her Instagram as she quickly searches and turns the phone to show me another account. "This is Libby. She's a single mom friend that I know from Hendricks's school. She's a total MILF, with the sweetest little boy that Hendricks is obsessed with. They're in the same class, and Theo's smart, too." She shows me a photo of a stunning brunette with huge blue eyes and a gorgeous smile, holding the hand of a cute little boy on a playground.

"Harlowe," I warn, as she scrolls through Libby's Instagram, showing me more photos of Theo and her mom friend looking like a down-to-earth and smoking hot woman who knows how to take a killer photo.

"The father's totally out of the picture, so no baby daddy drama, either. Ready-made family, win-win for company PR! She's a total sweetheart who I like, which is rare, but I've heard what she likes in bed and it's hot. Not at all saying she's easy, but if you hit it off, I could see it being mutually beneficial."

Paige chokes out an embarrassed laugh and claps a hand over her mouth, scandalized by Harlowe's brazen words. She's young and innocent, completely sheltered until she met Hayes who has likely corrupted her thoroughly at this point, but it's hard to remove the impeccable Southern manners forced into her. Harlowe is unapologetically herself and can be a bit much, especially for a prim and proper debutante like Paige. The fact they get along so well is still shocking, but everyone likes Paige.

"Damn, Harlowe. You're shameless. Do you even hear yourself? Libby's hot and that kid's super cute, but I'm not interested in dating anyone. Find her a good dude who will do her justice as a boyfriend, because it's not going to be me."

"You're impossible. You can't be the only Olsen brother without a partner. It's indecent."

"Indecent?" I scoff, feeling my smile slipping as Harlowe grows more insistent. I point at my younger brother. "Zander being a player for ten years was indecent. Not wanting to date your friends is far from that. Let me live my life on my terms and enjoy my work. I'll be fine." I'm keeping my words family-friendly due to the little ears around me, but I want to let her know how I really feel, which is irritated with her insistence.

"Fine." She rolls her eyes. "I think it's bad for business. You're the PR guy. You know better than anyone that being in a relationship would show the world that the men of Olympus are calming down, becoming more serious than ever, and committing to the stability of their company. Isn't that what Zander being married did? It's done wonders for your subsidiary stock prices. You're the lone holdout. We need to wife you up."

She wraps Zander's arm around her belly and laces her fingers with his. He pulls her back into his lap, fully on board with whatever she says. He's a stupid, besotted fool. I swear he loses his ability to think with his big brain whenever she's around.

"My love life's never been a problem for the company, like Zander's was, so you can't use that against me," I point out, gesturing at Zander who makes a face at me like he doesn't want me bringing up his past indiscretions in front of his wife who is all too aware of them. "As for being committed to the company's stability, there's a hacker I need to track down, and all of the operations to run. I'm putting in more time than ever to ensure the company's success, so obviously, I'm already doing my part. I don't need a wife, or girlfriend, to do that."

Harlowe's shoulders slump as I refute her arguments with ease, but she straightens and gets a gleam in her eyes I don't like the look of. "Just let me introduce you to a few people. Give them a shot and see what you think in person," she persists. "You need a girlfriend."

"Uncle Payton, do you want to borrow my girlfriend?"

I look over, surprised at the small voice chiming in, and catch Hendricks looking up at me from the rug where he's playing with more of his toy cars. "Oh, that's a nice offer, buddy, but I don't want to take your girlfriend," I say with an easy smile. "Your momma is playing around. I don't actually need a girlfriend, but thank you."

"It's okay, it's just pretend. Taylor and I play boyfriend and girlfriend on the playground, but it's not real. You could pretend to have a girlfriend and momma would be happy."

I chuckle at his suggestion. "That's very nice of you. I'm sure Taylor likes playing with you more than she'd want to be my girlfriend."

He shrugs and goes back to his cars, satisfied that he no longer has to be a part of the conversation. I turn back to Harlowe and give her a look.

"You see what your antics are doing? Your kid's trying to save me now. How about we leave this subject and get back to the cute baby and new mom we're supposed to be celebrating? I'm good on my own, there's no need for you to play matchmaker or meddle in my love life."

"Mark my words, Payton, a woman is going to come along and turn your world upside down and have you eating your words. I'm going to laugh my ass off when it happens."

Her words sound more like a curse than they should and I feel a tingle of unease run down my spine. "If that's the case, I'll laugh with you," I say, my smile feeling a little more apprehensive than usual after what she said. I need to plan for a future assault where Harlowe is concerned. She doesn't give up easily. I'm going to be an ongoing target for her machinations if that look is anything to go by.

Also By

Gods Of The Ice Series
Reckless On Ice
Temptation On Ice
Shattered On Ice
Southern Gods Series
The Bourbon Bride
The Bourbon Bargain
The Southern Thirst Trap
The Southern Submission
The Bourbon Duet
The Southern Gods Vol. Two
Drift Series
Drift Heat
Broken Drift
Standalones
A Taste of Bliss

Acknowledgements

To my readers—thank you for joining me on this incredibly emotional journey of reforming a fuckboy and taming a fierce Wildcat! I've loved creating The Southern Gods world and publishing the Olsen family this year for you. I hope you're loving this Southern high society take on Greek mythology and are ready for Payton's story, next. I can't wait to share more of this world with you!

Many thanks to the many people who took the time to encourage, beta-read, edit, and provide feedback to help me create this novel. You're all the real MVPs!

Billy—I love you, always. You selflessly let me be incredibly selfish and dive headfirst into my laptop, living with fictional people who demand all my free time and never complain. You're the best at understanding when I'm laughing to myself, sobbing over imaginary situations, and listening to me tell you about the crazy things my characters are doing like you actually care—and you do, because you care about what *I* care about. That is the gold standard, baby.

Sharon—whether climbing mountains, attending concerts & charity fashion shows, or sending Henry Cavil memes back and forth, you're my go-to girl. You keep life interesting *and* keep me sane – which is a full-time job on top of your real big girl job to add my bullshit to, so I appreciate you for taking me on. Thanks for being my bestie, my proofreader, my life coach, and for being inappropriate and laughing hysterically with me and scaring our husbands when we're all together.

Daddy Emm, AKA Emmerson Hoyt—Hell yes for our girl gang of badass authors always willing to lift each other up and ensure we're getting the best from life. Our unhinged texts, ADHD writing dates, and voice messages are the best things, and I'm so thankful for you! You're the only one I'll submit to for anything. Yes Daddy, whatever you say goes.

Stephanie Higgins—there is nothing better than having a local bookish friend who is always willing to hang out, talk story structure, travel with me to bookish events, and get eyes on a story before anyone else. You are a delight and I'm so thankful for you!

Rebecca—I am so thankful for our coffee dates and tea parties that helped me with my writing groove! It's wonderful to have a creative friend like you who inspires me in so many ways. May we continue our traditions and always embrace our over-the-top aesthetics and love of pretty locations for photos!

The amazing community I've built on Booksta—y'all are amazing, I love you all so very much and couldn't do this without you. I write for YOU and I'm so glad you found my stories. Whether it's shouting your love for my books and characters, making incredible edits, sharing reviews, or letting me into your DMs with my needy author ways and embracing me, you've all been so wonderful, caring, hilarious, and just so damn amazing! The internet is seriously the best for bringing your people together to create a community of some of the best ladies I know.

Website: www.adrianrhale.com
Newsletter: https://bit.ly/AdrianHaleNL
Facebook facebook.com/adrianrhaleauthor
FB Group https://bit.ly/AdriansGoodGirls
Instagram: instagram.com/adrianrhale/
TikTok: tiktok.com/@adrianrhale
Goodreads: goodreads.com/adrianrhale

About the Author

Adrian R. Hale is an enthusiastic lover of life who embraces big dreams, for herself and in her books. She writes new adult and contemporary romance featuring strong heroes with secret cinnamon roll sides, and dream-chasing heroines, with a little angst, a lot of swoon, and all the steam lovingly sprinkled in.

Adrian loves fast cars, baking sweet treats, hiking through Texas hill country, and is affectionately known as an agent of chaos to those closest to her. A self-professed caffeine addict, she loves a good vanilla oat latte, and will never turn down a tea party, especially in celebration of little milestones. When she's not writing or reading, Adrian can be found cuddling with her five dogs and husband, watching the 2005 Pride & Prejudice, DIY renovating her home near Austin, Texas, or listening to Taylor Swift.